Praise for Lori Foster's
Winston Brothers stories and Wild

"Funny, fast, and sexy."
—Stella Cameron

"A sizzling voyage of discovery . . . A sensual treat that combines fascinating character development with a terrific plot . . . [from a] masterful author's pen. A tantalizing and titillating delight, *Wild* lives up to its title with flair!"
—*Wordweaving*

"*Wild* lives up to its title."
—*Midwest Book Review*

"Her books [are] always sexy, with heroes to die for . . . Foster's books can help you heat up during the cold, dark days of winter."
—*BellaOnline*

"A talented author whose work shines, especially during erotic encounters."
—*The Romance Reader*

Praise for Lori Foster's other novels

"Fun, sexy, warm-hearted . . . just what people want in a romance."
—*New York Times* bestselling author Jayne Ann Krentz

"Foster out-writes most of her peers."
—*Library Journal*

"Lori Foster delivers the goods."
—*Publishers Weekly*

"One of the most dazzling authors in the industry, as she once again proves with her deft ability of balancing the wild side with strong integrity."
—*Wordweaving*

"Known for her funny, sexy writing, Foster doesn't hesitate to turn up the heat."
—*Booklist*

"Lori Foster delivers both heartwarming emotions and heart-stopping love scenes."
—Jennifer Crusie

Wildly WINSTON

Lori Foster

BERKLEY SENSATION, NEW YORK

THE BERKLEY PUBLISHING GROUP
Published by the Penguin Group
Penguin Group (USA) Inc.
375 Hudson Street, New York, New York 10014, USA
Penguin Group (Canada), 90 Eglinton Avenue East, Suite 700, Toronto, Ontario M4P
2Y3, Canada (a division of Pearson Penguin Canada Inc.)
Penguin Books Ltd., 80 Strand, London WC2R 0RL, England
Penguin Group Ireland, 25 St. Stephen's Green, Dublin 2, Ireland (a division of Penguin
Books Ltd.)
Penguin Group (Australia), 250 Camberwell Road, Camberwell, Victoria 3124, Australia
(a division of Pearson Australia Group Pty. Ltd.)
Penguin Books India Pvt. Ltd., 11 Community Centre, Panchsheel Park, New Delhi—
110 017, India
Penguin Group (NZ), Cnr. Airborne and Rosedale Roads, Albany, Auckland 1310, New
Zealand (a division of Pearson New Zealand Ltd.)
Penguin Books (South Africa) (Pty.) Ltd., 24 Sturdee Avenue, Rosebank, Johannesburg
2196, South Africa

Penguin Books Ltd., Registered Offices: 80 Strand, London WC2R 0RL, England

This is a work of fiction. Names, characters, places, and incidents either are the product
of the author's imagination or are used fictitiously, and any resemblance to actual
persons, living or dead, business establishments, events, or locales is entirely
coincidental. The publisher does not have any control over and does not assume any
responsibility for author or third-party websites or their content.

PRINTING HISTORY
The Winston Brothers (anthology comprising the three novellas): Jove mass market
edition / December 2001
Wild: Jove mass market edition / January 2002
Berkley Sensation trade paperback omnibus edition / March 2006

Library of Congress Cataloging-in-Publication Data

Foster, Lori, 1958–
    [Winston brothers]
    Wildly Winston / Lori Foster.
        p. cm.
    Contents: Tangled sheets—Tangled dreams—Tangled images—Wild.
    ISBN 0-425-20785-4
    1. Foster, Lori, 1958– Wild. II. Title: Wild. III. Title.

PS3556.O767W56 2006
813'.6—dc22
                                                                          2005055873

PRINTED IN THE UNITED STATES OF AMERICA

10 9 8 7 6 5 4 3 2 1

CONTENTS

Wildly
WINSTON

Tangled Sheets

To Cindy Hwang,
from the first Winston brother to the last,
working with you has always been a pleasure.
Thank you for making this so much fun!

She refused to spend her twenty-sixth Valentine's Day as a virgin.

Despite her circumspect upbringing, despite the well-meaning strictures of the maiden aunt who'd raised her, she was ready to become a woman, in every sense of the word. And Cole Winston—bless his gorgeous, sexy soul—was offering her the opportunity she needed to see her plans through.

Sophie Sheridan scanned the flyer again as she hesitated just inside the door of Cole's bar, previously called The Stud by some macho former owner, but changed to merely the Winston Tavern after Cole bought it. Heaven knew, the bar's reputation was notorious enough without a suggestive label. Though, to Sophie's mind, The Stud was pretty apropos, given what the Winston men looked like, Cole Winston especially.

All the neighboring shops had received a flyer inviting women to take part in a new Valentine's Day contest. Not that the Winston men needed an incentive to draw in the female crowd. Women loved to come here, to see one of the four brothers serving, tending bar, simply moving or smiling. They were a gorgeous, flirtatious lot, but Sophie had her eye on one particular brother.

The door opened behind her as more patrons hustled in, allowing icy wind and a flurry of snowflakes to surround her. For just a moment, intrusive laughter overwhelmed the sound of soft music and the muted hum of quiet conversation. Distracted, Sophie stepped farther inside the bar, then headed for her regular seat at the back corner booth, away from the heaviest human congestion. Since she'd met Cole some seven months ago after buying her boutique, he'd gone out of his way to accommodate her, to make certain her seat was available for her routine visit each night. He did his best to cater to all his customers' preferences, which in part accounted for his incredible success at the bar. Cole knew everyone, spoke easily with them about their families and their problems and their lives.

But he was so drop-dead sexy, Sophie spent most of her time in his company trying to get her tongue unglued from the roof of her mouth. It was humiliating. She'd never been so shy before; of course, she'd never received so much attention from such an incredible man before, either. Cole made her think of things she'd never pondered in her entire life, like the way a man smelled when he got overheated, so musky and sexy and hot, and how his beard shadow might feel on the more sensitive places of her body.

She shuddered, drawing in a deep breath.

While Cole believed she was timid and withdrawn, and treated her appropriately, Sophie had concocted some sizzling, toe-curling fantasies about him. Now, thanks to his contest, she just might be able to fulfill them.

Heat slithered through her, chasing away the lingering cold of winter, coloring her cheeks. Unfortunately, Cole chose that moment to set her requisite cup of hot chocolate in front of her. He'd put extra whipped cream on the top, and the smell was deliciously sinful. Almost as delicious as Cole himself.

"Hello, Sophie."

His low voice sank into her bones, and she slowly raised her gaze to him. Warm whiskey described the color of his eyes, fringed by thick, black lashes and heavy brows. She swallowed. "Hi."

Slow and easy, his grin spread as he looked down to see the flyer clutched in her hand. "Good." There was a wealth of male satisfaction in his rough tone, and his gaze lifted, locking onto hers, refusing to let her look away. "You going to enter?" he asked in a whisper.

Here was the tricky part, the only way she could think to gain her ends. Their relationship, already set by her tongue-tied nervousness, was hard to overcome. She couldn't merely go from reserved to aggressive overnight, not without confusing him and risking a great deal of embarrassment.

Her aunt Maude had drummed the importance of pride and self-respect into her from an early age. If she gambled now, and lost, she'd also lose the comfort of coming to his bar every night, the excitement of small conversations, and the heat of her fantasies. If he rejected her, she wouldn't simply be able to pick up and carry on as usual. Something very precious to her—their relationship—would have been destroyed. Everyone she loved, everyone she felt close to, was gone. She didn't want to risk the quiet, settling camaraderie she shared with him in the atmosphere of his bar.

But if she won, if she was able to interest him for even a short time, it wouldn't last. Cole was renowned as a die-hard bachelor; he simply didn't get overly involved with anyone. At thirty-six, you had to take his dedication to living alone seriously. The man obviously *liked* being a bachelor, had worked hard at staying that way.

His rejection could put a distance between them she wasn't willing to chance. So she had to use deception.

"I couldn't," Sophie said, laying the colorful flyer aside. She licked her lips in nervousness and toyed with the cup of hot chocolate, making certain it sat exactly in the center of her napkin. "I'd feel silly."

Cole's smile was indulgent and blatantly male. He pulled a chair over from the next table rather than sitting opposite her in the booth. He straddled it, his arms crossed over the back. "Why?" He sat so close, Sophie could smell his scent, cologne and warm male flesh, a combination she hadn't appreciated or even noticed until meeting Cole. She breathed deeply and felt her stomach flutter, as if his scent alone could fill her up.

Cole tilted his head at her, cajoling. "All you need to enter is a photo. I can even take your picture here at the bar. There will be dozens of other pictures up, too, you know. Already, we've had around twenty women sign up. I'll hang all the pictures in the billiard room, and on Valentine's Day, we'll vote on the prettiest picture."

"There's no point in it," Sophie said, though she hadn't meant to. She wasn't fishing for a compliment, but she realized that was how it sounded when Cole made a *tsking* sound.

His hand cupped under her chin, lifting her face, and his look was so tender, so warm, her heart tripped over several beats, making her gasp. "You're very pretty, Sophie."

Oh, to have him mean that! But Sophie had seen Cole treat everyone in the bar in the same familiar way. He was simply a people person: open, solicitous, and friendly. He teased the older women until they blushed, left all the younger women giddy with regret, and the men, regardless of whether they were businessmen, laborers, or retirees, all liked and respected him. They gathered around him and hung on his every word. Cole liked people, and he made everyone, male and female, young and old, feel special.

The heat from his hand, the roughness of his palm, was a wicked temptation, inciting sinful thoughts. She wondered what it might feel like to have that hard palm smoothing over other parts of her body, places no one had ever seen, much less touched. Her breathing quickened and her hands shook.

Clamoring to get her thoughts in order, Sophie held up the flyer and tried for a bright smile. "I think this might be more suitable for my sister. I don't photograph well, but she's in town for a brief visit and might like the idea."

For an instant, Cole froze, then he dropped his hand and studied her. "You have a sister?"

"Yes. A twin actually." The words slipped easily past her stiff lips. "Though we're not that much alike in personality. Shelly is much more ... outgoing."

"Outgoing?" He looked intrigued. Shifting slightly, he said, "A twin," and his tone was distracted, low and deep. "Tell me about her."

Sophie blinked at him. "Um, what's to tell? She looks like me, except she's not so ..."

That small smile touched his mouth again. "Buttoned down?"

"Well, yes, I suppose." *Buttoned down? What did that mean?* "Shelly was always the popular one in school."

Suddenly, he shook his head and his dark, silky hair fell over his forehead. Sophie loved his hair, how straight it was, the slight hint of silver at his temples, the way it reflected the bar lights. She wanted desperately to smooth it back, to touch him, to see if it felt as silky and cool as it looked. She clasped her hands tightly on the table.

"You should both enter. Maybe even together. The judges would love it."

"Who ..." She had to clear her throat. Cole suddenly stood, and his size, his strength, always sent her brain into a tailspin. She peered up at him, liking the differences in their sizes, imagining how they might fit together. There was just so much of him to appreciate, to tempt. "Who are the judges?"

Now his grin was wicked. "Me and my brothers. I think it's justice, given the way the media has taunted us this last year. Did you see that most recent article?" He snorted in amusement. "My brothers ate it up."

Sophie smiled, too. All the Winston brothers were superb male specimens. Cole owned the friendly neighborhood bar, but his brothers, Mack and Zane and Chase, helped work it. Mack was the youngest, and still in college, but at twenty-one, he had the quiet maturity of a much older man. Zane, at twenty-four, was the rowdiest and split his workload between his own computer business, which was still getting off the ground, with the sure paycheck from his brother. Chase, at twenty-seven, only a year older than Sophie, shared all the responsibilities with Cole. Though Cole owned the bar, he consulted with Chase on all major decisions. Chase, unlike Cole, was quiet, and more often than not, worked behind the bar, handing out drinks and listening, rather than talking.

In the seven months since she'd first met them, Sophie found the brothers got along incredibly well, and combined, they were enough to send the female denizens of Thomasville, Kentucky, into a frenzy.

"They actually suggested we should go topless," Cole said.

Sophie covered her mouth in an effort to hold back her mirth. The local papers had a fine time with their good-natured taunting of the Winston men. They teased them for their good looks and their overwhelming female clientele, constantly soliciting them to do an article on their personal lives. The brothers always refused.

Cole sounded disgruntled, but Sophie thought the idea had merit. Heaven knew, even with the business they had now, their popularity would likely double if the Winston men strutted around bare-chested. It was an altogether tantalizing thought.

"Zane has been threatening to take his shirt off all day," Cole added, "and the women have been egging him on. Knowing Zane, he just might do it. I have to make sure he doesn't end up doing a striptease that will get us shut down."

This time there was no stifling her laughter. She, too, could picture Zane doing such a thing. He flirted outrageously, and like the other Winston brothers, had his share of admirers.

"You don't laugh very often."

Sophie bit her lip. His look was so intense and intimate, her belly tingled. He had the most unique effect on her, and she loved it. No other man had ever listened to her so attentively, shown such interest in her thoughts and ideas and feelings. He made her feel so special. She had no idea what to say, then didn't have to say anything as his concentration was diverted by Mack, who had sauntered up to his side. "The delivery guys are here."

Looking back at her, Cole nodded. "I'll be right there." He waited until Mack had turned away, then leaned down, one large hand on the booth seat behind her, the other spread on the table. "Enter the contest, Sophie."

His breath touched her cheek and she jerked. She stared at the table, her hands, anywhere rather than meet that probing gaze at such close proximity. She'd likely throw herself at him if she did. "My sister will be in later tonight. She'll enter."

He straightened slowly and she heard him sigh. "All right. I'm not giving up on you, but you can tell her to come see me when she gets here. I'd like to meet her."

Sophie watched him walk away, loving his long-legged stride, the way his dark hair hung over his collar, the width of his back and hard shoulders. As he maneuvered around the tables, women watched his progress, their sidelong looks just as admiring. He stopped to speak to many of them, leaving laughter and dreamy smiles behind, and Sophie knew he'd convince them all to enter. That was just the way he was, attentive to everyone, easy to talk to.

He'd meet her sister, all right. Sophie could hardly wait.

"Here."

Cole started in surprise as Chase shoved the icy cold can of whipped cream into his hand, drawing his attention away from Sophie. He raised a brow. "What?"

"You've been standing there salivating ever since she lifted her spoon. I always wondered why you put so damn much whipped cream on her chocolate. Now I know."

Cole didn't bother to deny the charge. Hell, he'd been half hard since Sophie had lifted the first spoonful to her mouth. Such a sexy mouth, full and soft and—he was obsessing, damn it.

He remembered the very first day he'd met her, when she'd bought the boutique a few doors down and across the street. She'd come in after work, looking prim and proper and very appealing, and she'd ordered hot chocolate, of all things, even though the weather in July had been steamy. Amused, he'd put an extra dollop of whipped cream on top, then watched in sensual appreciation while she'd savored it, her small tongue licking out over her upper lip, her eyes closing with each small taste. She'd been unaware of his scrutiny, and for seven months he'd been allowing her to torment him nightly with the ritual.

"Since she's finished that up, you want to go for broke and give her more?"

Cole shook his head, choosing to ignore the jest. "Too obvious. If she had any inkling how much I enjoy watching her, she would never order hot chocolate again."

"Or maybe she'd put you out of your misery and take you home with her."

Cole slanted his brother a look. Usually, Chase was the quietest, but he was damned talkative tonight. "Any particular reason why you want to annoy me right now?"

Chase grinned. "Other than the fact you're hiding over here in the corner, staring at her like a kid in a candy store with a pounding sweet tooth but no money to buy anything? Nope. There's no other reason."

"She refuses to enter the contest."

"Well damn." Chase stepped away for a moment to fill an order, then came back to Cole's side. "You couldn't talk her into it?"

He shook his head, distracted. "She has a twin."

"Oh ho, *two* Sophies. Now that sounds interesting. They're identical?"

Cole elbowed him. "Yeah. And get your mind out of the gutter."

"Too crowded, what with yours already being there?"

"Something like that. She says her sister will enter, but she doesn't want to." He sighed in disgust. "What is it about Sophie that makes me start fantasizing all kinds of wild things?"

"You tell me."

Crossing his arms over his chest and leaning back against the wall beside the ice chest, Cole considered her. "She's so buttoned down, so serene. Not once in the seven months I've known her has she ever missed a night, which means she must not be dating at all." He studied her dark brown hair, parted in the middle and hanging to her shoulders with only the gentlest of curls. It looked incredibly soft; he wanted to bury his nose against her neck, feel that silky hair on his face, his chest, his abdomen.

He wanted to see it fanned out against his pillows as he covered her with his naked body, wanted to see it tangled and wild as she reached for the pleasure he'd give her.

He shuddered in reaction. "Damn."

"Care to share those thoughts?"

"No." Narrow shoulders, but always straight and proud, posture erect. Her skin could make him nuts, so smooth and pale. He wondered if she was that smooth all over, the skin on her thighs and bottom, her breasts, low on her belly. She would smell so sweet—he'd be willing to bet his life on that. Sweet and warm and sexy, just like the woman herself.

"Maybe her sister will give you a break. If they look the same, you could do a little imagining."

"I don't want her damn sister. I want her." He watched Sophie lift the mug of chocolate to her mouth now that the whipped cream was gone. She sipped, then patted her lips with a napkin. "It's more than just how she looks. It's *her*. She smiles at me, and all I can think about is warm skin, heavy breathing, and tangled sheets."

"You've got it bad."

"Damn it, I know it. But she shies away from me every time I try to get close. She's just plain not interested." He could easily picture the way her wide blue eyes would skip away, avoiding his, how her hands would twist together, how she'd bite her lip. God he loved how she bit her lip.

"Ask her why."

Cole glared at his brother. "Yeah, right. I can't even get her to enter the damn contest. How am I going to get her to open up her head to me?"

"There's a couple of days left. But if she doesn't enter, what are we going to do?"

Cole shrugged, angered by the prospect. "We'll pick a different winner. It's still a good contest. All the local papers have picked it up, so it's a great promo, even if we didn't need the publicity. And it'll only cost us drinks for a month."

"It'll also cost you a night on the town, lady's choice, because none of the rest of us are dumb enough to open that bag of worms. You're liable to find yourself with a permanent female escort."

Truth was, he wouldn't mind a permanent escort, if it was Sophie. He'd spent the better part of his life raising his younger brothers after his parents' deaths. He didn't regret the time he'd devoted to his brothers, just the opposite. Their closeness was important to him. But raising three boys, when he wasn't much more than a boy himself, had been a full-time job with no room for other relationships. He'd had to be content with fleeting female pleasure, the occasional night of passion.

Now Mack was in his last year of college, all the brothers were settled and secure, and Cole was finally free to live his own life. He wanted more. He wanted Sophie.

Damn her for her stubbornness, and for trying to pawn her sister off on him.

Cole walked away as Chase got sidetracked again with customers. He had some paperwork to do and might as well get started, but again, he paused in the hallway leading to his office and stared at Sophie. His plan had been so simple. Valentine's Day was a time for lovers, so therefore perfect for a contest that would bring the two of them together.

She was a shoe-in to win because his brothers knew how he felt about her, though they were amused because they thought it was mere lust. They didn't know he spent the better part of his day looking forward to seeing her when she closed her shop, when she'd spend a quiet hour sitting in her favorite booth, talking to him about everything and nothing. They didn't know he was obsessed with a woman for the first time in his life.

The winner of the contest not only got drinks at the bar free for a month, she would also have her picture taken with all the Winston men. The photo would be prominently displayed on a wall, and each year, another photo would join it as the contest became an annual event.

But best of all, the winner got a night on the town of her choice. Cole had visions of Sophie choosing a nice restaurant for dinner where they'd have plenty of time to talk without the bar's audience, followed by a little slow dancing where he'd be able to hold her close, move her body against his. He'd feel her thighs brushing his, her belly moving against his groin, her stiff nipples hot against his chest. And they'd eventually end up in bed with those tangled sheets he couldn't help seeing in his mind.

He didn't want to meet her sister. But at the same time, his curiosity was extreme. A woman who looked like Sophie, but wasn't. A woman who could be Sophie, but who wouldn't be so shy with him. He shook his head even as his body stirred. At that moment, Sophie looked up and their gazes locked. Even from the distance separating them, he felt linked to her, a touch that kicked him in the heart and licked along his muscles, a feeling he'd never experienced with any other woman.

Damn, he wanted her.

He wouldn't give up. Sooner or later, he'd get Sophie Sheridan exactly where he wanted her, and he'd keep her there for an excruciatingly long, satisfying time.

T W O

Mack gave a long, low whistle that effortlessly carried through the closed office door. "Will you take a look at that."

Cole glanced up from his desk and paperwork, wondering what had drawn his brother's attention. It had been a long, frustrating night, and his eyes were gritty, his head leaden.

"Hubba hubba. Who is she?" Zane asked as he, too, came to loiter in the hallway. Cole frowned and pushed away from his computer.

"Don't you remember her? I'll give you a clue. Cole is going to choke on his own tongue—once he gets it back in his mouth."

"No!" There was a considering pause, then, "Well, yeah, I suppose it could be her. But what did she do to herself?"

"Hell if I know. But she looks good enough to—"

Cole shot out of his chair, his curiosity too extreme to repress. He'd been determined to ignore the sister if and when she showed, and considering it was well after midnight, he figured he wouldn't have to worry about it.

He jerked the door open and Zane, who'd been leaning on it, almost fell on the floor. Cole helped to right him, then followed Mack's gaze across the room. Every muscle in his body snapped into iron hardness. He couldn't move. Hell, he could barely breathe.

Like a sleepwalker, he let go of Zane and started forward. He could hear his brothers snickering behind him, but he ignored it. God, she looked good. His heart punched so hard against his ribs he thought he might break something—and he didn't care.

As he got closer, she looked up, and her smoky blue gaze sank into his. She trembled, her chest drawing deep, quick breaths, and then she smiled.

"Sophie?"

A husky laugh sent fingers of sensation down his spine. "Of course not. I'm her sister, Shelly. And you must be the big, gorgeous owner Sophie's told me so much about." Her gaze boldly skimmed down his body, like a hot lick of interest, then back up again. "My my. I have to say, Sophie didn't exaggerate."

Cole was floored. Oh, he was interested; after all, he wasn't dead, and the woman standing in front of him, dressed all in black, was a surefire knockout. But she wasn't Sophie.

She could be Sophie, he thought, unable to keep his gaze from roaming all over her from head to toe, but the words out of her mouth were words he'd only imagined, not something Sophie would ever actually say to him. She held out her pale, slender hand, and he took it, painfully aware that he had all three of his brothers' rapt attention.

"Cole Winston," he said, and his voice sounded deeper than usual, huskier. Arousal rode him hard, making it difficult to form polite conversation. "Sophie told me you might want to enter our contest?"

Her hand lingered in his, small and warm and fragile. It felt just like touching Sophie, sent the same rush of desire pounding through him, and he felt like a cad, like he'd somehow betrayed her. Only Sophie's touch had ever sizzled his nerve endings this way, but now her sister's was doing the same.

"Yes."

That was all she said, and Cole stared. Amazingly, he could see her pulse beating in her slim throat, the fragile skin fluttering as if she were nervous. *Or excited.*

They were still holding hands. Cole cleared his throat. When he started to pull his hand back, she held on, stepping closer to him. She brought with her the scent of the fresh evening air, brisk and wintery, mixed with the warm, feminine scent of her skin, a scent he recognized. His nostrils flared.

"I didn't realize Sophie had a sister until today."

Her gaze lowered, and a wry smile curved her lips—lips the exact replica of Sophie's lips. His muscles twitched.

With a slight shrug, she whispered, "My sister is a little shy."

The urge to taste her rushed through him. He hadn't felt this primal, this turned on, in a long, long time. Even though she wasn't Sophie, she looked the same, only wilder, more attainable, and his beleaguered male brain reasoned that she likely even tasted the same. He couldn't seem to stop himself from pulling her up to his side, wanting to feel her close, wanting to see how her body lined up to his. "Why don't I show you the rest of the bar?"

Very slowly, her thick lashes lowered. "I'd like that."

Long-repressed desire for Sophie twisted in his guts. Every image he'd ever formed in his mind slammed into him at once. Slumberous, sated blue eyes, taut nipples and trembling breasts, open, naked thighs. *Tangled sheets*. He stifled a deep groan and put his hand on her narrow waist through her coat.

They turned, and all three of his brothers jerked around, running into each other, tripping, trying to pretend they were busy doing something besides staring. He could feel their cautious glances as he led Shelly to the back room where the billiard tables were housed, but it was a peripheral awareness; all his attention was on the petite woman beside him, the sound of her anxious breaths reaching his ears above the din of normal conversation and music. There were few people still in the bar so late on such a cold and snowy night, and the two men playing pool took one look at him, grinned, and put down their sticks. They left the room without complaint.

"Can I take your coat?"

Shelly smiled, then slipped it off her shoulders. As Cole stepped behind her to take it, he leaned close, breathing in the scent of warm woman. His stomach muscles knotted and he locked his knees. He tossed her coat—black leather, long and sexy—over one end of a pool table. She turned to face him again, slowly, expectantly. Her sweater was black, emphasizing her pale skin and the richness of her chestnut hair, now pulled on top of her head with a gold clasp, showing her vulnerable nape and small ears, little wisps of baby-fine hair. He wanted to press his mouth there, to watch her shiver in sensation.

His gaze dropped to her breasts, lingered, and amazingly, her nipples puckered, thrusting against the soft, fuzzy material of the sweater. Cole didn't dare look at her face, knowing he'd be lost, his vague control shot to hell. A few glossy curls had escaped the clasp, and one curved invitingly just above her breast, taunting him, forcing him to imagine her without the sweater. Her breasts were small, but they tantalized him, looking soft and sweet, and he knew her skin would be very pale.

Unable to help himself, he stepped closer. With the coat gone, he saw she was wearing the skinniest pair of black jeans he'd ever seen, jeans that hugged her bottom and showed the long length of her legs. He'd often wondered on the details of Sophie's build. Her clothing was always somewhat concealing, so that while he knew she was slim, he couldn't detect all the curves and hollows of her woman's body.

Shelly's outfit left little to the imagination, and he wondered if Sophie was built the same, so slight, but so damn feminine. His hands shook.

"Do you play?"

It took a second for his brain to comprehend the words, and when he did, his body stirred. He could easily imagine playing with her, spending long hours toying with her body, learning every little secret, every ultrasensitive spot. He would explore first with his hands, and then with his mouth. He gave her a hot look that made her eyes widen and her lashes flutter. In nervousness? Not likely, considering her bravado.

She stammered slightly. "Pool, I mean. I've . . . I've never played, but I've often wondered . . ."

"I'll teach you," he heard himself say, even though he knew he should get away from her. She wasn't Sophie, no matter that he was so turned on he could barely breathe. He couldn't imagine Sophie ever being so coy, teasing a man in such a way. *Damn, he liked it.*

"Are you good?"

He'd turned away to move her coat and rack the pool balls, and now he froze, his eyes closing, sexual innuendoes tripping to the tip of his tongue. Hell, he could banter with the best of them, make sexual sport of any conversation, no matter how mundane, but he didn't want that with this woman. If he ever hoped to make headway with Sophie, if he ever hoped to have her body under his, open to him, accepting him in all ways, then he had to curb his desire now.

He wasn't a horny kid incapable of maintaining control. He was a grown man and he wanted Sophie, not just for a night, though that was his most immediate craving, but possibly for a lifetime. He wanted to sleep with her every night and wake with her beside him in the morning. He wanted to know every inch of her, heart and soul.

As tempting as he found Shelly, she still wasn't Sophie. It was the way she looked, being the mirror image of Sophie, that was playing havoc with his libido. Nothing more.

So he summoned a calm he didn't feel and turned to face the sister. Determination made his guts twist in regret because at the moment, despite all he'd just told himself, he had an erection that throbbed in demand, and it wouldn't be going away anytime soon.

"Actually," he said, keeping his gaze resolutely on her face, "I'm a little rusty."

Her eyes, turning a darker blue, held his. "Then maybe we can warm up together." Before he could find a retort, she selected a pool cue and came to stand very close to him. "How do I hold the stick?"

With his heart thumping in slow, hard beats, Cole turned her so her back was to him, then guided her to lean slightly over the table, positioning the cue, placing her hands just so. She took her first shot and barely disturbed the colorful balls. One rolled about an inch. Shelly chuckled. "Sorry. I suppose I didn't do it hard enough?"

Cole felt as if he were dying by slow degrees as he once again racked the balls. "Try again, and this time, follow all the way through."

He straightened and she whispered, "Show me."

Damn. If he hadn't wanted to so badly, he could have said no. But for some reason, Shelly drew him as no other woman had, except for Sophie. It didn't make any sense. He hadn't even looked at another woman in a sexual way once he'd really gotten to know Sophie and realized how perfect they'd be together.

He walked behind her again, and this time, she bent without his instruction, her small bottom pressing into his lap while his body curved over hers. She wiggled, a soft sound escaping her, and he froze. Almost without his permission, his hands moved, from folding over her hands, to slowly slide up her arms to her elbows, then inward to hold her waist.

She was so narrow, so warm. His palms rubbed over the softness of the fuzzy sweater, then higher, feeling her ribs and then the warm weight of her breasts against the backs of his hands.

He hurt; his stomach knotted, his chest felt tight, his erection throbbed. He had to stop or he'd totally forget himself. With a stifled groan, he straightened away from her and took two steps back. Slowly, Shelly laid the cue stick aside and turned to face him.

She tilted her head, eyes wide; something in her gaze looked almost desperate. He ignored it and drew on his nearly depleted control. "Maybe it would be better if I got one of my brothers to instruct you."

Distressed, Sophie felt her stomach give a sick flip at his words. He didn't want her, even with her being so obvious, even with her making herself more appealing, he didn't want her. She turned away and bit her lip to keep him from seeing her hot blush of mortification. She didn't blush well, never had. While another woman might get a becoming pink flush to her cheeks, Sophie could feel hot color pulse beneath her skin, from her breasts to her hairline, turning even her nose and ears red. Her skin was so fair that any blushing looked hideous, not attractive.

Zane stuck his head into the room. His gaze skimmed her, his brows lifted curiously, then moved on to his brother. He spoke quietly. "Mack left a while ago. The bar is nearly empty, and Chase is ready to give the last call. I'm going to head on home."

She felt Cole approach behind her. "All right. Drive careful. I hear the roads are crap from all the sleet and snow."

With escape uppermost in her mind, Sophie turned to face Cole again, a smile planted firmly in place, her blush hopefully under control. He was closer than she'd suspected, and she took a hasty step back. "Oh, I'm sorry." A nervous laugh bubbled past her lips. "I, ah, suppose that settles the pool lesson. I should let you men finish up here and go home."

Cole looked cautiously undecided. Good manners won out. "We have about half an hour. Enough time for you to enter the contest if you're still interested."

He kept watching her, his golden brown eyes direct, almost probing. Sophie prayed he wasn't suspicious. If he figured her out now, she'd just die. To that end, she sidled close once more, doing things Sophie had always wanted to do but would never have the nerve to follow through on.

One hand splayed over his chest, and she was stunned by the feel of his hard muscle, of the heat emanating from him in waves. There was no need to deliberately lower her tone; it emerged as a husky whisper as her body seemed to soak up his nearness. "Of course."

He covered her hand with his own, paused, then carefully removed it, holding it to his side. "The camera is in my office. You can wait here—"

"I'd rather just come with you." Self-preservation warred with curiosity. She needed to get away from him, to accept the pain of his rejection in solitude. But she'd always wanted to see his office, an extension of the man, knowing it would reveal so much about him.

He had a thick, overstuffed couch in his office. Many times she'd heard one of the brothers joke about taking a nap, especially Mack, who had his schoolwork to contend with but insisted on carrying his weight at the bar. Cole had done such a fabulous job with the brothers. They were all exceptional, responsible men.

So many times, Sophie had pictured him in that office behind the thick wooden door, dozing on the couch or sitting at his desk going over papers. She now wanted to know if the reality was the same as the fantasy, since the fantasy was evidently all she'd ever have.

Reluctantly, Cole nodded. "All right." He released her, putting his hand at the small of her back and guiding her forward. Just that slight touch, so simple, made her think of other things. His spread hand spanned the width of her waist. He was large all over, his hands twice the size of hers. With a small shiver, she imagined those large, rough hands on her body, covering so much of her skin with each touch. Her breasts throbbed and an aching emptiness swelled inside her.

The light was out in his office, and the cool dimness enveloped her as they stepped inside. She didn't quite know how she managed it, but she turned as he closed the door behind them and their bodies bumped together. Her feet seemed glued to the floor.

"Shelly..."

His voice was husky, not at all unaffected. She didn't need to breathe deep to inhale his hot male scent, not when she was already close to panting, her lungs expanding in sheer excitement at the touch of his hard-muscled body against hers.

Slowly, unable to resist, she went on tiptoe and nuzzled her face into his warm throat. God, it was as wonderful as she'd always imagined, his smell brisk and hot and stirring, his skin warm to the touch.

His hands clasped her upper arms, his fingers wrapping completely around her, biting into her flesh. "The light is on the desk," he muttered, but he sounded desperate, the words shallow around thick breaths.

Sophie tried to pull back, knowing this wasn't what he wanted, struggling to accept her defeat, but he lowered his head, cursing so softly, and his jaw brushed her temple. She swallowed hard at the near caress, aching for something she'd wanted for so long now. Sexual craving was new to her; she'd never experienced it for anyone but him, and the overwhelming need to indulge the craving and answer the burning in her body was making her crazed.

He shifted slightly and then her belly brushed his lower body and she felt the iron-hard length of his erection like a thunderclap. It burned into her, solid and unmistakable and with a small gasp, she pushed closer, her body seeking out more contact, reassured by the discovery.

Cole cursed again. In the next instant, his hand turned her face up and he groaned harshly, even as his mouth covered hers. Devouring, eating, holding her steady for the frenzied assault of his tongue and teeth. She'd imagined a kiss, but never this carnal mating of their mouths. Her heart rapped against her breastbone, her stomach curled tight. Helplessly, she opened her lips and accepted his tongue, all the while pressing into him, loving the feel of his excitement, the way his erection ground into her.

He pulled his mouth away, but it wasn't to stop.

"Cole," she whispered as his lips burned across her jaw, her throat, nipping and licking. His hands slid down her back, roughly grasped her bottom, and lifted her into his pelvis, his fingers plying her flesh as he moved her against him.

She held onto his shoulders, dizzy with a building urgency and a tender relief. *He wanted her.*

She moaned as he adjusted his stance, pressing her legs open to make room for his long, hard thigh, pulling her higher so she rode him. Embarrassment couldn't quite surface, even with the newness, the intimacy of it all. This was Cole, and this was what she'd wanted since the first night she'd met him. He was all the things her aunt Maude had ever warned against, every temptation imaginable wrapped up into a gorgeous package of throbbing masculinity. But he was also the most incredible man, gentle and proud and caring. Strong in all the ways that counted most. Every sinful fantasy she'd ever had winged through her mind, and she wanted every one of them to come true with him.

His open mouth pushed aside the neckline of her sweater so he could suck her soft skin against his teeth. Sophie wondered if he'd leave his mark, and hoped he would. She tilted her head to make it easier for him, and her toes curled inside her shoes at the delicious sensation of his warm mouth and tongue.

He groaned. "Damn..."

Somehow, he seemed to know how her breasts ached, and keeping her close with one hard hand on her buttocks, he lifted his other hand and enclosed her breast in incredible heat, his palm rasping deliberately over her nipple until she gave a raw moan of pleasure, then cuddling the soft mound gently. His mouth found hers again, swallowing her broken gasp when he lightly pinched her nipple, tugged and rolled. His tongue, warm and damp, slid into her mouth and she greedily accepted it.

They were leaning against the door, the heat thick around them, the darkness shielding, when the knock sounded and they broke their kiss, both of them panting for breath.

"I've locked everything up and I'm taking off. Just wanted you to know." There was a low chuckle, then Chase added, "Carry on."

Cole's chest moved like a bellows. Her feet were completely off the floor as she straddled his thigh, her arms tight around his neck. One hand still held her behind, and it contracted now as he seemed to fight some inner battle. She could see the white gleam of his eyes in the darkness, could feel his scrutiny.

No, no, she begged to herself, holding the words inside with an effort. But then she was being set back on her unsteady feet and moved a good distance away—the entire length of his long, muscular arms. She felt cold, denied his body heat, and she wrapped her arms around herself. One of his hands still held her, making certain, she supposed, that she couldn't close the distance between them, while he raked his other hand through his hair. She heard Cole's head hit the door as he dropped it back, then twice more. His frustration was a palpable thing, shaming her, making her want to run.

He abruptly moved away from her and opened the door. He stepped out into the hall, and she could hear the murmur of voices as he spoke to Chase.

She wasn't at all surprised when Cole came back to tell her, his tone steady and detached, "It's time to go. Come on, I'll see you to your car."

He didn't touch her again, and she felt defeated. Until she remembered how wildly he'd responded to her. He wanted her. But for some reason, he didn't want to want her. Maybe, her thinking continued, it was because he feared she might require a commitment. Did he think because she was *Sophie's sister* he might be obligated to pay if he played? Did dallying with a friend's relative imply ties she hadn't considered? She'd led such a solitary life, she had no idea of the codes involved in male/female social relationships.

Sophie thought maybe he was only fearful of being trapped, and she felt newly encouraged.

The silence was almost oppressive as they slipped on their coats and Cole finished up a few last-minute things. The bar was pitch dark as they left, but when they stepped outside, the bright glow of a street-lamp lit the entire front of the building. Cole managed several locks, then turned toward her, and when Sophie glanced at him, again taking in his incredible body, she had to struggle for breath.

Cole was still excited. She could read it on his face: the color high on his cheekbones, the clenched jaw, the heat that burned in his eyes. Her gaze skimmed lower, beneath the hem of his coat, and she saw his erection still plainly visible beneath his fly. Oh, he wanted her, all right. All she had to do was reassure him, to make certain he knew there would be no repercussions to their lovemaking.

He took her keys from her and opened her car door. For the first time since leaving his office, he spoke. "You're driving Sophie's car."

Bolstered now by new confidence, Sophie smiled. "She insisted. We live on different schedules, with her an early bird and me a night owl, so there isn't a conflict. And," she added deliberately, hoping to entice him, "I won't be in town that long. Not more than a few days."

He didn't take the bait. "I see. Well, good night. It was...nice meeting you."

She almost laughed at that inane comment and the irony in his tone, but his face was hard, set in stone, and she didn't want to anger him. "Oh, we'll see each other again. You forgot to take my picture. I'll be back tomorrow night, okay?" Playfully, trying to be bold to ensure the credibility of her ruse, she reached out one leather-gloved finger and stroked his chest. "Maybe then we'll be able to stay on track. Or then again, maybe not."

His jaw locked, and as he turned away, she heard him mutter an awful curse. Sophie closed her door and started her car. Her heart was still beating too fast, her breasts still tingling, and there was a pulling sensation deep inside her, an acute emptiness that demanded attention. It felt delicious, and she wanted more. She wanted everything.

She wanted Cole Winston.

THREE

It had been an awful night. Cole sipped his coffee and tried to order his thoughts, but lack of sleep and extended, acute sexual frustration made his brain sluggish, hampering his efforts. The events at the bar, the sensual overload, and then the smothering guilt had conspired against him to make him toss and turn in between dreams of making love to a woman who looked and felt and tasted like Sophie but reacted like Shelly. Every so often, the two had combined to provide dreams so damned erotic he'd awake with his own raw groan caught in his throat, his body sheened in sweat, every muscle hard and straining.

He could still taste her, still feel the damp heat of her lips and tongue, and the warm softness of her mound as she'd worked herself against him. Her breast had felt perfect in his palm, small and sweetly curved, the nipple thrusting, eager for his mouth. And he'd wanted so badly to suck on her, to draw her deep until she begged for more.

He swallowed hard and closed his eyes, heat washing over him in waves. His hands trembled as he groped for his coffee mug and took a scalding gulp.

He had to talk to Sophie. When he admitted to her how he felt, how damned attracted he was to her, how badly he wanted her, she might bolt. If she wasn't interested in him, he could lose her friendship, and that wasn't something he even wanted to contemplate. But at least his confession should take care of Shelly, removing her as a temptation. He couldn't go through that again, couldn't chance the strength of his control. Hell, he'd been a hair away from laying her across his desk and stripping those damn flesh-hugging jeans down her long legs. He would have taken her hard, in a hot rush, and he had a feeling she'd have liked it.

But he couldn't exchange one woman for another; it wouldn't be fair to either of them. And the simple truth was, he wanted Shelly because she was the exact image of his Sophie. But she wasn't Sophie, and he didn't want to blow a chance with Sophie by missing that distinction.

He glanced at the clock as he finished his third cup of extra-strong coffee. He was seldom up this early, not with his hours at the bar, but sleep had been impossible. The caffeine hadn't kicked in yet, but it was almost nine-thirty, and by the time he got to Sophie's boutique, she should be there. Shelly was right about that, Sophie was an early bird. He'd better go before he lost his nerve.

That thought made him laugh because no woman had made him nervous since he'd turned sixteen. But then, no woman had ever mattered like Sophie did. He'd been waiting seven months for her. Ridiculous. It was time he put an end to things.

A half hour later, Cole opened the oak and etched glass door of the boutique, hearing the tinkling of the overhead bells. It was a classy little joint, filled with feminine scents and at the moment, lots of Valentine decorations. A small blonde-haired woman was perched in the corner, preparing to dress a nude mannequin in an arrangement of filmy night wear. She glanced up, looking at him over the rim of her round glasses.

"I'll be right with you," she said around a mouthful of straight pins that she held in her teeth.

"I came to see Sophie. Is she in?"

The woman straightened with new interest and quickly folded the garment in her hand, laying it aside and placing the pins on top. "No, I'm sorry. She's running a little late today. She called to ask me to open for her. Was she expecting you?"

Cole shook his head. It wasn't like Sophie to be late, and a flash of concern hit him broadside. "She's not ill?"

"No, I gathered she's just extra tired today." The woman smiled. "I'm Allison, her assistant. Aren't you the oldest Winston brother who owns the Winston Tavern? I saw your picture in the paper recently."

Cole twisted his mouth in a wry smile, well used to the feminine teasing. "Guilty. I hope you ignored the article. The paper loves catching me and my brothers unaware."

Allison's grin spread as she gave him a coy, slanted look. "It was a very nice shot. I saved the article."

Her blatant flirting didn't bother him; he'd deflected plenty of female interest in his days, gently, so he wouldn't ever hurt a woman's feelings.

Unfortunately, he hadn't deflected Shelly very well.

Cole abruptly changed the subject. "Do you know when Sophie will be in?"

"Sorry, I don't. She just said *later* around a very loud yawn. I think she's zonked and getting a late start this morning, judging by how she sounded."

"She was probably up late with her sister." He frowned with the thought. What if Shelly had already related the events of the evening to Sophie? What if she'd told Sophie how he'd kissed her...and more? They'd probably sat up all night gossiping about him and his cursed lack of control.

Damn it, Shelly had no business interfering with Sophie's rest. He knew Sophie worked long hours, and if anyone was going to disturb her sleep, he wanted it to be him.

Allison laughed. "Nope, that couldn't be it because she doesn't have a sister. Sophie is an only child."

Cole was surprised that Allison didn't know her employer any better than that, but then he thought of how private Sophie was, how little she talked, and he understood. "Shelly is her twin. She's in town for a short visit."

Allison shook her head and put her hands on her hips. "I don't know who's been pulling your leg, but Sophie is all alone. She lost her folks when she was just a kid. Her aunt took her in and raised her, but she died, too, about a year ago."

His heart flipped, then began a slow, steady thumping. Every nerve on alert, Cole asked, "Are you sure about that?"

"Positive."

Bombarded by a mix of feelings, most of all confusion, Cole braced his hands on the countertop and dropped his head forward, deep in thought. *No twin.*

"Hey, are you all right?"

He nodded. Hell yeah, he was all right. He was damn good. It was just that...He looked up at Allison again, trying for a casual expression to hide the emotions slamming through him, most of all sexual elation.

He felt off balance. On top of the carnal images crowding his brain, a swelling tenderness threatened to overwhelm him. Sophie was all alone in the world, not a single relative around. He'd lost his parents, too, so he knew how devastating that could be. But he'd always had his brothers, and they were closer than most complete families. He wanted to protect Sophie, to comfort her, to tell her she'd never be alone again.

His mind immediately skittered onto more profound thoughts, like the heat and sexual urgency of the night before. A hot rush of searing lust forced him to grip the counter hard. If Sophie didn't have a sister, then his entire day was about to take on a new perspective. Anticipation churned low in his abdomen. "You know Sophie well?" He was careful to keep the question negligent, not to arouse suspicions.

Allison shrugged. "Sure. I've been with her since she bought this place, around seven months now."

"I remember when she opened it." Cole could feel the heated, forceful rush of blood in his veins. His body hardened, pressing against the rough fly of his jeans, but he couldn't help himself. He shifted uncomfortably, remembering last night, how he'd touched Sophie, kissed *Sophie*. He knew what her breast felt like, how it nestled so perfectly in the palm of his hand. He knew the texture of her tight little derriere, the taste of her skin.

And he knew that Sophie Sheridan, actress and fraud, wanted him—enough to pretend to be someone else. His knees nearly buckled.

He cleared his throat twice before he could speak. "Sophie and I have gotten to know each other pretty well. But I could have sworn she told me she had a sister."

"No." Allison, bursting with confidence, perched on a stool by the cash register and leaned her elbows on the counter. "Her aunt was all she had, and they were really close. They've always lived together because the aunt got sick and Sophie had to take care of her. But then she died last year. It was an awful blow to Sophie and she took her inheritance and moved here, away from the memories." Allison tilted her head. "You interested in her?"

Oh yeah, he was interested. He knew his eyes were glittering with intent as he smiled down at Allison, making her blush. "We've been close as friends, but I was hoping to give her a surprise for Valentine's Day, something a little more…intimate. Could you do me a big favor, and not mention that I was here or that I asked about her? I don't want to ruin the surprise."

Eyes wide, Allison made a cross on her chest with an index finger. "I won't say a word. Sophie deserves a little fun."

Oh, he'd give her fun, all right. He mentally rubbed his hands together in sizzling anticipation. Sophie Sheridan was about to get what she wanted.

No, not sweet shy Sophie, he thought, remembering how she'd refused to enter his contest, how she froze every damn time he touched her. The sexy Shelly. Cole grinned, already so aroused he didn't know how he'd get through the day. Only the thought that the night would be an end to his frustration kept him on track with his plan. He'd deal with Shelly tonight—and then Sophie would deal with him in the morning.

He'd give her a Valentine's surprise she wouldn't soon forget.

Sophie was dragging by the time she'd gotten off work. The combination of the late night, the stress of deception, and the anticipation of starting it all again had her weary, both in mind and body. Aunt Maude had believed in early to bed, early to rise, and Sophie had always adhered to the philosophy, happy to do her best to please the aunt who'd raised and loved her. Yet she'd been up till almost two A.M. last night, and even after she'd gotten to bed, she hadn't been able to sleep, too filled with repressed desire. She wasn't used to the churning feelings that had kept her awake, and rather than sleep, her mind kept wandering back, remembering the delicious feel of Cole's hard, warm body pressed close, his muscled thigh between hers, his rough palm on her breast. She shivered anew. It had been a long, disturbing night.

Allison had been helpful, but too cheerful all day, smiling and humming, and Sophie had been endlessly relieved when she finally hung the CLOSED sign in the front window.

Despite her tiredness, she was anxious to see Cole, now that they shared a measure of carnal knowledge. She knew what his body felt like, how ravenous he was when kissing, his heady taste.

When she walked into the bar, shivering from the icy night, Cole immediately looked up at her, snaring her in his golden brown gaze. She had the feeling he might have been watching for her, and her heartbeat tripped alarmingly. His smile was different somehow, warmer and more intimate. Sophie wondered if it was Shelly's effect that made the difference.

For an instant, she was jealous of herself.

When Cole picked up a mug to fill with hot chocolate, releasing her from his gaze, she went to the back booth. Her belly tingled and her breasts felt heavy as she waited for him to serve her. She'd be herself, she thought, keeping her conversation to a minimum, drinking her hot chocolate without exception.

Only he didn't just give her the chocolate and leave after a few polite words. He set the cup in front of her, then seated himself opposite her in the booth, propping his chin on one large fist and smiling directly into her stunned eyes. He surveyed her until she squirmed, all the feelings from last night seeping into her muscles like an insidious warmth until her breath came too fast and shallow and her nipples puckered almost painfully tight. She hunched her shoulders in an effort to hide them.

Cole grinned, his gaze still a little too warm, too intent, slipping over her face as if he'd never seen her before. Just to break the tension, Sophie nodded at the steaming mug. "Thank you. I've been looking forward to this all day."

"Hmm. Me, too."

She paused with the spoonful of whipped cream halfway to her open mouth. His tone had been a low hungry growl. "Cole?"

He reached across the table and his large hand engulfed hers, then gently guided the spoon to her mouth. His gaze stayed directed on her lips, expectant, and like a zombie, Sophie obediently accepted the whipped cream. Slowly, Cole pulled the empty spoon away from her closed lips then laid it aside, his eyes so hot she could feel them touching on her. Using his thumb, he carefully removed a small dab of the cream from the corner of her mouth, and the gesture was so sensual, Sophie experienced a stirring of need low in her abdomen. His rough thumb idly rubbed her bottom lip, and for a few seconds her vision clouded and she had to close her eyes to regain her equilibrium.

She felt nervous and too tense. Much more of this and she'd be getting light-headed, fainting at his feet.

He pulled away, and his voice was low when he spoke, almost a whisper. "Have you ever dated, Sophie?"

His hands rested flat on the table, and she watched him shift, those long fingers coming closer to hers. She tucked her hands safely into her lap. If he touched her again, she'd be begging him for more, ruining her entire charade. "Why do you ask?"

"Oh, I don't know." His wicked smile was too sexy for words, but also playful. "Meeting your sister last night made me wonder why the two of you are so . . . different."

"You liked Shelly, then?" She already knew the answer to that. If Chase hadn't interrupted them, she had an inkling their intimacy might have become complete. What they'd done had been so satisfying in a way, but also very frustrating. The incredible feelings he'd created had been escalating, building, and she wanted to know what would happen, what the fullness of it all would be. She wanted to feel his body bare of clothes, to trace the prominent muscles she'd felt with her fingertips, skin on skin. His scent was stronger at his throat, and she wondered how it might be in other places, across his chest and abdomen, and where that thick erection had thrust against her.

Her breath caught and held as Cole reached across the table and fingered a curl hanging over her shoulder. "Yeah, I liked Shelly. But I like you, too."

She made a croaking sound, the best she could do with her thoughts so vivid and him looking at her like that. His knuckles brushed her cheek as he continued to toy with that one loose curl. "Well? Do you ever date?"

"No. I . . ." She tried a slight smile, but her face felt tight and strained. "You know how it is, how busy a business can keep you."

He nodded. "I raised my brothers, you know. Keeping them out of trouble and in school took up most of my time. I've just gotten to where I can have a serious relationship."

Sophie wanted to run away as fast as she could. Was he hinting that he wanted a relationship with Shelly? Good grief, she'd have to find a way to dissuade him of that notion.

Her jealousy swelled.

A smile flickered over Cole's mouth as he gave a playful tug on her hair. "Why don't you and Shelly get your picture taken together? I can't imagine anything prettier than that."

"Together?"

"Mmm. I could almost guarantee you'd win. And since you come in here every night, you could get your hot chocolate on the house."

And he could get his night on the town with Shelly. Words escaped her, so she merely shook her head. Winning the contest had never been her intent. She'd merely wanted to spend more time with Cole under the pretense of entering, using it as a way to introduce him to Shelly—on a temporary basis.

"All right. Suit yourself. But could you do me a favor? Ask Shelly if she can come in a little later tonight. Closer to closing. I have a lot of things to take care of and when she's here, I don't want to be distracted with work. Could you do that for me?"

Her mind raced. She'd probably have time to go home and catch a nap. She was absolutely exhausted, and as excited as she was about seeing him again, kissing and touching him again, she could barely keep her eyes open. A little sleep would refresh her and sharpen her flagging wits. "Yes. I'll tell her. There . . . there shouldn't be a problem. Her time is pretty free right now."

"Good. And Sophie?" He grinned, waiting for the questioning lift of her brows. "If you change your mind and decide to enter the contest, just let me know."

She could feel the embarrassed heat rushing to her cheeks and barely managed a nod. God, she hated it when she blushed. "Yes, all right. Thank you."

He walked away, whistling, and Sophie stared at her chocolate in abject misery. Most of the whipped cream had melted.

Well heck. She was horribly afraid her plans had just gotten irrevocably twisted.

Cole made it sound as though he hadn't stayed single by choice but rather by necessity. He'd even hinted that he wouldn't mind getting involved with a woman now.

And here she had stupidly given him over to her make-believe sister. Sophie covered her face with both hands. *The best laid plans*, she thought.

She finished up her hot chocolate and literally fled.

"You're grinning like the cat who just found a bucket of cream."

"Yeah." Cole turned to Chase and grinned some more. He'd been grinning all night, and with good reason. Damn, he felt good. *Sophie wanted him.* He kept reminding himself of that, but every time, it thrilled him all over. If he hadn't already known about her ruse, her last blush before rushing out would have done it. No one blushed like Sophie. He wanted to see her entire body flushed that way, hot for him and how he could make her feel. He'd been thinking and planning for hours now, ever since Sophie left, knowing that Shelly would return.

"So, what's up? You and Ms. Sunshine finally hook up, or was it that little rendezvous with the sister? That lady looked like she could put the grin on any guy."

Cole and Chase had always been as much like best friends as they were brothers, possibly because they were the two oldest, even though nine years separated them. They'd pretty much always confided in each other, but even so, if he'd had a choice, Cole would have kept Sophie's secret to himself. Problem was, Chase already knew she supposedly had a twin, so an explanation was in order. He sighed. "There is no sister."

Chase paused in the act of polishing a glass. "Come again?"

Damn, but he couldn't seem to stop grinning, the satisfaction almost alive inside him, bursting out. "Sophie doesn't have a sister." He said it slowly and precisely, relishing the words. "She's an only child."

Cole waited while Chase sorted that out in his mind, then a dumbfounded look spread over his face and he laughed out loud. "Well, I'll be." He gave a masculine nudge against Cole's shoulder. "Aren't you the lucky one?"

Relieved that Chase was going to view the circumstances in the same way he had, Cole nodded. "Damn right. But no one else knows."

"Not a problem. Mack and Zane were so busy tripping over themselves yesterday trying to figure out what was going on with you two, I just left them to their own imaginations. It's not often they get to see you tongue-tied around a woman."

Cole slanted him a look. "It wasn't my tongue that was knotted up. Hell, I think the Inquisition could have been easier than last night was."

"But tonight will be different?"

"Oh, yeah." Tonight he had no reason to resist Shelly's invitation. That expanding tenderness gripped him again, and his resolve doubled. When he thought of what Sophie was putting herself through, the elaborateness of her plan, he wanted to whisk her away and spend days showing her how unnecessary it all had been. Almost from the first day he'd seen her, he'd wanted her. All she had to do was smile, or order hot chocolate, and he was a goner. "If I don't miss my guess, Sophie is trying to get one thing without losing another."

"And you're both of those things?"

He nodded. "She's lived a sheltered life with an elderly aunt, and she hasn't ever dated much. She doesn't want to risk the comfort of coming here every night, which I gather is the sum of her social life, by causing an awkwardness between us. If we have an affair, things might change, at least that's how she likely sees it. But once I explain it all to her, she'll know how silly she's been."

"So you're going to admit to her you know she's an only child?"

"Hell no!" Cole scoffed at the very idea. Sophie, in all her innocence, was offering him a fantasy come true, and no way was he going to mess up her little performance. Besides, he wanted to see exactly how far she'd go with it. "I intend to show her that I want her, no matter who she is."

"Sounds like a dumb, hormone-inspired plan to me. And one guaranteed to tick the lady off."

"Like you're the expert?" Chase did even less honest dating than Cole. The death of their parents had hit him hard, and he'd been mostly reclusive ever since. Not that he was a monk, just very selective, and always very brief. Cole couldn't think of a single woman Chase had ever seen more than three times.

Chase shook his head. "It doesn't take a genius to figure out she'll be embarrassed. And women can be damn funny about things like that. You can accidentally bruise her while horsing around with some rough play, and she'll forgive you that. But hurt her feelings, and she'll never forget it."

Since that wasn't what Cole wanted to hear, he shrugged off the warning. Sophie had two sides, that was apparent now, and he intended to appease them both.

At that moment, she walked in, and incredibly, she looked even better now than she had last night. Of course, now he was looking at her with new eyes. This was his Sophie, so shy and sweet, yet now looking so sexy his teeth ached. The combination was guaranteed to blow his mind.

She wore the long, black leather coat again, this time over a loose, white blouse that buttoned down the front, tucked into a long black skirt and flat-heeled black shoes. She looked sensuously feminine and good enough to eat.

"Here comes Mutt and Jeff, so you better get your eyes back in your head and your tongue off the ground."

At Chase's muttered words, Cole pulled his gaze away from Sophie—*Shelly*—and turned to his brothers.

Mack was the first to speak, though he kept his fascinated gaze on Sophie. "What's going on with her lately? She's looking too damn fine."

"I'll say," Zane added. "Not that she wasn't a looker to begin with, but she never seemed aware of it before. She was always so...understated. Now her sex appeal is kind of up front, right in your face." He chuckled. "I like it."

Cole didn't bother responding to either brother. "I'm going to take her picture, so I'd appreciate some privacy while I'm in my office with her."

Mack's grin was so wide, it lifted his ears a fraction of an inch. "You need privacy to take her picture?"

Zane slugged him, which gained a disgruntled look, and a reciprocal smack. As Zane rubbed his shoulder, he said, "Don't tease him, Mack. Hell, I'm just glad to see him finally cutting loose a little." To Cole he remarked, "You act more like a grandpa than a big brother."

"Gee thanks."

Mack chuckled again. "We promise to give you all the leeway you need. In fact, given it's Friday, I can close up with Chase if you like."

"I was going to ask. Thanks."

"Sorry I can't stay too, Cole, but I already have plans. If you'd warned me—"

Chase gave his brother a distracted look. "Zane, you always have plans. What's her name this time?"

Unabashed, Zane straightened in a cocky way and said, "I never kiss and tell."

Cole figured Zane was more than old enough to manage his own love life, so he thumped him on the back and said, "Have fun," as he walked away to meet Sophie. She was still standing in the middle of the floor, and he realized she wasn't certain where to sit. From the beginning she'd always taken the back booth, which was the most secluded. But tonight, right this moment, she wasn't supposed to be Sophie and she didn't know how to act.

Someone turned on the jukebox just as Cole reached her and he had to yell to be heard. "I see you got my message."

She stared at him, devouring him with her eyes, and now he knew how to interpret that look. His lower body tightened in anticipation.

"Yes. Uh . . . Sophie told me to make it a little later. How soon will you close up?"

"Chase will give the last call in a few minutes." A couple shuffled past them, clinging to each other, barely moving their bodies as they feigned an interest in the music. Cole grinned. "Do you dance?"

As he asked it, he caught her hands and tugged her closer. She blanched. "Ah, no I don't. . . . That is . . ."

"No one is paying any attention," he cajoled. He pulled her into his arms, at the same time looking over her shoulder and seeing the rapt faces of his brothers. No attention, indeed. He frowned and shook his head at them. They all three nodded back, displaying various degrees of humor and curiosity.

Sophie tucked her face into his shoulder. "I've never danced much."

"You're doing fine." He nuzzled her temple, enjoying the feel of her warmth and softness so close, breathing in the sweet, familiar smell of her. She brought out his animal instincts, and he wanted to somehow mark her as his. His arms tightened and his thoughts rioted with plans for the coming night. "I like holding you."

Shuddering slightly, she leaned back to see his face. "I like having you hold me. Very much." She bit her lip, hesitant, then blurted, "And I liked what we did last night. Why did you stop?"

Cole felt poleaxed by her direct attack. He hadn't expected it. Lifting one hand, he cupped her cheek. "It was time to close the bar."

Sophie shook her head. "No, it was more than that. You seemed angry." Color in her cheeks deepened, but she held his gaze. "I want you to know, Cole, just because I'm . . . Sophie's sister, that doesn't mean I'd expect any more from you than any other woman."

"Oh?" *Silly goose.* She was so sweet and innocent, he wanted to pick her up and carry her away someplace private, then spend the long night reassuring her, making love to her, tying her to him. He knew his brothers were all watching, all alert, so he controlled himself. "What do other women expect from me?"

She swallowed audibly, but those smoky blue eyes never wavered, and he realized he admired her guts as much as everything else about her. Carrying out her plan couldn't be easy on her, and it directly indicated just how badly she wanted him. Lord help him, he'd never make it through the night.

"Nothing more than a nice night or two together, I suppose. I won't... won't be in town long. For the few days I am here, I'd like to share your company. But you don't have to worry about me hanging around afterward. I have my own life to live and I'm not interested in complicating it with a relationship. You don't have to worry that I'll make a pest of myself."

His chest tightened with some strange emotion he'd never experience before. He brushed her bottom lip with his thumb, then whispered, "Come into my office where we can talk. I'll have Chase bring us something to drink."

She looked more than a little relieved by his offer and smiled her thanks before taking the hand he extended to her. Her fingers were still chilled from the outdoors, and he gently squeezed, giving her some of his warmth. His body thrummed with excitement.

He turned and caught the flurry of movement as his brothers quickly found something to do. Zane was pulling on his coat, ready to leave. Mack was red in the face, studiously inventorying their stack of shot glasses. And Chase merely smiled, giving them both a brief nod.

As Cole passed him, he said, "A couple of drinks, Chase?"

"Sure thing." There was so much wickedness in Chase's tone, Cole felt obliged to add, "Colas please." He didn't want to give Sophie a hot chocolate, thereby giving up the game by showing her he knew her preferences. Beyond that, he wasn't at all certain his control was up to it right now. The way she drank hot chocolate was better than an aphrodisiac.

Luckily, Sophie didn't notice the byplay. Her gaze remained on her feet as they entered his office. This time, he'd left the light on. He wanted to see every small expression that might pass over her face. He locked the door and smiled at her. "Come here."

Slightly startled, her eyes rounded and her sweet mouth opened just before he covered it with his own. He vaguely heard Chase announcing the last call, and he felt his muscles tense. Soon they'd be alone; he'd have her all to himself, with all the privacy he needed to see about fulfilling every single wish she'd ever had.

He folded her closer, one hand cupping the back of her head, his fingers tangled in her silky hair, the other pressing low on her spine, urging her body into more intimate contact with his.

And just that easily, she melted. There wasn't an ounce of resistance in her. He parted her lips with his tongue, licking into her mouth, touching the edge of her small white teeth, stroking deep, claiming and exciting. Her hands fisted on his chest, pulling tight the material of his shirt.

"Cole..."

The knock on the door announced the arrival of their drinks. Cole took in her dreamy gaze, her flushed cheeks, and smiled to himself. "Don't move."

She merely nodded in response.

He opened the door and took the tray Chase handed him. "Thanks."

"Don't do anything I wouldn't do."

"What wouldn't you do?"

"Exactly." Chase slapped him on the shoulder and pulled the door shut.

When Cole turned back to Sophie, she was still standing in the same spot as if rooted there. He smiled, set the tray on the desk, and turned to her. He touched her cheek, her chin, smoothed her eyebrows. Her face was so precious to him. He kissed her again, then began maneuvering his way to the desk. She clung to him, following his lead, and when he lifted her to sit on the very edge, she did no more than sigh.

"I'm glad you wore a skirt, baby." He trailed kisses over her jaw and down her throat.

Breathless, she asked, "Why?"

He lifted his gaze, amused by her innocence, charmed by her heavy-lidded eyes and dazed expression. Slowly, he slid one hand down her side to her knee, then back up again, under her skirt.

"Oh!"

He grinned, but it cost him. Her slim thighs were warm, silky, and as his fingers climbed, he realized she wore stockings. He muttered a low curse and took her mouth, bending her back on the desk, hungry for her. With her skirt bunched up it was easy to nudge her legs apart and nestle his hips there. He gave up the exquisite explorations of her legs to cup one small, perfect breast. "I can feel your heart racing," he said against her mouth.

She pressed her face into his chest. "I love having you touch me."

"Then you'll love this even more." He slid the top button of her

V-necked blouse free. She sucked in a breath, then held it. The next button opened, and he could see the silky-smooth flesh of her chest, the beginnings of her cleavage. He traced a finger there, dipping and stroking both breasts, moving close enough to a nipple to make her shiver in anticipation. "God, there can't be anything softer or sweeter on earth than a woman's breast," he said as he continued to tease her. He shaped and molded her breasts in his palms, pushing them up, marveling at the resiliency of her soft flesh.

Sophie gave a quiet moan.

He tugged another button free. Her bra was white lace, barely there, and the sexiest damn thing he'd ever seen. He wondered if it matched her garter and panties.

Their foreheads were together, both of them watching the slow movement of his dark hand on her pale, delicate skin. He opened the last two buttons and pushed her blouse aside, lifting both hands to cup her breasts in his palms.

"So pretty," he breathed.

Her breasts trembled with her deep breaths; he touched the front closure of her bra with a fingertip.

And the music in the bar died. Sophie lifted her head, startled.

"Shhh, it's okay. They're just shutting down. It's time for everyone to go home."

She blinked, and her lips quivered. "Do we need to go, too?"

"Not if you don't want to." He kissed her, a warm, featherlight kiss. "But I'd like to take you home with me, sweetheart. My apartment is only a few blocks away. My couch is okay for a quick nap, but I don't have napping in mind, and I don't want anything about tonight to be quick." He touched her face, his fingertips barely grazing her downy cheek. "I don't mean to rush you. I know things are progressing awfully fast." His mouth tipped in a small smile and he added, "After all, we just met. But I want you, and you obviously want me. Will you come home with me? Will you spend the night?"

Her eyes went wide, her lashes fluttering. He could see the wild racing of her pulse in her throat. "Yes." She swallowed hard, then smiled. "Yes, I'd like that. Thank you."

Cole grinned at her perfect manners, wanting to tease her but unable to dredge up an ounce of humor.

The rigidity had left Sophie's shoulders by the time they were in his car, but she was far from relaxed. He'd barely managed to talk her out of driving herself to his apartment. He knew she'd wanted her car there as an avenue of escape.

He wanted her to trust him, to give him everything.

She remained silent as he parked the car and led her to the second floor of his apartment building. He didn't mind. The silence wasn't overly uncomfortable, but rather charged with tension and anticipation. Something very basic and primal inside him wanted to see Sophie in his home, on his territory, in his bed. He wanted to stake a claim, and he intended to do it right. He'd never been a barbarian before, but right now, he felt like howling, like slaying dragons to prove his affections.

She looked around as he unlocked the door and led her inside.

"My place is pretty simple. I'm not one for much decorating, and until recently, one or more of my brothers lived with me. Mack only moved on campus this past year and he was the last to go."

He watched as her gaze skimmed over everything, the dark leather furniture, the light oak tables, the awards and trophies set on a table that one or more of his brothers had won in sports and academics.

The eat-in kitchen was barely visible through an arched doorway. The bedrooms were down a short hallway.

"It's very nice," she said.

He pulled off his jacket, then took her coat, tossing both over a chair arm. "Zane teases me about being a housewife, but I like to keep the place clean, and now, he's no different. Teaching those three to do laundry and mop floors and cook was a chore, but they finally picked it up. We used to have a regular cleanup day, and there were no excuses accepted for missing it. Well, except for the time Chase broke his leg. Then we let him off the hook."

He grinned at her, wanting her to relax, to get to know him better. He was telling her things he'd never discussed with any other woman, and truth be told, she looked fascinated.

"How old were you when your parents died?"

"Twenty-two. I'd just finished college. Mack and Zane were still in grade school, but Chase was in junior high."

"It must have been awfully rough."

He nodded in acknowledgment, unwilling to rehash the past and all the problems that had cropped up daily. "We got through it. They were good kids, just a little disoriented by it all. It took time to get readjusted, to get past the loss." He wanted to ask her about her own loss, but because he wasn't supposed to know about it, he couldn't, and it frustrated him. They should be using this time to build a closeness, not hide behind secrets.

Abruptly, he asked, "Are you hungry? Or would you like something to drink?"

She hesitated only a moment and that intriguing blush turned her face pink. Then, suddenly, she launched herself at him. Her arms went tight around his neck, almost smothering him as he caught her. "All I want is to finish what we started at the bar." She pressed frantic kisses to his neck, his nose, his ear, making him laugh, and at the same time groan with an incredible rush of hot lust. "I want to lie down with you and touch you and—"

"Honey, shush before you make me crazy." To guarantee her compliance, he kissed her, holding her face still, thrusting his tongue deep, tasting of her, making love to her mouth. Her words had affected him, making his body ache in need.

He pulled her blouse from her skirt and quickly skimmed the buttons open, then pushed it off her shoulders. She helped, wiggling her arms free and trying to keep their mouths together.

Laughing again, he said, "Take it easy, honey. We've got all night. There's no rush."

He gentled her, stroking his hands up and down her bare back, placing small, damp kisses across her skin. Her hands clutched at his hips and he obligingly stepped closer to her, letting her feel his rigid erection, nestling it into her soft belly.

She made a small sound of mingled excitement and delight. "Cole?"

"Hmmm?" he muttered, distracted by the taste and texture and scent of her skin. The fact that this was his Sophie sharpened the pleasure to a keen edge.

"Will you take off your shirt, too?"

He hesitated, afraid he might lose control if she started touching him too much. But her eyes were soft and huge, inquisitive and excited, and he couldn't resist. His heart pounding, he unbuttoned his shirt and shrugged it off, then peeled his T-shirt over his head. He dropped them both on the floor. Sophie's gaze moved over him, warm and intimate.

"You can touch me, honey."

Still, she seemed timid, so he took her hand in his, kissed her palm, then laid it flat on his chest. Sophie licked her lips as she tentatively stroked him. "You're so warm and hard."

He laughed. Hot was a more apt description, and there was no questioning how hard he was. It felt like his jeans would split at any minute. He ruthlessly maintained his control and started on the side button to her skirt.

"Cole..." She stiffened, anxiety in her tone.

"I want to see you, baby," He searched her expression and read so much nervousness there, he paused. Cupping her face and leaning close, he whispered, "You're very sexy. I could spend a lifetime looking at you and it wouldn't be enough."

Her small hands curled over his wrists. "And we certainly don't have a lifetime, do we? I...I'm leaving in just a few days."

When would she give up that ridiculous tale? At this point, it almost annoyed him. It was so difficult not to call her by name, not to admit how much he cared. But this was her show, he reminded himself, and he was determined to let her play it as she chose, at the same time, helping to meet her goals, to give her everything she'd ever wanted. "Are you sure you won't be able to stay in town awhile?"

"No." She interrupted him quickly, firmly, then stepped against him to wrap her arms tight around his waist. "No, we can have tonight, but that's all I need. Just one night. An exciting experience for both of us, but no more than that."

His confidence started to dip. Had he misread her? Did Sophie truly only want a very brief affair?

Not even that, he thought, as her words *just one night* reverberated in his brain. Maybe, unlike him, she had stayed single by choice. God knew, the woman was more than attractive enough to draw men in droves. He'd seen the underlying sensuality beneath her quiet persona, so it stood to reason other men would have seen it as well. Even Zane had commented that she was a looker, and he was a connoisseur of women.

Anger washed over him. Her ruse no longer seemed so touchingly sweet, and he was met with a new determination, one to make her so deliriously satisfied, so sated with his lovemaking, she wouldn't be able to deny him ever again. He would give her what she wanted and more. Before the night was over, she'd be as addicted as he.

One night hell.

"Take off the skirt, sweetheart. Let me touch you." The growled words hung heavy between them until finally Sophie released her death grip on him and lifted her head. Cole stepped back just enough to allow her to move freely.

Her eyes looked more gray than blue as they held his, looking for reassurance. At his smile, she carefully released the button to the waistband of the skirt and slid the zipper down. It immediately dropped over her slim hips to layer around her ankles. Cole took her hand and she stepped out of it, leaving her shoes behind as well.

The dark, sexy stockings covering her long, slender legs were enough to make him groan, but it was the sight of her narrow waist, her flat belly, that shook his control. Her panties were pale, and the small triangle of chestnut curls could be seen beneath the sheer material, taunting him, making his palms burn with the need to touch her.

"Christ, you're beautiful."

He hadn't realized she'd been holding her breath until she let it out in a long shaky sigh. "I wasn't sure what you would think—"

"I think I'm one lucky bastard," he muttered, his tone none too steady. "Come here, honey."

He didn't mean to be rough, to startle her, but he didn't think he could take much more. He'd been imagining this moment for almost seven months, and the reality was much sweeter than any fantasy he'd dredged up. He supposed it was because he genuinely cared about her, because he liked and respected her, that sex between them seemed like so much more. To him, laying her down and burying himself in her would be more than physical, it would be emotional and mental, too, a bonding of more than just their bodies.

The softness of her skin drew him, and he touched her everywhere, his hands gliding over her shoulders, her waist, the back of her thighs above the stockings. He pulled his mouth away from hers as he slid both rough palms into her panties, cuddling her small buttocks. Sophie stiffened, and he kissed her ear, then nipped the lobe. She gasped and her fingers contracted on his arms.

"I like that," she whispered.

He smiled despite his roaring lust. "This?" he asked as he stroked her silky bottom again. "Or this?" His teeth closed carefully on her ear-lobe as his tongue teased. She arched against him.

"Yes, that."

"There are other places to nibble, you know. Places you'll like even more."

"Oh?" She was breathless, trembling all over. Keeping one hand on her bottom to hold her close, Cole slid the other hand back up her side until her reached her breasts. With only one flick, he opened her skimpy bra.

They both groaned as he cuddled the soft, delicate weight of one warm breast in his hand. She gave a rough purr of feminine pleasure but jerked slightly as he caught her stiff nipple between his fingertips and rolled.

"There's here, too." With that warning, he bent his head and caught the tip of her breast between his teeth, flicking with his tongue, just as he'd done to her earlobe. Sophie grabbed his head, her fingers tight in his hair as she cried out. Cole opened his mouth wide and drew her in, sucking strongly. His hands closed on her waist and he backed her to the nearest wall, then stepped between her thighs, deliberately forcing her legs wide.

His hand moved down her waist, over her belly, and his fingertips toyed with the edge of her panties. Sophie shivered and moaned, and he knew he was tormenting her as much as himself. Just as his fingers dipped inside he kissed her again, swallowing her moan of pleasure.

She was warm, wet, her tender flesh swollen, and his fingers gently caressed her until she was panting, her face pressed to his throat, her fingers grasping his biceps.

"Right here, honey," he whispered as he used his middle finger to ply her tiny, swollen clitoris.

"Oh God..." Her body jerked in reaction, pressing hard against him.

Cole kissed his way back to her ear, his teeth once again catching the lobe. His tongue stroked just as his finger did, and Sophie wasn't too innocent to realize the parody of what he did. She clutched at him and her hips began to move in tandem with the rhythm he set.

She was close, and he knew it. It surprised him, her immediate, unsparing reaction to him. It also made him nearly wild with lust. He'd always assumed Sophie had hidden depths, that once unleashed, her passion would be savage and uninhibited. His entire body pulsed with each small shudder she gave, each deep, raw moan. And when he whispered, "You would taste so sweet. Can you imagine my mouth here, honey, my tongue touching and licking—" she gave a stifled scream and climaxed.

Cole held her close, keeping the wild pleasure intense until she whimpered and slumped into him, utterly drained. Blood pounded through his veins, roaring in his ears. He scooped her up and hurried into his bedroom. He lowered her to the bed, laying her on top of the cool quilts, his own body coming down to cover hers.

He kissed her long and deep, caressing her breasts, her thighs, her belly. He leaned back to look at her, then removed her open bra and finished stripping her panties down her legs. She turned her face away, breathing shakily.

"You're perfect, sweetheart." What an understatement. He'd never seen a woman who stirred him like this one did. He kissed her breasts, sucking and nipping, his mouth gentle, his tongue rough. Sophie's body seemed to be designed with his sensual specifications in mind. He felt a near frenzy of need, but Sophie lay sated and limp beneath him, one hand in his hair, idly stroking. He shoved up to his side, pulled a condom from his jeans pocket, then held it in his teeth while he struggled out of the rest of his clothes.

His shoes went across the room when he kicked them off. He stood to shuck his jeans down his legs, and then turned back to Sophie. She immediately protested.

"I didn't get to see you," she said with a sexy pout.

Despite his need, Cole chuckled and moved her thighs apart, situating her for lovemaking. "Whereas I can see you very well. All of you," he added in a low, breathless growl, looking at her damp, soft curls and the tender flesh they protected. She still wore her stockings and the wisp of a garter belt, and she was so incredibly sexy he nearly lost his control. His fingers stroked over her again, easily now with her recent orgasm, feeling her slick dampness, her heat. Her modesty was gone and she simply allowed him to look, to touch. The sight helped to curb his rush. He could look at her forever and be happy.

She wasn't willing to give him forever. Damn this game.

She stretched like a small cat and smiled at him. "It's hardly fair, you know. I've been very curious about your body."

"You'll see me soon enough." He tore the silver package open and slipped the condom on. "But not now because I can't wait."

He caught her legs in the crook of his elbows and bent low over her, leaving her totally exposed and vulnerable to his possession. Sophie grabbed his shoulders to hold on, her eyes wide and dark, her breath coming in small, anxious pants. He probably should have taken more care, treated her more gently, with more restriction. Instead, he held her wide open and watched as he entered her body, as her delicate flesh gave way to his, slowly allowing him entrance. His muscles clenched even more, his heart thumping heavily. She was tight, resisting him, and he flexed his buttocks, forcing his way forward.

She said his name on a low moan.

"God, you're snug," he whispered through clenched teeth, and his forehead was damp with sweat. Sophie tipped her head back, biting her lip and squeezing her eyes shut. A rosy flush spread from her breasts to her throat and cheeks, not embarrassment, but sharp arousal. It fed his own. And then he sank into her, her body finally accepting his, squeezing him like a hot, wet, hungry fist.

He knew, of course, that she wasn't overly experienced, that she was mostly shy and withdrawn and therefore probably not all that practiced with men. But he hadn't expected her to be like this, so tight that he had to wonder if any other man had ever had her. The thought that he was the first, that she'd waited twenty-six years for him, broke his control, overwhelming him with a tidal wave of feelings he couldn't name and wasn't ready to deal with.

He withdrew, only to rock into her again, slow at first, but then harder and faster. "I'm sorry, baby," he said between rushing breaths, "I can't wait."

With no apparent complaints, Sophie reached for him, drawing his mouth down to hers, kissing him with a hunger that matched his own. Her small, feminine muscles held him tight, resisting each time he pulled away, then gladly squeezing as he pushed deep back into her, milking him, making him wild. When she pressed her head back, groaning in another immediate climax, Cole followed her. His mind went blank, his vision blurred, and his body burned. He felt a part of her, her scent in his head, his heart. He pounded heavily into her slim body until finally, he stiffened and his body shook as he emptied himself. He stayed suspended like that for long moments, then slowly collapsed against her.

Their rapid heartbeats mingled, and he could feel her breathing in his ear, soft, fast breaths. *God, he loved her.* The possessiveness nearly choked him; he wanted badly to whisper her name, to tell her how their lives would be from now on. To make her admit she cared also.

He'd gladly given up his personal life to care for his brothers. In that time, no woman had really appealed to him, to tempt him from his duty. But now he was free, and Sophie was here, as if sent by fate just when he was ready for her and needed her most. He wanted her, now and always. But he held back the words of commitment, unsure of her and how she would take such a declaration when she'd been so insistent on their time limit.

Slowly, carefully, he untangled his arms from her legs and heard her moan as her legs dropped. He'd been too rough, moved too fast for her, but she hadn't complained.

He managed a kiss to her neck by way of apology, but his mind was too sluggish, too affected, to do more than that. Her fingers sifted through his damp hair, and he could feel her smile where her mouth touched his shoulder.

"I hadn't imagined anything like that."

How the hell could she form coherent words? Cole struggled up onto his elbows and looked down at her, still breathing hard. She appeared smug and very satisfied. "So you thought it was okay?" he teased.

"Incredible."

He felt like a world conqueror at her words. He brushed his fingertips over her swollen lips. "I'm glad. I think you're pretty damned special, too. I always have."

She stilled for just a moment, her eyes wary. Her tongue came out to touch nervously on her lower lip, and she accidently licked against his finger. They both shuddered in reaction. "We only met a few days ago."

He was still inside her, her naked breasts flattened against the hardness of his chest, their pulses still too fast, and she continued the ridiculous game. She should have been admitting the truth to him by now. He'd all but told her how he felt.

Unless, of course, she didn't feel the same. If what her assistant, Allison, had said was true, her life had been so quiet, so sedate, she may have just hungered for a quick bite of adventure. Did she truly want him as a one-night stand? He'd assumed she'd concocted the absurd plan because she was unsure of herself and him. But it was possible the opposite was true, that she didn't hope for more involvement, but rather a guarantee of less. His stomach cramped at the possibility.

"Cole?"

"I was just thinking. It seems like I've known you a long time."

"Maybe that's because you've known Sophie. But we're nothing alike."

He smoothed her dark hair away from her face, wishing there was some simple, magical way to figure her out. He'd never suspected that his Sophie might be so contrary and complex. "I don't know about that," he whispered. "Sophie is—"

She laughed, interrupting him and quickly changing the subject before he could say the words that he desperately wanted to say, words he hoped would reassure her and gain a reciprocal declaration. "Are you ever going to get around to taking my picture?"

Momentarily distracted, he teased, "Like this?" He looked her over leisurely, the wild tangle of her hair, her sated gaze, the way her limbs were entwined with his. His hand smoothed over her hip. "You'd be a winner for sure."

She smiled. "How about just a head shot?"

He pretended disappointment. "I suppose it'll have to do." He pulled away, letting his hand linger on her thigh for a heart-stopping moment. "Don't move."

"I'm not sure I even can." But she did turn toward him, propping her head up on an elbow. "Where are you going?"

"I have a camera here."

Cole disposed of the condom, then slipped on his jeans before rummaging in his closet for the instamatic camera. He looked up to see Sophie posed there, her hair wild, the quilts rumpled beneath her, one long, stocking-clad leg bent, the lacy garter still in place. A new wave of heat hit him. She was his. One way or another, he'd make her admit it.

"I should have gone slower, played longer," he said as he surveyed the feast she made.

"Why didn't you?"

He shook his head and came to sit on the edge of the bed. "Because you made me so crazy I couldn't even think straight, much less wait very long. I meant to make our first time together really special."

She laughed. "You haven't heard me complaining, have you?"

He'd never imagined Sophie with that particular impish smile. He kissed her, loving her more with each passing moment. "So you feel satisfied?"

She stretched again. "Absolutely. It was more than I'd ever imagined. So stop worrying."

"All right." It was easy to convince him since he didn't want to waste a single second with her by debating the issue. The night was still young enough, he'd have plenty of time to prove his point to her.

He lifted the camera to his eye, sending her squawking and screeching, grabbing for the sheet. "Cole, wait! I have to comb my hair. I'm a wreck."

"No, you're beautiful." She crossed her arms over her breasts and laughed at him, and that's the picture he took. When it slid out of the camera, he lifted it out of her reach, then stood to put it on his dresser.

"Don't you dare consider hanging that anywhere!"

"I'm keeping that one for myself."

She relaxed again and studied him, her expression going soft and curious. "Why?"

"So I can look at you whenever I want." That was the truth, though not nearly close to how deeply he felt about it. "Now, if you want to put your blouse on and comb your hair before I take the entry picture, that's fine, but I swear you don't need it."

"I'm going to do it anyway."

He chuckled at her show of prim vanity. "All right. I'll go get us something to drink. You have about three minutes."

*   *   *

He was back in two, and Sophie had just begun to untangle her hair. She still felt languorous and warm and sated. She wanted nothing more than to curl back up on the bed with Cole and do all those things they'd already done, plus more. The bed smelled like him, and she could have snuggled into it forever. She pondered the possibility of stealing one of his pillows, but knew she'd be found out. She glanced at the clock and wanted to cry over the amount of time that had already passed them by.

Though she was enjoying their easy banter and intimate conversation—something she hadn't expected—she hadn't had near enough time to explore his body. It fascinated her, his perfect collection of hard bone and strong muscle. The few quick looks she'd gotten had made her insides feel like they were melting. She literally wanted to kiss him all over.

"What are you thinking about? There's a wicked gleam in your eyes."

Startled, Sophie looked up at him. He set a tray with two mugs of hot chocolate and a can of whipped cream on the dresser. His chest was bare and as he moved, muscles flexed and rippled. His jeans hung low, thanks to the fact he hadn't buttoned or zipped them, and his bare feet were large, braced apart, the tops sprinkled with dark hair.

She wanted to groan in pleasure; she wanted to tell him to stand there for about a year or so and let her look her fill. "I was thinking of your body, and how unfair it is that I haven't gotten to touch you much."

He froze for an instant, then shuddered. His eyes narrowed and grew dangerously bright. "You'll get your turn, if you're sure you want it." He loaded one mug of hot chocolate with whipped cream, forming a small mountain, then carried it to her with a spoon. Sophie scooted up against the headboard and balanced the warm cup between her palms. Leaning forward, she licked at the cream, more than a little aware of Cole's gaze.

His hand touched the side of her face, smoothing her hair back behind her ear. "I'd like to make love to you until morning, honey, if you're sure you're up to it."

Dark color slashed high on his cheekbones and his eyes were bright, glittering. He looked very aroused, and Sophie set the mug aside on the nightstand to give him her full attention. "I'd like that, too. I want this night to be enough to last a long, long time."

"You're not too sore?"

Such a strong wave of embarrassment washed over her, she felt even her nose turn red. "Of course not." It was a partial lie; she did feel achy in places she flatly refused to mention. But it didn't matter, not when compared with the pleasure of getting to hold him again.

"You were so tight," he whispered, his hands still touching her as if he couldn't help himself. "I know you haven't had much hands-on experience. No," he said, placing a finger over her lips when she started to object. "I'm not judging or asking for details. But I know women's bodies, babe. And you were either a virgin, or you've been a hell of a long time without a man. You were so damn tight I almost lost my mind. But either way, I don't want to hurt you."

Sophie felt touched to her soul. He was so wonderfully considerate, so decidedly male. Protective and virile, and she could gladly spend a lifetime with him. He'd hinted several times that he wouldn't mind continuing his relationship with Shelly, and she was so very tempted. But how could she ever manage such a thing? Keeping up the game for only a few days had worn on her. Already, she'd missed more sleep than ever before. Her boutique demanded all her attention in the mornings, so she couldn't keep up the late hours with Cole along with her normal shift at the shop. And the longer she was with him, the more risk she ran of being found out. If Cole knew she acted out both roles, what would he think? She shuddered at the mere possibility.

Softly now, because tears were so close, she whispered, "I want anything and everything you can give me tonight. What little discomfort I have doesn't matter at all, not in comparison to how you make me feel."

The muscles in his shoulders and neck seemed to tighten even more. Abruptly, he stood and grabbed up the camera. "Give me a smile, honey."

She did, though she knew it was a weak effort. His obvious arousal triggered her own. Once the photo was taken, he looked at the picture, nodded in satisfaction, then put it and the camera aside. "Now."

Shakily, her smile barely there, Sophie asked, "Now what?"

"Now we finish our drinks—after you get rid of that shirt."

Once again, he unbuttoned her blouse, playing with her, kissing each spot of skin that was uncovered, teasing her. Sophie relished his attention to detail. He also knelt in front of her to remove her garter and stockings. "I want you completely naked," he explained, and she hadn't cared to argue with him, too excited by the husky timber of his voice.

To her surprise, once that was done, he didn't attempt to make love to her again but instead wanted to assist her with her mug of hot chocolate. Sophie giggled every time he carried a spoonful of whipped cream to her mouth, but he was persistent, cajoling, and before the drinks were done, she had caught on and teased him unmercifully, licking at the spoon and sometimes his fingers, making him groan in reaction. She'd never been a flirt before, but she liked it.

And judging by his reactions, he liked it, too.

She thought of all the nights she drank hot chocolate at his bar and knew she'd never be able to order the drink there again. The chocolate always gave her a boost to get through the rest of her evening after a long workday, sort of like the caffeine from coffee did for others. She drank it year round, but now, she would imagine this scene, and if Cole so much as looked at her, she would recall his touch, his kiss. Though this was happening to Shelly, Sophie would be affected. No, she would never drink hot chocolate in front of him again. But it was worth it to lose the one small, routine comfort, when compared with the excitement of their present play.

"God, the way you do this ought to be outlawed for the sanity of mankind."

She merely smiled.

"You're such a tease," he whispered.

To which she replied, "Me? You're the one who still has his jeans on."

He leaned forward and kissed her, his tongue smoothing over her lips, then dipping inside before he pulled away. "An easy enough problem to fix." He stood and unselfconsciously shucked off the last of his clothes. Sophie caught her breath at the sight of him. He was already hard, thrusting outward, and her body warmed at the significance of that.

"I started something earlier that I didn't get a chance to finish."

She couldn't imagine what. Everything had felt very finished to her; her nerve endings all came alive as she remembered the ways he'd touched and kissed her. Her eyes rounded when he scooped her up and laid her flat on the bed, one of her legs across his lap, the other behind him. Without a word, he leaned over and very gently nipped her ear, his tongue touching, stroking. One hand closed on her breast, and his fingers smoothed over and around her nipple until she squirmed.

Her body thrummed in immediate excitement. She closed her eyes, thrilled by his touch, how quickly he could bring her to a high level of excitement. She'd never imagined anything like this in her life.

He moved from her ear to her throat, then her shoulder, which she hadn't realized was so sexually sensitive to his touch, but every time he kissed her skin, every little lick, sent a riot of sensation through her body, seeming to concentrate between her thighs.

"There's a lot of things I'd like to do to you, honey."

"Yes." Whatever he wanted was fine with her; he seemed to know things about her body she'd never guessed.

"You taste so sweet," he whispered as he neared her breasts. His breath was fast, his mouth hot as he covered her nipple and tugged. Her back arched, but he soothed her, murmuring to her until she relaxed again, though her heartbeat still galloped.

"Relax and let me make love to you, baby."

Relax? Her entire body felt too tight, too sensitive. Then his teeth closed on her nipple, just sharp enough to alarm her. He tugged and she cried out, but he didn't stop, gently tormenting her. She started to grasp his head, but he caught her hands in one fist and pinned them above the pillow. His rough, raspy tongue smoothed over and around her nipple until she cried, then he switched to the other breast.

He was in no hurry now and she could do no more than accept his unique brand of torture. Still, she tried to protest when he left her breasts to kiss her ribs, but he wouldn't be deterred. Sophie moved against him, wanting to feel him push inside her body, to fill her. She ached for him. The feelings were even stronger now that she knew what to expect, what to anticipate.

She stiffened when his mouth moved to the top of her left thigh and her breath caught in her chest. His fingers slipped between her thighs and cupped her. "Remember what I told you earlier, babe?"

One finger found her most sensitive spot and gently rubbed back and forth. Sophie couldn't find enough breath to answer him.

"Do you remember?" He lightly pinched her, tugged, stroked, and Sophie couldn't keep the long moan from escaping between her tightly clenched teeth.

"That's it. You do remember, don't you? Here, and here..." He kissed her ear again, her nipple. "And here." In the next instant, his mouth replaced the fingers between her legs and she couldn't believe it, couldn't control her reactions or her small screams. Her hands pulled free and knotted in his hair, keeping him close, and he moved closer still, tasting her, licking her, nipping with his teeth. He gently sucked as he worked one rough finger into her, then another. Pushing deep inside, slowly, adding to the building pressure and pleasure.

The contractions hit her hard and she screamed out her climax, vaguely aware of his hum of satisfaction, of the way he pressed his own body firmly against the mattress. Her hips bucked and he resettled her, his long fingers biting into her hips, holding her still. It seemed to go on and on and he wouldn't relent until she pounded on his shoulders and shuddered and begged.

Seconds later he was over her and he cupped her face between his palms, his fingers still damp. "Look at me, Sophie."

She managed to get her eyes open though it took a lot of effort. His words were indistinct to her muddled brain, but she knew he wanted her attention. Cole looked fierce, his face flushed darkly, his nostrils flared as he struggled for breath. And then he drove into her and once again her body reacted, her heels digging into the mattress as she strove to get as close to him as possible. Her climax, so recently abated, so utterly exhausting, came back to her in a flash of undulating heat and pinpoint sensation. She clung to Cole while he ground himself against her, his eyes never leaving her face, their gazes locked. It was a connection that went beyond physical, that joined their hearts as well as their bodies.

He groaned harshly and cursed and then she felt him coming, knew he'd locked his legs against the intensity of his climax. And he said her name again and again, as if he couldn't help himself. "Sophie, Sophie..."

This time when he collapsed, he turned so she faced him on her side, sparing her his weight. One heavy thigh draped over her own. His body was damp with sweat and radiated heat. For long minutes neither of them spoke. They allowed their heartbeats to slow, their bodies to cool.

Something, some vague unease niggled at the back of Sophie's mind, but she was too drained to identify the cause. She tried to ignore it, but it remained, vexing her like a dull toothache, prodding at the recesses of her mind.

Cole kept her close, locked in his arms, and then he whispered, "Sleep." His fingertips touched her nose, her cheekbones. "You look tuckered out, honey. Give in. I'll wake you when it's time to go."

Sophie sighed, comforted by his scent and the leisurely way he stroked her. She felt safe, protected. He snagged the quilts and pulled them over her, tucking her in. Within minutes she could feel herself drifting off, the long, restless nights two days past suddenly catching up to her.

Cole's hand cupped the back of her head, his fingers kneading her scalp, and that was all it took. She was aware of one last lingering kiss to her forehead, and then she was asleep.

F I V E

At first she was only aware of warmth and comfort, a coziness she'd never experienced before. She'd never awakened in a strange bed, and doing so now momentarily disoriented her. She sighed, mentally forcing herself from the depths of the deep sleep she'd enjoyed. Cole's scent and warmth mingled around her, stirring her senses. Even without full awareness, things felt almost perfect, except for one tiny problem. She frowned and concentrated on getting fully awake.

But the second she opened her eyes, she knew what had gone wrong. Oh God, he'd called her by name.

Sophie was afraid to move, almost afraid to breathe. Cole lay heavily beside her, his even breaths touching against her temple, disturbing the fine hairs there. He had one heavy thigh draped over her legs, one arm limp around her waist, the other cushioning her head. Their combined body heat had worked to glue their skin together and she knew, if she moved, he'd awaken.

Then the questions would begin.

She closed her eyes as dread filled her. *He knew!* The last time they'd made love, he'd called her Sophie, not just once, but over and over again. He knew she wasn't Shelly, but he'd made love to her anyway. She couldn't begin to comprehend the ramifications of such a thing. She was naked, in bed with the man she'd spent seven months fantasizing about, the man she'd slowly fallen in love with. They'd made love repeatedly and her body ached in tender places, reminding her just how new this all was to her, and how well he now knew her body.

Carefully, moving like a ghost, she turned her face to look at him.

His dark lashes cast long shadows on his cheekbones and beard stubble covered his lean jaw, chin, and upper lip. How long had they slept? His dark, silky hair fell over his forehead, and Sophie was amazed at how the sight affected her.

God, she loved him.

She closed her eyes as pain swelled inside her. Cole knew who she was, and now she had to deal with that. But she needed time. She couldn't sort out her thoughts with him so close, his naked body warming her own.

At that moment he yawned and stretched. Sophie froze, frantically praying that he wouldn't awaken. He put one arm above his head and rolled onto his back.

Her insides quivered in relief; she felt almost lightheaded. Not daring to move, she waited several moments, but he slept on. He, too, was exhausted. And his normal routine was to sleep later, since the bar kept him out at night. Slowly, holding her breath, she slid one leg to the edge of the bed.

When he remained motionless, she moved her other leg. Luckily, his bed was firm and didn't sag or rock overly with her motions. It took her nearly three full minutes, but finally she was standing beside the bed, staring down at him. He muttered in his sleep, scratched his bare chest, then sighed heavily.

What had she done?

Escape was the only clear thought in her mind. She needed time, time away rom him, from his magnetism. She had to think. On tiptoes, she gathered up her clothes and slipped out into the hallway. There she dressed hastily and grabbed up her coat. She didn't bother to look into a mirror, already knowing she looked a wreck. A night of debauchery had to leave a woman somewhat disheveled, but there was nothing she could do about it now, so she didn't want to dwell on it.

The lock on his front door gave a quiet snick as she slipped it open, and her heart almost punched out of her chest. But there were no ensuing noises, so she assumed he slept on.

She ran the few blocks back to her car still parked at the bar, the cold slicing into her, almost unaware of the tears on her face. Fortunately for her peace of mind, the streets were all but completely deserted. There was no one to witness her humiliation as she stumbled up to her car, then dropped her keys twice before finally getting the door unlocked.

She drove like a madwoman, anxious to be home in the comfort of familiar surroundings where she could sort it all out in private. When she finally pulled into the parking lot, her car was still cold and she was racked with shivers. It was almost six-thirty.

She couldn't bear the thought of working today, not sure if Cole would feel obliged to come and see her after the way she'd run off, more afraid that he wouldn't bother at all. The humiliation was too much. She called Allison and asked her to cover for her the entire day. It would mean paying the assistant overtime, but Sophie didn't care.

Once Allison had agreed, Sophie stripped off her clothes, took a warm shower, which did nothing to shake off the awful chill deep inside her, then she crawled into bed. She had to decide what to do, how to explain, what excuse she could use for such a dastardly trick.

But first, she cried.

"So what's wrong with you? You've looked ready to commit murder all night. The customers are giving you a wide berth."

Without answering, Cole stalked away from Chase. He felt heartsick and so damned empty he didn't know how to deal with it.

Of course, Chase wouldn't let it go, following Cole as he headed for the office, throwing the door back open and walking in without taking the obvious hints. He pulled out a chair and sat down. "Give it up, Cole, and tell me what's wrong."

His eyes burned and his gut clenched. Furious, he turned to Chase and said, "You want the goddamned details? Fine. She walked out on me."

"Sophie?"

Cole threw up his hands. "No, the First Lady. Of course I mean Sophie."

Carefully, Chase asked, "So you went after her and stopped her and told her how you feel, right?"

Sending his brother a look of intense dislike, Cole said, "I was asleep. She snuck out on me."

"Oh."

"After I woke up this morning, I went to her boutique, but her assistant said she called in sick. I don't have her home phone number or even know where she lives." He laughed, the sound devoid of humor. "After seven months—*after last night*—I don't have her damned address."

"Ask the assistant."

He growled, then said in a mock woman's voice, "It's against policy to give out personal information, but I promise to tell Sophie you asked."

Chase scowled. "She refused to give you Sophie's number?"

"Yeah. No matter what I said, she wouldn't give in."

"So that's it? Hell, I might as well throw dirt on you. If you're giving up now, you're dead and buried."

"I'm not giving up, damn it! I just don't know what to do at this precise moment. Waiting doesn't sit right. I have no idea what Sophie might be thinking."

"All right. I'll take care of it." At Cole's incredulous look, Chase added, "I'll go over there and talk to the assistant. I'll get Sophie's number for you."

"And how, exactly, do you plan to do that?"

"Never mind. Just figure out what you want to say to her when you do call her. If you blow this, I'm going to be really disappointed in you."

Mack and Zane approached the office just in time to hear Chase's comment. "Disappointed in Cole about what?"

Chase left the office to fetch his coat and get on his way. The three brothers followed him like he was the Pied Piper.

"What's going on with you two? Where's Chase going?"

When they were all behind the bar, Cole turned to his brother Mack. "On a blind mission, though he doesn't believe that just yet. But he will, after he meets Allison."

Zane stepped up, a look of confusion on his face. "Who's Allison?"

"Sophie's assistant."

"Oh yeah. I remember her."

Both Cole and Chase turned to stare at him. They started to ask, but thought better of it. The details of Zane's love life were often too boggling to deal with. Mack snickered.

After a moment, while Chase tugged on his coat and gloves, Zane asked, "Did you and Sophie have a falling out or something?"

"It's none of your business, Zane."

He shrugged at Cole. "Fine. But I just wondered if there was some reason you weren't serving her. If you'd rather I'd take her a drink, just say so. But I don't like ignoring a woman."

Cole's head snapped up and he stared over at the familiar booth. There sat Sophie, hands primly folded on the table, her expression cautiously serene, though her face was pale and her eyes were red. His heart twisted, then lodged in his throat.

Chase asked, "How long has she been sitting there?"

"About ten minutes now. Usually Cole serves her right off, so I didn't know . . ."

His words dwindled off as Cole climbed over the bar instead of going around it, sending several customers jumping out of his way, awkwardly snatching up their drinks so they wouldn't get spilled. Cole's stride was long and forceful, his gaze focused on his approach to Sophie's table. With each step he took, his pulse pounded in his ears until he almost couldn't hear. When he reached her, she looked up and he saw her eyes were puffy. God, had she been crying? He searched her face; words, explanations, all jumbled in his mind so that he couldn't get a single coherent thought out. Finally he just leaned down and kissed her. Hard. Possessively. He kept one hand on the table in front of her, one on the back of her seat, caging her in, keeping her from pulling away.

But she didn't try to pull away. Her small hands came up and grabbed his shirt, tugging him closer still.

He heard a roaring in his ears and realized it came from the bar. Lifting his mouth from Sophie's, he looked around and saw a majority of male faces laughing and cheering—led by his damn, disreputable brothers, of course.

He grinned, then faced Sophie again. She started to speak, but he covered her mouth with a finger. "I love you, Sophie."

Her eyes widened.

He leaned closer still, speaking in a rough whisper. "I've waited seven months to spend the night with you, and it was worth it. But I'll be damned if I'll wait anymore. I love you, I want you. Now and forever, regardless of what name you go by, or how you dress. You're mine now. Get used to it."

He waited, but her big smoky eyes never wavered from his. She was completely still except for the pulse racing in her throat. Cautiously, he lifted his finger. "Well?"

She swallowed audibly. "All right."

By small degrees, his frown lifted and his mouth quirked. She'd said yes. "You want me, too?"

"I've wanted you since the very first time I saw you."

He kissed her again, then asked, "Why the hell did you run from me today? Christ, I almost went nuts when I woke up and you were gone."

"I'm sorry. I felt stupid—"

"Damn it, Sophie—"

It was her turn to shush him, and she used her entire hand. Their audience chuckled. No one could hear what was being said, but Sophie's actions were plain enough. Cole grinned behind her palm.

"I felt stupid for pretending to be someone else instead of just being brave enough to tell you how I feel. So I decided to stop being a coward. Aunt Maude always told me adults should own up to what they do, to be responsible for their actions and accept the results. She also told me I should never be afraid to go after what I want."

Through her muffling fingers, he asked, "You want me?"

She nodded, tears once again in her eyes. "I love you."

His long fingers circled her wrist and he pulled her hand down. "I wish I could have met Aunt Maude. I have a feeling we'd have been good friends. Will you tell me all about her?"

She nodded, then forged onward. "I realized you must care about me, too, because you kept hinting about wanting a relationship. At first I thought you wanted Shelly. I was jealous."

His look was affectionate, full of love. "Goose."

"But then I finally remembered that you knew Shelly and I were the same."

"Not at first, and it almost made me demented. I wanted Shelly because she looked like you, made me feel like you do. I couldn't understand it because you're the only woman who makes me insane with lust and sick with tenderness." Then he growled, "Not to mention what you do to a mug of hot chocolate." He pulled her from her chair and swung her in a wide circle to the sounds of raucous cheers. "Will you marry me, Sophie?"

Very primly, she replied, "I was hoping you'd ask."

At that moment, Chase set two hot chocolates on the table. He winked at his brother. "Hey, might as well go for broke."

The Valentine contest went off without a hitch. Sophie was chosen unanimously by Cole's three desperate brothers, who wanted nothing to do with an arranged date for themselves. The local newspaper explained it away by saying Sophie and Cole had fallen in love during the contest, which put the perfect slant on the whole Valentine ambiance and gained them an enormous amount of publicity, some of it even covered by a local news station. Sophie, as the lucky winner, got incredible publicity for her boutique as well. Allison had her hands full fending off reporters who blocked the growing influx of new customers. She complained heartily, but Cole figured she was well up to the task.

Cole announced to the reporters that since he was soon to be a married man, next year one of his brothers would serve as escort for the winner. That brought about some bawdy comments from the women customers and some hearty groans from his brothers, who pretended to be terrified by the prospect but who nonetheless preened under the weight of feminine attention.

Sophie stood by Cole's side, elegant and serene and beautiful. He felt like the luckiest man alive. The contest really had been the perfect idea for both of them, even if they'd each indulged in ulterior motives.

He glanced up and saw the contest photo on the wall. As per the contest stipulations, Sophie had posed with all the Winston men. Their much bigger bodies crowded around hers, dwarfing her petite frame. She was laughing, and all the men looked smug.

In his nightstand drawer at home was a different photo, the one he'd taken of Sophie while her hair was still tousled and her cheeks flushed from his loving. But that one was private, for his eyes only. Forever.

Next year, he thought, grinning as he watched his brothers give one interview after another, the contest might work out as the perfect idea for another Winston man. He wondered which of them would be the lucky one. Then Sophie nudged his side and he forgot about everything but her. He led her to his office where solitude awaited—along with a carafe of hot chocolate and a can of whipped cream.

Tangled Dreams

ONE

Even though it was an incredibly busy night at the bar, even though he could barely hear the newest order over the din of loud conversation, music, and laughter, he heard her. Her every thought. Chase watched her, saw that her mouth wasn't moving, that she wasn't actually talking, but he could still listen to her.

She was on the other side of the bar, standing by a group of Halloween decorations that his sister-in-law had designed out of a bunch of pumpkins he and his brothers had carved. The haystack and jack-o'-lanterns were festive and provided an amusing backdrop to the serious expression on Allison Barrow's face. He'd known her several months now, ever since his brother had married her best friend and boss, but he'd never before noticed how cute her round, wire-framed glasses looked on her small nose or the fact that she had a tendency to straighten them needlessly.

He noticed now. But why?

His youngest brother, Mack, bumped into him. "Hey, Chase, orders are piling up here. You want to stop daydreaming and help me out?"

Chase gave Mack a distracted glance. "Come here a minute, will you?"

Mack paused. "What?"

"Over here. Come on. Now stop right there." Chase positioned him exactly where he'd been standing. Mack was in his last year of college, still studious and alert. Surely he'd pick up on something. "Now, look over there at Allison. See her, right past the redhead with the skinny guy in a suit? By that Halloween display?"

"Yeah, so?"

"What's she saying?"

Mack turned to stare at Chase in disbelief. "What's she saying? How the hell should I know? I can barely hear you, and you're only two inches away from me."

Frustrated, unable to really explain, Chase said, "Well, look at her, dammit, and try."

With a sound of disgust, Mack again stared toward Allison. Chase saw his gaze warm a little, then go over her from head to toe, and for some reason, that annoyed him. Now that he'd really noticed Allison, he didn't particularly want Mack doing the same. He'd always thought Allison was cute, in an understated, sort of just-there way, but suddenly she looked very sexy to him. She was twenty-five, on the short side, dark blue eyes, medium blonde hair. Nothing special. Certainly not the type of woman to appeal to his baser side. But tonight he couldn't pull his attention away from her. He suddenly heard her every thought when he'd sure as hell never been a mind reader before. And he only heard Allison, no one else. There was something going on between them, and it didn't make any sense.

"Well?" Chase prompted.

"She looks different, doesn't she?"

"It's the clothes," Chase explained, having noted the difference himself. It had taken him several minutes to finally pinpoint what made her look so unusual tonight, so...sensual. "She's wearing some sort of old-fashioned, vintage dress."

In truth, she looked like a woman straight out of a film noir. The dress was a deep purple gray, and even from a distance, Chase could see that the color did things for her eyes. Or were her eyes just brighter tonight, more alert?

There was subtle black beading on the top of the dress that caught the bar lights and drew his attention repeatedly to her less-than-outstanding bustline. At least, he'd never thought it outstanding before. But now...Now he was imagining her naked and almost going crazy because of it.

The waistline was tight, showing off her trim build, and when she turned, Chase not only saw that she had on seamed stockings but also that the damn dress had a flat bustle of sorts, a little layering of soft material that draped real nice over her pert behind, a behind that would feel just right against his pelvis if he took her from the back...

"It looks...I dunno, kind of sexy on her, doesn't it?"

"Mack." Pulled from his erotic thoughts, Chase said it as a warning, surprising himself and his brother. His tone had smacked of possessiveness, and he didn't like it, but he also didn't like another man, not even his brother, thinking Allison was sexy. He wasn't quite used to himself thinking it yet. "Pay attention."

"To what? From what I can tell, she's not saying anything. She's just standing there all by herself, looking sweet. In fact, she looks a little lost."

Chase rubbed his face. "So you don't hear anything?"

With a strange look, Mack asked, "What exactly am I supposed to be hearing?"

Damn. There was no way Chase could repeat the thoughts he'd picked up on so clearly. They were fairly... intimate. Explicit thoughts. Sexual thoughts. *About him*. He almost groaned. "Never mind. Forget I said anything."

Mack frowned at him. "Hey, you okay?"

"Yeah, fine. Go on before we get mobbed by disgruntled customers. You take that end of the bar, and I'll handle this end."

With one last curious look at his brother, Mack sauntered off. The bar, owned by the brothers, was especially packed tonight. It had gone from being a popular watering hole to a regular hangout. People not only drank there, they danced and played billiards and pinball. Cole, the oldest brother and recently married, was thinking of expanding into the empty building next door. He'd discussed his plans with Chase just the other day, and Chase was all for it, especially if it meant they'd hire in some help. The bar was plenty prosperous enough now to support several additional employees, and with Zane, the third brother, getting his own computer business off the ground, and Mack finishing up college, it was certain the two younger brothers would likely work less and less at the bar.

Cole had originally bought it to support the family after their parents had died. He'd worked damned hard, making ends meet and taking care of three much younger brothers. Chase, as the second oldest at twenty-seven, was still nine years younger than Cole, with Zane twenty-four and Mack just turned twenty-two. Chase had always tried to help out as much as possible, and he and Cole were friends, as well as being as close as brothers could be, but none of them had expected the bar to eventually be so popular. It had given them a great start in life and had guaranteed employment for the younger brothers, but it had served its purpose and it was time to think of the future.

Their clientele was as much female as otherwise, being that until Cole's recent marriage, they'd all been bachelors—according to the local papers, the most popular bachelors Thomasville, Kentucky, had to offer. A lot of women lamented Cole's altered state, which sent an overflow of attention to the remaining brothers. Chase smiled. He wasn't all that interested, being something of a recluse and extremely particular in his sexual appetites, but Zane and Mack sure appreciated all the female adoration.

The six to eight o'clock rush was finally starting to wind down when Chase was hit with another of Allison's vivid internal dialogues. He'd been fending off the stray thoughts, doing his best to ignore them, but there was no way to keep this one out. A tray in his hands, a dishrag over his shoulder, he paused on his way to the sink, like someone had frozen him in mid-step.

Such nice shoulders. So sexy. Probably hard and smooth to the touch. And hot. They'd move when he thrust, the muscles shifting...

And then a visual image joined the words, an erotic picture of him making love to Allison. It was carnal, sensual, and showed him exactly what she'd look like naked, laid out beneath him, straining against him while he drove into her. Her small breasts were flushed, her pale pink nipples were puckered tight. Her eyes were closed, her blond hair fanned out on a pillow, her hands desperately clutching his shoulders....

The tray almost slipped out of his hands, and he barely managed to catch it. He shook his head, trying to clear it, totally overwhelmed by a wave of raging lust and heated need. He turned to stare at her.

She was looking at him, and as he stared, gaze intent, her face turned pink and she ducked her head. Like a sleepwalker, Chase plunked the tray on the bar, threw the dishrag to the side, and started toward her.

She looked up at him, her eyes now rounding with alarm, and she took a hasty step back, but the haystack and pumpkins were there, crowded into the corner, making it impossible for her to flee. Which was just as well, because if she'd run, he'd have simply chased her down. All he could think of was getting his hands on her.

Chase stalked her, keeping her in sight, stepping around those people loitering or dancing in the middle of the floor, dodging tables and ignoring greetings. He didn't like being played with, and while he didn't know how she did it, he knew Allison was in some way responsible.

He stopped right in front of her and she looked up at him, one hand pressed wide over her heart as if to keep it contained in her chest. He started to question her, but then he noticed her lips, soft, pink, parted slightly, and he wanted so badly to kiss her he couldn't think straight. He could almost taste her on his tongue, hot and wet and woman sweet. His hands shook—hell, his whole body shook.

Like a wild animal scenting a female in heat, it took all his concentration to control his basic urges. He'd *never* felt this way before, not even with the most accommodating women, and they were rare indeed. His desires were usually specific, a little risqué to the average woman, something that needed to be catered to in order to achieve mind-blowing pleasure. He simply didn't get overwhelmed with lust at the mere sight of a woman.

Anger washed over him, making him tremble. He didn't want to notice her, dammit. She'd never affected him this way before, so why now? How did she do it? He stared down at her, at that tempting mouth, and every muscle in his body tensed. He cursed softly.

Oh God. Maybe I should have chosen Zane. He'd have been willing at least, and so much easier. He wouldn't question what was happening....

"Like hell!" Chase took her shoulders and shook her slightly. Through clenched teeth, he growled, "You're right, Zane wouldn't hesitate; he'd probably already have you in the back room with your little bustle in the air. But I'm not Zane, and I didn't start this, you did."

She stared at him, her shock apparent, her face draining of color.

Jealousy made him a little rougher, a little less discreet than he'd normally be. He took care to keep his private life private. Not that he was a monk, but he sure as hell wasn't the outgoing, obvious ladies' man that his younger brother Zane was. His hands tightened on her narrow shoulders and he leaned low to say, "You can just get thoughts of Zane right out of your head."

She blinked up at him, the pulse in her throat going wild. "What... what are you talking about?"

They were so close, her glasses fogged just a little, then slipped down the bridge of her nose. Chase could see small flecks of gold in her deep blue eyes, like little explosions of heat. His jaw worked for a moment, then he said with just a touch more calm, "How dare you even consider my brother?"

She gasped, putting both her palms on his chest. The touch burned him, making the lust that much worse. He wanted to howl. He had never in his adult life had this happen, had lust rage over him so suddenly, so uncontrollably. Hell, of the four brothers, he was the quietest, the most discriminating in outward appearances. And control, especially with a woman, was something he insisted on.

She glanced around, her movements nervous, then whispered in a rush, "Chase, what in the world is wrong with you?" Her face was flushed, her eyes round, and she looked embarrassed and alarmed and very worried.

Chase, too, glanced around. Several people were looking at him, including his damned brothers. *They must have radar,* he thought, wondering how all three of them had known he was going to make a fool of himself. But the fact that he had, that it was over a woman, was rare enough that he knew they wouldn't ignore it or let him forget it. He simply didn't cause scenes, ever, but especially not over women.

Turning back to Allison, striving for a pleasant look rather than that of a crazy man, he said, "I'd like to talk to you. In private." The words slipped out through his teeth and the parody of a smile he'd forced to his mouth.

She rolled her lips in and bit them, her gaze still wary, then nodded. But she looked far from willing. She looked nervous as hell. He could *feel* her nervousness, damn her, just like he'd felt everything else.

Holding her arm in case she changed her mind, Chase led her past the bar toward the back office. Mack stood behind the bar, shaking his head in wonder. Cole, standing in his path, frowned in concern, and Zane, surrounded by a group of women, grinned like the village idiot. Ignoring the two younger brothers, Chase stopped in front of Cole and said, "I need a few minutes of privacy."

Looking between him and Allison, Cole narrowed his eyes.

There was no way Chase could explain, so he said simply and firmly, "I'll be back out as soon as I can," and his tone alone forestalled any arguments.

Cole looked hesitant, then finally he nodded. "Take your time. We can handle things now."

"Thanks." Chase turned away, and Allison stumbled along beside him. He realized it looked like he was dragging her along, but that was only because she was holding back a bit. Chase glanced down at her. "You're causing a scene."

"Me?" They were now out of sight of the main room of the bar, and she again held back as Chase opened the office door. "You're the one doing the caveman routine. What in the world is the matter with you?"

He snorted. "Like you don't know." Hell, she'd been thinking about him all night, taunting him with those personal, private, *sexual* thoughts of hers. He didn't know how he knew it, but he did, and his conviction was so strong he didn't doubt it for a moment. He gently propelled her into the office and shut the door.

The lock turned with a quiet click.

Only one light was on, a small lamp sitting on the desk. Chase watched as Allison backed up a few steps, then stopped and braced herself. For what?

"Allison..."

You can do this, you can do this, you can...

"Do *what*?" Chase barked, advancing on her, again losing his temper. Startled, she jumped back and her knees hit the soft, slightly worn sofa that Cole had installed years ago when long nights sometimes made it necessary to nap at the bar. Allison lost her balance and she tumbled gracefully onto the sofa, the soft, flared skirt of that killer dress fanning around her. Her spine pressed hard to the back of the sofa in alarm. She started to jump up again, but Chase stepped so close she couldn't, not without plastering herself against him.

And judging by her expression, she didn't want to do that.

She eyed him, then whispered, "I don't know what you're talking about."

He leaned down, one hand on the back of the sofa next to her head, the other on the arm next to her side, pinning her in. "You want me. You've been thinking about me all night, distracting me, invading my head. Now you're trying to give yourself a pep talk and—"

Her eyes flared wide like saucers, and she fumbled with her glasses. Her mouth moved, but no words came out. Finally, she sputtered, "How on earth do you know that?"

He frowned, tilting his head to study her carefully. Her old-fashioned dress was a major turn-on for him, and he fully appreciated the feminine, sultry picture she presented. It affected him somehow, but he couldn't say exactly why.

"Chase?"

She sounded honestly surprised, and then he felt her shock roll over him and knew she'd had no idea he'd been listening in on her ruminations. She hadn't silently talked to him on purpose, he'd just suddenly been able to read her. *Why?*

Chase touched her cheek, feeling the heat of her blush. She was mortified to discover he knew her thoughts. Some of his anger evaporated, and he wanted to reassure her somehow, but first they had to figure out what was going on.

Standing up straight again, he said, "Don't move."

She shook her head, mute. Her thoughts were such a jumble he almost smiled. Poor little thing. She was as confounded as he. And now that he knew she wasn't controlling the situation, wasn't controlling him, he could almost appreciate the novelty of it.

He touched the tip of her nose, then a loose blonde curl by her temple. He liked touching her, he thought, then immediately withdrew. He didn't want to like touching her. "This is going to take some time to sort out. I'm going to go get us a couple of drinks, then we'll talk, okay?"

Her chest rose and fell rapidly, making the beaded bodice glitter. She looked away. "Okay."

"Allison?"

Her gaze came back to him reluctantly.

"It's all right." He searched her face, noticing how pretty her eyes looked, how they weren't just a dark blue, but a multitude of blue shades, complex and original. "That you want me. I mean."

Her lashes lowered, her hands fisted in her lap, and she whispered, "Oh God."

Smiling now, feeling like he was finally getting the upper hand, Chase walked out. Damn, he didn't know what was going on, but one thing was certain: Allison hadn't denied wanting him. She hadn't denied anything. She'd been too upset and embarrassed and confused to do more than stare up at him, letting him absorb her thoughts, letting him experience her desire.

And her desire sparked his own.

He was so hot, he thought he could breathe steam. His muscles were tensed, his abdomen tight. He felt like he'd been indulging in an hour of specialized foreplay, and in a way, he supposed he had, listening in on Allison's thoughts, seeing her small fantasies. They'd been almost real, and had affected him like a touch.

This whole thing went beyond the realm of reality. If someone had tried to tell him any of this was possible, he'd have laughed. Mind reading? Ha. He hadn't believed such a thing existed, but now he knew it did.

Even stranger than that was Allison, suddenly looking so appealing, suddenly wanting *him*. He'd always been polite to her but distant, because he'd instinctively felt she wouldn't meet his needs. She was mostly quiet, a little perky but in a cute, friendly way, not overtly sexual. A small woman with sweet features, not a single risqué or daring thing about her. She didn't in any way look like a woman who would indulge his sexual demands. So he'd been merely polite and she'd always been the same.

Now he knew her quiet facade hid some heated urges, and though they weren't on a par with his, they intrigued the hell out of him.

Hurrying, he went behind the bar and grabbed two colas. Cole tried to talk to him, but he put him off. Hell, there was no way to explain the unexplainable. Cole would think he'd gone off the deep end.

Mack and Zane started whispering, their heads together, but he ignored them, too, not even bothering to give them a second glance.

Even this far away from Allison, he still knew what she was thinking, and he wanted to get back to her, to reassure her. She was afraid of what he'd think, racking her brain for an explanation he'd accept. Her uncertainty was understandable, even endearing, given the bizarre situation.

For whatever reason, she suddenly wanted him, and he didn't really think he should turn her down. Hell no. Whatever was frightening her—and she was frightened—he'd take care of it.

Cole walked up to him again. "Chase . . ."

"It's under control, Cole. Don't worry."

Cole searched his face, not looking the least bit convinced. "But . . . *Allison?*"

Chase grinned. "Yeah, I know. Pretty surprising, huh? Maybe there's some black magic at work, considering it's almost Halloween, or there's a full moon out tonight or something. Who knows?"

Cole didn't respond to the joke. "Do you know what you're doing, Chase?"

Considering that a fair question since he wasn't behaving at all like himself, Chase shrugged. "I'm working it out. That's all I can tell you for now."

Cole still looked concerned, but he let it go, saying only, "Just remember she's my wife's friend and assistant. I don't want to end up in the doghouse because of you."

Chase laughed. As he headed back to the office, colas and napkins in his hands, he dodged under a black paper cat and an orange paper jack-o'-lantern hanging from the ceiling. Maybe Halloween really did have something to do with this sudden power of his to read Allison, to see things in her he'd never seen before.

If so, he intended to enjoy it while it lasted.

But first, he wanted some answers.

T W O

Allison paced the office as she waited for Chase to return. She'd never been in here before, and beyond her nervousness was a curiosity that kept her looking around. Cole mostly used the office, since he was the bookkeeper of the bar. Chase generally contented himself with being a bartender—and an unusual one at that. He wasn't chatty, was more of a listener than not. He had the incredible knack for keeping disagreements at a minimum, negating the need for a bouncer. The bar was a lively place, but it was friendly, and totally acceptable to a family man or woman.

The office was large with a massive desk at one end and a plush sofa against the adjacent wall. A few chairs were scattered about with a filing cabinet or two. Photos of the brothers at various ages hung on the wall, and with her heart pounding, Allison went to peer at an aged photo of

Chase. He was younger, but even then she could see the hidden fire in him, the repressed energy that everyone else seemed to miss, accepting him as the *quiet brother*. She shook her head. He was still incredibly gorgeous and her stomach knotted. It suddenly seemed like much too much.

"Darn it, Rose, I knew this was a bad idea. He's actually angry that I want him. Why wasn't Jack good enough? He couldn't read my mind, and we both know he was more than willing, even if he didn't exactly make my pulse race the way Chase does. He had no idea what you were planning. It would have been so much—"

The door slammed and she turned to see Chase, drinks in his hands and a frown on his face. "First my brother Zane, and now some bozo named Jack. How many men are you daydreaming about?"

He was angry again—

"Damn right I'm angry!"

Her own temper sparked, obliterating some of her nervousness. "Stop doing that! Stop reading my mind."

He stared at her, and very slowly his frown smoothed out. He looked disgruntled as he stepped into the office and set the drinks on the desk. "I can't help it. It's like you're screaming into my head."

"But why?" Her hands twisted together in nervousness. "I don't understand."

"Hell if I know. You came in tonight and just like that, I heard you thinking about me."

If her face got any hotter, her ears were going to catch on fire. Mustering her courage, determined to see this through—a thought he obviously read, judging by his smile—she admitted, "I've done that before."

"Thought about me?"

She swallowed hard and nodded. "Yes."

Eyes narrowed sensually, he stepped closer. His voice was low and heated when he asked, "Sexual thoughts?"

Her stomach did quick little flips of excitement. "Yes."

"I never guessed."

"I know. You've never even noticed me." That was painfully true, and there'd been many a night when she'd gone home feeling heartsick because she was all but invisible to him.

Chase reached out and touched her cheek again. "I'm sorry."

Darn it, she had to censor her thoughts a little better or she'd never be able to get through this.

Chase grinned. "Don't bother on my account. I kind of like reading your mind."

With the most ferocious frown she could muster, she said, "Well, I don't like it!"

He looked very annoyed again. "Because you're also thinking about Zane and this Jack person?"

"No!" She shook her head, flustered to the core. Seeing no hope for it, she admitted quietly, "I don't want Zane or Jack. Not like..."

His gaze softened. "Like you want me?"

"Yes. But none of it matters. I don't need to be a mind reader to know you couldn't care less about me. I'm sorry if my thoughts are suddenly intruding in your head, but I don't really know what I can do about it."

His frown was back, only now it looked more confused than angry. "You want me, but you don't want to do anything about it?"

Allison turned away. This was the tricky part—

Chase swung her back around and up close to his chest. His hands held her firmly, not hurting, but making certain she couldn't move away. Allison thought he'd shake her again, and she braced herself, but no sooner did she think it than he narrowed his eyes and sighed. "Dammit, I would never hurt you, okay?" When she didn't answer right away, he added, "I promise. Trust me."

Heart tripping at his deep, compelling tone, she said, "Okay."

"Good." There was a wealth of satisfaction in his heated gaze, but also determination. He tugged her the tiniest bit closer, until she gasped. "Now let's get something straight. I don't want you to try planning and plotting against me. It's only tricky if you're not honest with me."

Being so near to him was muddling her brain, making logical explanations difficult. "I...I can't be honest with you."

"Why not?"

"You won't believe me, and you'll think I'm nuts, and you won't want anything to do with me, but I need you to..." She closed her mouth, appalled by how much she'd just blurted out.

His gaze moved from a fascinated study of her eyes, to her mouth, then down to her breasts. His fingers on her arms turned caressing, persuasive. In a soft, gentle tone, he said, "This whole situation is nuts, so

I doubt you can add much lunacy to it. And to be truthful, I'm finding I want a lot to do with you. Maybe it's just a masculine gut reaction to knowing how much you want me, but I've had a hard-on since you first started thinking about me. And it's you I've got pictured in my brain, not any other woman."

Allison groaned. His words were like an aphrodisiac, making her blood race, her toes curl. Rose couldn't have planned this any better if she'd tried. But it was all wrong. Even if he was now willing to do what she needed him to do, it wasn't because—

Chase leaned down and pressed his mouth to her temple. "Tell me what you need me to do, honey."

Honey. He'd never called her that before. She liked it.

"I'm glad."

Her head dropped forward to bounce against his chest and she groaned again, this time thoroughly flustered at her wayward thoughts.

Chase chuckled, nuzzling against her crown. "I'm sorry. Would you rather I didn't answer your thoughts?"

She shook her head. This situation was so bizarre, it bordered on comical. But then, everything that had happened to her since moving into the house was beyond belief. "No. It's just...disconcerting."

His hands stroked up and down her back, and her eyes closed as she basked in the heat of his touch. He kissed her brow and said, "To me, too, you know. My brothers are probably out there huddled together, coming up with every wrong conclusion there is. It's for certain they're not anywhere close to the truth."

Alarmed, she pushed back to look up at him. "You're not going to tell them, are you?" It was bad enough that Chase had been drawn in, but she didn't want or need anyone else to find out all her secrets.

Chase cupped her cheek, his touch so tender she could barely find her breath. "I don't know. I'm not even sure yet what's going on. But if it'll make you feel better, for now I won't say anything."

Her eyes closed in relief. "Thank you."

"What secrets do you have?"

Darn. She hadn't meant to let that slip. Then realizing she might as well have spoken out loud, she said, "Just give me a little time, okay?"

"Time for what?"

"Time to figure out how to tell you, how to get used to this, how to prepare myself."

He didn't look like he wanted to agree. In fact, he looked very disagreeable, but he finally nodded. "Answer a few questions for me, then."

"If I can."

"Who's Jack?"

That was easy enough, though not a very desirable topic. "He's a man I've been dating. He wants to get serious, but I don't."

He looked far from pleased by her explanation. "Why?"

"He's not . . . right for me."

"In what way?"

Chase made it very difficult to talk when he kept touching her, his big hands smoothing over her shoulders, her back. And he stared at her mouth, making her self-conscious.

And he damn well knew it.

He shook his head. His voice was deep and affected, husky with desire. "I'm sorry. It's just that I can't stop thinking about kissing you—and a lot of others things. Things that'd likely have you hightailing your pretty little behind out of here as fast as you can."

Ignoring most of what he said only because it didn't make sense to her, she asked, "You . . . you really want to kiss me?"

"Oh yeah." His voice dropped even more and he stared at her lips. "But I can tell you don't really want me to. Yet."

Allison tried to step away, but he wouldn't let her go, so instead she covered her face. "This is so difficult."

She found herself hauled up against Chase's chest, his arms wrapped tight around her, comforting her. "I don't mean to make it—whatever *it* is—harder for you, honey. But I can feel your confusion. You want me, but you don't want to want me. Have I got that right?"

She sighed. He smelled so good, and it felt so good to be this close to him. More than anything she wanted to be with him, in every way imaginable.

He drew in a deep breath. "*Every* way?"

She stared at him, speechless. That had sounded too ominous by half. Still, she would have agreed, but there were stipulations that she couldn't ignore.

His eyes narrowed. "What stipulations?"

Darn it, she had no privacy at all! It took all her control to hold back her fist. She wanted really badly to punch him.

Chase held her tighter. "None of that."

This time she didn't even question his right to know her thoughts. Thoroughly disgruntled, accepting there was no way she could sort out her thoughts in her own head, she groaned and pushed back to glare at him. "Do you think I should be happy to want a man who doesn't want me?"

"But I just told you—"

"Right. That you...have an erection." Her face burned, but she didn't look away from him. "I know. But that's not because of *me*. Chase, you don't even know me, and you've never wanted to know me."

He was quiet, watching her closely.

"I think in the eight months that Sophie and your brother have been married, you've said about a dozen sentences to me, all of them mundane cordial niceties. How're you doing? Nice weather we're having. That sort of thing. Now, just because you know I've fantasized about you a little—"

"A lot."

"Okay a lot—"

One corner of his firm mouth kicked up. "Tell me some of the fantasies."

His voice was low, commanding, making her insides tingle. She frowned severely. "No. Besides, you'll probably know them soon enough as it is."

His brows lifted. "You've got plans, do you?"

She opened her mouth, then saw his taunting smirk and wanted to slug him again. "No! I meant that you'd probably just read my mind and know them, though I swear I'm going to do my best *not* to think about you at all."

"Party pooper."

"It's not funny, Chase."

He grinned and kissed the end of her nose. "From my perspective it is. There's not a man alive who wouldn't pay good money to be where I am right now. It's not often a fellow can actually understand a woman or know her thoughts."

She snorted. "Like you can even begin to understand."

He ignored that. "And I really am curious about these fantasies, but I'll wait, if you insist. Now, about that other nonsense you rattled off."

Her wariness returned. "What nonsense?"

"Me not wanting you. Okay, so I'll admit I'd never really paid much attention to you before. I never pay much attention to any woman, at least not for long, but especially not a woman who's a friend and assistant to my sister-in-law. I have no intention of getting involved long-term with anyone, and your relationship with Sophie puts you just a little bit too close to home for comfort. You're not the type of woman for a one night stand, and one night stands are about the only speed I go these days, so I ignored you. It really didn't have anything to do with you."

She stared at him, disbelieving such words had actually come from his mouth. "My goodness. All that? So your disregard for me was actually something of a compliment, because I'm above such casual notice?"

"Don't be snide."

"Snide? I don't believe a thing you said. Since I've known you, I've seen you with three women, and if they were any indication of the type of female you gravitate toward, then I have no problem at all understanding why you've always ignored me, and it didn't have a lot to do with my friendship with Sophie."

He'd stiffened at her first mention of the women. "Meaning?"

"Meaning the women you go for are always beautiful and...and well stacked." She winced at her own word choice, but it was absolutely true. While she was full through the hips, lacking in the upper works, and of a very ordinary appearance overall, Chase had shown a preference for tall, slim, busty women—none of which could be applied to her.

He chastised her with a shake of his head. "Women are so damn weird."

"Weird!"

"And so hung up on their bodies. Allison, there's absolutely nothing wrong with how you're built."

Her mouth twisted. She obviously didn't have a single sacred thought.

"No, absolutely not, especially when you're thinking all kinds of ignorant things."

"Ignorant things? Chase, I have mirrors in my house, and I know what I look like."

"You look fine, better than fine, and it wasn't the look of those women that drew me."

"Then what?"

He hesitated, studied her closely, then smiled. "Not yet, honey. But maybe, given half a chance, I'll explain it to you someday."

The deliberate secrecy annoyed her. "See? You're obviously just not interested."

His own temper sparked at her stubbornness. "Then explain why I still have a damned erection!"

He no sooner shouted that than a tentative tap sounded at the door. They both turned, appalled. Chase recovered first, saying in a bark, "What is it?"

There was barely repressed laughter in Mack's voice when he called out, "Uh, there's a guy here looking for Allison."

"Uh-oh." She cleared her throat as Chase turned slowly to glare at her, then she answered Mack nervously, saying, "I'll, uh, be right out."

Chase looked like a thundercloud. "Who the hell is looking for you?"

"Jack?" She posed her answer as a question, not sure how he'd react.

Working his jaw, Chase stood silent for a moment, then finally said, "You'll tell him to leave."

"No, I will not! Chase, we agreed to meet here tonight before I knew any of this would happen. I need to talk to him, to tell him—"

"That you want me."

"No! I'm not going to tell him that."

"Then I will."

He turned toward the door, and Allison launched herself at him, wrapping her arms tight around his waist and digging in her heels. "Wait! You don't understand!"

Chase easily pulled her around in front of him, then pinned her to the door with his hands on her shoulders, his hips pressed to her belly. Her heart skipped two beats, then went into frantic overdrive. His breath fanned her cheek and his gaze was hot. With his lips almost touching hers, he said, "I don't want you to see anyone but me."

His scent enveloped her, his nearness made heat bloom inside her. She'd wanted this for so long, but not this way, not when he'd more or less been coerced.

"No one is coercing me, Allison. I want you, plain and simple."

"There's absolutely nothing simple about this and you know it." Still, did she have any choice? Rose was counting on her, and so was Burke. She licked her lips and could almost taste him. "There's a lot I have to explain to you yet."

His hips pressed closer, letting her feel the long, hard length of his erection, making her gasp. "Like who the hell Rose and Burke are?"

Her glasses were crooked and she straightened them, staring at his throat rather than meeting his eyes. "Yes. And...and why I think you should come to my house and....and make love to me."

She peeked up at him. The heat of his gaze burned her up from the inside out. And then he kissed her, his mouth voracious, his tongue stroking. She clutched at him, overwhelmed and turned on and unable to rationalize what was happening. Unexpectedly, he caught her hands and pinned them over her head, then groaned deeply.

When he pulled away just the tiniest bit, he said roughly, "Get rid of the other man, Allison."

She practically hung there in his grasp, on her tiptoes, her arms stretched out, his pelvis pressed to her, keeping her still. "I...I will," she managed to stammer around her excitement. "But I have to do it right."

"Tell him to get lost."

"That would be cruel." She said it as a gentle reprimand, then quickly added, "He's a nice man, Chase. And he's serious about me. He asked me to marry him, so I can't just dump him like that."

Chase stared at her for a long moment, and she could see he fought an internal battle. Finally his eyes squeezed shut, and he whispered, "I've never been jealous before. I don't like it."

"You have no reason to be."

He kissed her again, softer this time, consuming, with so much tenderness it felt like her heart was swelling in her chest, nearly choking her.

"Don't let him touch you. Promise me."

"No." His kiss and his words left her nearly panting. "No, I won't."

With a sigh, he carefully, slowly released her wrists and stepped away from her. "Let's go before Mack starts telling everyone that I have a hard-on and I'm shouting about it."

Horrified by such a possibility, she asked, "He wouldn't, would he?"

"Hell yes, he would, if he thought it'd embarrass me. That is, he'd tell Zane and Cole. And they're the two I'd most prefer didn't know."

But when they stepped back into the bar, all three brothers stood there, grinning like magpies, and Allison knew Mack had already blabbed. Luckily, it was only Chase they seemed intent on teasing. But then Jack spoke up from behind them, drawing everyone's attention.

"Allison? What the hell's going on?"

She looked at Jack, silently begging for him not to start anything, but it was Chase who answered those thoughts, saying forcefully, "Forget it, honey," as he stepped forward. All three of his brothers crowded behind him.

Jack stiffened his spine. He was every bit as tall as Chase, topping six feet, but was Chase's exact opposite in every other way. While Chase was dark with golden brown eyes, Jack was blond with bright green eyes. They looked like two wolfhounds ready to bite each other. Allison was mortified.

"Cole, do something!"

He blinked at her, then turned to his brother. "Knock it off, Chase."

Both Chase and Jack ignored him. Cole shrugged at her, as if saying, *I tried.* But then he suggested, "At least make it private, Chase. You're embarrassing her."

Chase nodded agreement to that and turned to go back in the office. Jack followed him against Allison's protests.

Exasperated, Allison hurried in on Jack's heels, and shut the door behind her. "This is not necessary."

Chase said, "I think he disagrees."

In his most provoking tone, Jack said, "You're right, I do."

Trying desperately to salvage the moment, Allison said, "Jack, it's not even what you think."

Chase snorted. "Unless he's an idiot, it's exactly what he thinks."

Allison whirled to face him. "You promised, damn it!" Chase didn't even look at her, his attention fixed on Jack.

But he did say, "I promised to give you time to talk to him. But I didn't say anything about letting him yell at you."

"Allison?"

Jack sounded out of patience, and she turned to him again, saying in a whisper, "It was Rose's idea. I swear. I'll explain later . . ."

"Rose?" Suddenly Jack's expression relaxed and he even chuckled as he glanced at Chase with an amused look. "So you're letting Rose call the shots again, huh?" He shook his head, laughing at her.

Chase took an aggressive step forward. "Allison, maybe it's time you told me who the hell Rose is."

With a lift of his brows, Jack said, "I can explain, though I doubt you'll believe it any more than I do."

He was still amused, and seeing no hope for it, Allison decided she had nothing to lose. She frowned at both men. "Jack, you can forget our date tonight. In fact, you can forget any dates!"

Jack glared. Anger crowded his features, then a near panic. "Damn it, Allison..."

She crossed her arms over her chest.

Jack glanced at Chase, then narrowed his gaze on her face again. "I'll call you later when you've had a chance to calm down." And in a huff, he stormed out, slamming the door behind him.

Chase shook his head. Now that Jack was gone, he looked relaxed and under control again. His gaze lit on Allison, and he teased, "I thought you claimed he was a nice guy."

"And you!" She was practically fuming, she was so mad. Nothing had gone as expected, and she'd had more surprises tonight than one woman could bear. "I've decided you're not worth the trouble, no matter what Rose thinks!"

She turned to the door, ready to make a grand exodus, but Chase's hand flattened on it before she could get it open. Speaking close to her ear, he growled, "I don't get off till late tonight, so it'll have to be tomorrow morning. But we'll get together at ten to talk. Which is damned early for me, so I hope you appreciate the concession to my sleep."

"I won't—"

"We have a lot to discuss, and I think I'm showing a great deal of patience, all things considered."

She wanted to tell him to go to hell. She wanted to go hide somewhere, considering how horrible the evening had turned.

"But you won't, will you, honey?"

She turned the doorknob and he let the door open. As she stepped out, thoroughly defeated, she growled, "I suppose not. Good night, Chase."

"Ten o'clock, Allison. Don't make me wait."

Arrogant, obnoxious, controlling jerk...

She heard him laugh, and she groaned. Fleeing seemed her only option, and she did so quickly. But as she left the bar, she felt all four brothers watching her, and she knew, from here on out, nothing would be the same.

THREE

Chase was distracted as he finished closing down the bar. It was almost two in the morning, and he and Zane were alone. Mack had taken off hours ago to catch some sleep before his morning classes, and Cole always left early these days, now that he had a wife waiting at home for him. Chase grinned, thinking about Sophie. She was awfully sweet, and the way she'd played Cole just before they were married was something he'd never forget, the stuff fantasies were made of. Cole hadn't stood a chance, and Chase considered him damn lucky to have her.

But thinking of Sophie and Cole reminded him of something that had been niggling at the back of his mind ever since Allison had stormed out of the bar, her thoughts confused and her frustration level high. Hell, his frustration was through the roof. He was still mildly aroused, even though she was gone. He couldn't get her out of his mind, and though he couldn't read her so clearly now that she wasn't close, he still got the occasional glimpse of her thoughts and it kept his desire on a keen edge.

Small talk with customers had been almost impossible tonight.

Zane came out of the back room, whistling. Out of all the brothers, he was the rowdiest. Zane seemed to have a little wildness in him that no one would ever be able to erase. Cole had never really tried, preferring just to temper that energy whenever possible. It had never bothered Chase before, but now, he kept thinking of how Allison had briefly considered Zane, and it bothered him a lot.

Zane looked up and caught Chase staring. The whistling stopped. "What'd I do?"

"Nothing. At least, I hope not."

Reaching for his coat off a hook in the hallway, snagging Chase's also, Zane started forward. "What does that mean?"

"I want to ask you something, Zane, and I want a straight answer, okay?"

Zane tossed Chase his coat, then propped his hands on his hips. "At twenty-four, don't you think I'm a little old for a lecture?"

"I wasn't going to lecture you."

"Oh." He grinned. "Well, good. Because I wasn't going to listen."

Chase perched on a bar stool and stared at his brother. "You remember back when Cole and Sophie first hooked up?"

"How could I forget?" Zane lifted himself onto the edge of the bar. "Hell, Cole was so damned amusing, I worked extra hours, neglecting my own business, just to get to watch him fumble around."

Chase grinned, too. "He did have a hard time of it, didn't he?"

"Aw, well, Sophie made it worth his while."

"You knew Allison back then, didn't you? I mean, even before Sophie and Cole hooked up." He'd sort of blurted that out, but he was getting edgier by the minute, prompted by some unknown discontent, like something was wrong, but he didn't know what.

Zane shrugged. "I know just about every woman in town, Allison included, but probably not the way you're thinking, judging by your frown." He grinned. "I asked her out, but she turned me down flat."

That surprised Chase. "She did?"

"Yeah, several times, in fact."

So Zane had asked her out more than once? He didn't like that. "You never said anything."

"Like you expected me to brag that I was turned out cold? Get real. Besides, from the way the two of you carried on today, I have to wonder if she wasn't hung up on you way back then. You can be damn blind when it comes to women, Chase."

"What's that supposed to mean?"

"It means a lot of women try to get your attention, but you don't take the bait."

Because they were nice, conservative women who most likely wouldn't meet his appetites. He shook his head. "I date."

"Yeah, about five times a year." He snorted. "That's barely enough to keep a man alive. I figure every so often your libido takes over, and you cave. Other than that, you're a man of ice."

"Maybe I just don't like to spread myself so thin."

Zane chuckled. "You were sure spreading it around today. The way you corralled Allison into the back room reminded me of a stallion herding a mare. Not at all subtle."

Chase made a disgusted face and muttered, "Yeah, well, I don't know what got into me today." But even as he resolved to regain his iron control, his uneasiness grew, prompting him to leave. He stood up and pushed in the bar stool.

Zane slid off the bar and buttoned up his coat, preparing to follow Chase out. "If I'm not mistaken," Zane said, "I think it's called lust. And about time, I'd say."

Suddenly, Chase had to see Allison. The urge to go to her was overwhelming, as bad as the turbulent lust had been. He had to fight to keep from rushing out, making a fool of himself again. Only the fact that he didn't have her exact address held him back. He glanced at his brother and wanted to wince. Zane was giving him a rather knowing look.

"I don't suppose you know—"

Zane chuckled. "She lives on State Street, not too far from here. It's a big old cream-colored clapboard farmhouse, and you can't miss it because the roof sticks up way higher than any of the others."

Narrowing his eyes, Chase asked, "How do you know?"

"Well, I haven't been there wooing her, if that's what you're worried about. Besides, like I already told you, she wasn't interested in me. From what I understand, she inherited the house from an old spinster aunt. I helped out about a month ago when Cole and Sophie moved her in there."

"Thanks." Chase headed out the door, driven by some vague urgency he couldn't suppress. He tossed a quick look at Zane. "Lock up, will you?"

Zane blinked in astonishment. "You're not going over there now, are you?"

Chase didn't answer him. He didn't have time. Before he was completely through the door, he was flat-out running. He had to get to Allison. Why, he didn't know, but the panic was real, making his heart race and his jaw lock. Within minutes he was in his car, driving too fast, and just as he turned the corner on State Street, he was able to clearly hear her again, her every thought, her every word. And what he heard caused him an unreasonable amount of anger.

It's not that I mind you being here, really. It just makes me a little nerv-

ous because it's not something I'm used to. Especially when I'm trying to bathe. Couldn't you go away for just a little while until I finish up?

Someone was with her while she was trying to take a bath? And he refused to leave?

Allison's nervousness was real, flooding his senses. In fact, her nervousness bordered on fear, and Chase was suddenly so enraged, a red haze crowded his vision. He parked his car in the driveway with a screech, thankful that she didn't have any near neighbors on the older, quiet street. He jumped out of his car, stormed up the paved entry walk to the immense wooden front porch decorated with a huge jack-o'-lantern and some cornstalks, but as he started to pound on the door, he noticed a narrow window to the side of the front room was opened just a crack. In late October, the evening air was cool enough that all the windows should have been shut, especially considering she was a woman alone, on a dead-end street, and it was nearing three in the morning. His instincts kicked in.

Chase crept to the window and slid through it silently. Once inside, he closed and latched it, then looked around. He seemed to be in a parlor of sorts with carved, embroidered furniture, plenty of crocheted doilies, and lamps with fabric shades. Even though the room was dim, enough light came from the hall chandelier to let him clearly see the flocked, flowery wallpaper. He felt like he'd stepped back in time.

The house was dated enough to boggle his senses.

He explored cautiously, leaving the parlor and sneaking a peek into the adjacent rooms, one a library lined with dark, heavy wooden shelves, the other a more modern family room with a TV and overstuffed couch. The rooms were long and narrow with arched doorways and heavy drapes, and they opened to a central hall. At the end of the hall he could see a spacious country kitchen, and next to it, a small bath with black and pink ceramic tile on the floor and walls. Right inside the front door, to the left, was an incredible winding, ornate wooden staircase that led to the second floor.

Hearing a creak from above, Chase looked up. From the sounds of it, Allison was up there talking quietly with someone.

Jealousy, hot and dark, raced over his nerve endings, along with the need to protect. He could still feel her unease, and when he found out who was responsible, they'd be sorry. He crept upstairs. Each damn step seemed to groan beneath his weight, the typical speakings of an old house. The urgency suddenly quieted, replaced by annoyance—not his annoyance, so maybe it was hers?

The stairway ended with another hall. At one end was a large, narrow, diamond-paned window showing the dark night beyond, with two bedrooms, one on either side of the hall, in between. At the other end was a master bedroom and a larger bathroom, and that's where Chase headed. He could hear Allison clearly now, and his brows drew tight. Who the hell was she talking to? He paused outside the bathroom door and listened.

"Really, the idea is ludicrous. I can't sleep with Chase when he doesn't truly want me. And before you say it, you know it's just that darn trick you played on me, letting him read my mind, that has him reacting right now." She groaned. "When I think of all the stuff I imagined, it's *so* embarrassing. If it wasn't for that, he'd still think I was invisible.

"Oh, no. That dress had nothing to do with it, though I admit I liked wearing it. It made me feel sexy, whether it actually worked or not." She laughed slightly. "The underthings were great. I loved them."

Chase peeked around the open door, his eyes narrowed. But there was no one in the room. Just Allison. Naked. In a tub of bubbles.

Her blond hair was pinned on top of her head, little ringlets falling free, and her bare arms rested along the sides of the free-standing, claw-footed white porcelain tub. Her eyes were closed and her soft mouth smiled.

She sighed deeply, and one small pink nipple appeared above the froth of bubbles. Chase stared, mesmerized, unable to speak, barely able to breathe.

"I appreciate your efforts, guys, I really do. But I'm not at all sure I can go through with it, so let's just forget about Chase, okay?"

Chase stepped completely into the bathroom, his body pulsing with need. "Let's don't."

With a loud squeal and a lot of thrashing and splashing, Allison turned to see him. She knelt in the tub, her hands crossed over her chest, her eyes wide. She didn't have her glasses on and she stared at him hard.

Automatically, he said, "It's me, Chase."

"I know who it is! What in the world are you doing in here! This is my bathroom. How did you get in?"

He opened his mouth, but she interrupted him, shouting, "Never mind that! Just get out!"

He frowned. "Who were you talking to, Allison?"

She groaned. "Oh God, I don't believe this. I don't believe this, it isn't happening. . . . "

"Are you going to get hysterical on me?"

"Yes!"

She glared up at him, her big blue eyes rounded owlishly as she tried to see him without her glasses. She was still crouched in the tub, the bubbles reaching her hips, and her hands somewhat inadequate to completely cover her breasts. She was small, but the soft, white, rounded flesh showing from around her crossed arms was very distracting. And here she'd thought herself lacking. . . .

Chase cleared his throat. "I'll step out in the hall, but make it quick. You have some explaining to do."

He walked out and dropped back against the wall, his eyes closed, his stomach muscles pulled tight. He'd left the bathroom door open and heard her growl, "Don't you dare peek!"

He just shook his head. "Hurry up, will you? My patience is pretty thin right now."

There was a flurry of splashing and mumbled cursing, then Allison, leaving a trail of water, padded barefoot out of the bathroom, an ancient embroidered chenille robe wrapped tightly around her, her glasses once again in place. Bubbles clung to the end of a ringlet over her right ear, and her throat and upper chest were still wet. The robe covered her, but the neckline dipped low enough that he could just make out the edging of white lawn underwear. Again, something vintage? When she stomped over to face him, the robe parted over her legs and he saw old-fashioned drawers that just reached her knees. His heart rate accelerated, but she quickly pulled the robe closed again.

She greeted him with a pointed finger poked into his chest. "How dare you barge in here, intruding on my privacy!"

Chase grabbed her hand, pulled her close, and gave in to the need to kiss her. She was still warm and damp, and she smelled like flowers. He held her head between his hands, urging her to her tiptoes, then kissed her long and soft and deep, eating at her mouth, capturing her tongue and drawing it into his own mouth. She groaned softly, and the hallway lights blinked happily around them.

"What the hell?" Chase looked up, but there was no one there. "What happened to the lights?"

Her hands remained fisted in his shirt, her expression dazed, her lips still parted. Around panting breaths, she said, "Hmmm?"

"The lights blinked, almost like a strobe."

"Oh." Very slowly, she pushed herself away from him, then straightened her glasses. She looked around with a frown. "It's an old house. The wiring is sometimes...temperamental."

Chase stared at her, saw her trying to gather herself, and shook his head. "Damn, honey, you look sexy as hell." He lifted an edge of the robe. "What have you got on under there?"

Her eyes widened and she clutched the robe. "Chase, stop it."

He stepped toward her, and she backed up. "Who were you talking to, Allison?"

"Myself?"

He shook his head. "I'm not believing it. Try again."

"You can see there's no one here."

"The window downstairs is open."

"It is?"

"Yes." He couldn't quite keep his gaze on her face, not after seeing her practically naked—and liking very much what he saw. He was so hard he hurt, and his imagination was going wild, thinking of all the things he'd like to do to her. "Don't you think that's a little risky, being you're here alone?"

"I didn't open the window, Chase."

His brows pulled down again, because she sounded totally unconcerned as she said that. Then she added, "What are you doing here, anyway? It's kind of late for a social call, isn't it?"

Why was he here? Damn, how could he tell her he'd been worried? That he'd felt something was wrong? He started to say just that when suddenly the lights flickered again, almost going crazy, and seconds later there was a crash downstairs. Chase grabbed Allison's arm, shoved her into the bathroom, and shouted, "Lock the door," before rushing down the stairs. His instincts were screaming an alarm, and he didn't wait to see if Allison would do as she was told. He just took it for granted that she would.

Bounding down the steps two at a time, an awkward task given the lights danced wildly, he reached the bottom in just a few seconds. He heard another noise, like a distant thump, and followed the sound into the parlor where he'd entered. As he bolted into the room, he saw that the wind had picked up a heavy curtain hanging over the window he'd climbed through minutes before.

He distinctly recalled closing and locking that window. Someone had just left the house.

He moved silently across the room, his gaze searching everywhere, checking out every corner. But the fact that the window was open when he got here, and then opened again, led him to believe someone had been in the house and had now left. Otherwise, how did the window get open, when it locked from the inside and he himself had just locked it?

He turned to go back to check on Allison and ran right into her. She would have landed on her sweet behind if he hadn't caught her upper arms and steadied her.

"Dammit! I thought I told you to stay upstairs." He wasn't at all pleased that she'd disregarded his orders.

She glared right back at him. "This is my house. And besides, I knew nothing was wrong. A house this old makes all kind of noises. There was no reason to be alarmed."

He wanted to shake her. This propensity he had for losing his temper and rattling her teeth was disturbing in the extreme. He'd never really lost his temper with a woman in his life, and he'd sure as hell never taken to shaking them. In fact, he took extra pleasure in maintaining icy control, in holding the reins of command gently. It was a big turn-on for him.

But Allison made him forget all that.

He leaned down close until their noses almost touched and said in a low growl, "Someone was just in your house."

She scoffed.

"Dammit, Allison, how much proof do you need? When I got here, the window was open, which was how I got in, by the way. But then I closed and locked it. Only now it's wide open again and a table's knocked over and there's a broken dish on the floor. So unless you're going to tell me this house is inhabited by ghosts, you'll have to admit—"

"It is."

Her blurted statement and small wince had him verbally backing up. "It is, what?"

She drew a long breath and he felt her shoring up her courage, preparing herself, then she whispered, "It is inhabited by ghosts."

He had the horrifying suspicion she was serious. "Come again?"

With another deep breath, she looked up at him, then said, "The house comes with two ghosts. If you'd like, I could introduce you to Rose and Burke."

F O U R

Allison waited anxiously while Chase did no more than stare down at her. He looked skeptical and a little concerned. Finally he said, "Are you all right?"

"Chase." She took his hand and led him to a couch, forced him to sit, then turned on a few lamps. He was right. There was a knocked-over table and a broken dish. She frowned and said to the room at large, "Very funny, Rose. If you wanted to scare him off, you're succeeding."

"Uh, Allison—"

She waved him to silence, propped her hands on her hips over the soft robe, and looked around. "Well, Rose? You got him here, so the least you can do is come out and show yourself. What? No more blinking lights? No more parlor tricks?"

Nothing. She frowned again, then glanced worriedly at Chase. He watched her like she'd grown an extra head. She raked a hand through her disheveled bangs, somewhat embarrassed. Darned aggravating ghosts.

"Uh, listen honey." Chase spoke very gently, very softly. He patted the couch cushion beside him. "Why don't you sit down here for a minute and I'll go see if I can get us something to drink."

When she shook her head at him, he left the couch to stand beside her, trying to urge her to the seat he'd just vacated.

She made a sound of disgust. "It must have been Burke. Rose is pretty nice most of the time, though she's sometimes a little crotchety. But Burke"—and here she raised her voice to make certain he'd hear— "can be a real pain!"

A cold draft filled the room, making her shiver. Chase looked around, then chafed her arms roughly to warm her. "Do you have another window open?"

"No, that's just Burke. He hates it when I insult him."

He eyed her dubiously. "On second thought, I don't want to leave you alone. Why don't we go into the kitchen together?"

Allison laughed. "Chase, you can read my mind. Can't you tell I'm not making it up?"

She might have been made of fine china, the way he now handled her. "I can tell you think you're actually talking to ghosts." He put a rather brotherly arm around her and urged her into the hallway. "But don't worry about that right now. Let's just go to the kitchen, and while you get something to drink, I'll check the other windows. There's definitely one open. Your hair is blowing around."

She lifted one hand and shoved a loose curl behind her ear. Her gaze searched every corner of the hallway and all the rooms as she passed, but Rose and Burke were hiding for some damn reason.

"Shhh. It's okay. Here, just sit a minute while I go check the windows and doors."

Allison sighed. "I'm not going to break, Chase."

"I know that." Then he very carefully smoothed her hair in a way that reminded her of a puppy being petted. "I'll be right back, honey." He jogged out of the room.

Allison looked around her empty kitchen and wanted to scream. She said aloud, "Well, I hope you're happy now. He thinks I'm loony. And I seriously doubt discrediting my mental faculties is going to inspire him to lust."

A warm breeze blew over her, taking away the chill. "Thanks. I hate being cold." Then she covered her face. "Guys, this is never going to work. I know you thought it would, but—"

Chase walked back in, a severe frown on his face. She knew he wanted to say something about her conversation with ghosts that he didn't believe in, but he refrained. "Everything on this floor is closed up and locked. I didn't check upstairs yet, but the breeze seems to be gone."

She eyed him carefully. "Of course it is."

"Actually, for such an old house, the locks are pretty secure. Were they changed recently?"

A safe enough topic, she decided. "My aunt, whom I inherited the house from, had never married. She lived alone here, and it made her nervous. I think she updated the locks every two years, and she had them all checked regularly." Allison added with a grin, "Living with ghosts made her really nervous. She didn't accept it nearly as well as I have."

Pulling a chair up close so that their knees almost touched, Chase seated himself. He took her hands and stared her in the eye. "Forget your ghosts for a second, okay? You have a real problem."

"What?"

"Honey, I opened the front door and right off the edge of your porch, there are footprints in the dirt. Big prints. Not yours." He glanced down at her small bare feet, then with another frown, added, "Someone went out the window in a hurry, then leaped off the porch. Not a damn ghost, a flesh-and-blood man. Someone was here in the house with you."

Every small hair on her neck stood at attention while she stared frozen, straight into Chase Winston's dark, serious gaze. So that was why she'd been feeling so nervous and why Burke and Rose had invaded her bath.

Chase made an impatient sound. "Allison, I don't understand—"

She waved him to silence, finally ungluing her tongue from the roof of her mouth. "Don't you see? Usually they respect my privacy. They're around, but they don't intrude—at least, not much—and certainly not when I'm changing clothes or bathing. But tonight they kept hanging around the bathroom, and even though they're just ghosts, it really did make me nervous. I mean, I was *naked.*"

Chase blinked slowly. "Yeah, I noticed."

She ignored that and continued to reason things out. "At least, I thought that was why I was nervous. But now I think it must have been the intruder. Rose wanted me to be nervous, to understand...Oh God." The enormity of it hit her. "Someone was in my house!"

Chase bit the side of his mouth, and she could feel him thinking, sorting out what he'd say, how to address what he considered sheer fancy on her part. Finally, he lifted a hand to her cheek and tried a small smile. "Honey, you're telling me there're ghosts in your house, but that doesn't bother you. It's only the idea of a real man—"

"Oh, for pity's sake, Chase. You're a real man, and I'm not afraid of you. But then you don't sneak in through windows!"

His thumb brushed over her temple, distracting her. "Actually, I did."

She struggled to get her mind back on track and away from that big, warm thumb. "You know what I mean. You came because you were worried about me. Hey! That's it. Just like Rose transferred my thoughts to you at the bar, she must have let you know about the intruder. Can you just imagine what might have happened if you hadn't shown up?" She shuddered in very real fear. "I guess I owe Rose my thanks."

Chase appeared to be considering everything she'd said. "Okay, let's deal with that first. Why did you leave the window unlocked?"

Allison huffed. "I'm not an idiot, Chase."

"But . . ."

"I didn't leave the window open," she insisted. "And before you even think it, Rose or Burke would never do such a thing."

Chase lifted his gaze to the ceiling. "I wasn't going to suggest they might."

"Oh, that's right. You don't believe in them."

"What I believe is that someone broke in here, and they got in through the window. It didn't look to me like they'd broken in, rather they just opened the window because it wasn't locked."

"But they're always locked."

"This one wasn't."

She pondered that. How could such a thing have happened? The lights flickered again and both she and Chase looked up at the old Tiffany-style chandelier hanging over the kitchen table. Allison pursed her mouth. "See there? I think Rose or Burke have an idea, but because they're fickle and determined on their own course, they won't just come right out and tell me about it."

"They, uh, talk to you, do they?"

"I don't know if I'd call it talking. I mean, I hear them, but I don't know that they're actually saying anything. You understand?"

His expression was ironic. "Certainly. What's not to understand?"

She narrowed her eyes at him. "You claim to hear me when I'm not talking to you."

"But you're not a ghost."

"So?"

He opened his mouth, then closed it.

Satisfied that he'd listen, Allison stood to pace. "The thing is, they didn't come right out and tell me, but they did do the next best thing, which was to send you here." Then she glanced at him again, and the look on his face didn't encourage her. "I'm sorry you're out so late tonight. You must be exhausted after working all day."

Chase looked like he either wanted to strangle her or lay her out on the table and do wickedly sexy things to her. She gulped, knowing which she'd prefer.

"I know which I'd prefer, too," he said pointedly, staring at the way her robe gaped at her throat, "but I think we need to get a few things straightened out here first."

"Like my sanity?"

"I'm not suggesting you're insane—"

She began pacing again. "I'm not confused or making it up or imagining it, either. You saw the lights. Well, they do that to show they're agitated or excited. Which proves Rose and Burke are real. Or, that is, they're as real as ghosts can be."

"Because of some flickering lights? Honey, I hate to tell you, but this old house probably has lots of glitches in it. It's ancient enough to be falling apart. Damn, just look at the kitchen."

There was a touch of criticism in his tone as he looked around at the kitchen she loved so much. She saw his gaze linger on the old-fashioned free-standing sink with the hand pump at one end. Protectiveness for her house rose like a tide within her. "I happen to love my house."

He shook his head. "It looks to me like it needs some major fixing up."

No sooner did the words leave his mouth than a large plastic bowl filled with fruit toppled off the top of the rounded refrigerator to pummel his head. Chase jumped up, cursing and looking around, his body tensed. A plump orange rolled across the floor, stopping when it hit Allison's bare foot. She bent to pick it up. Several apples, a banana, and a few grapes were littered around him. Chase's look of insult was replaced by disbelief. "How the hell did that happen?"

"Burke?" When Chase scowled at her, she shrugged. "He loves this house. He bought it for Rose after they married, sort of a little love nest, though in this day and age the house would be considered huge. But anyway, Burke doesn't take kindly to someone insulting it, so if I were you, I'd be careful what I say."

"Dammit, Allison, that's ridiculous. Besides, I wasn't insulting the house, only commenting on the obvious."

"I guess Burke didn't like your comments."

He shook his head. "The floor slants, that's all. Even the walls are crooked. The bowl was bound to topple sooner or later. It was just coincidence that it happened to fall on me just then."

"If you say so."

He crossed his arms over his chest and leaned back against the refrigerator. It was such an old, squat appliance, his head was above the top now that he was standing. "I'd just gotten off work when I had the feeling you were upset about something. What are you doing up this late, honey?"

She fidgeted, wondering how much to tell him, but one look at his face and she knew he'd just read her mind if she attempted to hold anything back. Still, it was so embarrassing...

"Out with it, babe. All this hedging will just make it worse."

She bit her lip, knowing he was right but resenting him all the same. She should have had at least until tomorrow to get her thoughts together. "I couldn't sleep. I kept... kept thinking about you and that you'd kissed me and how wonderful it was." His gaze darkened, and his look became almost tactile. She shivered again, this time in reaction. Then she added softly, "And I kept thinking that it was all wrong."

His shoulders tensed while he looked her over from head to foot. "What's wrong about it?"

He sounded gentle again, but determined. Allison cleared her throat. "You don't really want me, Chase. I think Rose has done something to you to make you think you do. It's kind of a long story—"

"Do you have to be at work early tomorrow?"

"No. Not until noon. Sophie's opening up tomorrow."

"So, we have plenty of time for you to explain this long story to me then, right?"

Unfortunately, she couldn't think of any reason to refuse him.

He smiled. "First, I think we need to call the police about the break-in."

"No!" Even as she said it, the lights flickered crazily.

Chase's expression hardened as he glared at the lights. "Allison, a man was in your house. If I hadn't shown up when I did, you might have been hurt—"

"It was probably just a prankster, you know, a kid messing around because of Halloween."

"It isn't Halloween yet."

"But you know that sort of thing always starts early. And now he's gone, and I'll be sure to double-check the windows every night from now on, so there's really no reason to worry. And no reason to bother the police."

Chase wasn't an easy man to fool. He leaned over and trapped Allison against the butcher block counter. "What's going on, Allison? Why the aversion to the police?"

With him this close, she could see how thick his eyelashes were, could smell him . . .

"Dammit, forget my eyelashes! I'm not trying to seduce you. At least, not yet. I want to know why you won't call the police."

She looked at his incredibly sexy mouth, saw it quirk slightly, then blurted, "Rose and Burke hate having people rummage through the place. It makes them nervous."

His eyebrows shot up incredulously. "Nervous ghosts?"

"Well . . . yeah."

Straightening again, he rubbed the back of his neck. But Allison's gaze dipped over his body—so gorgeous—and her attention got stuck on the fact that he was hard again. His jeans fit him snugly and the soft, faded material hugged that part of his body, making heat explode inside her, her stomach twist in need.

He groaned. "You're making me crazy, babe."

"I . . . I think you need to see something." She gulped. "Before we go any farther, I mean."

He leveled a look on her, hot and expectant.

"It's . . . it's upstairs. In my bedroom."

He smiled.

Shifting nervously, Allison said, "I'll just go up and get dressed, and then I'll show you—"

Chase took her arms and half lifted her off her feet. He shook his head. "I like you just the way you are," he whispered, then kissed her gently, showing a lot of restraint. "You look sexy as hell with your hair pinned up, that soft robe giving me sneak peeks every now and again of that sexy cotton underwear, and your glasses perched on your nose that way."

She clutched the robe shut to rid the possibility of any further sneak peeks, then asked with a squeak, "You like the corset cover and drawers?"

"What I've seen of them, yes. Do you intend to model for me?"

Her brain went blank at the idea of dropping her robe for him. He grinned, and she quickly asked, "You think my glasses are sexy, too?"

Pulling her up flush against him, he said, "I think everything about you is sexy, and your damned ghosts don't have a thing to do with it."

"But . . . my glasses?"

He smiled again. "Let's go upstairs, honey. I think I've waited long enough."

Eyes wide, she said, "But I have to show you something before you start getting . . . um . . . amorous."

One large hand stroked her waist. "I'm already amorous."

"Chase . . ."

"You can show me what you think is so important, but it won't make any difference."

Allison turned to nervously lead the way to her bedroom. Under her breath she muttered, "Wanna bet?"

But Chase heard her, and he rewarded her sarcasm with a small smack on the bottom, then left his hand there, caressing. It took all her resolution to climb the stairs. And once they were in her bedroom, she avoided looking at him, knowing if she did, she'd jump his bones and they'd never get around to the important stuff.

Hurrying to her nightstand, she opened the top drawer and pulled out an old, red leather-bound journal. She thrust it toward Chase. "I haven't shown this to anyone else. But I think you should read at least part of it before we do anything."

He stared at the book, stared at her, and then stared at the huge, four-poster mahogany bed, and he sighed. Taking the book, he said, "I sure don't have any complaints on your bed, honey. It looks plenty big enough, and the four posters are giving me some interesting ideas." He looked at her, searched her face, then asked, "How about you?"

She gulped. "How about me, what?"

Nodding toward the bed, he asked, "Any interesting ideas?"

She could just tell he was reading her mind, and what was in it was too explicit for words. Ideas? Heck yes, she had ideas, and all of them had him naked for her pleasure.

Chase grinned, then sat on the edge of the mattress. "Not exactly the images I'm having, but we'll work on it." He held up the book. "Just as soon as I finish this."

He settled himself comfortably with a pillow behind his head, at his leisure. With one last glance at Allison, standing there with her mouth open, he murmured, "You're just damn lucky that I'm a fast reader."

And there was a promise to those words that had her catching her breath and shivering from the inside out. "I think I'll go get us those drinks we kept talking about."

"And something to eat? I'm starved."

"I'll see what I can dredge up." She fled the room, unable to look at him as he read the damning words in the journal that told what his purpose tonight would be.

F I V E

Allison made four peanut butter and jelly sandwiches and poured two large glasses of milk. Rose and Burke were mysteriously absent, and she had the feeling they were watching Chase read. She felt so bad for them, she sincerely hoped Chase would be able to accommodate what needed to be done.

She'd been downstairs over twenty minutes and decided putting it off any longer was just plain cowardly. Still, she dragged her feet as she went up the steps. Sure enough, when she entered the bedroom, she saw both Burke and Rose hovering over Chase, who still had his nose buried in the journal. Now, however, he'd taken off his boots and had his sock-covered feet crossed at the ankle, with one long arm behind his head. He was so tall, his stretched-out form went from the head of the bed to the very end, when she often felt lost in the incredible size of it.

When she stopped in the doorway, his gaze lifted to her, but otherwise he didn't move. His expression was speculative and lazy.

She cleared her throat, ignoring Rose and Burke. "I, ah, made you some peanut butter and jelly sandwiches. I hope that's okay?"

He laid the open book on the mattress, spine out, and rolled to his side, propping his head on a fist. He still didn't say anything.

"Um, interesting reading?"

"Very."

"How far did you get?"

"Far enough to know now what it is you want me to do."

"Oh." Her face heated and she inched closer to hand him the tray of sandwiches.

Chase set it in the middle of the bed, then patted the other side, indicating she should sit down with him. Very tentatively, she slid onto the mattress. She smoothed the robe over her outstretched legs, kept her back straight, and settled her hands in her lap. Just to give herself something to do, she picked up half a sandwich and took a small bite while staring at her bare feet.

Chase, knowing exactly how nervous she was, waited until she had her mouth full to say, "I'm supposed to be your *grand passion*, right?"

And Allison promptly choked.

Chase made no move to assist her, instead picking up his own half of a sandwich and eating it in two bites while watching her struggle for a breath.

Allison wheezed and snuffled and when she could finally talk without rasping, she asked carefully, "Did you get to the part about the jewels?"

"Um-hmm. Burke gave Rose jewels as a sign of his love, but when he died with the measles, and she, too, got sick from never leaving his bedside, nursing him until his death, she hid them in the house so none of her damned relatives could steal them. They were, in Rose's words, a symbol of *grand passion*, and neither she nor Burke wanted them getting into the wrong hands."

Allison toyed nervously with a curl that had escaped her hairpins to hang to her shoulder. "That's right. And in fact, Rose did die of the same thing, only she went a little faster than Burke did because she was already so weak from taking care of him." She glanced at him. "Isn't that sad?"

Chase shrugged. "I suppose a wife who loved a husband would do exactly that. Or vice versa."

His answer obviously pleased the ghosts, considering how the lights twinkled happily and a warm glow seemed to fill the room. This time, Chase didn't even seem to notice the lights. All his attention was on Allison.

She cleared her throat. "They're not really a symbol of everlasting love or anything like that." She peeked at him through her lashes. "But Rose and Burke at least want the female relative who inherits the jewels to be...um...*passionate*. So far, there's been no one they feel fits the bill, so they've kept the jewels hidden, and they've been stuck here, not wanting to leave until the legacy of the jewels has been passed on."

"So it's an actual legacy of passion?"

Allison wasn't sure if he was teasing or not or if he believed any of it or not. His expression gave nothing away. "When they both died, they left the house to one of Burke's sisters, Maryann. But Maryann's young husband had already died, and she never remarried. Her only daughter, Cybil, inherited next, but she never even seemed interested in the idea of marriage. Rose didn't consider either of them women of... um...*fire*. Like herself. The women didn't believe in the ghosts and weren't that interested in men. It's Rose's worry about the jewels getting into the wrong hands that's keeping them both gounded on this plane instead of finding peace."

Chase ate another sandwich and drank half his milk, still looking at her in that watchful, curious way, as if waiting to pounce on her. "Rose didn't have any other relatives that suited her?"

Allison shook her head, and two more curls tumbled free. She tried to stick them back up, but somewhere along the way, she'd lost a pin or two. Chase's gaze skimmed her hair, lazy and hot, then came back to her face.

"I, ah...no, Rose's relatives all thought she'd married beneath herself, and most of them disowned her. That's why the jewels were so important. Burke had to work really hard to afford something for her that he thought her family would find adequate. But Rose never wanted anything material from him. Still, he bought her this house and the jewels and—"

"And they had a very passionate marriage."

Allison ducked her head. "Yes." Then in a smaller voice, she added, "That was all Rose ever expected from him. But he was an entrepreneur, and it wasn't long before they were actually doing pretty well. Rose had always believed in him, so she wasn't surprised. And it didn't make her love him more. And by then her family all wanted her back, but she was devoted solely to Burke and didn't want to associate with a family that hadn't accepted him based on the wonderful man he was rather than his material worth."

The last sandwich was gone, wolfed down by Chase. She'd only eaten a half. Chase finished his milk, then set the whole tray aside on the nightstand. He reached for Allison, and she stiffened, both in excitement and wary nervousness. She squeezed her eyes shut.

Chase paused, his hand now gently rubbing her arm. "I take it you're willing to fulfill the role of the passionate heir?"

Not quite meeting his gaze, she said, "Rose thinks I would suffice, though truth is, I've never considered myself a particularly passionate woman."

"No?" His fingers trailed up and down her arm, then across her throat.

Allison swallowed hard. "You'd probably find out soon enough, considering things are progressing right along here, but I'm actually still a . . . a virgin."

Chase froze, then with a growl he dropped back on the bed and covered his eyes with a forearm. "I don't damn well believe this."

Allison peered over at him. He seemed to be in pain, his body taut, his mouth a firm line, his jaw locked. "Chase, are you all right?"

His laugh wasn't at all humorous. "A damned virgin," he muttered.

"Well, I'd hardly consider myself damned. I just never met anyone . . . um, except you . . . that I wanted to get all that involved with. Sexually I mean. And being as you weren't interested . . ."

"This is incredible. A *virgin*."

"You don't need to drive it into the ground."

Just that quick, Chase was over her, causing her to yelp in surprise before her breath was completely stolen away by the look in his eyes and the pressure of his wide chest over hers. He caught her hands in one of his and raised them over her head, effectively pinning her in place so she could do no more than blink. Through clenched teeth, he muttered, "Do you have any idea what I wanted to do to you?"

She opened her mouth but could only squeak.

Chase gently smoothed her hair away from her face, the careful touch in direct contrast to how he held her and the roughness of his tone. "You know so little about me, sweetheart."

Suddenly the lights turned dazzling bright, making them both squint against the glare. Allison turned her head to look in the corner at Rose—and her mouth fell open in shock. "Oh my God."

Chase shielded his eyes with a hand and barked, "What?"

She turned back to him, so surprised even the light couldn't bother her. "Is it true?"

"Is what true, damn it?"

"What Rose just said."

"I didn't hear her say a damn thing. Are you telling me the ghosts are here with us now?"

He couldn't see them. Allison registered that fact and wondered how she'd ever convince him. Then just as quickly she realized that if what Rose claimed about him was true, he probably wouldn't need much convincing.

Chase pressed his chest closer, effectively pulling her from her thoughts. With a near sneer, he asked, "And what exactly is it that Rose has said about me?"

She almost couldn't utter the words. It took two swallows, and a great deal of effort to whisper, "She says you're . . . you're kinky."

"Kinky!"

Allison nodded. "She says you like to . . . to dominate in bed." Chase's expression was almost comical in his disbelief. "She says that's why you're so choosy about who you sleep with, why you ignored me, because you didn't think I'd get into sex games with you or that I wouldn't indulge your preferences for a little bondage and—"

Chase laid a hand over her mouth, halting the flow of words. He whispered, as if he didn't want anyone else to hear, "There really are ghosts?"

Allison nodded.

The look of disbelief left his face to be replaced by outrage. He glared and thrust himself away from her, rolling off the bed and onto his feet in one quick, fluid movement. He searched the room, but the lights were dim again and Rose and Burke were hiding. Chase turned his accusing gaze on Allison, who hadn't moved a single muscle. She was still too fascinated by the idea of being at Chase's sexual mercy. She didn't know exactly what he'd do or how much mercy he'd have, but she was more than a little anxious to find out.

"Oh no you don't! Don't start trying to distract me again with sex." He pointed a finger at her. "You expected me to make love to you tonight, and you knew all along they'd be watching? You set me up as entertainment for them? Rose and Burke can't just be normal ghosts, oh no, they have to be damned voyeur ghosts!"

A pillow shot off the bed to hit Chase square in the face. He slapped it aside, but another took its place. Chase cursed and said, "Oh great. Now I've pissed off a ghost! It doesn't get much better than this, does it, Allison!"

Still lying there, feeling a lot more confident about the situation now, Allison grinned and said, "Then you believe in them?"

Running an agitated hand through his hair, Chase said, "Why not? It makes as much sense as anything else."

She looked ready to giggle. Chase realized he was behaving in an absurd way. There was Allison, spread out on a bed, looking so damned ripe and ready it made his teeth ache. And he was provoking ghosts.

It also dawned on him that she didn't seem overly repelled by the idea of him dominating her. In fact, if he was reading her right—and he knew he was—she was intrigued. *Well, how about that.*

Another pillow hit him.

"I think Rose wants you to apologize. She said she kept her eyes closed whenever Burke made love to her, so she sure as certain doesn't have any urge to watch you."

A reluctant smile curved his mouth. The uniqueness of the situation was finally starting to sink in. "She said that, did she?"

"Yes." Allison hesitated, then added, "But Burke says it isn't true, that she used to devour him with her eyes when they made love. He says Rose has the most beautiful, expressive eyes in the whole world."

Despite himself, Chase was touched by the sentimental words. *Ghosts.* And not just any ghosts, but passionate ghosts who joked and teased and loved. Who would have believed it? Allison had to be telling the truth because how else could she have known? And the damned pillows had literally flown off the bed without her help. She'd done no more than lay there, watching him. Waiting.

In a way, he was grateful, because Rose and Burke had given him

Allison. Without their interference, he never would have seen the depths of her, and seeing her now, so anxious to take part in everything he wanted to do with her, he couldn't imagine not being with her.

He stepped over closer to the bed. "Tell me something, honey. Did you think to try this with Jack?"

She wrinkled her nose but apparently felt there was no point in lying. "I needed to do something passionate so Burke and Rose could move on. They don't mind being here, but they're not settled. Only they didn't want me with Jack—and I have to admit I'm glad. He's a nice guy, despite how he acted at your bar, and he's been very considerate, very helpful to me. But I couldn't quite get into the idea of . . . of . . ."

Chase felt his heart swell at her pink cheeks and stammering tone. Very gently, he said, "You couldn't imagine being passionate with him?"

She nodded, then added in a whisper, "I tried to think about him that way, but it always ended up being you in my fantasies. And somehow Rose just sort of knew that. She insisted I should go after you, even though I told her it was useless. She even selected the stuff I'd wear—"

"Ah, that killer dress from yesterday?"

She nodded. "Rose found it in the attic."

"Was it hers?"

"No. She told me she really likes this modern, shorter style though." Allison smiled. "To Rose, it seems really risqué."

He lifted a brow and looked her over slowly. "To me, too."

"Really?" She gulped, then forged on. "Rose even picked out the stuff I'm wearing now, but at the time, I didn't know you'd ever see me in it."

He knelt on the bed beside her and without a word, unknotted the fabric belt to her robe to pull it open. He stared down at the soft-as-silk cotton chemise and drawers. There was a flawless rose crocheted on the neckline of the chemise right above a row of tiny shell buttons, and more roses on the front of each leg. The drawers closed up in front with a wide, intriguing flap—big enough for a man's hand. Chase breathed hard. "You can tell Rose I heartily approve."

Allison smiled. "You just told her yourself."

He stared down at her soft breasts, her small nipples hard and straining against the cotton material. He felt his nostrils flare, felt a twisting in his guts. Without lifting his gaze, he said, "Beat it, guys. Allison and I have some business to attend to."

The lights dimmed so that only a soft glow touched the bed, then a slight warm breeze passed over him and he knew Burke and Rose had given them privacy. He wasted no more time. Straddling her hips, he stared down at her body, at the way her chest rose and fell with her deep breaths. He unbuttoned his shirt and shrugged it off.

Allison groaned at the sight of his bare chest and started to reach for him. He smiled and caught her hands.

"No, I have a certain way I like to do things, sweetheart. And seeing as we'll be doing this a lot—"

"We will?"

"Oh yeah. Definitely. So we might as well start out right." He pulled her into a sitting position and removed her glasses, tossing them aside, then stripped the robe off her shoulders. Holding her wide gaze, he pulled the soft, chenille belt out of the belt loops.

He could feel her trembling, both alarmed and excited. "Don't ever be afraid of me, Allison," he ordered quietly. She licked her lips, eyeing that soft belt, then nodded.

"Good girl." Her acceptance pleased and provoked him. "Now, lie back down."

She was practically panting, her eyes unblinking, her lips parted. Chase couldn't help but smile at her. "Put your arms over your head, as far as you can. Try to reach the top of the bed."

She gulped, but she slowly did as he ordered. Blood rushed through his veins at her compliance. And better still, he could feel her excitement, almost as great as his own. It was like she was his exact match, a perfect soul mate, and his body and mind recognized that fact, making all the feelings more acute, more important.

Taking his time, making the anticipation build, he held her wrists together and looped the belt around them, then tied it to one of the sturdy posts at the top of the bed. When he was confident that the knot would hold, he trailed his fingers down her bare arms to her armpits, then over her collar bone. She shivered slightly, twisting, and he whispered, "No, don't move."

She stilled instantly.

He eyed her taut form. "Are you uncomfortable?"

"No."

That was the tiniest voice he'd ever heard from her, and he recognized the aroused tone. He touched the rose on her bodice. "I'm going to look at your naked breasts now, Allison."

She started to close her eyes, but again, he reprimanded her. "I want you to watch me," he instructed gently.

Her teeth sank into her bottom lip, but she kept her gaze on his face. The tiny buttons slid easily out of the silk loops, and little by little, he bared her. Her breasts were small, some of the fullness removed by her stretched-out position. He felt her touch of embarrassment but refused to allow it to interfere with her enjoyment.

Closing his fingers around one taut nipple, he said, "You're more beautiful than any woman I've ever seen."

She started to speak, and he pinched lightly, tugging. Her words evaporated into a gasp.

"You like that?"

"*Yes.*"

He lifted his other hand, plying both breasts. Her back arched, ignoring his order to remain still, but he let the small disobedience pass. She looked sexy as hell writhing under his hands, and he enjoyed watching her, enjoyed feeling her waves of carnal pleasure pass through him.

Without a single word of warning, he leaned down and replaced one hand with his mouth. She cried out at the sweet, soft tugging and the stroke of his tongue.

"Shhh." He blew softly on her now wet nipple.

"Chase, I can't stand it."

"Yes, you can."

He felt her frustration explode, felt her body tensing even more. She was drawn so tight, her entire body jerked when he lightly nipped her with his teeth. He tightened his thighs around her hips, holding her still, forcing her to his will.

He switched to her other breast, treating it to the same sensual torture. Around her nipple, he whispered, "I learned early on how much I love controlling a woman this way, being in charge of her pleasure, mastering her with sex. But I love controlling you even more."

She groaned and tried to lift her legs but couldn't. He smiled. "None of that now. I told you to be still."

"Chase..."

"It's all right. Let's see what we can do about these bottoms."

Sitting up, he positioned himself so that her upper thighs, clamped tightly shut, were accessible to his hands. Through the soft cotton, he stroked one finger over the center seam of the drawers.

Allison's head twisted from side to side and she tugged on the bindings of her wrists. It was an instinctive reaction, he knew, to try to free herself even though she didn't really want to be free. He could feel everything she felt, and it doubled his pleasure knowing his own unique form of foreplay drove her crazy with need. She was already wet, the drawers damp where his finger continued to stroke. He was careful to barely touch her, to avoid letting her get too close to the edge.

Her belly hollowed out and her breasts thrust upward as she tried to strain closer to his taunting finger. He watched her face as he asked, "What do you want, Allison?"

"I don't know," she answered on a wail.

"Yes, you do. Don't lie to me."

She squeezed her eyes shut and he lifted his hand. "I told you not to do that."

Gulping air, she forced her eyes open again. "I want you to touch me."

"Like this?" His finger slid down, dipped, came away.

A great shudder passed over her. "No. Under...under the drawers."

His body rocked with his heartbeat. He slid his hand inside the seam, barely touching her. "Like this?"

She tried to thrust against him, but he pulled away again. "Oh, please."

"Tell me, honey."

"I want...I want your fingers inside me."

Her face was bright red, both with frenzied need and embarrassment. Chase was so pleased with her, he leaned down and kissed her mouth hungrily, thrusting his tongue deep, his control almost shattered by her innocently whispered words. When he pulled back again, she stared at him expectantly, her breath held. He opened the seam of the drawers, laying the material wide.

Her feminine curls were dark blond, damp, and he wanted to taste her very badly. He locked his jaw against the temptation and insinuated one long finger between her folds, feeling her wetness, the warmth of her. His penetration was eased by her excitement, but the tightness of her nearly did him in.

Allison let out a low, keening cry as he forced his finger deeper. "Is this what you wanted, baby?"

She didn't answer, her hips working against him, almost lifting his weight from the bed. He pulled back, watching her face closely, then thrust again, hard and deep.

She screamed with pleasure. *His name.*

Cursing viciously, Chase levered himself to the side. He pushed her legs wide, then held them there when she instinctively tried to close them again. The material of the drawers was in his way and he ripped it open wider, wanting to see all of her, vulnerable, open and ready for him.

Allison was stunned. He could feel her sudden confusion and anticipation. He slipped his finger into her again, then added another. Her hips bucked, and that was all the provocation he needed. Bending down, he took her in his mouth, his tongue hot and rough and insistent. He found her small clitoris and sucked gently.

Allison climaxed with a shock of incredible pleasure that shook her whole body, and he felt it all, felt her trembling, her emotional turmoil, her greed. He cupped her hips, lifting her tighter against his mouth, refusing to let her orgasm fade despite her cries and weak struggles. When finally she stilled, going boneless beneath him, he climbed off the bed and furiously stripped off his jeans and shorts.

"Allison?"

Her eyes barely opened—until she saw he was naked. Then her big blue eyes flared wide, looking him over in great detail. "Are your arms okay, sweetheart?"

She squinted at him, trying to see him more clearly, and he smiled. "I want to touch you, Chase."

"That's not what I asked."

Her legs shifted restlessly, then she nodded. "I'm not in any discomfort, if that's what you mean."

"Good. And don't worry. You'll get your turn. But for now—" His gaze burned over her again. Her legs were still open, her damp curls framed by lacy cotton. "—For now, I like you just the way you are."

He slid a condom on and moved over her. After gently lowering himself onto her, he held her face and said against her mouth, "I like making love to you like this, Allison. Will you mind if we do this often?"

She blinked at him, then mutely shook her head.

"Good. I think I'd enjoy keeping you tied to my bed forever."

"Chase..."

He could feel the questions she wanted to ask, questions about the future. But he couldn't even explain to himself what he felt, the rightness of being with her, the intensified pleasure of his naked body touching hers. She felt like his soul mate, like just being with her would be enough to make him whole. He realized how alive he'd felt since last night, when he'd first started sparring with her, wanting her, trying to understand her and get to know her better. He felt unbearably possessive, and he knew the feeling wouldn't go away anytime soon. Probably never.

He kissed her to stop any further questions and calm his own tumultuous thoughts, then reached down and carefully opened her to his first thrust. The bed rocked gently and she moaned into his mouth.

"So tight, honey. So damn wet. God, you feel good."

Her body resisted him at first, then, as if being welcomed home, she accepted him, his size and length, letting him in until he filled her completely. She gasped, arching her neck back, her tied hands curling into fists. Her muscles clenched and unclenched in small spasms, her entire body trembling. It was incredible and mind-blowing, and he couldn't pace himself, couldn't hold back to tease further.

He met her eager gaze as he balanced himself on his elbows and tried to control the depth of his steady thrusts. His jaw locked with the effort, his shoulders straining.

The damned bed, apparently on uneven legs, rocked back and forth with his every movement. He slid his hands over her breasts, felt her nipples tight against his palms, felt her hips lifting, seeking, her muscles squeezing around his erection as he thrust harder and faster, and he was gone, closing his eyes against the too intense pleasure of it.

Nothing in this life had ever felt so right.

He knew then that he couldn't ever lose her.

SIX

Long minutes later, Chase became aware of Allison shifting beneath him. Good lord, had he fallen asleep? Appalled, he lifted himself to stare down at her. Her face looked so precious to him, glowing, flushed, happy, and also a little timid. He smiled and kissed her gently, then smoothed her mussed hair, now more unpinned than not. "Are you all right?"

She ducked her head shyly and attempted a restrained stretch. "I'm wonderful."

He looked up at her wrists, then reached to untie her. Lowering her arms carefully, he began to rub them, easing any tenderness she might feel. "I've never made love to a virgin before." He grinned at her. "It was a uniquely satisfying experience."

She gave him a quick glance. "I've never been tied up before. I doubt I would have enjoyed it with anyone else but you."

"And with me?"

"It was...incredible. You're incredible."

Chase rolled to his back and pulled her on top. She wasted no time in doing some of the exploring she'd missed out on due to her restraints. Her hands coasted over his chest and she sighed in wonder. "You are one devastatingly beautiful man, Chase Winston."

Satisfaction settled into his bones. Life didn't get any better than having a naked Allison sprawled over him, his body replete from loving her, his mind at peace with the knowledge that she was his.

When she bent to press her soft lips to his chest, he laughed and resettled her against him. "Behave, woman. It's almost four in the morning. Don't you think we need some sleep?"

She made a pouting face at him. "I thought you said I'd have my turn."

"You will. Tomorrow."

She looked his length over greedily. "Will I get to tie you up?"

"Hell no." The frown she gave him now was mutinous, and he kissed her thoroughly in between chuckles. "The effect isn't at all the same, I promise. Besides, there are a few things I still want to do to you."

"Chase..." Her eyes were suddenly glowing warmly again.

He touched her cheek. "You're an intelligent, independent, sexy woman, Allison Barrows. I wouldn't have you any other way. Except," he added when she looked flustered at his praise, "in the bedroom. In here, I'm in charge. And I already know how much you like it, sweetheart, so don't bother protesting."

Allison picked up a pillow to smack him with it. The bed teetered. Chase caught the pillow, then frowned. "Has this damn bed always been uneven?"

Still looking disgruntled that he could so easily know her thoughts, she muttered, "Not that I've noticed. But then you probably weigh a hundred pounds more than me. I don't think I could make this bed move if I tried."

Chase sat up and rocked experimentally, then felt the enormous bed wobble again. With a dark suspicion, he climbed off the mattress and looked down at the thick posts supporting the massive bed. Placing one hand on the edge of the mattress, he pushed. The bottom left leg of the bed lifted and fell because it was almost a quarter inch short. Chase noticed a small corner of cloth poking out. He bent down, but it was stuck inside the bottom of the leg. "Allison, come here a minute."

"What is it?" She peered over the side of the bed, squinting in an effort to see clearly without her glasses. Her gaze was on his naked body, not the bed.

Chase shook his head in amusement, then tugged on his jeans so her attention wouldn't be divided. "See if you can pull that piece of material out when I lift the edge of the bed."

Chase was momentarily diverted from his quest when Allison scrambled off the mattress, breasts bare, drawers gaping open and hanging low on her lush hips. He felt a fresh wave of heat and almost forgot his purpose, especially when she went on all fours in front of him, then looked up. "Well?"

Damn. The erotic images that crept into his mind were probably still illegal in some states. It took all Chase's resolution to reach down and heft the edge of the heavy bed. He barely managed to lift it two inches, but Allison quickly tugged out the thin piece of white lawn. It had something written on it.

"What did you do with my glasses?"

Chase reached for the small square of material, but she held it out of reach. "I got it. I want to look first."

"Allison..."

She narrowed her eyes at him, still sitting on the floor. "You can control the sex, Chase, but that's all."

With a slow, satisfied grin, he picked up her glasses, then sat on the floor beside her, his back to the bed. "That's all I want to control, babe, so I guess we're in agreement." He slipped the glasses on her nose while she watched him warily.

"Somehow I'm not sure I won that one."

He leaned closer, eyeing a pert breast. "Later, when I'm showing you a position I'm particularly fond of, you'll be more certain."

She reluctantly pulled her gaze away from him and stared at the scrap of material. "Oh my God! Do you realize what this is?"

"Since you won't let me look, no."

"It's the directions to where the jewels are hidden!"

Despite himself, Chase felt the rise of enthusiasm. "A map?"

"Not really. I mean, it just directs us to a certain spot in the basement. And judging by how complicated this is, without the note, we'd never find the jewels."

The laughter erupted, so hearty he almost fell over. Allison smacked his shoulder. "What?"

"Don't you see?" He wiped tears from his eyes and chuckled some more. "The note is hidden in a leg of the bed, and the only way anyone would know about it is—"

Her eyes widened. "If they indulged in some pretty passionate activity in that bed! Otherwise, the bed is so heavy, it would never rock, and no one would ever notice the hidden note."

"Exactly. You have to admit, Rose was pretty damned clever."

Allison jumped to her feet. "Come on."

"Whoa." Chase held her hand and pulled her back to stand between his wide-spread legs. "Don't you think you should put something on first?"

"Why?"

"Because if you don't," he said succinctly, leaning forward to kiss her belly, "I won't be responsible for the fact that we never make it to the basement."

"We won't?"

He stared at one taunting nipple. "No, we won't."

Allison grinned. "You make me feel very sexy, Chase."

"That's because you are very sexy. Incredibly sexy."

"And here I'd always heard virgins weren't supposed to enjoy their first time."

Chase cupped both her breasts, his interest in cold jewels fading quickly. "You're not the average virgin, honey."

She flashed him a coy smile and stepped away toward her closet. "Or maybe you just have a rather unique way about you that…stimulates my sexier side." She wiggled out of her drawers and pulled a dress off the rod. She slipped it on over her head. Chase stared.

It was another old-fashioned dress, fitted across the top, calf-length. It had no collar, just sort of scooped down in a narrow *V* over her naked breasts. There were about a zillion little tiny covered buttons down the front that fit into narrow, covered loops. Chase watched her start buttoning and knew it would take an excruciatingly long time to get her back out of that dress. To him, it looked like an opportunity for endless foreplay.

He already looked forward to the effort.

She pulled out chunky heeled shoes, then said with a wink, "These are my Brighton Beach hooker shoes."

Chase narrowed his gaze. "You're naked underneath."

"I know." And just that easily, she sauntered out of the room. "Come on, Chase. I'll show you the way to the basement."

Chase grinned as he followed her, watching the tantalizing sway of her behind in the full skirt.

Allison had the foresight to grab a flashlight from the kitchen. Once in the basement, they had a hard time maneuvering across the packed-dirt floor. The one bare bulb hanging at the bottom of the stairs wasn't adequate to light their way. The basement was musty, the walls damp. They followed the directions carefully, counting off steps, making abrupt turns, steering around the odd pipe. They came to a stop in the far corner where the rough edge of a protruding, homemade laundry chute was just visible from the ceiling beams. Chase stared down at a rusted tub beneath it.

Fascinated, Allison paced around him. "That's the old laundry chute, from when Rose used to have to do the wash with a wringer-type washer. Burke built it for her. When they first got this house, they couldn't afford a maid of any kind, so he tried to make it as organized for her as he could. The chute starts under the sink in the hall bathroom, but a former heir had it boarded up when a modern laundry room was built off the kitchen."

"We need something to climb on," Chase said, moving to stand just beneath the chute. He aimed the flashlight at the square of linen in Allison's hand. "It says the jewels are directly up from here."

The flashlight beam bounced over the long, deep chute, then inside it. About two feet up, taped flat against the inside, was a narrow box. "Well, I'll be damned," Chase whispered slowly.

"Is it the jewels?"

"I think so."

Chase felt Allison's excitement roll over him, and then a thought occurred to him. "Where are Burke and Rose? There hasn't been a single light flicker or breeze or anything. Not since..."

Allison froze. "Not since you asked them for some privacy."

Chase gently touched her cheek. "Maybe they realized things would work out."

Allison bit her lip, her eyes huge behind her glasses, then she whispered, "Will they?"

They both jumped when a third voice intruded, amused and condescending. "Don't tell me you actually believe in that ghost nonsense."

Allison whirled around. "Jack?"

Chase stepped forward, forcing her behind his back. Jack stood at the bottom of the steps beneath the feeble bulb. In his hand was a gun. Very calmly, Chase asked, "Visiting again?"

Jack merely smiled. "Yes. That was me you found in the house tonight. I thought Allison would be in bed, and God knows, I never figured on you visiting that late. But not only did you visit, you stayed." His expression hardened and he glared at Allison, who stood on tiptoe to peek over Chase's shoulder. "After you sent me off without the slightest regret, I never suspected it was so you could have another man over. Somehow I had the impression you were a nice girl."

Allison gasped, but it wasn't the insult that shocked her. "How did you get in? I locked the front door behind you myself!"

"Ah, but first we went to the parlor and talked, and while you were busy explaining to me why we couldn't see each other anymore, I unlocked the window. You thought I was staring despondently, when I was actually planning." He smirked. "Your door is now a little damaged by the way."

"But why?"

"For the jewels, of course. You told me they were here somewhere. I want them. They must be worth a fortune."

Chase said nothing. He was busy watching the bulb over Jack's head dim slightly, then turn bright again. A small smile touched his mouth. "You want the jewels, you bastard? Fine, they're up there."

He pointed at the chute, but Jack just shook his head. "I think you can fetch them down for me. And Allison can come over here by me to wait."

"No."

Jack raised the gun. "I'm not asking, bartender. I'm telling you."

Before Chase could stop her, she darted around him toward Jack. He saw her glance up at the light. He hoped like hell they weren't both nuts, trusting in ghosts that might not even be around anymore.

Once Allison was pinned to his side, Jack said, "Well, hurry it up. Get the damned jewels."

Not willing to waste a single moment with Allison so close to the other man, Chase turned over the heavy, rusted-out laundry tub and climbed on top of it. His fingertips could just barely reach the package. He used the edge of the flashlight to work it loose, and finally, after several minutes, it fell down into his grasp.

"Give it to me."

Jack held out one hand, and Chase started toward him, but the gun lifted. "No, toss it to Allison." He shoved Allison forward, and she stumbled, then righted herself. Staring at Chase, she held out her arms. He carefully tossed the heavy package and she caught it in both hands.

Jack grinned and snatched it away from her. "Excellent. You know, I'm thrilled to finally have these, but I swear, Allison, I would have enjoyed having you, too."

She shuddered in revulsion, then sneered at him. "I didn't want you, though, and that's all that matters."

He laughed. "Because your damned ghost said it had to be *passionate*?" He gave Chase a man-to-man look. "Can you believe that nonsense? When she first explained it to me, I went along. I mean, what the hell, she's pathetically naive, and I figured it'd be fun."

Chase turned his molten-hot gaze on Allison. "You actually planned to sleep with this bastard? You went so far as to explain to him why?"

Allison's face turned bright red. "I didn't think you would be . . ."

"Obviously. Hell, Allison, even Zane would be preferable to him."

She lowered her head, chagrined.

Chase inched closer. He didn't know quite what Jack had planned, but he didn't doubt for a minute that it wouldn't be pleasant.

Before he could take two steps, Jack snarled at him. "That's enough. Both of you, over in the corner."

Allison stared up at him. "What are you going to do?"

"I'm going to lock you both down here until I can get away, that's all."

But Chase knew he was lying. His brow furrowed as he realized exactly what Jack would do. Had Rose let him read another mind? "You're going to set the house on fire."

Jack looked abashed at first, then wary. "How did you know?"

"Rose told me."

Jack began backing carefully up the steps, keeping the gun on Chase the whole time. He tried for a sneer but wasn't overly successful. "I don't believe in ghosts."

The lightbulb flickered, almost going out, then blazing so brightly, Jack had to lift one hand to shield his eyes.

Chase smiled. "Neither did I, until I met two of them."

"It a trick! How the hell are you doing it?"

"I'm not. Rose and Burke are. And if you're smart, you'll put the gun away and give Allison back her jewels."

"Ha!" He had almost reached the top step. "So she can sell them?"

Allison gasped. "I would never do that!"

Jack stopped on the top step. A cold wind blew down the stairs with an eerie whistle. Jack's breath frosted as he shouted, "Stop it!" He lifted the gun. "I don't know how you're doing it, but—"

Suddenly he was pushed forward and his gun hand went up in the air, then resounded with a loud crack as Jack instinctively pulled the trigger. Allison covered her ears, while Chase covered her with his body. Jack lost his balance and tumbled head over heels down the hard stairs, squealing the whole way. He landed in a heap, the gun skidding a good three feet from him. Chase jumped up and grabbed it, then leaned over Jack. The man was unconscious but alive. Judging by the twist of his right leg, it was broken. He turned to Allison and held out his arms.

With a small gasp, she ran to him, and it felt so good to hold her, to know she was again safe, he knew for certain he'd never let her go.

Suddenly there was a flurry of footsteps from above. *"Chase!"*

Chase lifted his brows. "Cole? What the hell are you doing here?"

Not only Cole filled the open doorway at the top of the narrow stairs. Zane and Mack, both wide-eyed, joined him. "What the hell happened? We walked in, and here's this maniac, holding a gun and shouting."

"It's just Allison's old boyfriend," Chase explained, and though he was still holding her close with one arm, she managed to punch him in the side. He grinned and pulled her closer, then started up the stairs.

Zane peered down at him. "We were rushing over to help, but then..." He looked at Cole. "Did you, uh, push him down the stairs?"

Cole stiffened. "Me? I thought you did it somehow."

"Well, no." They both turned to Mack.

"Don't look at me!"

Chase chuckled as he joined his brothers upstairs. "It's a long story."

"Then you better make it quick. I, uh, called the police."

"Why the hell did you do that?"

Cole shook his head, then looked away. "Damned if I know. I was sleeping with my wife—which is usually enough distraction to block out the rest of world—and suddenly I just...knew you were in trouble." He shrugged. "It was the strangest damn thing. I called the cops, then Zane and Mack, and we all met outside."

The kitchen where they had all clustered suddenly glowed with warmth. The brothers looked around. Mack turned to Zane. "I think I'm ready to get the hell out of here."

Zane nodded. "I'm with you." They both turned to go. "If you need us for anything later on, just give a holler."

Mack snickered as they walked out. "First Cole, and now Chase. I can't wait to see what the hell you get into."

"Ha! I hope you're not holding your breath, because you'll be the next entertainment, not me."

"I'm still in school!"

"And I'm having way too much fun to start acting crazy over one particular woman."

Their voices faded as they went through the house to the front door. Cole, Chase, and Allison stared after them.

After shaking his head, Chase raised a brow at Cole. "What about you? You going to stick around?"

Cole sighed. "Well, I did leave a rather warm, willing female in my bed." Then he laughed. "But I suppose Sophie will wait. Hell, I'm anxious to see how you rationalize this to the cops."

It was several hours before the police left, content with the explanation that Jack was simply an insane intruder, the story neatly shored up by his loud claims of ghosts.

Allison and Chase were alone, back in the massive bed. It had taken Chase quite some time to get the dress off her, but the end result had been spectacular. Allison curled up at his side, then sighed.

Chase smoothed her hair. "What are you thinking, sweetheart?"

She froze, turning quickly to look up at him. "Don't you know?"

The expression on his face was comical. "Uh, no."

Her heart pounding madly, she asked, "You can't read my mind anymore?"

Chase frowned, then shook his head. "I don't have a single clue."

"Oh, God. Does that mean Rose and Burke are really gone? Have they moved on?"

Chase touched the modest emerald and diamond necklace around Allison's throat. The jewels weren't ostentatious or enormously valuable, except maybe to a collector. But they were beautiful, and she'd cried as Chase hooked the latch at the back of the necklace and helped her to slip the pierced earrings in. The ring was a little big for her fingers, so it was now on Chase's pinkie.

He kissed her cheek. "The jewels are where they belong, sweetheart. It's only right that they find peace now."

"I'll miss them."

"But you still have me."

His small jest didn't make her feel much better. Would she have Chase? A thought occurred to her, and she asked, "Could you read my mind while we were, you know. Making love?"

Her face felt bright red, thinking of the way Chase had lingered over removing the dress, how he'd positioned her on the edge of the bed, how she'd eventually pleaded with him to take her.

He pulled her up over his chest and framed her face with his hands. "Come to think of it, no. But I didn't need to read your mind when your little moans told me everything I needed to know."

She swallowed hard. "Chase? Do you really like my old-fashioned dresses? I mean, there's trunks full of them, left over from one of the spinsters, and I like wearing them and—"

He placed a hand over her mouth. "Hell yes, I like them. They're the type that inspire fantasies, sweetheart. At least, they do when you're wearing them."

She pulled his hand away and asked, "Do you like my house? Because I don't ever want to leave here. I know it needs some work, but—"

Again, he covered her mouth, this time grinning. "I like your house. A lot. I think it'd be fun to do some repairs, without changing the looks of things."

With her words muffled against his palm, she asked boldly, "Do you like me?"

Very slowly he shook his head. "No. I don't *like* you." Her heart nearly punched out of her chest, and it was all she could do not to wail. The disappointment seemed like a live thing inside her. Then he lowered his hand and kissed her and he whispered, "I love you. All of you."

"You love me?"

"I've never known a woman like you, Allison. How the hell could I not fall in love with you? You casually converse with ghosts, defending them, fighting for them. Befriending them. You burn me up in bed, taking everything I have and giving it back tenfold. But you make the rest of the world think you're such a good little girl. You even turned down Zane, and that makes you unique as hell." He grinned, tangling his fingers in her hair. "You're smart and independent and brave, and best of all, you love me, too."

With tears threatening, she whispered, "Did you read my mind to know all that?"

He very slowly shook his head. "No. It's right there, in your pretty blue eyes for me to see. You do love me, don't you, sweetheart?"

"Yes. I have, almost from the first time I saw you."

"Will you continue to indulge me in the bedroom?"

She bobbed her head. "Oh yes."

This time he laughed out loud. "You sounded awfully eager when you said that."

She pressed her forehead to his rock-hard shoulder. "I'm so glad Rose tangled up my dreams and sent them to you."

"I'm so glad you had the good sense to dream about me in the first place."

They both grinned, and then Chase rolled her beneath him. Neither one noticed, but there was one last, happy flicker of a light—and then it was gone.

Tangled Images

Mack Winston was minding his own business, as usual. His thoughts were focused inward, mostly on career choices and disappointments, but he whistled carelessly, unwilling to let anyone witness his concern. The day was snowy and cold, getting colder by the moment, and his nose felt frozen. He was distracted enough not to care.

But the second he entered the family-owned bar he saw them, all three of his damned older brothers and his two sexy sisters-in-law, huddled together at a single tiny table. They looked...conniving.

They'd been working on him lately, trying to cheer him when he didn't want them to know he needed cheering. It irritated him. He liked being known as the carefree brother, the fun brother. It suited him.

Since it was early and the bar was not yet open, they all glanced up at him when they heard the door close. Then they did a double take. The women suddenly smiled, and their smiles were enough to make the slowest man suspicious. And despite his brothers' ribbing, he wasn't slow.

Mack's whistling dwindled. He thought about making a strategic retreat, but then Zane, only three years his senior, called out, "Ha! A lamb for the slaughter! What perfect timing you have, Mack."

Cole, the oldest brother and the most protective, shook his head, looking somewhat chagrined that Mack had shown himself at this precise moment. Chase, the second oldest and the quietest, glanced at Mack and snorted. Both their wives looked as if an enormous problem had just been solved. Whatever the problem, Mack knew he didn't want to be the solution.

Zane grinned. "I tried to save you, honestly, but I'll be out of town."

Cole rolled his eyes. "You're too damn willing, Zane. It unnerves me."

Chase merely snorted again. His wife, Allison, patted his arm. "You were never even considered, honey, so relax. There's no way I want the female masses of Thomasville ogling your perfect body. You're a married man now, and that means I'm the only one allowed to ogle."

Mack backed up two steps.

Sophie, Cole's wife, now seven months pregnant, ran over to Mack and latched on to his arm. "You understand, I couldn't let Cole do it. Not that he would have, anyway. You know how reserved he is. But my God, it would have started a riot! Can you just imagine how the women would react to Cole?"

Mack didn't know what she was rambling on about, but he almost smiled anyway. Sweet Sophie harbored this absurd notion that Cole was perfect, and that every female he met wanted him in the most lascivious manner imaginable.

Mack had to agree that in many ways, his oldest brother did border on perfection. Cole had pretty much raised him and Zane, with Chase's adolescent help, after their parents' deaths, and he'd done a great job of it. But Cole was so over the top in love with his wife that he no longer even noticed other women. They could riot all they wanted, and Cole wouldn't care.

Both Cole and Chase had only recently married, and Zane swore Mack would be next, that the Winstons had somehow been either cursed or blessed, the two remaining bachelors still uncertain which it was. Oh, their brothers felt blessed, and the sisters-in-law were wonderful. It was just that Zane didn't ever want to marry, and Mack didn't want to marry anytime soon.

He'd been very cautious around women ever since Chase had unexpectedly succumbed, proving the virus to be very real. Of course, Mack had been shunning the dating scene for other reasons as well. While he was in college, his studies had taken precedence over everything else. Well, everything except one very sexy, very enticing woman—who hadn't wanted a damn thing to do with him. There were still times when he dreamed of her, and someday he hoped to meet a woman like her, one that could turn him on with just a look. But until then . . .

Sophie's hand tightened on his arm, and Mack tried to step away. He didn't get very far. Though she looked small and delicate, Sophie had a grip like a junkyard dog hanging on to a prized bone.

Zane sauntered over, his eyes glinting with humor. "I still think I'd have been the best choice. But you know I'm going out of town for that convention, so that leaves you, little brother."

Mack swallowed, eyeing each relative in turn. "What exactly does that leave me to do?"

Sophie squeezed a little closer, and her tone became cajoling. "Why, just a little modeling."

His brows shot up. "Modeling?"

"Yes."

Chase snorted again.

"All right." Mack decided enough was enough. "Sophie, turn me loose, I promise not to bolt. Zane, I'm going to flatten you if you don't stop grinning. And no, Chase, there's no need to snort again. I already gather this isn't something I'm going to enjoy."

"Nonsense!" Allison, his other meddling sister-in-law, whom he adored to distraction, leapt to her feet to join Sophie. Mack felt sandwiched between their combined feminine resolve. He assessed their wide-eyed, innocent stares warily.

With a sigh Cole came to his feet, too. "Sophie has some harebrained idea of offering a new line of male lingerie at her boutique."

Male lingerie! Mack stiffened and again tried to back up. The sisters-in-law weren't allowing it.

"It's not lingerie, Cole," Sophie insisted in a huff. Since her pregnancy had gotten under way, she huffed more often. "It's loungewear. And it's very popular."

Mack's head throbbed the tiniest bit. "Loungewear?"

"Yes, you know, like silk boxers and robes and—"

Zane leaned forward. "And thongs and lace-up leopard-print briefs and leather skivvies and—"

Allison slapped her hand over Zane's mouth. "Women appreciate those nice things on a man."

Zane, Mack, and Cole all stared at Chase, who immediately started to bluster, while frowning at his wife. "Oh, no. You can forget those thoughts right now! That's just an assumption on Allison's part. You wouldn't catch me dead in any of that goofy stuff."

Disappointed, they all returned their attention to Mack. He looked around at their expressions, which varied from amused to resigned to hopeful, and he shook his head. "Hell, no."

Sophie glared at him. "You don't even know what it is that I want yet."

"Honey, I don't need to know. If it involves this...this...*male loungewear,* I want no part of it."

Her eyes narrowed in a calculating way. "All I need you to do—"

"No."

"—is to let the photographer get a few pictures of you in the clothing to advertise it in a new catalogue."

"No!"

"Because there's no way I can afford to hire a real model, who would probably have to come all the way from New York or Chicago, and I have the feeling you'd look better anyway."

Well, that was a nice compliment, but...he shook his head. "No."

Zane pried Allison's hand away. "Not as good as *I'd* look, but as I said—"

Three voices yelled in unison, "Shut up, Zane!"

Zane only chuckled.

Sophie continued, her voice coercing, her eyes wide. "This is a great opportunity for me, Mack. The photographer is a friend of mine, willing to do this cheap for the exposure it'll bring the studio. I'm getting a special deal here. It'll only take two or three days—"

"*No.*"

"—so it won't really interfere with your schedule or anything—"

"Damn it, Sophie—"

"—and Valentine's Day would be the perfect time to advertise the new line."

Mack groaned.

"So it's all set, then. And Mack, I *really* appreciate it." She gave him a sideways, very calculating glance. "You can consider this payback for all those study sessions with me for your college science classes."

He felt doomed. He could only mumble, "Unfair, Sophie."

She batted her pretty blue eyes at him and said, "You'd never have passed anatomy without me."

Cole's mouth fell open. "All those late nights she helped you study, it was for *anatomy*?"

Mack rolled his eyes. "Just female reproduction. That stuff's confusing."

Zane roared with laughter, and this time Chase and Allison joined him. Cole, still huffing, pulled his wife possessively to his side while Mack groped for a chair and fell into it.

"Well, hell." He looked to the heavens, but all he saw was the ceiling of the bar. He supposed there was no help for it at all.

He tilted his head toward Zane. "You'd actually have done this if you weren't going out of town?"

"Are you kidding? The women will love it. You'll have so many new dates, you won't have time to be in a funk."

"I'm not in a funk."

Chase snorted.

Rubbing his brow, Mack tried to ignore them all. He knew Zane probably would like to flaunt himself a little. He was a born exhibitionist and wallowed in the female attention heaped upon him. But Mack wasn't that way—at least, not as much so as Zane. There'd been only that one woman he'd ever wanted to wallow with.

He glared at Sophie and said, "I'm not wearing anything stupid."

She glared right back. "I wouldn't carry anything stupid at my boutique!" Then she softened. "But don't worry. There'll be a selection available, and you and the photographer can decide together which things to photograph. Other than a few definites that have to be in the catalogue, you can pick and choose."

"Gee, thanks."

Sophie handed him a card that read "Wells Photography," and listed a downtown address. She gave him a huge hug and kissed his cheek. "Be there Friday at two o'clock, okay?"

At least that gave him two days to get used to the idea. Or rather, two days to dread it.

Mack parked in the small lot to the side of Wells Photography, as directed by a hanging wooden sign. He'd checked his mail before leaving his apartment, but still no word from the board of education. He'd been a good teacher, damn it. The best. The kids had loved him, the parents respected him. His class had scored much higher than past averages, much higher than expected.

But the principal still hadn't recommended him.

His hands fisted in his coat pockets as he walked across the broken-concrete lot. He stared at his feet, ignoring the blustering wind, the beginning of wet, icy snow as it pelted the back of his neck. The sky was a dark gray, matching his mood. He'd never felt so helpless in his life, and he hated it. The principal's judgment of him, as well as her decision not to recommend him, were beyond unfair, but there wasn't a damn thing he could do about it.

Finally, after Mack had crossed the nearly empty lot to the front of the building, he focused his thoughts enough to realize that the studio wasn't a studio at all but rather an older home. The redbrick two-story house was stately in a sort of worn-out way. It was hemmed in by the empty lot to the right and another older home advertising apartments for rent on the left.

Squinting against the freezing January wind, Mack bounded up the salted concrete steps to the front door and knocked briskly.

A thin, freckle-faced girl of about thirteen answered. She grinned, flashing a shiny set of braces. Mack grinned back. "Hello."

"Hi."

"Ah . . . I'm looking for the photographer?"

She nodded. "Are you here for the two o'clock shoot?"

"Yep. I'm Mack Winston."

The girl opened the door and let him in. "You can follow me. My mom is just finishing up another session, so you won't need to wait long. We had two cancellations because of the storm. Our receptionist is sick, so I'm sorta filling in."

She closed the door behind Mack, then started down a short hardwood-floored hall. To the right was an open set of curtained glass doors, revealing an office of sorts inside, though the outside wall was mostly used up by an enormous fireplace. To the left of the hall was a flight of stairs leading to a closed door that separated the upper story. Mack continued to look around. "You say your mother is the photographer?"

The girl tucked long brown hair behind her ear and nodded, while stealing quick peeks at Mack. "Yeah. She's real good."

They entered a room that had a utilitarian beige couch and a single chair in it, a table full of magazines, and a coffee machine. To Mack, it looked to be converted from a kitchen, judging by the placement of the window and a few exposed pipes.

The walls were decorated with dozens of incredible photographs, ranging from babies to brides to entire families. There were outdoor scenes with animals in them, indoor scenes around a Christmas tree. Babies in booties, men in suits, children in their Sunday best.

All of the photographs were beautiful, proof of very real talent.

Another set of glass double doors, these closed with opaque curtains, apparently separated the studio. Mack shrugged off his coat, hung it on the coat tree, and then chose the chair in the far corner.

The girl smiled shyly at him. "You want some coffee or something?"

"No, thanks." He returned her smile. "What did you do? Skip school today?"

"We had a half day for teacher in-service."

"Ah. Lucky for your mom, huh? I bet she really appreciates your help with the receptionist missing." He grinned his most engaging grin. The girl blushed and again tucked her hair behind her ear.

Before she could say anything, the phone rang, and she dashed off to answer it. Mack chuckled. He just adored kids, which was one reason why he was determined to get a teaching position.

Of course, at the moment, his teaching possibilities looked grim. That thought had him scowling again, ready to sink into despair. God, he hated brooding—it didn't suit him at all.

Fortunately the photographer chose that moment to open the door. Mack heard two sets of feminine voices and his senses prickled. Something about one of those voices was familiar, sending a wave of heat up his spine. There'd been only one woman who had ever affected him that way, but it couldn't possibly be her. Still, he leaned forward to peer around the coffee machine.

A young woman holding a squirming baby faced him, while the photographer had her back to Mack, displaying a very long, very thick braid hanging all the way down to her bottom. *Oh, damn, he knew that braid!* He leaned a little more, feeling ridiculously anxious, holding his breath. Then she turned slightly, giving him her profile, and Mack felt like a mule had kicked him in the ribs.

Jessica Wells.

His heart slowed, then picked up speed. It was a reaction very familiar to him. Just like the last time he'd seen her, he felt his muscles tremble, his stomach knot, his body go simultaneously hard and hot.

He hadn't seen her since college, almost two years ago, and hadn't suffered such an extreme reaction to a woman since then. But Jessica had always been unaware of the turmoil she caused him regardless of how he'd tried his best to be friendly with her, to get her attention. She was maybe six, eight years older than he was, quiet and very serious. Even a little withdrawn. He'd always thought her adorable with her standoffish ways and reserved manner.

She had beautiful chocolate-brown eyes that made him think of soft, warm things—like the way a woman looked after making love. She had a narrow nose slightly tilted up on the end, high cheekbones, and a small, rounded chin.

She also had the most impressive breasts he'd ever laid eyes on. They made his mouth go dry and his palms sweat. Not that he was hung up on physical attributes...except that he'd dreamed about her at night, about getting her out of her conservative sweaters and her no doubt sturdy brassiere so he could see her naked, touch her lush flesh and taste her nipples....

He swallowed hard, still staring, taking advantage of the moment, since she remained unaware of him.

Mack had always felt intrigued by her. She'd been so different from the flighty girls who'd flirted with him continually. But the few times he'd tried to talk to her, she had turned her small nose up in utter disregard.

Well, she'd have to talk to him now. *Thank you, Sophie.*

Jessica spoke easily with the woman, who struggled to control the chubby baby boy dressed in a miniature suit. She smiled, and Mack felt the impact of it clear down in his gut. In the time they'd spent together in class, he didn't think she'd ever smiled, not even a glimmer of a smile. No, she was the epitome of seriousness, and it had made him nuts.

Mack was a natural smiler. He liked being happy, friendly, courteous to everyone. But trying to wheedle a smile out of Jessica had been like trying to get a fish to sing.

He still recalled the first day he'd seen her, when she'd walked into the same photo tech class, loaded down with books, looking conspicuous and nervous and uncomfortable. He'd been sitting in the front, and she'd sat as far in the back as she could get. He'd twisted all the way around to see her, but her gaze had met his only once, then skittered away.

He'd taken the photography class out of casual interest, thinking it might be a way to make some of the lessons more fun for his students. And it had. But obviously it had been much more for her.

While tickling the baby's chin, she said, "I'll call in about a week after I get the proofs together, and then we can set up an appointment for you to make your choices."

The woman sighed gratefully. "You're a saint, being so patient with him. I don't know why he was so fussy today."

Mack figured any guy stuffed into a suit had a reason to be fussy.

The baby kicked, prompting his mother to hurry along. After they'd gone, Jessica checked her watch, rubbed her brow, then headed for the coffee machine. That's when she noticed Mack.

Drawing up short, she stared, her dark eyes widening, but only for a single moment. Then, with a carefully blank expression, she stepped forward and extended her hand. "Mr. Winston?"

Mack resisted the urge to mimic Chase's snort. There was no way she didn't recognize him. *Was there?* Surely he'd made some sort of impression! But when her expression remained fixed, he started to wonder. Narrowing his eyes, he slowly stood and extended his hand. Here he was, indulging in erotic daydreams, and she didn't even remember him. "That's right," he said, keeping his voice moderate. "Actually, we met in college a few years ago."

She blinked lazily as his hand enclosed hers. He felt her tremble the tiniest bit as she summoned a look of polite confusion. "We did?"

Okay, so she'd always ignored him. She'd been as far from impressed by him as a woman could get. She'd still been aware of him, he was sure of it. And two years wasn't so long that she could have totally forgotten him.

He held her hand when she would have pulled away and tried for a cocky grin. "Yeah. We had a class together. Photo tech. Remember?"

Suddenly she smiled, a very phony smile that set his teeth on edge. "Ah, I remember now! Mack Winston. You were the class Romeo who kept all those silly coeds in a tizzy."

She tugged hard and he let her hand go. "Class Romeo? Hardly."

She waved his words away, as if he were only being modest. "Yes, yes, I remember now. All those foolish girls crowded around you. Half the time I couldn't hear the instructor for all their whispering and giggling. I think you probably dated every one of them. I was always rather amazed by your . . . stamina."

Every single word she said, though softly spoken, sounded like a veiled insult. It wasn't something Mack was used to. But of course, nothing with Jessica, including his feelings, was ever as he expected.

He rocked back on his heels and slowly looked her over, from the form-fitting jeans to the loose white sweater and braided brown hair. Physically, she hadn't changed at all. She still turned him on. Even now, he could feel his muscles tightening, the heat beneath his skin. He wanted her, and all she'd done so far was insult him.

Carefully gauging his words, he said, "I remember you being a recluse—and maybe just a little stuck up."

Her expression darkened, her brown eyes turning nearly black. "I was not stuck up! It was just that, compared to you...well, I was there to learn, not to socialize."

She sounded defensive, and he wondered about it. He also wondered what it would be like to kiss the mulish expression away from her lips. "This may surprise you, but I learned. I just had fun doing it."

"Now, *that* I can believe. The fun part, that is."

There was nothing distracted about Mack's brain at the moment. No, he felt razor-sharp, focused, full-witted, and aroused. He prepared to coach her on his idea of fun, when the young girl suddenly raced into the room. When she saw her mother and Mack facing off, she skidded to a halt. "Uh, Mom, I don't mean to interrupt—"

With obvious relief, Jessica turned away, effectively dismissing Mack. "That's all right, honey. You're not interrupting anything...important."

Her choice of words made Mack feel relegated to the back burner. He almost laughed because he recognized her efforts to distance herself. Yeah, she remembered him. She could deny it all she wanted, but he wasn't buying it.

"Well..." The young girl played with her hair, sneaking looks between her mother and Mack. "Since you don't have any more appointments today, I was thinking of going to Jenna's. Her dad will pick me up. She...uh, invited a few friends over."

"Friends, as in guy-type friends?"

The girl grimaced, then leaned forward and said in an excited stage whisper, "Brian's going to be there!"

Mack watched as Jessica fought with her smile—another genuine smile this time. "Oh, well, in that case, how could I possibly refuse?"

Before Trista could work up a loud squeal, she added, "I assume Jenna's parents will be there the whole time?"

"Yeah."

"All right, then. Call when you're ready to come home and I'll come get you."

Trista ran forward and hugged her mother, then with the energy exclusive to the early teens, charged out of the room.

Mack chuckled. "She's really cute."

"Thank you." Jessica said it with pride, and for the first time Mack felt her defenses were down.

"I gather Brian is a guy she likes?"

Jessica almost laughed. "My daughter is suffering her first crush. And so far, the 'totally awesome' Brian hasn't even noticed her."

"It's a tough age for kids."

"You're telling me! She went from wanting Barbie dolls to pierced ears overnight. Shopping has become an all-day expedition. And she absolutely hates her braces."

She seemed so natural, so at ease discussing her daughter, that Mack felt encouraged. He stepped a little closer, appreciating the softness in her eyes, the slight smile playing over her lips. He wanted to touch her, but of course, that would be over the line. "I didn't realize you had a daughter. Especially not one that old."

Jessica immediately stiffened. "No reason you should know."

"Are you married?"

She ignored him. "Sophie told me she was sending a male model."

"She sent me." He held his arms out to the side.

"Are you a professional?"

"Not at modeling."

She didn't take the bait. "This might be a problem. Getting just the right pose isn't easy."

"I think I can manage—with a little direction."

She continued to eye him, then shook her head. "I've known Sophie for a while, knew that she married, but I never connected the last name."

Mack followed her as she started into the studio. Her jeans did interesting things for her bottom, and hazardous things to his libido. Jessica Wells was a lushly rounded woman. "Hmm. Why would you have? You didn't even remember me, right?"

She stalled and he almost bumped into her. His hands settled on her straight shoulders, but then she hurried away. "That's right. Now, we should get started." Again she checked her watch. "We've got a lot to get done today."

Mack folded his arms over his chest. "Sophie told me it might take a couple of shoots to get everything done."

"Oh, no. With any luck, I can finish up today." She sounded nearly desperate as she said it, then rushed over to a long, narrow table and picked up a folder. "I have the catalogue layout right here. We'll need about thirty pictures. Some of them just of your...uh..."

Her gaze skimmed his lap, then darted away. "Just of the garments. Others will need all of you in them."

She seemed nervous, flitting about, grabbing up various papers and carrying them from one table to another. Mack leaned against the wall to watch her. For the first time in a long while, he felt totally absorbed in something other than worries about his future teaching position.

The room was interesting. Props occupied every corner and filled several shelving units. One entire wall was empty except for large pull-down screen devices that held various backdrops. All of the camera equipment was centered at the far end of the room.

The studio was at the back of the house and had two windows each on three walls. Dark shades kept out any sunlight, and bright lights had been turned on instead. Finally Jessica seemed to get herself organized. She began hauling a large box toward the table. Mack stepped forward to help her.

Against her protests, he picked up the box and asked, "Where do you want it?"

Resigned, she motioned toward the table. "Set it on the floor there. We have to figure out which things you'll model. There's a pretty good sampling of the, uh, briefs inside, and on the rack there's other stuff."

She wouldn't quite meet his gaze. Suspicious, Mack opened the box and peeked in. He immediately slammed the cardboard lid down again, then stared at Jessica.

"What?" She leaned toward the box, but he pulled it out of her reach.

Damn. He cleared his throat. "Let's start with some other stuff."

She looked equal parts curious, hesitant, and determined. "Why? Sophie wants at least eighteen shots of briefs, to give a good sampling of what she'll be offering. We're supposed to do nine shots to a page."

Eighteen shots of him in tiny scraps of material? When he was already half hard? Ha! "Couldn't they just be shot on a mannequin or something?"

Her efforts at indifference weren't overly effective. Her cheeks had turned a dusky-rose color and she wouldn't quite meet his gaze. "Wouldn't matter to me. But Sophie might not like it. She said she wanted her customers to see a real man wearing this stuff, to prove real men look good in it."

Mack grinned. "A real man, huh?" The color in her face intensified, and Mack totally forgot his own hesitation. He shoved the box toward her. "All right. You pick."

"Me?"

"Sure. You have a trained eye, so you should probably be able to tell what'll look best on me." Feeling a little outrageous, he stood up to tower over her. He widened his stance, spread his arms out to his sides. "You might want to, ah, *study* my form first, right? I mean, so you have a good idea of what would look most complimentary on my particular physique." She'd know he was aroused, but so what? He wanted her to know how she affected him.

He watched as stubbornness surfaced in her expression. She stared back at him, hard, her gaze never leaving his face. Then without looking away from him, she reached into the box. She felt around and finally tugged out a teeny-tiny pair of paisley-print thong briefs. She thrust them toward him like a challenge.

Mack almost laughed. With his baby finger, he accepted the briefs, which had no apparent backside and were so sheer that they weighed about as much as a hankie. Trying to sound earnest, he asked, "Do they, perhaps, come in a larger size?"

Pretending to take him seriously, Jessica searched through her papers. "Nope. One size fits all."

Mack gave the outrageous briefs a dubious inspection. "Hmmm. I must be unique, then, because there's no way these puppies are gonna fit me."

She lifted one slim brown brow. "Oh? They're too . . . big?"

Mack choked, but quickly recovered. He liked it that she now felt comfortable enough to tease. "Jessica, I don't think you actually looked at me when I told you to."

She shrugged. "I did, but then I guess my mind wandered."

"Ah. Got you thinking of *other things*, did it?"

"Actually, I forgot my glasses so I couldn't really see the insignificant things. . . ."

This time Mack did laugh. She hadn't looked at his body, only his face, or she'd have seen some *very* significant things. "You're very damaging to a man's ego, you know that?"

She made a rude sound and shook her head. "As if your ego needed any help."

Just that easily, she went from playful to insulting again. He squatted down in front of her and leaned over the box to make certain he had her attention. "Why do I get the feeling you've made some assumptions about me, and none of them are particularly favorable?"

With him so close, she looked startled and breathless. She jerked way back—and toppled onto her bottom. Amused by her telltale response, Mack stood up and pulled her to her feet. She quickly shook him off, as if his touch bothered her more than it should, then took two hasty steps back.

"This is ridiculous," she protested. "I don't have all day to banter with you."

She was suddenly so flustered, he knew damn well she couldn't have been as indifferent to him as she'd claimed. Only a woman aware of a man could be so affected by a simple touch. Why did she continue to deny it?

He didn't understand her. They'd been joking like old friends, having fun, and then suddenly she'd seemed to realize it and retreated back into herself. He crossed his arms and gave her a curious stare. "If you're pressed for time, then we should probably get this cleared up right now."

She turned away and stalked to the clothes rack. She yanked down a hanger that held a black silk kimono robe with red piping and matching pull-on pajama pants. She thrust them toward him. "I have a better idea. Let's just get some photos taken, like we're supposed to."

Mack refused to take the garments. "Since you claim to barely remember me, and I know damn good and well I never did anything to make you dislike me, your animosity seems pretty strange."

"Look, Mr. Winston—"

He barely choked back his laugh of disbelief. "Mr. Winston? Get real, Jessica. At least admit you remember my damn name."

There was a second of vibrating silence, then she seemed to explode. She tossed the clothing aside and thrust her chin toward him. "Well, with the girls all talking about you all the time, I suppose it'd be hard to forget!"

Her sudden anger inflamed him. Her dark eyes were impossibly bright, her chin firmed, her cheeks flushed. Her lush breasts rose and fell in her agitation, and she had her fists propped on her rounded hips.

He wanted to kiss her silly.

He wanted to watch all that anger and frustration turn into passion. Just the thought made him catch his breath. He wanted to howl, because she made him hotter than a sultan's harem, but she refused to let him close.

Never in his life had a woman reacted to Mack the way this woman did. She seemed more comfortable ignoring, antagonizing, or insulting him than she did just getting along with him. It didn't make sense—and for some insane reason, he felt more intrigued than ever.

Marshaling his limited control, Mack shook his head and managed a relatively calm reply. "I'm definitely missing something here, and it's not your hostility, because that's pretty damn clear. So why don't you just spell it out, Jessica? What's the problem?"

She struggled in silence, her nostrils flaring, and then, after a deep, calming breath, she nodded. "All right."

She looked so serious, Mack held his breath.

After licking her lips nervously, she said, "I resented you. Back then. Not now. As I said, I barely remember you."

Her breasts were still doing that distracting rise-and-fall thing that was making him nuts. He tried to pay attention to her words, but it wasn't easy. "Uh-huh. So why did you resent me?"

"Because I worked my behind off in college. It wasn't easy going back, being so much older than everyone else and having so many more responsibilities. And I was raising Trista alone, and half the time the class was interrupted by the instructor fawning over you, or one of the girls asking me to pass you a note, or you making eyes at the girls—"

Mack blinked at her, pleased by her admission. "If you'd been paying attention to the instructor, instead of me, you wouldn't have noticed me making eyes, now, would you?" He watched her face heat again, the color climbing from her throat all the way up to her hairline. She had very delicate skin, not overly pale, just smooth and silky-looking.

He wondered if she would flush like that during a climax.

Her eyes, clean of any makeup, almost exactly matched the golden-brown shade of her hair. And that hair...he'd always noticed it in college. She kept it long, but he'd never seen it out of the braid. It was so thick, the braid so heavy, he could only imagine what it'd be like loose. He used to wait to take a seat until she had, so he could occasionally sit behind her. Without her knowing it, he'd touched her braid, felt how warm and silky it was.

At least, he'd thought she didn't know—until she started sitting in the middle of a cluster of students, ensuring he couldn't get close.

He watched her now as she gathered her thoughts. Little wisps of hair escaped her braid to float around her face, teasing him. He wanted to reach out and smooth them down, to reassure her, but judging from her expression, she'd probably sock him if he tried it.

"Jessica?"

She worried her bottom lip for a moment, then finally sighed. "You're right, of course. And I did try to ignore you. But you were a terrible distraction and I suppose I resented that more than anything."

Cautiously, drawn by an inexplicable mix of emotions he'd never dealt with before, Mack stepped closer. "Why?"

She laughed. "You'll think this is nuts, but you remind me of my husband."

That wasn't at all what he'd been expecting. He stilled. She'd said that she'd raised her daughter alone, so he assumed she wasn't married. He *hoped* like hell she wasn't married. *She'd better not be* . . . "Are you widowed?"

She shook her head hard, causing her braid to fall over one shoulder and curl along her left breast. Mack gulped, forcing his gaze resolutely to her face.

"No, divorced. For quite some time now. But just as you seemed to be the life of the party, so was he. Nothing mattered to him but having a good time. Even when Trista was born, he refused to grow up and settle down, to be a husband or a father. And he was about your age when I stupidly married him."

"I see." But he didn't, not really. He wasn't a husband or a father, but he knew in his heart he'd take those responsibilities very seriously.

She smiled, and again shook her head. "I'm sorry. It's none of my business if you choose to make life fun and games. That's certainly your choice, and I had no right to sit in judgment of you. Whew. I feel better now."

She felt better? Mack clenched his jaw, he was so annoyed. He wasn't irresponsible or immature. He knew what his priorities were, and he kept them straight. No one had worked harder in college or taken his lessons more seriously than he. Yet she automatically labeled him because he'd managed to make school fun. Enjoyment was the standard he'd set for his students, his teaching method for making information stick. It was also one of the reasons the principal hadn't recommended him for the available teaching position. She and Jessica evidently had a few things in common. They were both self-righteous and far too somber.

Only the principal didn't turn him on, but Jessica most certainly did. She always had.

Mack kept his expression impassive. "So now your conscience is clear?"

"Exactly. Imagine, a woman my age reacting to a two-year-old resentment, especially toward someone so young."

"I'm twenty-four."

She nodded, as if that confirmed her suspicions. "It's ludicrous. Why, obviously your outlook would be different from my own."

"Because you're so . . . old?"

"Well, if thirty is old, which I suppose to someone your age, it is." She smiled again. "So, can you forgive my surly attitude? Do you think we can start over and go ahead with the shoot?"

He didn't want to; he wanted to keep talking to her, to get to know her better. But he had promised Sophie. And he had no doubt Zane would ride him forever if he let his reactions to this one woman keep him from getting the job done. He could console himself with the fact that she'd noticed him, she just didn't like noticing him.

When he hesitated, she sighed again. "I don't blame you, I guess. But really, I'm not one of those bitter divorcées who can't talk about anything else. I promise not to even mention it again. And to tell you the truth, I was really looking forward to this shoot. It'll be a nice opportunity for me, more than I've ever done before, since my work usually only includes portraits."

"So you want this job?"

"Yes, of course."

Mack nodded. Now he had something to work with. "I'll stay."

He saw the subtle relaxing of her shoulders, the relief she tried hard to hide. "Good."

"We only have one problem."

"Oh? And what's that?"

"You promised not to mention your husband or your divorce again."

"That's right."

Mack smiled, and he knew damn good and well his eyes were gleaming with intent. Good. Let her know he wouldn't be brushed off. "I want to know about your husband. And your divorce. I want lots of little details. Since I remind you of the guy, it only seems fair. Don't you think?"

T W O

Jessica stared at Mack Winston, caught between wanting to laugh and wanting to smack him. She was used to that particular reaction—and other, more sexual reactions as well, if she was honest with herself.

He was so incredibly gorgeous, so young and handsome and sexy. He'd whizzed through college, not caring about his grades, always joking, always having a good time, while she'd been forced to struggle to make mediocre B's.

His carefree attitude and abundant charm did remind her of her ex-husband, and that's why her attraction to him scared her so much. Why couldn't she be drawn to a staid, mature man, one that would be steady and responsible? She'd tried dating a few times a year after her divorce was finalized, but the men she wanted to be interested in didn't stir a single speck of interest in her.

And the one who did, the one who made her feel young and alive again, was exactly the type of man she knew she should stay away from.

When she'd graduated, she'd thought to never see him again. It had been both a relief, because he was a terrible temptation, and a crushing pain, because she still thought of him often, still awakened in the night after dreaming of him. And now, here he was, in the flesh, and if anything, two years had added to his appeal. *Darn Sophie Winston, anyway.*

Drawing a deep breath and dredging up another nonchalant smile, she asked, "What exactly would you like to know?" She had no intention of letting him see how uncomfortable he, and the conversation, made her feel.

Mack picked up the sexy pajamas with a smile. "How about I change while we talk? That way I won't hold you up."

He'd gotten his way, so now he'd be accommodating? She swallowed her huff of annoyance. "That's fine. You can change behind that curtain."

He gave her a smile that she was certain had melted many a female heart. When Mack Winston smiled, you saw it not only on his sexy mouth, but in his dark eyes that always glittered with humor, in the dimple in his lean cheek, in the warmth that seemed to radiate from him. She expected that nearly every female in Thomasville, Kentucky, had fantasized over him at least once.

But fantasizing was all she would ever do.

While he was occupied, Jessica rummaged through the cardboard box, looking in vain for items that wouldn't expose his body overly.

"Tell me why you divorced him."

She glanced up and saw Mack's flannel shirt get slung over the curtain rod. She gulped as a sharp twinge of excitement raced down her spine. A white T-shirt and belt quickly followed, making her imagination go wild.

"Jessica?"

"I, ah . . . I told you. He wouldn't settle down. He kept losing jobs, running through our money. Trista was not quite seven when I filed for divorce, eight before everything was finalized. I decided to go back to college so I could bone up on the newest photography techniques. It was something I'd always wanted to do, but I'd worked to get Dave through college, and then Trista was born, and, well . . . I just never got around to it. After the divorce, I needed a way to support us both—"

"Is he still around?"

His worn, faded jeans landed on top of the flannel, and her tongue stuck to the roof of her mouth. *Mack was naked behind the curtain.* "Who?"

"Your ex."

"Oh. Uh, no. Well, sometimes. He lives in Florida, and every so often he remembers Trista and sends her a card or a gift." She looked down at the pile of so-called briefs and quickly tried to decide which ones would conceal the most.

"He doesn't pay child support?"

"Ha!"

"You could sue him for it, you know."

Everything she picked up was far too scanty, too revealing, to actually suggest that he wear it. She was a thirty-year-old woman who'd been celibate for too many years to count. Her heart wouldn't take the strain. "But then I'd have to suffer his presence. This way, he's almost completely out of my life, and he's not messing with Trista's emotions."

"What have you told her about him?"

She stared at the damn briefs, imagined them filled out by his masculine flesh, and felt flustered. "Only that we didn't get along, but it had nothing to do with her. When she asks me why he doesn't come around more, I tell her that he does love her, it's just that some people have a hard time settling into domestic roles."

"That's pretty wise of you, you know. So many times, parents are bitter and they force their kids into the middle of things without even meaning to. And the only ones who get hurt by it are the kids."

"I would never tell Trista what a jerk her father is. Hopefully, by the time she gets old enough to figure things out on her own, he'll have gotten his act together."

She glanced up as Mack stepped around the curtain—and froze. He adjusted the waistband, leaving the sheer pants to hang low on his lean hips. The robe was draped over his arm. He was barefoot, his hair appealing mussed, his hairy chest wide and sexy and hard. His abdomen was sculpted with muscle, and a line of silky hair led from his navel downward. She wanted to look away, but she couldn't quite manage it. Her heart beat so hard it hurt, and her stomach did strange little jumps that felt both sweetly tantalizing and very disturbing.

Oh, Lord, it had been so long since she'd seen a mostly naked man. And she'd *never* seen a man like Mack Winston.

He paused in the center of the floor, then simply stood there, hands on his hips, and let her look. His eyes narrowed, direct and hot and probing, and his smile tilted in a sensual, teasing way.

Finally, when it dawned on her how long they'd both been silent, she jumped to her feet. An impressive array of colorful, silky underwear fluttered off her lap and onto the floor, like a platoon of male butterflies folding ranks. She looked down, realized she'd been practically buried in the damn things, and almost groaned. She swallowed, staring at the heap on the floor. "I was . . . was looking for which ones you should pose in."

She felt more than heard him move closer. "It's not going to be an easy job."

Didn't she know it! "We'll figure out something." She cleared her throat roughly. "Now, would you like to put on the robe?" She contrived a polite smile, managed to raise her gaze to his face without lingering too long on all the exquisite male flesh in between, and then wished she hadn't bothered. He was just so handsome, he took her breath away.

"The robe is a little tight in the shoulders. I'll put it on when you're ready to take the picture."

She nodded dumbly, stared some more, then shook herself. She was not, and never had been, a giddy coed. She was a mother and an independent businesswoman. "Right. Uh, just let me get a few things ready."

It took her only seconds to arrange the set as she wanted it. She pulled down a background that looked like a kitchen, set a tall stool and a coffee mug nearby, then motioned him over. "You're going to pretend you're just out of bed, okay?"

"I'm supposed to have slept in this stuff?"

"Is that a problem?"

"I sleep naked."

Jessica faltered, verbally stumbled over a few gasps, then glared at him. "It doesn't matter what your normal sleeping habits really are. This is just to show the clothing to advantage."

"Jessica, no man in his right mind would try to sleep in this stuff. Have you felt it?" He offered his thigh for her to test the material. She backed up, feeling foolish, yet utterly appalled at the thought of actually touching that thick, hard thigh.

Mack blinked lazily at her, his look so knowing she felt another blush. "It's slippery. And there's no give to it. No man would sleep in it—"

"Then pretend you just pulled it on after you got out of bed!"

"When I'm alone? Why would I do that?"

She closed her eyes and counted to ten, doing her best not to imagine Mack traipsing around his home impressively naked. She failed. The image flashed into her mind and refused to budge.

It felt like a Bunsen burner had been turned on inside her, especially low in her belly, where the heat seemed to pulse. "Mack." She said his name through her teeth. "Just sit on the damn bar stool and sip your coffee, okay?"

He shrugged. "If you say so, but it's a dumb pose."

She gave up. "Okay, how do you suggest we set it?"

"Maybe in the evening, in front of a fire." His gaze met hers. "With company."

"Company?"

He stepped closer, and the lamplight shone on his hard shoulders, heating his skin. "Sure. This stuff is supposed to appeal to women, right? So wouldn't a guy only wear it for a woman?"

She hated to admit it, but he had a point. "All right. Let's try this." She replaced the kitchen backdrop screen with one that featured a glowing stone fireplace. With Mack's help, a plush easy chair replaced the stool. Jessica used the stool to situate a female mannequin's arm, holding a wineglass, just to the side of the chair. The arm would be visible from the elbow down, as if a woman were offering the glass to Mack.

He approved.

They got several nice shots of him lounging at his ease, smiling in the direction of the phony woman. The robe was open to show his hard belly, his sculpted pecs.

She probably took more shots than she needed, but he was such a natural, she could almost feel jealous of the damned plastic arm.

After that, they took two sets of photos of Mack in drapey silk boxers. He admitted to liking them, and she admitted, only to herself, that he'd definitely draw in the female customers, just as Sophie had expected.

Though the snow continued to fall and the temperature continued to drop, Jessica felt much too warm. She realized she was turned on just from photographing him, and prayed he'd never know.

"What now?"

"Reading the morning paper on the terrace—and no, don't tell me you wouldn't go outside in your underwear."

"Sure I would."

She almost laughed, he was so incorrigible. They arranged the set together, using a small bistro table and chair, a pot of silk flowers, and a screen showing morning sunshine and blue sky.

"Now we need to pick the underwear."

Mack glanced doubtfully at the pile she'd left on the floor. "I don't know..."

She hesitated as well. She didn't *want* to see him in nothing more than a strip of silk or mesh or vinyl. Her pulse raced just at the thought. The damn boxers had been difficult enough, though at least they weren't so blatantly suggestive. They hung over his masculine endowments, rather than hugging them. But the skimpy briefs...

She really had no choice.

And, she thought, if it was any man other than Mack Winston, it wouldn't even be an issue.

She glanced at her watch, dismayed to see that they hadn't gotten nearly enough done, then struggled to achieve a level of professionalism in her voice. "After this shot, we'll just take some of the various briefs. The photos will show only your navel to your upper thighs."

Mack blinked at her, and no wonder. Her voice had sounded like a frog being ruthlessly strangled.

She forged onward. "Would you like to choose the briefs or should I?"

Mack waved at the pile. "Be my guest."

Bound and determined to get it over with, she grabbed the pair closest to the top. "Here."

Mack frowned. "What's wrong with them? They're kind of bunched up."

She looked at the thin blue underwear carefully, then wanted to kick herself. Lifting her chin, she explained, "They have a seam down the back."

"Why?"

"It's...it's a...well, here. I'll just read the description to you." She rushed over to the table and picked up her file. After flipping through a few pages, she found the item number. "It says, 'cheek-enhancing feature with rear seam to shape comfortably—"

"You can damn well forget that pair!"

There was no way she could look at him. "Mack..."

"My backside doesn't need enhancing, thank you very much."

She couldn't have agreed more. "Ah, fine. You pick. You're the one who has to wear them. But keep in mind, if you choose a thong, you'll probably have to shave."

"Why? I thought the shots were only from my navel down."

It felt like her heart lodged in her throat. "Yes, and that's where you'd have to shave. Too much body hair—"

"You can forget the damn thongs, too!"

Relief made her chatty. "All right. Good. I mean, fine. We can maybe take a shot of you hanging them on a clotheslines—"

He grunted, as if that idea didn't appeal to him at all either, but he'd accept it rather than the alternative.

"Are you almost ready?" The longer he took, the edgier she got.

"I'm looking. But I can tell you right now, no thongs, no animal prints, and no vinyl."

She peeked out of the corner of her eye, pretending to rearrange her papers, while Mack held up pair after pair, finally choosing the one with the most fabric.

"I'll be right back." He stomped off behind the curtain, and Jessica held her breath until her lungs hurt.

Ridiculous, she told herself. She was thirty years old. She'd been married and divorced. She was an independent woman. She'd more than learned her lesson about run-around, frivolous men who...

Mack stepped out.

Her wits scattered, every logical argument vanishing in an instant. *Impressive.* She no sooner thought it than she squeezed her eyes shut. Good grief. She was not a sex-starved woman who went about measuring men's endowments. But—well, he looked incredible. Better than incredible. Perfect. A very impressive male specimen.

He cleared his throat impatiently, and she opened her eyes again. It was an effort, but she essayed a look of outward indifference, when inside her body was dealing with numerous responses to his appeal.

Then he stepped into the harsh lamplight, and she saw that the material miraculously turned transparent. *Oh, my God.*

"Jessica, you're staring."

The black briefs now looked like a mere shadow on him, and she'd never seen anything so enticing.

"If you continue to stare, I won't be responsible for what happens."

She swallowed hard and tried to get her gaze to move, but the effort proved more than she could manage. The man was all but naked. Surely no sane woman would look away.

"It's a perfectly natural response, you understand, when a sexy woman stares at a man like she wants him."

That got her attention. Her gaze shot to his face. "Sexy woman?"

He didn't move, except to frown slightly. "You."

"I'm not—"

"Yes, you are." He sounded very positive and his eyes glowed hotly. "Very sexy. Just about as sexy as a woman can possibly get." When she gave him a blank stare, his expression turned tender. "You didn't know?"

"But . . . that's ridiculous."

"Afraid not."

"You never paid a bit of attention to me," she said in near desperation.

He started forward, prompting her to back up. But at least he was moving away from the light, and his briefs were once again opaque. The relief afforded her a modicum of sensibility.

"Mack, we were in the same class for two semesters. Other than a few smiles tossed my way, you ignored me."

"That's not the way I remember it. And I bet if you think real hard, it's not even the way you remember it." He kept moving forward until he stood a mere foot in front of her. He searched her face, his gaze lingering on her lips. "Jessica, you always fascinated me. I tried my damnedest to get your attention, but all you ever did was turn your nose up at me."

She'd backed up so far, her bottom was pressed to the edge of the table. She reached back and gripped the table for support. "You had about a million girlfriends. All young and silly and—"

"They were *friends*, honey. That's all."

She snorted as rudely as Chase ever had. "You expect me to believe that?" Before he could answer, she added, "Not that it matters, anyway! You could have slept with the instructor and I wouldn't care."

"I think you do care."

"Well, you're wrong."

"Jessica, I have a lot of friends, a lot of female friends. That doesn't mean I'm sleeping with them all. And that doesn't mean I react to them all the way I'm reacting to you, the way I've always reacted to you."

Her heart rapped up against her breastbone and she trembled. "I don't know what you're talking about."

One side of his mouth kicked up in a very boyish grin. "I have an erection, honey. In these stupid flesh-hugging briefs, it's not really something I can hide."

Of course she looked, just as he knew she would.

He chuckled softly. "Your staring is what caused that in the first place. If you hope to take any more pictures today, I think we need to cool things down a bit."

He wanted her? The truth of that hit her like a thunderclap. Her hands shook, and she curled them into fists. Her breathing became shallow, her skin too warm. She drew in a slow, uneven breath, but it didn't help.

"Then again," he said, his voice a low, rough rasp, as he watched the signs of arousal blooming in her features, "maybe not."

She felt the heat pouring off him, felt his sexual tension. She looked up, and it was her undoing. His eyes had darkened, narrowed intently. His cheekbones were flushed. He touched her chin with the edge of his hand, raising her face more. Then slowly, giving her a chance to pull away, he leaned down.

She didn't want to pull away. It had been so long since she'd been with a man, long before the divorce became final. Though she did her best to deny it, there were times when her body ached with need. But never so much as it did right now. Mack affected her in a way she hadn't even known was possible; every nerve ending felt acutely alive and needy.

His mouth barely touched hers, moved away, came back. The kiss was tentative, exploring. He skimmed her lips, teasing, moving over her jaw, the tip of her nose, her chin. She panted, following his mouth, hungry for it. She went on tiptoe to bring his mouth closer.

He only touched her with that one hand, holding her face up, keeping her expectant. Rational thought was nonexistent. She stepped away from the table to get closer to him.

Their bodies brushed together, and he groaned. "Damn, I've dreamed about this."

"Mack..."

He settled his mouth against hers, and she felt drowned in the moist heat, the delicious taste of him. His hand opened, his calloused fingertips sliding over her jaw and into her hair. His hand curled around her head, tilting it slightly. His mouth moved, urging her lips to part for his tongue.

Her hands were still fisted at her sides, and she realized he wouldn't come closer until she invited him to do so. In a near daze, mindless with heat and lust and desperation, she raised her arms. His shoulders were hard, his flesh incredibly hot and smooth under her palms, and she felt him, greedy for more. She stepped closer still, pressing her breasts into the hard wall of his chest. The low, harsh sound he made sent goose bumps dancing up her spine. She clutched at him, and he wrapped one muscled arm around her waist, practically lifting her off her feet.

His erection throbbed against her belly.

"Mack..." She pulled her mouth away, gasping.

In between kissing her throat, her shoulder, he whispered, "I love hearing you say my name." He pressed his forehead to hers and sighed. "Am I moving too fast, Jessica?"

She could only groan, which he evidently took as encouragement. Kissing her again, he slid one hand down her back to her bottom, then urged her closer, moved her against him. She felt his fingers caressing, cuddling, squeezing. His hand was so large, and she could feel the heat of his palm even through her jeans. He lightly bit her bottom lip. "God, I'm about a hair away from losing control. You feel so good, so sexy and soft."

No man had ever told her such things. Her husband had wanted her in the early part of their marriage, but he hadn't indulged in much pillow talk. And not long after they were married, he'd gotten bored and started to roam.

Remembering caused her to stiffen. Mack immediately noticed the change. Even as he continued to nuzzle her, he cradled her face in both large palms. After one more light kiss, he looked at her intently. "What is it, babe? What's wrong?"

It was so difficult to get the words out. He appeared to be consumed with tenderness, with desire. He was on the ragged edge of desire—she could feel his muscles quivering—but he was also concerned. And the dual assault of a man wanting her and caring about her made her vulnerable. She looked away from him so she could gather her wits. She absolutely could not do this. Not again. "This is insane," she whispered.

His thumb brushed her temple, and he turned her back to meet his gaze. His smile was gentle. "It doesn't feel insane to me." He searched her face. "It just feels right."

"Mack." She caught his wrists and lowered his hands, then stepped away. Her legs didn't seem too steady, so she kept one hand braced on the table. "How can it possibly be right when we barely know each other?"

"Jessica..."

"No! You've only been here a few hours, and we're carrying on like... like animals."

He gently tugged on her braid, and she knew without looking that he was smiling. "You say that like it's a bad thing."

Here she was on fire, and he found the wit to tease. It was just like him, just like the man she knew him to be, and it reinforced her impression of him. Swallowing hard, she said, "You're only out for a little fun, aren't you?"

He gave a short, incredulous laugh. "Well, hell. If it wouldn't be fun, why do it?"

She groaned and covered her face.

"Jessica?" His tone dropped, became more intimate. "You *would* have fun, sweetheart. I'd make sure of it."

Shaking her head furiously, more to convince herself than him, she said, "Is that all you think about? Having fun?"

His fingers touched her hair, trailed down the length of her braid next to her breast. "I think about you. I've always wanted you."

She wouldn't look at him, not when all he wore was a heated look and what amounted to mere decoration. She knew her own limits, and she didn't want to tempt herself. After a deep, steadying breath, she whispered, "I'm a little embarrassed, if you want the truth. You might be used to women throwing themselves at you, but I swear I'm not usually like this."

"Which only goes to show that we're both very aware of each other, because despite what you think, I'm not usually this way, either."

Oh, he was good. Not that she would buy it. He was just so experienced that he knew exactly what to say and when to say it. She bit her lip, then forged onward, searching for a credible explanation, something to defuse the situation.

Nothing, not even the truth, seemed overly redeeming. "It's... it's just that it's been a... a long time for me, and I guess that's why—"

"How long, honey?" He continued to play with her hair, and it was maddening.

She wanted to step away but couldn't quite get her feet to move. That overwhelming hot need still pulsed inside her. "Since before the divorce."

He stared, leaning down to see her face. He looked shocked, but also fascinated. "You're saying...*years?*"

She turned her back on him. If he laughed at her, she'd...

He stepped closer, and she could almost feel him touching her back. All her nerve endings seemed to scream, and she wasn't sure if it was an alarm, or a plea.

"Not that you'll believe me, but it's been a damn long time for me, too. Not as long as you, but...well, long enough. I didn't expect this any more than you did. No one in his right mind has indiscriminate sex these days." She nearly choked over that little truism, prompting him to give her a squeeze. "I know you don't think much of my morals, but I'm not an idiot."

"I never said...!"

"You called me the class clown, a goof-off, remember?"

She could feel her bottom lip starting to tremble, but she would have died before she'd cry in front of him. "I didn't mean to insult you."

"Well, now, I think you did. And you know why? Because we're having a little fun together, and that scares you."

"No."

"And because you want me." She could feel his breath on her nape, the touch of his warmth. "You were as aware of me two years ago as I was of you. And you didn't like it any more then than you do now."

She turned without thinking. "That's not true!"

His expression softened. He looked at her face, down the length of her body and up again. Her breasts tingled when his gaze lingered there, and she knew her nipples were stiff, pushing against the sweater. His smile seemed ruthless, when she'd never thought of Mack that way.

"You want me still," he growled. "Why don't you admit it and let's see what happens?"

She felt cornered with him standing there so tall, so strong, his body all but bare. She'd forgotten all the wonderful differences men afforded, the incredible scents, the heat. Or maybe no other man had been like this. Though she'd tried to deny it, there had always been a chemistry between them, a sexual awareness that had taken her by surprise and stormed her senses. When they'd shared the class, she'd been painfully aware of every small move he made. And he was right—that awareness frightened her.

"I think we're done for the day."

He sighed. "I'll go. But promise me you'll think about what I've said, okay?"

"There's nothing to think about."

"There's this." He bent and kissed her again, a short, quick kiss that curled her toes and made her heart leap. Then he turned and walked away, unconcerned with his near nudity, with the tempting display he made as muscles and sinew shifted under his smooth flesh.

Jessica stepped out of the studio. The room, changed over from a master bedroom and bath, had always seemed immense to her. But with Mack inside, it was almost crowded, and at the moment she needed some space.

She waited by the window in the outer room, watching the ice and sleet fall, hearing it tap against the windowpanes. Confusion swamped her, but also shame, because despite what she knew was right, she didn't want him to go.

She heard his footsteps come up behind her. As he was pulling on his coat, he asked, "When do you want me again?" She stiffened, then heard his soft laugh. "To finish the shoot, I mean."

God, she didn't know. She needed as much as wanted the job. Even with giving Sophie a deal, she'd stand to make a lot of money off this. And adding the catalogue to her portfolio would bring in other commissions, would expand her possibilities. She shook her head, unable to sort through all the ramifications. And then the phone rang.

She felt so tense and edgy, she nearly jumped out of her skin. Mack watched her as she stepped around him and hurried down the hall to the phone. He silently followed.

"Hello?"

"Mom, can you . . . can you come pick me up?"

She frowned at the strained tone of her daughter's voice. "Trista? What's wrong, honey?"

"I just wanna come home now."

"All right. Hang on, sweetie. I'll be right there."

"Thanks, Mom."

Mack looked at her as she laid the receiver back in the cradle. "What is it?"

"Trista." She headed out of the room to get her coat and keys, and Mack again followed. "Something's wrong. She sounded about ready to cry. I...I have to go pick her up."

Mack nodded. He didn't question her decision to walk out with things still unresolved. He just kept up with her hurried pace, even helping her to slip on her coat. "Do you think it's anything serious?"

"No." He opened the door for her and she stepped out into the biting wind. "Jenna's parents are nice people. It's probably just an argument with a friend, but..."

"You have to go. I understand."

"I know we have...unfinished business, but..."

"Jessica." He squeezed her shoulder. "She's your daughter. If she needs you, of course you have to go."

He sounded so sincere, she blinked up at him. "You mean that, don't you? You don't think it's silly for me to rush out to get her?"

He gave her that endearing crooked smile again. "If you say she sounded upset, then I'm sure you're right. If I had a daughter, I'd do the same thing."

And he would. Though it amazed her, she could tell he did understand, and a small knot of regret settled in her belly. Maybe she had judged him too quickly. "My husband used to say I spoiled her."

As soon as the words left her mouth, she gasped. Good grief, she hadn't meant to share that.

Mack touched her cheek. He kept touching her, as if he couldn't help himself. "You can't spoil a child with too much love."

They had circled to the side lot, and as she neared her car she looked up at him. "Thank you."

Mack stared at her car with a frown. "Don't thank me yet. I have a feeling you're going to need my help."

Confused, she followed his gaze and saw her car was literally frozen beneath a layer of ice. The old house didn't have a garage, so her car was at the mercy of the elements. And since she hadn't driven it in a couple of days, she knew it would take a while to get it ready to go.

Mack held out his arms like a sacrifice. "Behold, your white knight. Or maybe I should say your chauffeur."

She didn't want to prolong her time with him, but she was already shivering, and it didn't make sense to stand out in the cold arguing about it. Especially not when she knew Trista was upset and waiting for her.

Mack stood there, determined to come to her assistance despite what had happened between them. Unlike most men, who would have stormed away mad over being rebuffed, he wanted to play the gallant. Frost collected on his dark hair and his cheeks turned ruddy. He looked young and strong and capable; she'd almost forgotten what it was like to have a man share her burdens. She'd wanted to forget, to prove herself independent, capable of handling anything alone.

Right now she was simply relieved to have a good excuse to keep him close.

Knowing that her own nose had to be cherry-red, she lifted it anyway and said, "Fine. Let's go."

T H R E E

Since he'd been expecting more stubbornness, Mack was nearly bowled over by her compliance. But only for a moment. He took her arm and quickly ushered her toward his truck. He held her close and said, "Be careful. The pavement's slick."

There was a coating of ice on his truck as well, but he easily forced the doors open. Once inside, Jessica huddled into a corner. Her long braid was tucked beneath her coat, and she shivered uncontrollably. He wanted to pull her close, to share his warmth, but she'd already made it clear what she thought of that idea.

It was his own fault for going too fast. Not that he could have helped himself. He'd simply wanted her for too long, dreamed about her too many times, to pass up such an opportunity. She'd looked at him with her soft doe eyes filled with lust, and he'd damn near exploded.

She'd tasted better than he'd expected, felt better than he'd imagined. All the fantasies he'd stored up hadn't prepared him for the reality. Damn, but she packed one hell of a carnal punch.

Yet for some reason she'd apparently sworn off men. He wouldn't give up on her. He wanted her too much for that.

Her breath frosted the air between them as she watched him fasten his seat belt, start the truck, and ease out onto the road. She was silent, but he could almost feel her thinking. He glanced her way as she gave him directions, and noticed how cute she looked with a red nose and rosy cheeks.

It was already dark, and the streets were in terrible shape, but they made the few blocks to where Trista was waiting in less than five minutes.

Mack sat in the truck, relieved that the thermostat was finally warming up, while Jessica climbed out to get her daughter. Trista saw her from the doorway and met her on the sidewalk, looking curiously at the truck. Mack gave her a smile of encouragement as she slid into the seat between him and Jessica.

"Can you get the seat belt okay?"

She nodded, and kept sneaking glances at him. She looked utterly morose, and Mack smiled, remembering how life-altering everything felt when you were a teenager. "You're wondering why I'm here, right?"

Her answer was a cautious look toward her mother.

"Hey, I like your mom, and she was all in a dither to get to you, and her car was completely frozen over, so I offered to drive. I hope you don't mind. Just pretend I'm not here."

Both Jessica and Trista stared at him. He chose to take it as an encouraging sign.

The silence was heavy, so he asked, "It's got to do with that Brian guy, right?"

Trista tucked in her chin, watching him warily.

"I could be a big help, you know. I mean, who better to understand the warped-guy psyche than a guy? Think of all the insight I can give you." He leaned closer and whispered, "I was thirteen once myself."

Jessica cleared her throat. "Uh, Mack..."

He interrupted her with a wave of his hand. "We could discuss it over hot chocolate. What do you think?"

He'd rushed the physical side of things earlier. Now that he wasn't holding Jessica, now that he was fully dressed and his body was back under control—thanks mostly to the frigid February weather—he could think more clearly. Or at least, he could think without salacious intent clouding his judgment.

He wanted her. He wanted to make love to her, to explore her body, especially those incredible breasts of hers. He wanted to taste every inch of her and listen to her moan his name. More than anything, he wanted to see her beautiful dark eyes as she climaxed with him.

But he also wanted to talk to her, to tease her and listen to her huff and watch her face when she blushed. He wanted her to share her sharp wit, the love she felt for her daughter. He wanted to know more about her work, her divorce, how she felt about things, and what her life had been like.

Despite their moment of intimacy, she was determined to push him away, hesitant to get involved on any level. But it wasn't because of lack of mutual appeal, that much was certain. He could still feel the burning touch of her stiff little nipples against his chest when she'd rubbed against him, the way her fingers had dug into his shoulders, how hot she'd tasted on his tongue. He shuddered with the memory.

All he needed to do was keep his cool, ignore her occasional insults, and figure out why she had such an aversion to men in general and him in particular. She'd said he reminded her of her ex, but it had to be more than that; he felt sure of it. She was an incredibly sensual woman, yet she'd been years without a man. The very thought boggled his mind.

Patience, that's what he needed.

Patience, and a lot of determination.

Trista tucked her hands between her knees and said to the windshield, "I don't care what Brian does. He's a jerk."

Pretending offense, Mack said, "Well, give me some credit! I already figured that out."

"You did?"

"Of course I did. You left with a smile, but came back with a frown. Only a jerk could cause that."

Trista gave him a half smile before remembering she was piqued. "He called me a dummy."

"He's a jerk. I rest my case."

"I don't do too good in science, and we're going to have a big project coming up. I thought he'd be my partner, but he asked Jenna today instead."

Jessica reached over and squeezed Trista's hand. "Let me guess. Jenna said yes?"

"She only likes him because I do."

Mack pulled into the lot behind the house, parking as close to the brick structure as he could in hopes that some of the icy wind would be deflected. "You know, I had a lot of trouble with science, too. My sister-in-law used to help me study. Sometimes all you need is a little help."

Jessica patted Trista's leg with a smile. "I can't claim to be a whiz at seventh-grade science, but I'm sure we can study up together."

Mack cleared his throat in an imperious way, and though it was sneaky, he spoke directly to Trista. "Well, now, considering I'm a bona fide teacher, and I've finally mastered science, I *can* claim to be a whiz. So whatdya say I tutor you a little? Not so you can prove anything to Brian, because what he thinks doesn't really matter, right?"

Trista grinned. "Right."

"But this way, you'll know he's wrong if he ever says anything so obnoxious again."

Trista immediately turned to her mother. "Could I?"

Mack knew he had her. He added, just for good measure, "I need to be here a couple more times anyway to get the magazine photos all taken care of. We could work on that while Trista is in school, then I could stay after and do some studying. What do you say?"

She looked like she wanted to smack him, but since Trista sat between them she held back. "If you're a teacher, won't you need to be at school?"

That stumped him. He hated to admit he hadn't landed a permanent job yet, but he really didn't see any way around it. He hedged just a bit instead. "I'm still waiting for my final placement. The school board has to go through several interviews, and until that's done, my days are free. Unless, of course, someone calls for a substitute, but that doesn't happen that often."

Trista looked excited. "Are you going to teach at my school?"

"Nope, sorry, kiddo. I've sort of specialized in inner city. That's where good teachers are needed most because the kids have so few advantages. I'm hoping for a permanent placement at Mordmont." He glanced at Jessica. "And I'm a very good teacher. That's where I did my student teaching, and I'm kinda close to the kids now, so I'd like to go back there."

"Bummer. It'd be cool to brag that we had a model for a teacher."

He could just imagine how that info would go over with the school board. Not that it would really matter to them. They'd tried using his family connection to a bar as a reason to get rid of him, but that didn't carry any weight, considering the backgrounds of some of the other teachers. Most of them were questionable old relics who wouldn't know a modern method if it bit them in the butt, and that's why they hadn't wanted him. He challenged their outdated methods, refused to conform, and any nonconformity scared them shitless, even when they could see the advantages to the students.

If worse came to worst, he'd have to go out of the area. But that would be a last resort, because in the inner city he'd felt he made a real difference, and that's what teaching was all about for him.

The truck had gotten toasty warm, but they couldn't keep sitting in it forever. He looked at Jessica and said, "About that hot chocolate..."

She stared him straight in the eye. "Not tonight, Mack. I'm sorry, but it's been a long day. I started early this morning and I spent all day in the studio. I still have tons of household chores to get done. And my weekend, as well as a good part of next week, is already booked. I was going to see if Thursday morning would work for you to do our next shoot. That'll still give us plenty of time to get everything together for the catalogue."

And it would give her plenty of time to forget about him. He needed to make a diplomatic withdrawal, before she could refuse him everything, but no way would he withdraw enough to let her rebuild all her defenses.

He smiled at her. "No problem. I wouldn't want to get in your way." She looked slightly dazed at his easy acceptance, and he added, "But Trista and I don't need you to help us study, anyway. Saturday I'm busy, but I could come Sunday and the rest of the week until you're ready for me."

Her eyes narrowed, and he could just imagine what she thought he'd be doing on Saturday. He had no doubt her thoughts included sexual indulgence and wouldn't be overly flattering. If only she knew what a recluse he'd become. Working at the family bar on Saturday had been the highlight of his social life lately.

Trista filled in the gap of silence. "I'll bring home the instructions for my science project on Monday. Maybe you can give me a few good ideas?"

"I'd be glad to." He turned off the motor and walked around to open Jessica's door. "Come on, ladies. I'll see you inside."

Trista giggled, but he thought he heard Jessica growl, "We don't need you to—"

Mack looped an arm through each of theirs and proceeded onward, ignoring Jessica's protest while practically gliding her across the icy ground. "Hang on tight. The walk is pretty slick."

She huffed, but had no choice except to hold on or fall. "I gather you think you're steadier than we are?"

"Sure. I've got bigger feet, don't I?" Jessica wasn't amused, but Trista chuckled.

When they reached the door, Jessica fumbled with the key while Mack turned to Trista. "I don't suppose you have your science book at home, do you? It'd help if I could see where you are in it."

"I don't have my book, but I have all my papers from last week."

"How about I take them home with me and look them over? Then we can get started right away on Sunday afternoon."

"I'll go get 'em!" She dashed inside and Jessica, still with her back to him, started to do the same.

Mack caught her arm. "Whoa. Can we talk just a second?"

Reluctantly, she turned to face him. She didn't look pleased, and the second she spoke, he knew why. "I don't like being manipulated, Mack."

Though he knew he'd do it again in a heartbeat, he did feel bad about cornering her. He wasn't in the habit of forcing his company on women. "I'm sorry."

She gaped at him. "You're not even going to deny it?"

"Why should I? I want to see you and this seemed like my only chance. You didn't really think I'd give up that easily, did you?"

She looked astounded and chagrined and, if he was reading her right, a little complimented.

"This is ridiculous—"

"You keep saying that, but damned if I see what's so ridiculous about it."

"I'm too old for you."

He laughed.

"Will you be serious!"

His smile disappeared, but she could still see the slight amusement in his eyes. "Okay, how's this for serious? If I kissed you right now, would you think about me tonight?" She drew a deep breath and he added, "Try being honest with me for once, okay?"

Her chin lifted. "All right. Yes."

"Yes, you'd think about me?" He was so pleased with her he wanted to lift her in his arms, swing her in a circle. He wanted to kiss her silly, to touch her all over. He wanted to devour her, actually, and not even the damn cold could temper his lust.

"Yes, I probably would. But you're not going to kiss me, Mack, so it's a moot admission."

There was no way he could contain his grin. "I bet you'll think about me even if I don't kiss you."

She made a disgusted sound. "Oh, for pity's sake."

"Won't you?" He ducked his head, trying to see her averted face. "Jessica? Tell me you'll think about me, because I'll damn sure be thinking about you."

"No."

"No, you won't tell me or no, you won't think about me?"

She laughed, covering her face with her gloved hands. "You're impossible!"

He pulled her hands down and kissed the end of her icy-cold nose. "I'm infatuated." She started to back up and he let her, pretending it didn't bother him. "I really will enjoy working with Trista. Don't think I'm not serious about that, because I am. Even though I used it as an excuse to spend more time around you, I do think I can help her out. I'm a good teacher." Modesty kept him from total honesty. In truth, he was an *exceptional* teacher.

"It's hard for me to imagine you at the head of a classroom."

He looked away. "Yeah, well, the principal has the same problem."

Tipping her head back to look at him, she asked, "What does that mean?"

He was saved from any morbid confessions by Trista's return. She looked embarrassed as she handed him a stack of papers. "Some of the grades on those aren't too good."

He'd seen the same uncertainty on dozens of different adolescent faces, and it always filled him with compassion. School, in his opinion, shouldn't be about failures so much as accomplishments. He neatly folded the papers in half and stuck them in his pocket. "Did you do your best?"

"Yeah."

"Good girl. No one can ask for more than that, regardless of how you scored on the paper. Let's forget about these grades and concentrate on the next ones, okay?"

"You really think I'll do better?"

"We'll both give it our best shot."

When she smiled, the streetlamp reflected off her braces. He loved making kids smile. Sticking out his hand, he said, "Trista, it was a distinct pleasure."

She shook his hand, giggling, then said a proper good night. With a quick, calculating look at her mother, she ducked back inside and pulled the door shut. She even turned off the porch light. Jessica groaned.

Without conscious thought, Mack moved closer to her, sharing his warmth. Their breath mingled. "Your daughter likes me."

"My daughter doesn't really know you."

He bridged both hands against the brick wall on either side of her head. He felt her nervousness, her excitement. "This may surprise you, but you don't really know me, either."

She lifted her chin. "I know what I saw in college. There's not only a big age difference between us—"

"A few piddling years."

"—but we also have very different outlooks."

"Because I want to have fun and you don't?" He'd leaned down so close, his nose brushed her soft, cold cheek. She smelled sweet and fresh and like the brisk outdoors. He nuzzled against her, drinking in the wonderful scent.

"Mack."

It was a weak protest, and they both knew it. But he was a gentleman and he didn't want to push her. He wanted her to want him, to admit she felt the same incredible things he felt. He rested his forehead against her crown for just a moment, relishing the simple enjoyment of holding her. "If you change your mind over the weekend, call me."

"I won't change my mind."

She sounded less than certain about that, and he smiled. "Sophie has my number."

"I won't change my mind."

He leaned back to look at her. "Tonight, when you're in bed alone, think about me." Her brown eyes were huge in the darkness, and she stared at him without answering. He opened the door and gave her a small nudge in the right direction. "Sleep well, honey."

Just before she pulled the door shut, she whispered, "Mack? Be careful driving home." Stunned, Mack stood there a moment until he heard her turn the lock. Then, slowly, he started to smile. He even laughed out loud, but the sound seemed more ominous than not in the cold, quiet night.

Damn, he felt good.

And then he remembered the Winston curse.

Sophie was ringing up a customer when Mack walked in. The little bell over the door jingled, and she looked up with a smile of welcome. Three other women looked up as well, then proceeded to stare rudely, as if he'd invaded their private territory. Mack merely grinned, sauntered over to some lacy bras, and began browsing.

Allison came out of the back room and spotted him. "Hey, Mack. How did the photo shoot go?"

Why did Allison look so suspicious when she asked that? He narrowed his gaze at her, then shrugged. Maybe she was waiting for the curse to hit him. She couldn't know that he'd already resigned himself to his fate. Hell, he was half anticipating it.

"It went okay. Though some of that stuff isn't coming anywhere near my body."

"Spoilsport."

Sophie joined them, looking indignant. "Which stuff?"

"G-strings? Those filmy briefs with the see-through front? And what about those clear vinyl thingies—"

Laughing, Sophie put a finger to his lips. "Hush. Every lady in here is eavesdropping."

Allison looked at him over the rim of her round glasses. "See-through vinyl?"

"Yeah. You should get Chase a pair." He tried to hide his amusement, but it was impossible when Allison seemed to be seriously considering the idea.

Sophie took his arm and dragged him to the other side of the room, where there were fewer ears to listen in. "Some of those things are just for fun. They're not meant to be taken seriously."

"Well, I'm seriously not modeling them."

"Is that why you're here? You're not going to back out on me just because a few of the items are a bit . . . risqué, are you?"

"No, I'm not backing out."

She suddenly stiffened, then grabbed both his hands. "Oh, wait! Did you hear from the school board? Did you get the position?"

"No, I didn't hear anything yet." He almost wished she hadn't reminded him. His preoccupation with Jessica had driven away much of his frustration. Which was just as well, because he absolutely hated to sit around fretting like an old schoolmarm.

Sophie looked ready to embrace him, and he quickly sidestepped her. She had this mothering tendency that sometimes made him uncomfortable. It had been especially noticeable since she'd gotten pregnant. "I'm fine, Sophie, really. It's not a big deal."

"Baloney. I know how hard you've worked to be a great teacher."

"Yeah, well. A lot of good it's done me."

"Oh, my God. I just thought of something. What if the school board sees you in the catalogue?"

"That's not an issue. Nothing I wore is that revealing, and I seriously doubt they'd ever see it, anyway, since they're two districts away. No offense, hon, but it's not like your boutique is well known across the state."

She sniffed. "No, it's a quaint local shop."

"Very local. And the school board can't touch me on morals charges. Not when one of the teachers moonlights at a strip club and another has been picked up twice for brawling. Their big gripe is that I don't follow their procedure, even though I've proven my procedure to be more effective."

Sophie gave him a sad smile. "This matters a lot to you, doesn't it?"

Damn. How had he let the subject get so sidetracked? "It matters," he admitted, "but that's not why I'm here." He suddenly felt a little self-conscious and reached out to touch a satiny-soft camisole hanging on a rack. "I, uh, I wanted some advice."

Allison crept back over to them. "Oh, good. I love giving advice."

Mack ran a hand through his hair. "The thing is, I know Jessica."

"No!" Sophie put a hand to her chest.

Allison nudged her, then cleared her throat. She gave Mack her undivided attention. "You know her? From where?"

Something wasn't right, but damned if Mack could figure out what. He'd never understand his sisters-in-law, and he'd given up trying. "I knew her in college. We took a class together. I always liked her, but she—well, she's not too fond of me for some reason."

Sophie raised her brows in theatrical surprise. "Wait a minute! Jessica isn't the woman you always talked about when I helped you to study, is she?"

"One and the same."

Allison leaned back against a display table of panties. "Fascinating coincidence."

Frustrated, Mack paced away, then back again. "Yeah, I know. I didn't think I'd ever see her again. But now that I have seen her again, I want her."

Allison straightened at that. "Maybe I'm too young to hear this."

Sophie smothered a laugh. "I'm not. Go ahead, Mack."

He stared at both of the women, then blurted out, "Which of those goofy lingerie things do you think she'd like the most?"

They looked at each other before Sophie asked, "You want us to tell you which things will be likely to . . . uh . . ."

The women were staring at him so wide-eyed, he felt his ears turn red. He wanted to get this over with so he could get back to his planning. "To turn her on. Yeah. So what do you think?"

Sophie choked, but Allison gave it serious thought. "I like the soft cotton stuff. Cotton feels so good on men and it hugs all those sexy muscles. Chase looks just adorable in cotton boxers, especially the snug-fitting kind." She turned to Sophie. "Weren't there a few of those in the box?"

Sophie tried unsuccessfully to get rid of her grin. "Um, yes. They have little"—she gestured toward Mack's fly—"silver snaps up the front."

Allison patted his arm. "With your dark coloring, try the black ones. Or the forest green."

Sophie shook her head. "I rather like the silky ones. In white."

"So you think if I wear those for Jessica, I mean for the shoot, she'll . . . ah, enjoy the sight?"

"Most definitely."

"Absolutely."

Mack shook his head, grinning. "Why do I get the feeling you two are up to no good?"

Sophie shrugged. "You obviously have a suspicious nature."

She looked too innocent, and he didn't like it. "Where exactly did you meet Jessica?" He didn't think he had ever shared her name with Sophie, though he had described her on numerous occasions. Hell, for a while there she was all he could think of, until he'd resigned himself to never seeing her again.

"She shops here."

Mack felt like someone had doused him in fire. He looked around at all the sexy stuff on mannequins, hanging in displays, stacked softly on tables, and his heart thumped. He pictured her stretched out on a bed, *his bed*, her lush body barely covered in black satin or white lace. "She really wears this stuff?"

Allison gave him a pitying look. "What did you think she wore? Burlap?"

"No, but . . . which stuff?"

"Ah, now that would be telling, and I can't do that."

"Sophie?"

Sophie crossed her arms and lifted her chin. "Allison's right, Mack. If you want to know what kind of lingerie Jessica wears, you'll just have to find out on your own."

He damn well intended to.

A few minutes later Mack walked out the front door, thinking what lucky dogs his brothers were. He glanced back once and saw Allison and Sophie collapsed against each other, laughing hysterically. He smiled. He didn't mind their ribbing at all since they'd been totally honest with him. Poor Jessica. She didn't stand a chance.

FOUR

Jessica felt so confused, she didn't know what to think, or precisely how to handle her new decision.

Mack had been hanging around all week, working with Trista, laughing and joking, making his presence unmistakably known. When he was around, Jessica felt it in every pore of her body. She'd catch herself listening for his laugh, or looking to catch a glimpse of him in between appointments. He and Trista mostly worked in the office, but after the first day Trista had asked if Mack could go upstairs with her to help make lunch. The upstairs was where they lived, and Jessica didn't want him invading her home as well as her office, but she couldn't find a reasonable excuse to deny him. And after that, they often went upstairs, getting drinks or looking for books, or using the computer. Trista adored him, and already she had new confidence in her abilities at school.

Often, when Jessica's workday was over and Mack had gone home, she'd find signs of him upstairs still. Notes he'd scrawled for Trista, a hat he'd left behind, even his scent lingered. Sleeping was difficult, because no matter how she tried, she couldn't stop thinking of him and how he'd made her feel. He'd only kissed her and barely touched her, yet she'd been more aroused than she could ever remember. She wanted him, and the wanting wasn't going to go away.

He hadn't been especially familiar with her since that first day. He was, in fact, a perfect gentleman, talking politely, minding his manners, respecting her wishes to be left alone.

Though it shamed her to admit it, she hated it that he'd given up so easily. Or had he?

She hoped not, because she'd already decided she wanted, needed, to know what it was like to be with him. He looked at her and it affected her more than a physical touch. She hadn't felt like her old self since he'd first kissed her, and she saw no reason she shouldn't indulge herself for once. But just once.

Today he'd be back for the shoot, and she didn't quite know what to expect or how to make her declaration. Since that first day Trista had been close by to act as a buffer, and she supposed that could possibly account for part of Mack's restraint. When he was studying with her, his attention was undivided. But now Trista would be in school, and she and Mack would have quite a few hours alone and uninterrupted.

And Mack would be wearing those damned seductive undergarments again.

Just the thought of it made her palms sweat, her heart jumpy. She looked around the studio, making sure everything was in place. With any luck, they could finish up early and then, if Mack was still willing, use the rest of the afternoon to make love.

The doorbell rang and she jerked around, feeling guilty about her thoughts even though no one would know. She hurried out of the room, but at the door she stopped to compose herself, feeling like a foolish coed yet unable to help herself. She pasted on a smile and pulled the door open.

Mack leaned on the door frame, arms crossed over his chest, his breath frosting in front of him. At the sight of her he smiled lazily. "Hey."

Just that small smile, and her insides fluttered in anticipation. "Hello. Right on time." She opened the door wider and he came in. Only he didn't step to the side of her. He came right up to her. He cupped her face in his gloved hands and, casual as you please, he kissed her.

"I missed you," he whispered against her mouth.

Flustered, she stammered, "You've seen me all week!"

"Hmmm. Seen you, but not been able to touch you." He kissed her again, a light, barely there kiss, making her want more. "Did you miss me, too?"

"Mack. This is—"

"Ridiculous?" He touched the tip of her nose and stepped around her, then peered into the empty office. "Where's the receptionist?"

Swallowing nervously, Jessica tried to remind herself that she was thirty years old, an experienced woman, a divorcée who knew how to handle herself in any situation, never mind that she hadn't been in this situation in too many years to count, and never with a man like Mack.

She laced her fingers together to keep her hands from shaking. "You're the only appointment I have today, so there was no need for her to come in. She helps out mostly with appointments to view proofs or to pick up packages."

Mack looked at her intently, one brow raised. "Then we're here all alone?"

Now he would probably kiss her again. She licked her lips, anticipating his unique taste, the heat of his mouth. "Yes."

He nodded, still looking at her. "I suppose we should get started?"

Disappointment filled her, but she hoped it didn't show. "Yes, of course." She didn't understand him at all. He seemed to still want her, but if he did, then why was he waiting? She started down the hall and for the first time questioned her choice of clothes. The scoop-neck, cream-colored sweater was soft, and her plaid skirt almost reached her ankles. True, she often wore long skirts to work in because they were so comfortable, but today it had been a deliberate choice; she'd wanted to look more feminine for Mack. That decision now seemed beyond pathetic, and she had the irrational fear that he'd know it.

She cleared her throat once they were in the studio. "Sophie called and mentioned a few other things she wants you to wear."

His brow shot up a good inch. "She did?"

"Yes. There's some snap-front boxers and matching ribbed undershirts she definitely wants in the catalogue."

Mack grinned, and an unholy light entered his eyes. "I see."

Jessica handed him the first change of clothes, and Mack went behind the curtain. While he was there, she readied her camera and set up some scrims to filter the light, making the scene softer, more intimate. This particular scrim, or mesh filter, had denser spots, which provided a dappled look, like sunlight through leaves. She placed an old-fashioned quilt on the floor over artificial grass, then added some props to give it an outdoor look. She used a birdbath, a small bush, some flowers.

Mack stepped around the curtain just as she smoothed the quilt one last time. She smiled at him, barely managing to still her sigh of appreciation. The snug boxers and ribbed undershirt showed his big muscled body to perfection.

"For this shot," she said, her voice just a little husky, "it's going to look like you're resting outside, enjoying the sunshine, totally at your ease. It's to sort of show how comfortable the clothes are."

"I can buy that." He rubbed one large hand over his abdomen. "They do feel nice."

She swallowed hard, wondering how it would feel to her hand—not just the fabric but his body beneath it. With a sigh, she looked him over from his tousled dark head, his intent eyes and stubborn, clean-shaven jaw, to his broad shoulders, lean hips, and long legs, all the way down to his big feet. She couldn't imagine a man who looked more perfect or more sensually enticing than Mack Winston.

Her heart beat a little too fast, and she had trouble drawing an even breath. Mack watched her face, and after a moment, he said softly, "I like it when you look at me like that. You know, I memorized your features back in college. You'd sit there, refusing to look at me, staring at the instructor as if she spoke gospel, and I'd study you. Every little angle, the tilt of your nose, the slant of your jaw, how your lashes left shadows on your cheeks. I'd go nuts looking at the profile of your breasts."

Jessica knew that was always the first thing men noticed about her, and it annoyed her. From the time she'd hit puberty, she'd worn a C cup. It had always been more of a nuisance than anything else. "All women have breasts."

"All women aren't you." He came closer, then dropped to his knees directly in front of her. With only one hand, he touched her jaw, smoothed her hair back to her braid, then trailed his fingers down her neck to where it met her shoulder. He lifted his other hand and cradled her head, using his thumbs to stroke her jaw. Jessica felt herself trembling in anticipation, and knew he felt it, too.

After a moment of heavy silence, he tilted his head to the side. "What is it about you, Jessica, that makes me feel this way?"

She stared at his collarbone, at where the low neck of the undershirt showed just a bit of hair on his chest. This close, she could smell him, the musky smell of aroused male. She swallowed hard and asked in a whisper, "What way?"

"Like I have to have you." His hands drifted down to her shoulders, then inward, his fingers spreading wide over her upper chest. "*Have* to, just like I have to breathe, or eat. It was pure torture in college, trying to concentrate when I had a hard-on all the time. And all you wanted to do was snub me."

She shook her head, unwilling to be pulled in with lies. "How could you have been thinking of me when all those skinny girls kept throwing themselves at you?"

He was looking at her breasts, and his hands skimmed over her sides to her waist. "I didn't—"

Jessica scrambled back, wrinkling the quilt. "You did. You flirted and played around, and all the girls adored you."

Mack dropped back to sit on his heels, studying her closely. "I also got straight A's. Which I earned."

"That's impossible!"

"Ah, surprised you with that one, didn't I? I guess you figured I coasted through with the lowest passable grades possible? Did you think that's why I was interested in teaching inner-city kids? Because no influential school district would have me?"

She shook her head. "I don't know." But of course she had thought it.

"You're confusing me with him," he said gently. "I'm not the one who hurt you, not the one who used you." He lifted one shoulder, and his look was sad. "Honey, having fun doesn't make you a bad person. It doesn't make you irresponsible or frivolous. It's okay to enjoy everything you do—your schoolwork, your friends, your job. Life."

It hurt her to admit he might be right, that she might have been the one with the wrong outlook. "I guess that's easier for some people than others."

"Why? Why can't you have a little fun?"

Despite herself, she smiled. "Fun, as in fooling around with you?"

"No fooling to it. Sometimes you need to take your fun very seriously."

She had no idea what to make of that. His look was direct, hot, and very sensual. She shivered, then admitted, "I . . . I want to."

His eyes gleamed, and though he didn't quite smile, she saw the dimple in his cheek. "But?"

"It's not easy to explain."

"Well, now. I can be a pretty good listener when you give me a chance."

No doubt Mack would be good at anything he did. But talking about her inhibitions, the problems that had nearly suffocated her just a few years ago, wasn't easy. Talking about them with Mack was doubly hard, because she suddenly cared what he thought. He scooted closer, crossed his legs Indian style, and gave her a look of encouragement.

He looked young and sexy and caring and considerate. His body was hard and beautiful, his smile gentle. He was a female's fantasy come to life, the epitome of temptation and magnetism. And he sat before her, waiting.

With a sigh, she gave in. "My husband and I met when I was a high school senior and he was in his second year of college. I'd always been sort of mousy, real quiet, and he was the first really popular guy to pay attention to me."

Mack picked at a loose thread in the quilt. "It's tough for me to imagine you as mousy." He glanced up and caught her gaze. "You're so damn sexy now."

She blushed. "Mack..."

"Go on."

He flustered her so with his compliments, it was hard for her to gather her thoughts. "He was so much...*fun*. I was completely overwhelmed by him, and like a dummy, I wasn't as careful as I should have been. I got pregnant."

Mack snorted. "He was older, and no doubt more experienced?"

She shrugged, a little embarrassed to have to admit it, but she did. "I was a virgin."

"So why the hell wasn't he being careful? Any man who cares about a woman protects her as well as himself. My brother pounded that into my head when I was about fifteen, long before I ever got around to even trying anything with a girl." He grinned slightly. "I guess after Zane, who's more wild than not, he wasn't going to take any chances."

"Your brother is older than you?"

"Yeah, by about fifteen years. My mom and dad died when I was young, so Cole pretty much raised the rest of us."

"Oh, Mack." Her heart swelled. She was still so close to her parents, she couldn't imagine losing them. "I'm so sorry."

He gave her that adorable boyish grin. "It's okay. It was a long time ago, and Cole made certain we had everything we needed. He was a mom and dad and big brother all in one."

Fascinated, she asked, "How many brothers do you have?"

"I'm the baby." He grinned shamelessly at that admission. "Then there's Zane, who's a complete and total hedonist, but we forgive him because he's a damn good brother, too. And Chase, who's pretty quiet, except maybe not so much now that he's married to Allison. And then Cole. He's married to Sophie."

"You're all pretty close, aren't you?" At his nod, she said, "I was an only child. My folks are great, but I know they were a little disappointed when I got pregnant. They wanted to help out, for me to stay at home and go to college, but I really thought I loved Dave and that we'd have a good marriage."

"Didn't work out that way, huh?"

"No. Dave was never very responsible. Oh, he married me, but then I couldn't go to college because we needed me to work to pay his tuition. He said his studies took up too much time for him to hold down a job. Only his grades were never very good, and then he flunked out the first semester of his third year. I hated to admit how badly I'd screwed up in marrying him, so I made excuses for him and told everyone what a great job he'd gotten. But then he lost that for missing too much work."

Mack's eyes had narrowed, but his tone remained calm. "He sounds like a real winner."

"That's just it. Everyone thought so. He was the life of the party, a real charming guy. People met him and they naturally liked him. Especially the women. I always came across as a terrible nag. His relatives complained about how I had dragged him down, because he was saddled with a wife and a kid, and they said that was why he'd failed college, because he had too many responsibilities."

Mack touched her cheek. "I can only imagine how that made you feel."

"It wasn't *fun*, I can tell you that."

"Not for you, but it sounds like he did all right."

Jessica pulled her knees up, making sure her long skirt covered her legs. She crossed her arms over them and rested the side of her face there. She didn't want to look at Mack. She didn't want to see his pity at the stupid girl she'd been. "He did better than all right. He ended up with a nothing part-time job that left him plenty of free time to run around. I worked full time at a restaurant, and my parents watched Trista for me. Dave had a lot of friends, and they all thought I was a bitch if I suggested he should skip hanging out. Then one day Trista got sick and I needed him to get medicine. I called the house where he was supposed to be playing cards with his buddies, but when a woman answered, I could tell it was a huge party. I went to get the medicine myself, and on the way home I stopped by there."

Mack scooted around to sit behind her. He pulled her back to his chest, closed his arms tightly around her, and kissed her temple. "He was cheating on you."

It wasn't a question, so she didn't bother to answer. "Here I was, still wearing my stained, wrinkled waitress uniform, Trista beside me. I looked horrible from working all day, and Trista had a runny nose and red eyes. But Dave looked great. He was laughing and having a good time. When the woman on his lap looked up, I didn't want to admit to being his wife. They all stared at me, and I could tell they felt sorry for Dave. They thought he'd gotten a bum deal with me. I just turned around and walked out."

She could feel the tension coming off Mack, only this time it was anger. She twisted around to see him, but the minute she was turned, he kissed her. His mouth opened on hers, and his tongue stroked her lips, making her gasp. He seemed almost desperate, his hands in her hair, holding her close, devouring her. His urgency alarmed her a bit, overwhelming her. His hands stroked everywhere, down her back to her bottom, over her stomach and up to her breast, and then his fingers found her stiffened nipple, making her shudder and gasp. A thick, low groan erupted from his throat and she felt him tremble.

All her reservations vanished. She wanted him, and there would never be a better time than now.

Mack cursed roughly when Jessica suddenly relaxed, her arms wrapping around his neck, her breast pressing into his palm. "Jesus. I feel like I'm going to explode."

"Mack..." Her small, cool hand touched his jaw, bringing his mouth back to hers. He couldn't think of anything he'd ever wanted as much as he wanted her right now. He understood her so much better after all she'd told him, and he wanted—needed—to prove to her that he was different. He wanted to stake a claim. He kissed her, long and deep.

Then he pulled away, struggling for control. "Sweetheart, we need to slow down. I'm sorry. It's just that...damn, I'm jealous."

Her slumberous eyes opened to stare at him. Her pupils were dilated, making her eyes look nearly black. She looked dazed and aroused and beautiful, so damn beautiful.

"I don't understand."

How could he tell her everything he felt? Her ex was an idiot, but Mack was glad, because if he hadn't screwed up, Jessica might still be married, when Mack knew in his bones she belonged with him. Even now she clung to him, her breath hot, her body quivering with need. And he'd barely touched her. The thought made him frantic with lust.

Easing her down slowly, he laid her on the quilt. Her chest rose and fell, and she opened her arms to him.

"Shhh. Let's get these clothes off you. I'm all but naked, and you're bundled up from head to toe."

He reached for her sweater, and she turned her head away. Mack stilled. "Jessica?"

Her eyes squeezed tightly closed. He wanted her so bad, his body burned, but damned if he would do anything to make her uncomfortable. "Tell me what's wrong, honey."

He saw her slender white throat tense as she swallowed, saw her hands fist. "You're used to beautiful women."

He stroked her shoulder, keeping the touch feather light. "And you think you're not?"

"I'm...I'm thirty years old, not twenty with long legs and no hips. I've had a baby and..."

"And because you're a mother, you can't be sexy anymore?"

"That's not what I'm saying and you know it!"

He stroked her cheek, smoothed back her hair. "I'm sorry, babe, but you're being silly. I think you're the sexiest woman I've ever known. Do you think I walk around with an erection for every woman on the street?"

She made a sound that was a cross between a groan and a laugh. "I wouldn't put it past you."

"Well, you'd be wrong." He reached for the hem of her skirt and slowly began dragging it up her legs. She stiffened, but she didn't say anything. Mack stared at her shapely legs and tried not to be affected. He wanted his tone to remain calm, not rough with lust. But it wasn't easy. She wore some kind of elastic-topped nylons that ended just above her knees and left her pale thighs bare. The elastic was decorated with small cream-colored roses. His breath rasped unevenly as he touched her knee, urging her legs to part just a bit. "Did you buy these stockings from Sophie?"

Her eyes popped open. "What?"

"She told me you shop in her boutique, that that's where she met you. Did you get them there?"

"Yes."

Things were starting to come together, the goofy way Sophie and Allison had acted. The reason *he'd* been picked to model. It was a setup—and he owed them both more than he'd realized.

The bright photography lights were still aimed at them, illuminating the square of quilt and the two people stretched out atop it. Mack smiled. "I can see you, all of you, very well. I like this."

His fingers trailed above the stockings, moving the skirt higher and higher, until the pale sheen of her silky beige panties reflected the light. The material looked damp between her legs, and he groaned. Without even thinking of her reaction, he bent and pressed a heated kiss there.

She nearly leapt off the floor. "Mack!"

He nuzzled closer. "Damn, you smell good." In a rush, he sat up and unbuttoned the skirt, then tugged it down her legs. "I think I'll leave the stockings. They turn me on."

She panted, staring at him in mingled embarrassment and need. He laid a hand over her belly. It wasn't concave, sinking between her hipbones, but it was soft and silky and . . . "How could you think this isn't sexy? Do you have any idea how you feel to me?" He closed his eyes, stroking her, relishing the touch of her warm, satiny skin, then slid his fingers into her panties and tangled them in her feminine curls. Her hips lifted, and he pulled away.

Straddling her upper thighs, he cupped her face and smiled. "I feel like a teenager again, having to pace myself so I can last long enough to get inside you. God, woman, you affect me. Forget any other man you've known. Right now there's just me. Okay?"

She looked him over, then whispered, "Will you take off your shirt so I can see you again?"

"Hell, yes. And then yours." He pulled the undershirt over his head and tossed it aside. Her hands were immediately there, caressing his shoulders, touching his small nipples to make him shudder. He gave her time to look, to touch him, and when he couldn't take it anymore, he jerked her sweater up. He was awkward and trembling and laughed even as he cursed. Jessica lifted her arms so he could pull it free, then rested back on the floor. She watched him anxiously, her soft brown eyes wide and uncertain, her breath held.

The bra she wore was incredible, beige satin to match the panties, but with a lace overlay, looking sexy as sin and making his heart race. He could just see the dark shadows of her erect nipples beneath the sheer fabric. He locked his jaw, fighting for control, and with one finger he circled a nipple and watched her shiver. He looked up and met her eyes. "I want to take you in my mouth. I want to lick you and suck on you."

Her body arched as she moaned.

"Can we take off the rest of our clothes now, babe?" His voice was a rasp, a bare echo of sound.

For an answer, she sat up so he could reach the back closure on the bra. His hands shook as he expertly slipped the bra open, then slowly slid the straps off her shoulders. Her breasts were so full and white, resting softly against her body. He'd never considered himself a breast man, at least not in any sort of preference and not when he loved everything about women's bodies, but with Jessica... The sight of her made his insides twist with need.

He cupped both breasts in his palms, closed his eyes as he felt her, and whispered, "You thought you didn't compare to other women?"

"I... I breast-fed. And it shows. I'm not as firm as I used to be. Dave used to tell me—"

"Forget Dave." He looked and saw a few faint lines on her breasts and imagined her swollen with milk, mothering her child. *"God."*

He smoothed the lines with his thumbs, then bent and took one nipple into the heat of his mouth. Jessica moaned, and her fingers tangled in his hair. He switched to the other nipple, sucking strongly, making her cry out. She tried to pull away, but he held her securely, greedy, lifting her breast high, continuing to lick and suck until he knew he had to stop or he'd come.

She collapsed back against the quilt, panting, her body warm and rosy, her nipples drawn tight, wet from his mouth.

She gasped at the look in his eyes, then blurted out, "Dave never wanted me much after Trista was born. I had picked up weight, and my body looked different. He said that's why he started going to other women...."

"What a goddamn fool." Heat clouded the edges of his vision and he knew he was near the end. "I'm not him, sweetheart. I didn't break your heart, and I never will. You're beautiful, all of you, in so many ways. I can't imagine ever not wanting you."

"Oh, Mack."

He could see the small quivers in her body, the way her lush breasts shimmered with each ragged breath. "Be right back."

Never taking his eyes from her, he stood and then back-stepped to the curtain where he'd left his jeans, blindly reached for them, and came back to her. With the jeans bunched in his fist, he pressed her legs apart and knelt between them. She looked almost pagan lying on the quilt with the bright lights flooding down on her. Her skin appeared translucent, her breasts swollen and rosy, her thighs open. He hadn't known for certain what love was, but now he knew this had to be it, because seeing her total acceptance of him meant more than he'd ever known was possible.

His heart slowed with the realization that despite all her efforts to fend him off, despite her resistance, he'd fallen head over heels, and he liked it. The Winston curse be damned. He felt blessed. After locating a condom in his wallet, he tossed the jeans aside. He laid the condom nearby, knowing he was near the edge of his control.

He touched her chin, down her chest to circle both breasts, pushing them together, gently rasping his beard-rough cheeks against her. He tickled his fingertips down her belly and watched her squirm, then stopped at the edge of her panties.

"I'm sorry, Jessica," he said, forcing the words out around the constriction in his heart, "but I can't wait much longer. Usually I'm pretty good at this, but now..."

She choked on a laugh. "Pretty good at what?"

"Waiting. Making the anticipation build. But you make me burn." He dropped the jeans and hooked both hands in the waistband of her panties, then bent to kiss her belly as he slowly tugged them to her knees. Her laughter turned to a ragged moan. "Lift your hips."

She did, but rather than just removing her panties, he slipped both hands beneath her buttocks, raising her, and tasted her again, this time without the barrier of cloth. Jessica twisted on the quilt, making incoherent sounds of pleasure. Her fingers tangled in his hair, tugged.

"Easy," he whispered, then kissed her again, using his tongue to stroke deep. "Damn, you're so wet. You want me, don't you, Jessica?"

Her body bowed, her head thrown back. He could feel the fine quivers running through her, but he wanted to hear her say it, wanted her to admit that what was happening was special. He blew softly against her heated flesh, ruffled the curls with his fingertips. Slowly, watching her face, he worked one long finger into her. Her thighs tensed and her buttocks flexed.

"Tell me, honey. Tell me you want me."

"Mack. *Yes.*"

His finger pressed deeper, and he was shocked at how tight she felt, proof of her long abstinence. She sobbed, straining toward him. He kissed her sweet female flesh, drowning in her scent, and demanded, "Tell me this is special for you, too, babe."

"Yes, Mack, please..."

He broke. He couldn't wait another minute, and for the first time in his life, he resented the time it took to use the condom. Jessica shook beneath him, squirming, needing him. As he came over her, she gripped his shoulders so tightly her nails stung, then she strained up against him, trying to hurry him along. Mack entered her with one long, even stroke. They both groaned, but Jessica didn't give him a chance to wait any longer, locking her thighs around him and holding him tight. He began moving into her with a hard rhythm, loving the feel of her lush breasts against his chest, her hot breath fanning his throat. She accepted him, wanted him, and the knowledge drove him over the edge. As he gave a stifled groan of release, he felt her internal muscles clamp tight around his erection, intensifying his pleasure and assuring him she'd found her own climax.

He sank into her, sated, awash in burgeoning emotions, and then he heard her soft sob.

Jessica tried to cover her face, but Mack wouldn't let her. She'd barely made a sound, and she'd assumed he'd be too far into his own pleasure to hear her anyway. But now he was over her, his expression alert, his hands holding hers so he could search her face.

His brows drawn in concern, he asked, "What's wrong? Why are you crying?"

"Mack, I want you to go now." He had to leave before she totally fell apart. God, she'd been so stupid. She'd thought she could make love with him, enjoy him for a time, then get back to her staid, responsible existence. She knew now that that was impossible, and she felt the sharp bite of panic. How could she ever go back to her old ways after having been with him, after knowing what it could be like?

She'd felt so alive while he loved her, so mindless with pleasure, she knew she'd been existing in a void. All she'd managed to do was show herself what she'd missed.

Mack's frown grew ferocious. "Like hell! I'm not going anywhere until you tell me what's wrong."

But she couldn't tell him. That would be like the final indignity, proof of how desperately pathetic she'd become. She shook her head and pleaded, "Please. You need to leave now. Trista will be home soon—"

"Not for at least another two hours. And we haven't finished the shoot." He smoothed her hair in that gentle way he had, making her heart ache. "Did I hurt you?"

Appalled that he could even think such a thing, she shook her head. Her voice was choked, strained, but she said, "It was wonderful. You were wonderful."

With a slight smile, he pulled her braid loose from behind her and played with it. "I love how you feel, the warm silk of your hair, the texture of your skin." His big hand cupped her breast, stroking it possessively. His gaze locked on hers, too intent, too compelling. "Everything about you excites me. You smell too good to describe, and you taste even better."

She blushed slightly, remembering the places where he'd tasted her. Mack smiled. "I love you, Jessica."

Her eyes widened. "Don't be—"

"Ridiculous?" Slowly, he pulled the tie from her hair and dragged his fingers over it, untwining her braid. "I know what you're going to say. That we don't know each other well enough. That nonsense about you being older than me." He laughed. "Do you realize how much influence your ex had on you? He convinced you somehow that you're old and worn out, but when men look at you, they see a young, very sexy woman. Not a housewife. Not a mother. A woman."

"How would you know what other men think?"

"I'm male." He drew a deep breath. "I dreamed about you even after we were out of college. It was like I knew something very important had slipped through my fingers. We hadn't talked a lot, but I'd studied you every chance I got. I knew you were serious and withdrawn and shy and a little wounded. I knew you were so sexy you made my teeth ache, and I saw how all the other guys looked at you. It made me nuts. I knew even then you were the woman I wanted."

Tears gathered in her eyes despite her resolve. She didn't know what to say, except to be honest. "I did the same."

"Yeah?" He looked pleased, then leaned closer to whisper, "Did you ever touch yourself . . . you know, while you were thinking of me?"

Her face went hot, her breath catching. "What kind of question is that?"

He shrugged, looking mischievous. "I did, thinking about you. I wanted you so damn bad, no other woman even interested me. I won't lie to you and tell you I stayed celibate, as you did, but my sexual encounters were few and far between. And I haven't been with anyone for almost six months. I was so disgusted over this teaching business that I haven't been able to think of much else. I guess that's why my meddling family set us up."

She was still embarrassed—and intrigued—over his very private admission, but managed to clear her mind enough to ask, "What are you talking about?"

His hand slipped down her body, stroking her, petting her. "Sophie used to help me study, and I told her all about you. Not your name, but everything else, like about your incredible breasts, your sexy braid, your beautiful brown eyes. She sympathized with me, in between badgering me enough so I'd learn that damned science that I hated so much."

He lifted her hand and kissed her fingers. "Did you ever tell her which college you went to?"

Jessica thought about it, then reluctantly nodded. "And what years, and that there was this annoying, utterly distracting young stud who kept interrupting my concentration. But she was Sophie Sheridan then, not Winston, and after she married I just never put the names together."

Mack barked a sharp laugh and bit her finger. "A stud, huh? Well, I think Sophie put two and two together, with some help from Allison, my other meddling, very adorable sister-in-law, and the result was this cooked-up catalogue of goofy men's lingerie."

Jessica licked her lips, then admitted, "I don't think it's goofy at all. I think you look downright scrumptious in this stuff."

"Is that right?"

She nodded.

"Scrumptious enough to give me a chance? To give us a chance? Because I really do love you, you know. At first I thought it was just an obsession, that eventually I'd get over you. But I didn't. And now, after being inside you, feeling you squeeze me tight, watching you come, I know it's more. I know I don't want to do that with anyone else but you, because it could never be as good."

She bit her lips to keep them from trembling. Could it be true? Could he really love her? He kept touching her and looking at her body, and she could feel him, hard again against her thigh.

He sounded just a tad uncertain as he continued. "I don't have the teaching position nailed down yet, but I'll figure that out one way or another. In the meantime, I work with my brothers at the bar. Cole bought it long ago so he could support us all, give us jobs as we got older. I worked there to pay my way through college, as did Zane. Now that we're getting other jobs, Cole and Chase have expanded and hired a few outside people. You'll love the place. It's incredibly popular, especially with the women, but it also has a nice family atmosphere."

Talking was impossible. Even swallowing was too hard to manage. Jessica launched herself against him, squeezing him tight. "Mack, I'm so sorry. I've been so wrong about you."

He rolled onto his back and held her close. "Ah, babe, don't cry. Please."

"You're the most amazing man and I don't deserve you."

"Now there's where you're wrong. Tell me you won't boot me out, honey. I'm in an agony of suspense here."

She kissed his face, his ear, his throat. Mack moaned, so she continued, and then she moaned too because he tasted so good she wanted to kiss him all over.

"Is this a yes, Jessica?" His voice shook and his hand held her head as she kissed his belly. "Does this mean we can have an honest-to-goodness relationship? You'll quit expecting me to be some kind of bum you can't depend on?"

Her hand wrapped around his throbbing erection and she kissed his navel. "Yes," she whispered. And in the next instant, Mack had her beneath him, kissing her, exciting her. *Loving her*.

EPILOGUE

Mack barely got in the door before Trista leaped up, waving her report card in front of his face. "I got three A's," she yelled, and Mack, so proud he thought he'd burst, lifted her up for a massive hug. When he set her back down, she stayed glued to his side and walked with him down the hallway as he perused her report card.

"Three A's and three B's." He put an arm around her and smiled. "I sure hope you're proud of yourself, especially since one of those A's is in science."

Her braces shone brightly when she grinned and confided, "I got the highest score on my science project. Higher than Brian's!"

He couldn't help but laugh. Then Jessica was there, her hair loose down her back, swishing around her hips, distracting him. Just the way she knew he liked it.

"Hey, babe." He leaned forward for a kiss, which she freely gave. God, he loved being greeted this way. "You don't have a shoot right now?"

"Nope. I took the rest of the afternoon off."

His brows lifted. "Oh ho. Any special reason?"

"Yes, but first, how did your day go?"

He realized she was anxious, worried about him on his first day back, and his love doubled. He tossed a few papers on the coffee table in the waiting room and dropped into a chair. "It was great—except for the principal poking her nose in every hour to check up on me."

Jessica perched on his lap, affronted on his behalf. "She didn't!"

"She did. Seems that even though she gave in to the parents' demands to have me back, she's still not happy about it. But I also got a visit from the head of the school board, and he told me they're behind me one hundred percent, so I'm not going to let the principal get me down. Especially now that I know the parents won't hesitate to lobby in my defense." He grinned shamefully, still amazed that the parents had taken on the school board to get him back.

Trista leaned forward and in a low tone meant to mimic his own, said, "Well, I hope you're proud of yourself."

"Come here," he growled, and pulled her onto the arm of the chair, close to his side. In the past few weeks, he'd grown to love Trista like she was his own. And she treated him as naturally as if he'd been around forever.

Mack couldn't imagine being any happier than he was now. Since he had been with Jessica, time had gone by like a dream. The parents of his students had organized and appealed to the school board, which had gotten him hired in the position he wanted, despite the principal's continued opposition. Sophie's catalogue, delivered in time for the Valentine's Day sale, had proved a huge hit. The women swamped her boutique every day now, and the main topic was the model. But with Jessica's insistence, all the photos had been cropped, so only Mack's body was visible. She'd gotten very huffy over the idea of other women knowing it was him in the racy loungewear, once she'd staked a claim.

Zane found the whole situation beyond hilarious.

"So what's your good news?" He toyed with a long lock of Jessica's hair, knowing that she'd left it loose for him.

"I'm going to be shooting another catalogue—this one for kids' clothing."

She looked so pleased with herself he kissed her again, making Trista giggle.

She pulled away with a sigh. "I also heard from the church today. Our wedding date is set. June sixth."

"It's official?" He had to hide his excitement. His damn nosy sisters-in-law had been insistent that Jessica deserved a big wedding this time around. He didn't mind that, because he would do anything to make her happy. But every time they'd come up with a date, they'd run into a glitch. He was beginning to think the Winston curse would fail him.

She looped her arms around his neck and said, "*Everything* is official for June sixth—the hall, the flowers, the dress, the guests, everything. Sophie will have the baby around the end of March, and Allison isn't due until November. The only problem, and it's only a tiny one, is Zane."

"What the hell has Zane got to do with this?"

"Well, your brother keeps complaining about a Winston curse, and he says if he comes to the wedding, it's liable to get him. But I know you want him there. . . ."

Mack laughed and hugged her close. "Don't worry about my damn brother. He'll be there, probably with bells on. And I have no doubt he's up to tackling any curse there is."

Trista tilted her head at him and leaned close, fascinated by the talk of curses. "Did you tackle the curse, Mack?"

He touched the end of her nose and grinned. "No, honey. I welcomed it with open arms."

Wild

To my agent, Karen Solem.
Your drive, energy, and vision matches my own.
Everything you contribute is very greatly appreciated.

ONE

"I want you."

The suggestive, husky whisper stroked over Zane Winston with the effect of a soft, warm kiss to his spine. It devastated his senses.

He froze, then clenched hard in reaction, his muscles tightening, his pulse speeding up. He nearly fell off the stepladder.

The motherboards balanced precariously in his arms started to drop, but Zane managed to juggle them safely at the last second.

He didn't want to look, didn't want to acknowledge that soft whisper. He knew without looking who had spoken to him. Still, as was generally the case where *she* was concerned, he couldn't *not* look.

His gaze sought her out, and found her standing a mere two feet away, her eyes downcast, her waist-length, black hair partially hiding her face like a thick, ebony curtain.

People shuffled through the small computer store, taking advantage of the sale he was running, grabbing at clearance items, storing up on disks. Yet no one bumped into her, no one touched her. Alone in the crowd, she stood to the side of his ladder, and Zane could feel her intense awareness of him. It sparked his own awareness until his breathing deepened, his skin warmed.

Damn it, that always happened when he was around her—which was one reason why he tried to avoid her.

She didn't say anything else, didn't even bother to look at him, so Zane went back to restocking the shelf. Perhaps he'd misunderstood. Perhaps he'd even imagined it all. He hadn't been sleeping well lately— or rather, he'd been sleeping too hard, dead to the world and caught up in lifelike, erotic dreams that left him drained throughout the day. He felt like a walking zombie—a *horny* walking zombie—because the dreams were based on scorching carnal activities.

With *her*.

Zane's computer business had done remarkably well the past year, and it required a lot of his attention. The location in the small strip mall was ideal. Her antiquated two-story building stood right next door, only a narrow alley away, and the scent of the sultry incense she burned often drifted in through the open door of his shop. Worse than that, the pulse-thrumming music she played could be heard everywhere, and it made his heart beat too fast. With all these distractions, concentrating on software and modems wasn't always easy, no matter his level of resolve. And now with the damn dreams plaguing him, his iron control was fractured.

His brothers had taken to heckling him, tauntingly accusing him of too much carousing. Zane didn't bother to correct them. No way would he tell them the truth behind his recent distraction—that his carousing had only been in his dreams, and his distraction was a little Gypsy he didn't even find appealing.

Especially since he was determined to deny any such distraction.

The last thing he needed was a face-to-face visit with her.

Though he wasn't looking at her, Zane felt her inch closer; he was aware of her all along his length, in his every pore, even in the air he breathed. The ladder had him several feet above her, which placed her face—her mouth—on a level with his lap. *Damn damn damn*. He tensed, waiting, and more images drifted into his mind.

"*I want you*," she repeated, a little louder but still low enough that no one seemed to notice.

He hadn't imagined it.

Anger erupting, Zane glared down at her, this time catching and holding her dark, mystical gaze. Her long, coal-black lashes fluttered, but she didn't look away from him. Staring into her eyes, he felt her thoughts and emotions invading his mind. Her nervousness touched him bone deep; the way she forced herself to remain still affected him, too.

How the hell did she manage to toy with him so easily? It outraged Zane, left him edgy and hot and resentful. Despite what some of his female associates might think, he was always the pursuer, not the pursued. He subtly controlled every intimate relationship, took only what he needed, gave only as much as he wanted, and no more.

Zane realized he was breathing too hard, reacting to her on an innate level. Deliberately he jammed the boxes of motherboards onto the shelf before climbing down the ladder.

Facing her, his arms folded over his chest, he did his best to intimidate her while hiding his discomfort. He needed her to leave. He needed to stop thinking about her.

He was nearly certain his needs didn't matter to her in the least.

"What do you want?" He sounded rude to his own ears, obnoxious and curt. But this was a battle for the upper hand, and he intended to do his best to win.

Her full lips, painted a shiny dark red, were treated to a soft, sensual lick of uncertainty. Filled with tenacity, her gaze wavered, then returned to his. Her chin lifted. "As I said, I want . . . you."

God, she'd said it again. This time straight out, to his face. Zane braced himself against the lure of her brazenness and her bold request. She looked like walking sex, like a male fantasy—*his fantasy*—come to life. He would *not* let her suck him in with obvious ploys.

"For what?" *There*, he thought, *deal with that, Miss Gypsy*. And she *was* a Gypsy, no doubt about it. He almost believed the signs, painted in the front window of her shop, that claimed she could read palms and predict the future. The signs, backlit by the eerie glow of a red lamp and dozens of flickering candles inside, also said she could cast spells and enlighten your life.

It was the spell-casting part that made Zane most uncertain. After all, he was familiar with curses firsthand. And he didn't like them worth a damn. At least, not when applied to himself. For his brothers it had worked out just fine. Better than fine. *For his brothers*.

Agitated, she shifted her feet, and the tinkling of tiny bells rose above the noise of the crowd. Zane found himself staring at her small feet beneath a long gauze skirt of bold colors and geometric designs. The skirt was thin and would be transparent if she stood in the right light.

Luckily for his peace of mind, they were more in the shadows than not. But that didn't stop him from imagining what he couldn't see. And it pissed him off that he could guess just how she'd look.

Twin ankle bracelets of miniature silver bells had produced the music when she moved. Dainty silver rings with intricate designs circled her painted toes.

On her hands, each finger was adorned with a silver, pewter, or gold ring. A multitude of bracelets with inlaid colored stones hung on her slender wrists and jingled when she clasped her hands together.

Around her neck, and disappearing into the neckline of her midnight blue peasant blouse, were strands of small beads: jet black, bright amber, ruby red.

He noticed the necklaces, then immediately noticed that she wasn't wearing a bra. Her breasts lay soft and full beneath her blouse.

An invisible fist squeezed Zane's lungs, stealing the oxygen from his body, making him light-headed. For God's sake, they were only breasts—and not all *that* impressive. But he could see the faint outline of her nipples beneath the dark, thin material, and it set him on fire.

He wanted to curse, but that would give too much away, so he refrained.

When he took a deep breath, trying to relieve some of his tension, that musky, earthy scent of incense filled his head. He stared at her hard, intent on keeping his gaze on her face. "I'm waiting."

She glanced at the surrounding crowd. Her large, heavily lined eyes looked mysterious and sensual. No one paid any attention to them. She said low, "I want you for sex."

Her gaze melted into his, touching his soul, reawakening those hot, taunting dreams that had plagued him nightly. In his sleep, he'd already taken her every way known to man. Now she offered to let the dream become reality.

Breathing was too damn difficult. He was nearly panting.

"I want you," she boldly continued, fanning the flames, "to share your body with me, and let me give you mine."

Slowly, hypnotically, she lowered her lashes and added, with a small shrug, "That's all."

That's all? That's all. Urgency throbbed through his veins, as if he'd spent hours on leisurely, detailed foreplay. Zane wanted to smack her.

Even more than that, he wanted to drag her into the backroom and lift her long, flirty skirt and take the body she so willingly offered. He wanted to inhale her scent, wanted to taste her in all her hottest, sweetest places. And he wanted to bury himself deep inside her.

Damn it all, he had a hard-on to end all hard-ons, and here he stood in the middle of his shop with hordes of people ready to spend money and purchase his wares.

Nostrils flared, and with as much disdain as he could muster, given his acute state of arousal, Zane growled, "Thanks, but no thanks."

Her gaze clashed with his, startled, upset. Her lips drew in, got caught by her teeth, and color scalded her cheeks. She took two slow breaths, then asked in a wavering voice, "You're certain you're not interested?"

He was so damn interested it wouldn't have taken much more than a few touches to make him insane. Zane locked his knees, clenched his fists, and hardened his resolve. "Positive."

Her long, silky hair hung to her thighs as she bowed her head. For a suspended moment, Zane feared she might actually cry—or cast a hideous spell on him. He wasn't entirely sure which would be worse. Not that he normally believed in such things as spells and incantations. But there was the Winston curse. He believed in it, had seen its effects on his brothers as one by one they'd been caught and married off. Happily.

One curse per family was more than enough. Little Gypsy could just take her mesmerizing voice and her intrusive sexuality and leave him the hell alone. He liked his life just as it was, just as he'd made it.

Without looking at him again, she turned and left. Her departure struck him like a punch in the gut. She hadn't been crying, he thought with concern, but she'd been so silent. . . .

Oh, hell, she was always silent. She used it as part of her mystique. He refused to be drawn in by her and her feminine cunning and what amounted to no more than theatrics to shore up her ruse as a Gypsy.

The gentle, enticing sway of her skirts as she slowly retreated held his attention. She might be leaving, but her scent remained, circling around him, filling his head and his heart. Her effect remained, too, keeping him hot and tight and far too aware of his physical needs. And that last look on her face remained, making him curse himself for being such a bastard.

He was good with women, damn it. *Great* with women, in fact. He always treated them gently, whether he was interested or not. So why the hell had he been so rude to her? Why had he felt compelled to grind her down with his rejection? He'd been out to prove . . . what? That she didn't affect him after all?

Zane snorted at that. The tent in his pants proved otherwise, no matter his behavior toward her.

Now that she was gone, only the essence of her remaining without the threat of her appeal, he was ashamed of himself.

A customer touched his arm, causing him to jump. With great effort Zane brought his mind back to the job at hand. Even with two employees in to help, they were swamped. The line at the register was long and continuous. People had questions, and the shelves constantly had to be restocked. He couldn't afford to be distracted by his witchy neighbor. He would run the register—where he could hide his arousal behind the counter—and do his job.

But for the rest of the day, she lingered in his mind, an unwelcome invasion that kept him jittery and taut, the same way he felt when he'd gone too long without sex.

He hated what he knew he would have to do.

But since he was resigned to doing it, he'd damn well put himself in charge. No more letting her toy with him, no more letting her overwhelm his senses. It was Thursday, the weekend fast approaching. He'd have time to spend with her, and on her. And if anyone would be overwhelmed, it'd be her.

That thought finally had Zane smiling.

In anticipation.

Tamara Tremayne flipped over the CLOSED sign in the front door of her shop and turned all the locks. Luna, her assistant, had left an hour ago. Her relatives had called a few times but hadn't come by, which was strange. But she was thankful for the quiet. She was finally alone.

For a moment, she leaned her forehead against the glass in the door and looked at the FOR SALE sign stuck in the scraggly strip of lawn in front of the old building.

She didn't want to sell, but she had no choice.

Walking around the shop, she pinched out the many candles she always kept lit, and snuffed out the stems of incense that continued to smolder, filling the air with sweetness. Smoke clung to the ceiling, giving added ambience to the small shop with its colorful cloths over every tabletop and the glittering beads on lampshades and curtain trims. A dark drape separated her reception area from the two small rooms she used for her sessions. She pushed it aside and made sure all the lamps were turned off.

One of her favorite estate sale finds, a polished, curving mahogany countertop with ornate trim, concealed the traditional and quite modern CD player. Tamara clicked it off, killing the sensually stimulating New Age music. It felt like her heartbeat died with the last strumming note. The silence lay heavy in the air.

As she strolled away, feeling lazy and defeated, Tamara trailed her hand over a large crystal ball, wishing it could, indeed, predict the future, wishing she could see if Zane Winston would ever give her the time of day. But the beautiful glass was empty. And she already had all the answers she needed.

Thanks, but no thanks.

Four little words had never hurt quite so much. Each one had felt like a sharp dart piercing her heart, stealing her breath, making her lungs constrict. They'd dashed her dreams, her fantasies. They gave her nothing to look forward to but a continuation of the long, sexually frustrating nights and her endlessly hopeful dreams.

Zane was known for his seduction successes. Out of the four Winston brothers, Zane was the most blatantly sexual, the most outrageous, the most . . . wanted. At least by the ladies. There was an earthy wildness about him, a primal masculinity that drew women in, a hot sexuality that kept them coming back.

Intelligent, driven, Zane was, in her mind, the most handsome of the brothers. And that was saying a lot, considering the Winstons were a virile and sinfully gorgeous clan.

Cole, the oldest, struck her as the most somber. He took his responsibilities seriously and loved with a depth of emotion Tamara had never seen before. And she didn't need to be a mind reader to figure that out. It was there on his face whenever he looked at his brothers, and especially when he looked at his wife or his new baby boy.

It was a look that made her long for things she'd never have—a husband, a family of her own. A normal life.

Tamara had visited the Winston Tavern a few times, and she loved it there. She loved blending in with the rest of society as if she were just a woman running a shop, just a woman out for a relaxing evening.

Not a Tremayne.

Not a Gypsy.

She had so little time for socializing or frivolity.

Chase, the second oldest, was the bartender, and she'd seen

through him right away. Tamara smiled. She wasn't a true psychic, as her advertisement claimed. She couldn't read minds, just as she couldn't predict the future. But she was much more intuitive than most people. Throughout her life, there had been certain people whose emotions were clearer to her. Generally, she thought them to be people with acute feelings: loving with their whole heart, or hating with fanaticism.

The Winstons, with their zest for life and open honesty, were often quite clear to her. Chase gave the impression of being quiet and serene, but he was a deeply sensual person and very erotic, maybe even bordering on kinky. His quiet persona hid some of his fire, but Tamara could see the heat in his gaze, and knew that his thoughts regularly focused on the sexual. Luckily, his wife was the perfect match.

Tamara liked Mack Winston the best. He was the youngest, the most playful, a man who knew how to laugh and have a good time. She'd watched him at the bar, moving from table to table, a smile always on his face. He saw joy in everything and everyone, especially those he called family. You couldn't be near Mack and not smile, too.

Yes, she liked Mack best, but it was Zane she wanted.

Even though his driving sexuality scared her just a bit—or maybe *because* it did—she wanted him. She wanted him so much she could barely sleep at night. She'd lie awake for hours, imagining all the ways Zane might want to make love, and all the ways she could enjoy him. Sometimes the dreams were so real, almost as if he were with her, guiding her, telling her what he liked and how he liked it, showing her what she'd like, too.

In her heart, she knew dreams would never compare with the reality.

For the few years that his shop had been there, Tamara had watched Zane open in the mornings, and close at night. She'd watched women fawn all over him. She'd gotten to know his brothers better just by observation, and she'd gotten to know Zane better, too.

He was an overachiever, though he'd never admit it. He preferred the label "playboy." He was a combination of his brothers' better traits with a naughty, rambunctious streak thrown in, a man who prided himself on individuality, a man who struggled to be his own boss in all ways—but especially with women.

When she'd turned eighteen, Tamara had known it was time to settle down, to lay claim to a location and make it her own. The old building had appealed to her on several levels; not only was it perfect for her shop, but the living quarters upstairs were quaint and cozy. She'd been there for six years now.

In that time, she'd seen other shops in the adjacent strip mall try to make a go of it, but they were never able to stay afloat for long.

Zane hadn't let the failures of others keep him from trying. He'd taken the empty store and quickly made a success of a fledgling computer business. He sold products and did repairs, and even built computers to customers' specifications. He worked long hours, sometimes far into the night. From her bedroom window above the shop, Tamara had seen his lights on past midnight. Yet he'd be there bright and early the next morning, looking sexy as ever and not in the least worn down.

He must have incredible stamina, she thought, then shivered as a lustful fever crept into her bloodstream. She'd never get to know, because Zane didn't want her at all. Any other woman might have had a better chance. For some reason, he'd taken an immediate dislike to her. Even over the past year, as she'd tried to be friendlier, that hadn't changed.

Shaking herself out of her melancholy, Tamara pulled a long, thin chain decorated at the end with a silver finial displaying a couple entwined in a sensual embrace. It was another of her finds that added to the mystical illusion of the shop.

The mellow, overhead light flicked off, leaving the shop in moonlight and shadows as she made her way to the back stairs and her apartment above. There was also an outside entrance, but Tamara rarely used it unless she went out at night. Tonight, all she wanted to do was shower and go to bed and try to figure out where she'd gone wrong with Zane. The software manuals she usually worked on in the evening to give added income to the family and to help add balance to her crazy lifestyle, could wait. It looked like she might have the whole weekend to sit at home and work on them.

She wanted to read the journal again, to see if she'd somehow mistaken the instructions. It had seemed so clear-cut, almost guaranteed to work. But not for her. Not for a Tremayne.

Even before Tamara had opened the door at the top of the stairs, she knew the book—and all her fantasies—would have to wait.

The family was there to visit.

She had given Olga a key ages ago, to be used only in an emergency. To the Tremaynes, everything constituted an emergency, and now they felt at ease to let themselves in whenever they wanted. With her family of self-proclaimed black sheep, counterfeit clairvoyants, and bona fide con artists, visits were seldom a casual thing. They usually meant that the family had ganged up on her with the intent of making her change her mind about something.

Not that they could. She'd been running the family since her sixteenth year, but not necessarily by choice. Someone had to do it.

Pinning a fat smile on her face, Tamara pulled the door open and said with false enthusiasm, "Uncle Thanos! Aunt Eva! Aunt Olga!"

Aunt Eva, at age seventy, the oldest in the group, and the most dramatic by far, was the only one who didn't still help out in the shop on occasion. She visited it, but usually just to criticize. She said, "So we are selling. We're being run out by demons!"

Uncle Thanos, his voice booming to match his great size, disagreed with Eva's sentiment. "It's a good thing to sell! Things'll be changing again. Finally, adventure, excitement, new travels. I'm more than ready."

Both Eva and Olga nodded, and Olga admitted, "It's for the best. We're not meant for the dormant life."

Tamara shook her head as she began removing all her jewelry and placing it on the small mahogany entrance table. So Thanos wanted to move? Ha! Getting the three of them packed up and mobile again would be a chore. Just thinking about it gave Tamara a pounding headache.

Despite the image they liked to project, her relatives were no longer the wandering Gypsies of her youth. As a child, she'd lived in more places than most people did in their entire lives. Tamara had always been grateful to them for raising her after her parents had died. They'd taken her in without hesitation, given her love and laughs, if not stability. Living with them had provided an interesting education.

But Tamara knew for a fact that they liked the settled, mostly sedate lifestyle she'd been able to give them since she'd become an adult. They took turns working with her in the shop, mostly on the busier weekends, and that was about as much excitement as they could handle these days.

Thanos now preferred to tend the tiny garden behind the house she'd bought for them, and amazingly enough, Eva and Olga knitted. They hid their projects from her, but Tamara still knew. She always knew what was going on when it came to her family.

Just as she knew their visit was for bluster. They didn't want to move, but they tried to hide that from her. And Tamara loved them all the more for their consideration.

Aunt Olga, so thin she looked like she could be folded away, announced in tones of premonition, "It's Uncle Hubert. He hasn't forgiven us for not forewarning him of his imminent death." Her frail hands covered her face. "Now we've angered him. You're right, Tamara. We must go. Before it's too late."

Tamara dropped back against the wall, so tired she wanted to collapse. Her colored contacts were starting to burn, and the ridiculous sandals pinched her beringed toes.

In as reasonable a voice as she could muster, she said, "Uncle Hubert died months ago. It was a freak accident, certainly not something we could have predicted."

"It was an omen," Olga cried.

If it had been an omen, Tamara thought with a smirk, someone had a warped sense of humor, because Hubert had expired at an outdoor concert when a vicious storm had overturned the portable toilet in which he was seated. He'd sustained a hard hit to the head and a true blow to his dignity, considering his pants had been around his ankles at the time.

"He was on the West Coast," Tamara reasoned. "We're in Kentucky. It wouldn't make much sense for Hubert to come all this way just for a little haunting over something we had no control over. Besides, it's not like we hadn't all warned him that he needed to quit partying so much. One less concert, one less drink, one less groupie, and he might have still been with us."

The wig tickled and without caring what her relatives might think, Tamara pulled it off and vigorously ruffled her short blond hair. Immediately her head began to feel better.

At least it did until Aunt Olga objected to Tamara's rationale.

"Mind powers," Olga insisted, "aren't affected by distance. Ghosts can damn well go wherever they please!"

Throwing up her arms in a display of frustration, Tamara stalked away. None of them had mind powers, much as they'd like to convince themselves otherwise, so there was no way they could have warned Hubert. Hubert knew it, so he had no reason to haunt them.

No, their troubles were rooted in a flesh-and-blood human, not a ghostly manifestation. But not knowing why anyone wanted to cause them trouble was what really bothered Tamara. So far as she knew, she had no enemies, and neither did her relatives. They were cons, but they were harmless cons. And it wasn't like the shop would be of value to anyone but a group of sentimental, aging Gypsies.

"I'm going to shower," she called over her shoulder, needing a few minutes of solace to shore herself up for the rest of the visit. She knew the relatives were night owls, and they wouldn't think twice about keeping her up so they could continue to lament the supposed haunting. "I'll be back in a minute."

More objections followed her down the short hall. Her living quarters consisted of a family room that opened to the outside stairs on one wall, and to the stairwell leading down to her shop on another. Next to that, separated by an arched doorway, was the kitchen, which also opened onto an L-shaped hallway. To the right was the part of the house she'd closed off. To the left was another short hallway that led to her bedroom and the bath.

Tamara could hear the buzz of the aunts grumbling, along with Thanos's booming contribution, but the closing of the bathroom door mostly drowned them out. Despite her dejection over failing with Zane, a small smile touched Tamara's mouth. *Her demented family.* She should have known they'd find a way to dramatize the problems with the shop and their grief for Hubert. They lived to put on a show.

She loved them so much, even if they were all nuts. And perhaps their visit was propitious after all. She certainly couldn't pine for Zane while dealing with her relatives' extravagant tales of vaporish ghosts and spurious hauntings.

But even as Tamara tried to convince herself of that, her body warmed with the mere thought of Zane. She wanted him, needed him.

One way or another, she'd have to figure out how to have him before the house sold and she left town. She'd study the manual in minute detail until she found a way to win Zane over.

She deserved at least that much.

Twilight had come and gone by the time Zane locked up the store for the night. It had been a great sale, very successful, and he was pleased. So why did he still feel so on edge?

Little Gypsy.

The large, ancient building housing her shop on the ground floor sat across the alley from the newer, more modern strip mall. Zane turned and, as usual, there was a light on in her upstairs window, the room he somehow knew was her bedroom. His stomach tightened, his muscles loosened, his body warmed.

They were extreme reactions that he couldn't control, and he hated that. In part, he'd avoided her for that very reason. She got close, and he felt it in his every nerve ending. He couldn't bear it; it smacked of a weakness he refused to accept.

Even as he told himself that he wouldn't allow her to get to him, he wondered what she'd look like stripped of those ridiculous long skirts and colorful blouses. Her hair was so long, it could easily cover her nudity. And that in itself was hotly erotic.

Except that he didn't like her hair. Normally long hair was a turn-on for Zane, the ultimate in femininity. But on the Gypsy, it seemed overdone, too much along with everything else. Her hair was thick and straight and inky black—and didn't suit her at all.

Without intending to, he walked toward the building, his hands on his hips, his head tilted to stare up at that lit window. He was diagonal with the front of the shop when he noticed the sign.

Zane stared at the bold black words FOR SALE for a long minute, refusing to believe what his eyes told him. She was moving away? Leaving for good?

"Shit." He stood there, feeling dazed and angry as the night breeze drifted over his heated skin, ruffling his hair, fogging his breath. He shook his head, a sharp, decisive movement. "No!" His voice sounded ominous in the quiet of the night with all the shops closed, the street mostly empty. It was an apt reflection of the turbulence smothering him. "*Hell, no.*"

With a hard stride, Zane started toward the stairs at the side of the house. He'd prove to himself and to her that *he* was in control; no curse or spell—*no small Gypsy*—could make him do things he didn't want to do, or feel things he didn't want to feel. He wouldn't allow it.

Determined, even a little anxious, he took the metal steps two at a time. What he'd say to her, he had no idea, but by God she wasn't going to walk away without a few explanations.

Like how the hell she'd managed to get into his head when he didn't even know her name.

And how she could dare to proposition him in the middle of a busy sale, as if she'd been asking what time it was. He'd known a lot of bold women, and appreciated them for that very quality. But what the little Gypsy had done really crossed the line.

And now she dared to invade his dreams, to the point that he couldn't sleep anymore for craving her.

If she had cast a spell, she could damn well uncast it.

That's what he'd tell her. That and a little more, like how she was far too brazen, and how she grated on his nerves even from a distance.

And how he wanted her, too.

Each footfall on her steps clanged louder and louder, until Zane was literally stomping up to her door, the stairs rattling and shifting beneath his feet. He lifted one fist, rapped hard, and waited. He didn't realize he was holding his breath until he saw the curtain covering the door window move, and a pale face peeked out.

The curtain dropped immediately.

Anticipation, charged and smoldering, sizzled in the humid evening air. It shot through his veins and made his skin prickle. Zane sucked in a deep breath, and he was just about to knock again, through with waiting, when he heard the lock click.

The door opened a crack and a thin, small, blond woman slipped out, pulling the door shut tight behind her. The landing at the top of the stairs was narrow, partially covered by a thick welcome mat. They stood close by necessity, her nose even with his throat, her hands still behind her, clutching the doorknob.

In utter silence, Zane looked her over. She wore slim jeans faded nearly white, a loose, untucked shirt, and no jewelry.

He didn't understand, didn't know who she was or why she was staying with the Gypsy—and then the breeze shifted and her scent, hot and sultry and compelling, filled him up and he went rigid.

The sweet smell of incense was gone, but the more basic aroma of woman remained, unique and tempting. Like any alert male animal, Zane drew it in, savored it, and recognized her by scent alone. Confusion swamped him, and then she looked up at him.

Large, dark green eyes fringed by impossibly long brown lashes ensnared him. Even the air he breathed seemed heated.

Zane shook his head. He knew, and yet he whispered, "Who the hell are you?"

"Tamara." She released the doorknob and shifted nervously. Her gaze never left his; like him, he doubted she could look away. "Tamara Tremayne."

Zane watched a soft, pale curl blow across her cheek. She quickly tucked it behind her small ear. His heartbeat stuttered.

"I'm sorry," she murmured, "I never introduced myself properly. Then again, you never really gave me the chance." Her voice was shaky, husky, and oh so familiar.

Zane watched her lush mouth move, now clean of the shiny red lipstick. The corners tilted up in an uncertain smile that he felt clean down to his groin.

Jesus. He knew lust, knew what it felt like, had wallowed in the intensity of it, the fiery pleasure of it.

This was something more.

This was so damn powerful he shook.

"Tamara." He touched her cheek, still staring into her eyes, unable to look away for more than a few seconds at a time. She looked so different. His mind was alert to deception, not understanding why or how she'd changed so quickly, but his body had immediately known her—and reacted to her. The erection he'd fought since her visit to the store was back in full force, straining against his slacks.

Tremulous, she smiled again, and that was all it took. She was as irresistible as the air he dragged into his lungs. Zane meant to kiss her gently, to let her get used to his deep sensuality and his agreement to her proposition by small degrees.

It didn't quite happen that way.

As he leaned toward her, her lips parted, and with a groan Zane took her, his mouth hungry, starving. She made a small sound of surprise, of acceptance, and her eagerness licked over him. He felt ready to ignite with the pleasure of it.

Insane, he insisted to himself, even as he held her face still and, with one hard move, pinned her to the door with his hips. She was small, delicate, *pretty* . . . and she tasted better than anything he could remember. Her mouth was sweet and damp, her tongue stroking against his, accepting his, as eager as his own yet less practiced.

Her hands clutched the front of his shirt, then drifted lower to his waist, sliding slow and easy, exploring with a hunger that fueled his own. As if relishing the feel of him, her fingers spread and her small, hot hands teased. Zane threw his head back, panting, praying she'd touch him where he craved it most, trying to encourage her to do so.

And the door opened behind them.

Zane tried to catch her, but his sluggish brain was slow to react, his body too overheated to be cooperative. Tamara fell flat with a small yelp, and Zane tripped over her. He was barely able to keep from landing on top of her, smashing her into the carpet. He stumbled hard against an enormous solid object, and then was lifted off his feet and dangled in the air.

Confused, he stared down into the most ferocious face he'd ever seen on human or animal.

The man—if this was a man and not a damned yeti—sported a full, black bushy beard, a gold earring in one ear that matched a gold front tooth; his eyes were black as midnight.

Mean black eyes.

Immediately concerned for Tamara and intent on protecting her, Zane reacted on instinct. He brought his knee up in a sharp, solid blow, forcing the giant to gasp and drop him. As the man bent forward, holding his gut and wheezing, Zane grabbed him by his bushy head, ready to bring his knee up again, this time to smash a nose or break a jaw.

Zane's leg flexed, readying for impact—and something wiry jumped onto his back, clawlike fingers digging in for a good hold.

Twisting around, Zane saw a small, wrinkled face, wild, gray hair pulled loose from a bun, and another set of fathomless ebony eyes. Their gazes locked; the wizened face scrunched up, then let out a screeching war cry that made the skin on Zane's body crawl and his eardrums reverberate with pain.

Before he could figure out how to get the demon off his back, Tamara had crawled around in front of him. She threw her arms around his thighs and pressed her face to his abdomen.

"Don't hurt him, Thanos!" she pleaded.

Don't hurt him? Indignant, Zane heard her words, and everything male in him rebelled. *He* was protecting *her*, not the other way around! Hadn't he already felled the giant? Why the hell was she worried for him? Or was Thanos a name for the witch on his back, yanking at his hair and bellowing into his ear until he thought he'd go deaf?

It was a miracle he could think at all with Tamara on her knees in front of him. Her supplicating position registered with the force of a thunderclap, and he nearly lost awareness of everything else. Even the pain in his scalp as the witch continued to yank on his head couldn't quite dispel the lascivious images.

Through the cotton of his pants, Zane could have sworn he felt the warmth of her breath.

Damn, he was in deep.

Zane touched the back of her head with one hand, amazed at how soft her blond curls felt, and heard her say in an evil voice, "I mean it, Uncle. Put the cane down."

Cane? Zane looked up from Tamara, still in her imploring position, and observed that the giant now held a cane in one meaty fist, and the cane had a lethal blade on the end. He was also rubbing his stomach where Zane had kneed him, and he looked mad as hell.

Oh, shit.

Well, yeah, maybe he could use her intervention after all, especially since she seemed to know these lunatics.

"Tamara?" He deliberately tried to ignore the heaving behemoth ready to skewer him, despite Tamara's pleas. Zane tangled his fingers in her hair and urged her face up to his.

She blinked at him, and those green eyes nearly did him in once again. *Green, not black.* "Yes?"

Uncertain how to deal with such an overwhelming craving, Zane concentrated instead on the bizarre circumstances. "Do you think you can get this monkey off my back? I prefer my hair to stay on my head, rather than being strewn around the floor."

Gasping, Tamara leaped to her feet. She snatched the cane away from Thanos—*thank God she, at least, was thinking straight*—and ran behind Zane to remove the old lady who grasped him so tenaciously. It took Tamara a few minutes to get the old woman to disengage, and during that time, Zane lost a little more hair, even while he tried to hold perfectly still.

Thanos no longer held the cane, but he looked more than capable of removing body parts with his bare, hamsized hands. Zane silently took the giant's measure; he didn't want to hurt anyone unless he was forced to.

"Aunt Olga," Tamara scolded in that beguiling voice he knew all too well, "what were you thinking, attacking him that way? You could have been hurt."

Olga waved a fistful of hair. "Ha!"

It was a cry of triumph. Zane rubbed his head and winced. He was lucky he wasn't bald.

Somehow he'd walked into a circus. Tamara wasn't Tamara anymore; she was better, and more mysterious than ever. And she had giants and witches for relatives. The best thing to do would be to walk right back out, to forget this day had ever happened.

But he wasn't a weak-spined coward, ready to turn tail and run at the first sign of mental instability. So her relatives were certifiable? He wouldn't let that stop him. Not when there was something, or someone, he wanted.

And right now, at this moment, he wanted Tamara Tremayne bad. That fact had been driven home to him in no uncertain terms.

Even in the midst of bedlam, he was aware of the vibrating tension in his muscles, and the sexual fever pulsing in his blood. He was too drawn to her to walk away now. But he could handle things his own way, refusing to give her the upper hand.

Zane raised one brow, keeping a close eye on Thanos-the-missing-link, and said, "Tamara, would you mind telling me what the hell is going on here?"

The giant stepped forward and thundered, "You were mauling her! We all saw you."

Zane couldn't very well deny that, because he had been all over her—never mind that she seemed to be going along with it, even enjoying herself. And perhaps doing a little mauling of her own.

Not since his second woman had Zane abandoned all finesse during a seduction, but with Tamara, for that brief moment, he'd been aware only of his need for her. Nothing else had registered. They'd been on a stair landing, for God's sake, but if no one had interrupted them, Zane suspected he'd have taken her right there, with only the night shadows to conceal their activity.

And from all indications, she'd have let him.

As he started to nod in assent, ready to accept the truth of Thanos's claims, Tamara gasped and said loudly, "I *wanted* him to."

That sure got things quiet.

While they all, Zane included, stood there staring at her with their mouths open, she asked, "What were you all doing watching, anyway? I specifically told you to give me a few minutes of privacy."

"Your apartment isn't big enough for privacy," Thanos told her.

"It's big enough if you don't press your nose to the door window and snoop."

Zane was surprised not only by what she said, but also her vehemence and the number of words she'd used to say it. In the time he'd known her, Tamara had managed to be mysteriously soft-spoken and far from chatty.

Olga, brushing Zane's hair from her hand, shrugged her narrow, frail shoulders. "We heard you hit the door. We thought he was attacking you."

Another woman, a bit older but looking just as mean, harrumphed as she came up next to Olga. "He *was* attacking her."

Olga narrowed her eyes. "Now that I think about it though, she didn't seem to be fighting him off."

Zane rubbed the back of his neck. This was too much for him. Way too much. It had been a long time since he'd had to deal with a woman's relatives. "Look, I'm sorry I jumped on her that way. I've never done that before."

Tamara took immediate offense. "Don't you dare apologize, Zane Winston. You didn't jump on me, you kissed me." She stepped closer to him, pointing that lethal cane at his chest. "And it was wonderful." Her fierce expression was enough to melt his insides.

Zane's libido stirred, and he fought to keep his responses at bay. Not here, not now. It had been bad enough dealing with an erection in the store, with swarms of customers moving around him. In front of her less than reasonable relatives, it would be impossible.

Zane didn't move except to let his eyes shift, taking in all the curious faces surrounding them. Thanos looked bemused. Olga and the other woman were pressed together, eyes wide, staring at Tamara.

"Uh . . ." Zane knew he had to regain control somehow. "Care to introduce me, Gypsy?" He figured if he was to be accosted and threatened and put on display, it should at least be on a first-name basis.

Tamara clapped a hand over her luscious mouth. "Ohmigosh. I'm sorry, Zane. Of course I should introduce everyone."

She stepped to his side and clasped his arm, providing a united front against the others. Zane refused to dwell on the emotions that her action stirred, how her stance pleased him. Plenty of women had stood at his side throughout his life, but none had ever seemed quite so *right* there. That realization disturbed him.

"Zane Winston," she said, now smiling, "this is my uncle, Thanos, and my aunts, Olga and Eva Tremayne."

The relationship was easy enough to see. Though they didn't look anything like Tamara now, they certainly looked like her when she wore her Gypsy getup. And while their eyes were black, and hers were green, the slanting, cat-eyes shape was the same.

"You called her Gypsy," Eva accused with a smile. She looked very pleased by it.

Zane shrugged. He wanted to touch Tamara again; he wanted to find out what the hell had happened with the long black hair, the penetrating black eyes. In the most basic ways, she was the same woman without the unusual clothes and makeup, yet she was also doubly intoxicating.

Now she seemed more real, more attainable, and that played havoc with his senses. She wasn't that gorgeous, and she certainly wasn't stacked. But she was still so intrinsically sexy that his temperature had automatically gone up three degrees the second he'd seen her.

He was starting to sweat.

"She claims to be one," Zane explained, and hoped he was the only one to notice the gravelly, aroused tone to his voice. "But seeing her like this, I have to wonder."

"There, you see," Olga said with satisfaction. "Without the right props, no one would know your heritage. You're far too fair, too slight, and plain. We were right. You need the enhancement."

Tamara frowned at Zane, and her eyes were lit with a touch of disappointment. At him?

"They insist I wear the dumb costume—"

"Not dumb," both women exclaimed, obviously appalled that she'd utter such sacrilege.

"—otherwise, I'm like the white sheep in the family."

Thanos shook his huge head and laughed. The windows rattled at his exuberance. "Little Gypsy, even without the costume, you're still a white sheep." To Zane he added, "She's too good, too tenderhearted. She has a conscience as big as the moon. How she came to be in our family is a miracle."

Eva added, "It's amazing she plays the game so well, considering her romantic nature."

"The game?"

Nodding, Eva said, "Fortune-telling, palm reading, and the rest."

Olga went on tiptoe to murmur into Zane's ear, "She comes from sure stock, yet doesn't like fooling people. Can you imagine?"

Zane wasn't exactly sure what they were all prattling on about, but he could feel Tamara's distress. He knew he was partly responsible, and regretted it. The last thing he wanted to do was hurt her.

Didn't these people—her own family—know they were upsetting her? It angered him, and made him feel not only protective, but defensive. They weren't emotions he normally associated with anyone other than his family. He frowned with that realization. "I'd like to talk to Tamara alone now, if you wouldn't mind."

Thanos barked a rough laugh. "It's not talking you have thoughts for, man. Your lust is there for all to see."

Olga sighed dreamily. "For our little Tamara."

"It's about time," Eva added.

About time? What the hell did that mean?

Tamara, her face coloring hotly, whirled on them all. Zane had never seen her angry, never heard her loud.

Never seen her blond.

"Don't any of you even *think* of interrupting me again, do you understand?" She pointed toward a hallway and said, "We're going to my room, and if I hear even a creak of a footstep"—her voice dropped to a demonic growl—"I'll make you all *so* sorry."

As far as threats went, it wasn't specific enough that Zane would have worried. She was one small woman. What could she possibly do to them?

Thanos gave her an approving nod, unmistakably pleased with her show of anger. "The Tremayne temper. She has it in spades."

The two old women twittered.

Exasperated, Tamara grabbed Zane by the arm and practically dragged him down the hall. He felt the gazes of her aunts and uncle boring into his back like fiery brands. Without any of them uttering a word, he heard *their* threats loud and clear, and they were a lot more specific than Tamara's had been.

If he hurt her, they *would* make him sorry.

Zane shook off his uneasiness. He was about to be alone with her, and that filled him with undeniable expectation; there was no room for anything else.

Tamara dragged him inside a room and shoved the door shut. Bright, overhead lighting, centered above a huge, modern computer desk, nearly blinded him, drawing his attention first.

She flipped a wall switch, and there was only moonlight filtering through her window, and light from one small lamp on a table beside her queen-size bed.

Zane stilled. He was in her bedroom. They were relatively alone. He looked at Tamara and caught her bewitching smile.

Oh, no. He wouldn't make it so easy on her. She'd led him in here, and now she was smiling at him, her eyes filled with promise. Teasing, taunting, using her Gypsy tricks and her curses. He was on to her.

Now was as good a time as any for him to take control. She claimed only to want sex. Fine. He'd give it to her, in abundance. He'd brand her in the best way known to man.

His gaze raked over her, seeing the thrust of her pretty breasts beneath her top, the gentle slope of her belly, and the curve of her hips in the snug jeans. There wouldn't be a single part of her he left untouched.

He'd see to it that she experienced the best damn sex she'd ever had. When all was said and done, she'd be as emotionally raw and hotly wired as he now felt.

Having made his decision, Zane gave Tamara his own slow smile, and watched her eyes widen in wariness. She swallowed, and said softly, "Oh, my."

Zane had the awful suspicion she'd just read his mind, and anticipated his intent.

Christ, what had he gotten himself into?

THREE

"Oh, my, what?" Zane demanded.

She licked her lips, tried for a negligent shrug, but her eyes told it all. She had beautiful, incredible eyes, the green much nicer than the darker contacts had ever been.

"I was . . . just . . ." She gestured with her hand. "You look so . . ." Clearing her throat, she said, "Never mind."

Refusing to let her see his unease, purposely shifting the mood, Zane glanced around the room and was amazed by what he saw. In direct contradiction to what he'd seen of her shop through the large front window, her private room was plain—and modern.

Neither the desk nor the computer fit his original image of her. As a Gypsy, she used candles and incantations as her tools, not a state-of-the-art computer complete with fax and scanner and copier. Yet the system arranged neatly on her desk was most impressive. Zane eyed it with appreciation, wondering what she did on that computer, if she'd learned to cast spells through the Internet.

There were no ornate fixtures or candles or lace overlays. No smoldering incense, no colored lights. Her bedspread was plain blue, her carpeting a solid beige, her furniture sturdy light oak in a style of clean, simple lines.

There was no clutter anywhere, nothing fancy, nothing exotic or seductive. It amazed Zane, and further confounded him.

This room matched her as she was now, a petite blonde scrubbed clean of makeup, barefoot, wearing well-worn jeans. An innocent earth child, and doubly sexy because of it.

Tamara took in his frown and stepped away. For the moment, Zane let her retreat, knowing if he reached for her, they'd be back at square one, with her body flush against his where he most wanted it to be. He needed some answers first; he needed to know her at least a little more.

Zane watched her pace the length of the airy room. She went to the window that faced his store and moved the curtains aside to look out. How many nights had she done that? How many nights had she watched him from that window? Maybe he'd felt her gaze, maybe that accounted for his sleepless nights and vivid dreams.

In a soft, agonized whisper, she said, "I'm so, so sorry."

Zane's chest constricted tightly at her low apology, at the embarrassment and upset he could hear in her tone. "For what?" he asked, keeping his tone gentle, hoping to soothe her, to gain her confidence.

"Everything." She shrugged helplessly. "Shocking you as I look now, letting my relatives attack you, even my bold proposition this afternoon."

Panic ripped through him, and he growled, "I won't let you take it back."

She turned to face him, lips parted in surprise.

In three long strides, Zane reached her. *"I won't let you take it back."* He clasped her shoulders, drew her up to her bare toes. "You said you wanted to sleep with me."

Her chest rose and fell, her eyes widened and glittered with moonlight. "I do."

"You said you wanted sex with me." Zane didn't want any misunderstandings. He wasn't sure he could survive a misunderstanding.

Tamara licked her lips slowly, cautiously. "Yes."

Rather than easing his tension, her confirmation drew him tighter until his every muscle strained and he could count the hard beats of his heart. Knowing he was close to losing it again, Zane forced his fingers to open, to release her, and he stepped away.

He felt like a damn fool. How did she keep doing this to him, pushing him over the edge, making him act like a man he didn't recognize? How did she make him so aware of her every thought and emotion, until they became his own? He didn't want any woman to affect him that deeply.

"Good." He gave a sharp nod. "Then that's settled."

"Is it?" She looked him over, taking in his features with a kind of hopefulness that nearly made him groan aloud. "Is it, really?"

"Oh, yeah." Zane couldn't quite get over his amazement at her appearance. He could have looked at her all night long and it wouldn't have been enough. "There's no backing out for you now."

Her blond curls bounced silkily as she shook her head. "I don't want to back out. I want you."

In that moment, Zane decided Tamara would have been a valuable addition to the Inquisition. "Damn, don't say that."

"Don't say . . . what?"

"That you want me." He scrubbed his hands over his face, paced up and down. "I don't know why, I don't understand this at all, but I'm hanging on by a thread." He stopped and glared at her. "A real thin thread."

Tamara came a tiny bit closer. It was too close. He could detect her scent again, and it called to him in some primal way, tightening his testicles, filling him with a surge of hunger until his vision blurred and narrowed on her features.

"You want me, too?" she asked.

Her naïveté would have made him laugh in different circumstances. Plainly visible if she only looked, his cock filled his pants, straining for release, straining for her. And even if she missed that rather obvious sign, lust was written all over his face. Hell, even Thanos had seen it, and that's when Zane had thought he was successfully hiding it.

"I want you," he confirmed, then added, "And I intend to have you, since you were gracious enough to offer."

"Thank you."

He knew women, knew all their tricks, all their ploys. But he had no idea what Tamara was up to—or, for that matter, who she really was. A blonde who pretended to have raven hair? A modern woman who gave the illusion of Old World values? A wild temptress who now looked too sweet to bear?

Slowly circling her, Zane studied Tamara from every angle. Wearing a loose pullover shirt and trim jeans, her blond hair mussed, her extreme makeup and the abundance of jewelry gone, she looked like innocence personified.

Yet she'd liked being mauled by him on the stairs when he'd only just learned her name. Her sexual nature matched his, or at least came close enough that she'd been as unaware of the surroundings as he had. All that had mattered was getting closer.

But there was something he was missing. Since he'd known her, which had always been in a peripheral way, Tamara had presented herself as a free-spirited Gypsy wrapped in mystery and superstition. Her clothes said as much. Her shop said as much. Her every smile and teasing glance said as much.

And now, by pure chance Zane had caught her looking entirely different. Not like a Gypsy siren, but like a damn schoolgirl.

"How old are you?" he asked abruptly, suddenly uncertain—she appeared so young, so inexperienced, so hopeful.

She tucked her fair hair behind her ears, inadvertently shoring up his perceptions, then said, "Twenty-four. And you?"

"Twenty-seven," Zane answered, distracted by his thoughts. She didn't look twenty-four. Of course, she hadn't really looked like a black-haired Gypsy, either. Perhaps that accounted for his edgy reaction to her. He'd suspected she was hiding behind a dark facade.

Would she have gone on deceiving him if he hadn't made his impromptu visit tonight?

Was she deceiving him even now?

"This is your natural look?" At her blank expression, he clarified. "The blond hair is natural?"

She touched her hair. "Yes."

"There are ways I can tell, you know."

Her brow lifted. "How?"

"When I see you naked."

She blinked at him, and then, as realization dawned, her face heated and her hand dropped to her side. "I'm a . . . a natural blonde."

Zane sensed her discomfort as he continued to circle her, continued to study her in minute detail. "I *will* see you naked, you know."

Nodding, she asked, "And I'll see you, too?"

Zane hesitated, taken aback by her question. "Did you think I made love fully dressed?"

"Have sex."

"What?"

He stood behind her, paused momentarily. She replied without looking at him. "We'll have sex, not make love. We . . . you and I barely know each other, so there won't be any love involved."

She annoyed him. Zane narrowed his eyes and said through his teeth, "Yeah, I'll be naked. And it's fine with me if you want to look your fill."

Again she said, "Thank you."

"I'll be looking my fill, too. Will you like that, Tamara?"

She nodded, but said, "I don't know."

Because she had something to hide? For certain she didn't have a shy bone in her luscious little body. Zane began circling again.

Her fair skin and glittering green eyes went along with the golden hair, so she was likely telling the truth about that. But he wasn't quite satisfied; there were too many things that didn't add up.

Would she have worn that black wig to bed with him when he made love to her? Would black eyes have smiled up at him when he was inside her, riding her slow, stroking deep?

Eyes like green fire watched him now, wide and wary at his prolonged silence. Zane stopped in front of her and smiled.

"Just like that?" he asked, keeping his voice silky and smooth. "You ask me to have sex with you, I agree, and you're . . . grateful?"

Her gaze wavered, embarrassed, then bravely came back to his. "Well, you did say no at first."

That wasn't the answer he had expected. It wasn't practiced or flirtatious or challenging. It was . . . honest.

It threw him off. Zane stared at the ceiling, trying to organize his thoughts. It was a mistake. Tamara took swift advantage of his preoccupation and moved against him. Her arms slipped around his waist, squeezed him tight.

"I've wanted you," she whispered, "since the first time I saw you."

His knees nearly gave out. "Did you cast a damn spell on me or something?" he growled, needing to know.

Her cheek rubbed his chest as she shook her head. "No. I can't do that." She glanced up at him. "But I probably would have if I was able."

Too much honesty, he decided. He wasn't used to it, didn't know how to deal with it. Thoughts warred with his instinct, and instinct won. He couldn't resist cuddling her closer. Everything about the embrace felt right: the way the heat of their bodies melded together, mingling their scents; how her head tucked neatly into his shoulder; how her breasts crushed against his ribs. And that bothered him even more. It shouldn't feel so right. No embrace had ever felt like this before.

If she hadn't done something magical to him, then what was going on?

"Why have you waited to say something?" Zane asked. "Why ask me now?"

Her arms tightened. "Every other woman in town has had you," she complained softly, "So why *not* me?"

She sounded logical, a woman utilizing a sensible argument. Only there was nothing sensible about Tamara Tremayne or the circumstances.

"So now, today, you decided to pull out the big guns?"

"Big guns?"

He rubbed his chin against her hair, feeling the warmth and softness of it. He wanted to devour her, and he wanted to hold her gently all night. "No man can resist a direct attack. You said you wanted me, which made me want you." That was only a partial truth. In his dreams, he'd wanted her for a long time.

"You've always ignored me," Tamara said, tilting her head back to see his face. "And I hated it. I tried everything to get your attention, but you always looked through me, or past me." She drew a deep breath. "Now I'm going to have to leave, and my biggest regret was that I wouldn't have another chance to be with you, to fulfill a few of my fantasies. So yes, I felt a direct attack was my last resort."

Zane was still aroused, but now some other emotion prevailed. He didn't know what it was, so he couldn't fight against it. "I haven't been with *every* woman in town." For some reason, he wanted her to understand that.

She laughed. "Okay, so there are a few you're not interested in. I've been to the Winston Tavern. I've seen the women hanging on your every word. And I saw how much you love it."

Zane pushed her back a bit, frowning. "You've been to the bar? When?" His oldest brother, Cole, ran the bar, and Chase was the bartender. He and Mack worked there part-time, more so back when they were in college. Now Mack was teaching and Zane spent the majority of his hours at his computer store. But the bar was a comforting haven when be wanted to be with friends and family, and it still seemed natural to serve drinks or wipe tables whenever he was around.

Not once could he recall seeing Tamara there.

"Off and on," Tamara hedged.

"Off and on when?" A thought occurred to him, and his hands tightened on her shoulders. "You were there dressed as you are now, or as the Gypsy?"

As if his question had somehow insulted her, her chin lifted. "Neither. I dress the Gypsy when I work. You heard my relatives. I'm not a very convincing fortuneteller as I really look." Her upturned nose wrinkled. "I look too young and gullible. So it's necessary."

Zane wanted to tell her she was a pretty damn convincing femme fatale no matter how she dressed, but he held the words back.

"You caught me getting ready for bed," she explained, "so I'm sort of a mess right now. But when I go out, I do know how to clean up proper."

Zane stared down at her. He was very aware of her body against his, but he had control of himself, and he meant to keep it that way. Talking with her seemed like a good way to maintain that control. "The ghastly makeup?"

"Is like the jewelry and the dark contacts and the wig. I wear makeup, just as most women do, but it's not so dramatic."

Zane looked at her mouth, naked and full and so sexy. He touched the corner of her lips with his thumb, brushing softly until she opened, until he could hear her accelerated breathing and see the tip of her pink tongue. "You don't need makeup."

Carefully, he lifted his hands to her hair and tangled his fingers in the fine, silky curls. She was baby soft, and it made him wonder about other parts of her, if she was so damn soft all over. His blood surged hotly.

"Answer me this." His large hands easily held her immobile. "If I had agreed this afternoon, how would you have come to me?"

Her lashes lowered, hiding her eyes. "I don't know what you mean."

Zane gently tugged on her hair until her face tilted up at him. Restraining himself, he kissed her—a light, teasing kiss—then whispered against her lips, "Yes, you do. Would I have been sleeping with the sultry Gypsy or the sweet little blonde?"

Tamara strained closer, trying to gain full access to his mouth again, but Zane stayed just out of reach, only his breath caressing her lips. She made a soft sound of frustration. "I don't know. I hadn't thought that far ahead."

"Tamara . . ." He loved saying her name, loved the lyrical sound of it, the suggested eroticism, the mystique. It suited her perfectly. "Don't ever lie to me."

"A . . . a book said I should be bold, that men love boldness in a woman." She waited for his nod of agreement, then continued. "Especially men who are slaves to their primitive nature."

"Primitive nature?"

"Men who are ruled by their libidos." She said it against his mouth, then licked his bottom lip in a suggestive way that made his erection swell and strain against his fly.

Holding himself in check had never been so damn difficult.

"I'd have been the Gypsy," she whispered, "bold and sensual." Her green gaze snared his, mesmerized him. "And you'd have loved it."

Zane took her mouth hard, further scattering her wits, doing it deliberately. It was a great effort not to give in to the demands of his body, but her comment about a book, about slaves and boldness, swirled in his head. He wanted explanations, and he intuitively knew the best way to get them would be to keep her off balance.

She gasped when he ended the kiss. "You think I'm a slave to my sexuality?" As he spoke, he pressed hot, damp kisses against the tender skin of her throat.

Her head tilted back, exposing her to him. "I know you are."

Zane smiled, nibbling his way down to her shoulder. He was the master, not the slave; she'd understand that soon enough. Spells and curses be damned, he would do as he pleased, and not be caught.

It was what she wanted anyway, what she'd asked for, so there would be no call for him to feel guilty.

Impatience rode him hard, and he decided to get this interview over with. He wanted to take her to his place, where they could be alone, without the twin banshees and a dark behemoth waiting outside the door.

He wanted her naked, stretched out on his bed. With nothing between them except excitement, it wouldn't matter who she chose to be, the Gypsy or the innocent. He'd take either one.

And listen in satisfaction while she screamed his name, begging for more of the pleasure he'd give her.

Zane nuzzled her throat, inhaling her increasingly potent scent. "Tell me about this book, Tamara."

Suddenly she stiffened. A second later, before Zane could reclaim her thoughts, she pushed away from him. He let her go rather than chase after her. Her reaction to a mention of the book was interesting, even if his body rebelled at the distance now between them.

Looking horrified, Tamara backed up and shook her head. Moonlight poured over her in a silver glow, showing her wide eyes, the gentle slope of her narrow nose, her rounded chin. When she was several feet from him, her back to the wall near the door, she said, "The book is—"

A crash from far away echoed in the room. Zane heard the relatives just outside the bedroom door, scrambling around and muttering obscenities. A fist—likely Thanos's, given the way the door frame rattled—demanded their attention.

"He's back," Thanos thundered.

"Hubert is downstairs." Olga wailed. "Lord almighty! He's come for us!"

Tamara flipped on the bedroom light and opened the door. "*Hubert is dead!*"

"It's his ghost," Eva insisted, her hands clasped to her chest, her black eyes filled with dramatic horror.

"There's no telling what he's capable of doing in this form!"

"Oh for the love of . . ."

Tamara, still muttering to herself, started away. Zane rushed after her. He wondered who Hubert was, and what he had to do with ghosts and the racket that had come from downstairs.

Like a parade, the other three hustled into line behind him.

"What the hell is going on?" Zane asked to Tamara's retreating back.

She kept moving, forcing Zane to keep up as she raced on light feet for the stairwell that would take her to the main shop.

"Shh," she cautioned, and then quietly opened the door. It gave an ominous creek, as if tuned for the effect. "I have an intruder, a live one, though my aunts insist on thinking it's my deceased uncle Hubert."

He knew he shouldn't have been surprised at this new turn of events, but just when he thought things couldn't get more bizarre . . . "Your deceased uncle Hubert?"

"Tragic," Olga whispered from behind Zane's right shoulder. "Just tragic how he died."

"And now he wants revenge," Eva predicted in mournful tones while edging close to Zane's other side.

Tamara turned. "Stay back, all of you." Incredibly, she included Zane in her order. Her uncle and aunts obediently stopped in midstep. Zane gave her a ferocious scowl.

"This time," Tamara said with relish, "I'll catch him for sure."

Zane snared a fistful of her shirt and jerked her up short just as she started to turn away. "The hell you will!"

She tried to shush him, which only made him angrier. "You mean to tell me," he growled, his other hand now wrapped securely around her upper arm, making sure she wouldn't slip away from him, "that you think someone has broken in downstairs and you're determined to go investigate?"

"Someone *is* downstairs," she whispered anxiously, "unless your big mouth has just scared him away."

His big mouth? Zane couldn't remember a woman ever outright insulting him before. Usually they showered him with sweet compliments.

He'd never met a woman with a more stubborn independent streak, either. Most females would have had enough sense to send an available male downstairs to check things out. But not Tamara. No, she ignored Zane's presence—except when it came to the subject of sex.

His scowl turned a little blacker. He glared at Tamara, then thrust her toward Thanos. "Hang onto her. I'll be right back."

Olga and Eva looked at him like he was true hero material.

Thanos, beaming at him in approval, asked, "What will you do if it is a ghost?"

Knowing the big man deliberately baited him, Zane said, "I'll kick his ass," and he trotted down the steps. "Just keep the women upstairs."

He was surely in bedlam, Zane decided, hearing Thanos laugh as Tamara insisted on being turned loose. But with the mood Zane was in, any intruder, ghost or otherwise, would be smart to get the hell out of his way.

Zane fully expected to walk through the downstairs without a single disturbance.

Unfortunately, things didn't quite turn out that way.

FOUR

Tamara heard a loud thump, then a husky groan. Her heart shot straight into her throat, nearly strangling her. "Zane!"

In his sudden concern for Zane, Thanos became preoccupied and loosened his grip just enough. Tamara didn't even think twice; she bolted away, intent only on getting to Zane.

"Damn it, Tamara," Thanos groused as he made a wild grab for her and missed, "come back here this second!"

Tamara ignored him, leaping down the stairs two and three at a time. Behind her, she heard Olga chanting and Eva cursing.

Zane hadn't flipped on any lights, but the moon was bright enough that the shadows were gray rather than black, and large objects were outlined by an opalescent sheen. Tamara knew her shop—every knick-knack, curio, and tattered rug—without the benefit of lights.

She also knew Zane Winston, much better than she'd thought. Her intuitive abilities were far from psychic, but every time Zane had looked at her, she'd felt him. She'd shared his feelings.

She'd known his desires.

And boy, was the man hot-blooded! Tamara hadn't expected to be wanted like that—in fact, Zane's graphic, blatant hunger alarmed her. She'd hoped he would agree to share sex with her, but she hadn't expected him to crave her. She wasn't exactly afraid of him, but his intensity was startling. And exciting.

No way would she let some blasted intruder hurt him.

Crouching by the long counter, she stopped and listened, but it was difficult to hear anything over the pounding of her heart and the racket of her relatives upstairs.

Then a faint grunt reached her ears. *Zane!* She felt his pain, slight but nagging, and she accepted it, took it in, made it her own.

Without hesitation, she followed her senses toward the backroom. She slithered past the counter, slipped through the partially open curtain.

There was only one narrow window in the backroom, shadowed by the other buildings, and she didn't dare turn on a light. It was so dark she couldn't see her hand in front of her face.

Reaching out, she felt for the wall, then the door frame. The door was wide open, and she darted inside—and promptly toppled over a large, hard object sprawled out around her feet.

With a grunt, she landed hard. One of her elbows cracked on the concrete floor, making her wince, and the other—

The lump on the floor reared up with a bellow, then collapsed with a long, shuddering, pain-filled moan.

"Zane?" Tamara twisted around, trying to find his head so she could see how badly he was hurt.

His hand caught her bare foot, stilling her movements. "Christ almighty, woman! Are you trying to make me a choirboy?"

Tamara's eyes adjusted to the dark, and she realized she was facing the wrong end of Zane. He was the hard thing she'd tripped over, sprawled flat on his back in the middle of the floor. "Zane? What in the world are you doing? Are you hurt?" Then, with extreme menace: "Did someone hit you?"

Zane laughed. "I'm just bruised." His fingers were still around her foot. "There's no one here. I fell over a damn box of books."

"You're bruised?" She tried to turn so she could evaluate his injuries.

Zane tightened his hold. "Bruised, and getting more so by the second. Will you hold *still*?"

Tamara froze. She'd just realized her head was directly over his lap.

Her hands twitched. She squinted hard, trying to see more clearly through the inky blackness. "Um . . . I guess that wasn't your stomach I elbowed."

He growled. "My stomach is *not* soft."

No, she knew it wasn't. She'd seen his washboard abs a few times when he'd been helping unload a truck behind his shop. Watching Zane Winston lose his shirt, seeing the sweat dampen his upper body as he worked, had been a particular kind of provocation, doing much to embellish her fantasies. His chest was lightly covered with springy dark hair, and his jeans always rode low, showing off his navel, occasionally even his hipbones.

Groaning, she gave in to temptation and put both hands on his fly. He jerked, and a low, raw groan reverberated softly in the room. Tonight he wore casual khaki slacks, which did nothing to hinder her inquisitive fingers.

He filled her hands.

Eyes closed so her senses could fully absorb him, her stomach flip-flopped, heat pulsed and swelled beneath her skin. He was soft down low—probably where her sharp elbow had landed—and hot and hard and heavy above. She traced the rigid length of his erect penis with her palm and felt his legs flex, shift. Her breath shuddered in and out. So hard, so long. So very nice.

Zane lifted his hips just a bit, then made another low sound, this one more pain-filled than any of the others. It struck Tamara that she was copping a feel off an injured man! She wanted him, but she didn't want to take advantage of him. Not like this.

Mortified by her uncharacteristically brash behavior, she was just about to lever herself up—never mind that his hard body felt very nice beneath hers—when the bare lightbulb overhead clicked on.

There was a startled moment of silence before Thanos roared at Zane, "*What the hell do you think you're doing with her, man?*"

Tamara started to object, but Zane just dropped his head back and laughed. He still held her foot, his long fingers fastened around her ankle so tightly she knew she couldn't do a thing until he let her.

She looked down at his erection, appreciating the bird's-eye view now that she could see him, and regretting the interruption.

Thanos took a step forward, his eyes almost red. Zane said, "She's on top, Thanos. All I'm doing is trying to protect my more vulnerable body parts from elbows and knees."

No sooner did he say it than she moved again and her heel made sharp contact with his chin.

Thanos chuckled.

Zane didn't find anything humorous in the situation. He sat up and used her leg to drag her around to face him, then held her cradled on his lap. The new position effectively hid his arousal from her uncle, and it felt really nice against her backside.

Using the tip of one finger, Zane brought her gaze around to his.

His brown eyes, shadowed by his lashes, were dark with annoyance. "Do you have a problem following orders?"

Unsure whether she should be outraged or incredulous, Tamara leveled a look on him. "You've got to be kidding, right?"

His brows snapped down. "I specifically told you to wait upstairs."

Tamara leaned back to stare at him in disbelief. "Surely you never, for one second, thought you could give me orders?"

Zane glanced up at her uncle, who held out both hands, wisely refusing him any help. Tamara waited.

With an exaggerated sigh, Zane said, "I can see we're going to have to work out a few ground rules."

"Absolutely, but later." She was beginning to notice the mess around her. An enormous box of erotic books she'd purchased from an estate sale had fallen from a top shelf. They were everywhere, a few of the spines broken, some pages torn.

She hadn't had a chance to assess the value of all the books yet. Some of them seemed very old, maybe even antique. A collector might pay a high price for them—if they hadn't been destroyed by the fall.

Thank God she'd already moved the journal upstairs. In truth, it was probably worth less than any of the other books. But Tamara found it fascinating reading, and beyond value to her personally. "What happened here? Are you sure no one hit you?"

Zane worked his jaw as if only the clench of his teeth held his temper at bay. "No, there was no one here. No intruder, no spirit. You must have put the books too close to the edge of the shelf, and they fell. That's the racket you heard. I tripped over the damn things, and you tripped over me."

It seemed very unlikely to her that the books would have fallen suddenly. She'd bought the box of books almost two months ago, and they'd been on the shelf ever since. They hadn't shown any sign of toppling before now.

Tamara rubbed her bruised elbow. "Where are you hurt?"

"I conked my head is all. It dazed me for a second." Zane took her hand and pulled her arm straight so he could examine her elbow. "At least you landed on me rather than the hard floor."

Tamara blinked at him. "News flash, Zane. You're not exactly cushiony."

To her amazement, he brushed off her elbow, ran his thumb over it twice, then pressed a soft kiss to the red spot. In a voice far too intimate, considering her uncle stood close by at full alert, he asked, "Does it hurt?"

She nearly melted on the spot. Her insides turned to liquid, problems faded away under the impact of his touch.

The intruder had been at it again, she just knew it. But for the first time since the trouble had started, she really didn't give a damn.

Zane Winston wanted her. For tonight, that was enough.

Thanos hauled them to their feet. "None of that, now," he said to Zane. "You keep your lips to yourself until Tamara's aunts and I have had time to consider this."

Zane raised a brow at Tamara, who sighed theatrically. "There's nothing to consider, Uncle Thanos, so back off."

"Not this time, sweetie. There's a lot going on here, what with the trouble and ghosts." He eyed Zane. "How do we know who's involved and who isn't?"

"Thanos!" Tamara looked prepared to have a full-fledged fit, and Zane meant to forestall that occurrence. Already his head ached from connecting with the concrete floor, and other parts of him ached, thanks to Tamara's bold curiosity and soft little hands. He couldn't take a family brawl right now.

"I'm here because she asked me to be," Zane pointed out, "and I wouldn't do anything to her that she didn't want me to do." He hoped to reassure Thanos, and at the same time spoke only the truth. From what Tamara had said to him, she wanted a lot, all of it sexual. That suited Zane just fine.

Tamara gasped as if she'd known his exact thought, but Thanos laughed out loud. "Ah, now there's the rub. What our little Gypsy lacks in dark looks, she makes up for with darker passion and an imagination that boggles the mind."

Zane eyed her. "Dark passion, huh?" He wasn't sure he liked hearing that. How many men had come before him? Had she seduced them as the Gypsy, or as the angel? And exactly what had her imagination dredged up that could boggle the mind? His mind was pretty damn creative, all on its own.

"That's enough out of both of you!" Tamara looked beyond

Thanos, then put her hands to her head. "Here come Eva and Olga. This night is never going to end."

Zane felt his smile slip. Did she mean her relatives intended to hang around a little longer? That wouldn't do. He wanted her now. Right this instant. He was willing to wait a few minutes more . . . but the whole night? He snorted.

Tamara gave him a pathetic, helpless look, and nodded. Damn it, if she didn't stop reading his thoughts, he'd—

Olga suddenly came around Thanos and threw her skinny arms around Zane with an exuberant hug. "Zane! Thank God you were here, young man." Then she thrust him back and demanded shrilly, "What did you see? What did Hubert look like? Is he well?"

Eva shook her head. "Olga, Hubert is *dead*. How can he be well, for pity's sake?" Then to Zane. "Was he ethereal? Wispy? Or was he as solid and substantial as ever?"

She turned to Tamara without waiting for Zane to answer. "You know Hubert always was a stocky man. Thick in the chest."

He'd landed in bedlam, Zane decided. In precise tones, so no one would misunderstand, he said, "There was no ghost. No Uncle Hubert. No intruder." Waving a hand, he indicated the books scattered everywhere. They were dusty and old, some of the yellowed pages lying loose. "The books fell, that's all."

Olga peered at the books. "Wonder if Hubert pushed them down."

Eva nodded enthusiastically. "Probably did. Hubert never was one much for reading."

"No." Tamara stood like a small amazon, hands on her hips. "For the last time, it's not Hubert. It's a . . . well, a man, probably, though I suppose it could be a woman."

Zane surveyed her serious expression and swallowed his impatience. "What makes you think a man would break in here? For what purpose? To steal your books?"

"No, of course not. But . . ." She hesitated, then shrugged. "Never mind. It's not your concern, and I don't want to involve you."

Zane felt like he'd been slapped. Damn her, he hadn't even wanted to be involved, not until she tried to exclude him. First she'd propositioned him, then insulted him, and now she was shutting him out. He matched her stance, fists on his hips, legs braced apart. "I'm making it my concern."

"No."

That did it. Zane's temper exploded and he glared down at her. In a near shout, he said, "You're saying that cursed word more and more! I think I liked it better when you stayed quiet and mysterious."

Eva clapped her hands together. "That's what we keep telling her! She's not nearly mysterious enough."

Olga agreed. "She's too . . . blond."

Laughing to himself, Thanos added, "And green-eyed."

Zane wished her meddlesome relatives elsewhere, but obviously his wishes meant very little.

"That's enough on my appearance." Tamara's tone was stern, bordering on brittle. She started to smooth her wayward curls, then caught herself and sent Zane a crooked smile meant to placate. "I guess you should be going." She nodded toward her aunts. "The family and I have a lot to discuss."

Now she hoped to dismiss him. Crossing his arms over his chest, Zane propped himself against the door frame and stared impassively.

Tamara frowned. She turned and took two steps toward the door. "C'mon, Zane." She sounded like she was enticing a pet. "It's time to go." She took two more steps.

Zane yawned, then asked Thanos, "So what's been going on?"

"Mischief," Thanos told him without hesitation. Tamara rushed back to her uncle's side.

"Uncle Thanos, our family problems don't concern anyone else. I'll thank you—"

Thanos threw a meaty arm around her shoulders and squeezed her till she squeaked. Zane started to protest, but Tamara had a long-suffering look on her face, as if she was quite used to the rough affection. "You can thank me later, little one. For now, why don't you take your aunts upstairs and get them settled while Zane and I talk things over? They've had an upset."

"Tea," Olga hinted elaborately, "would be just the thing to settle the nerves."

"Oh, no." Tamara pried herself out of Thanos's embrace and glared at him. "I'm not going to be dismissed like a . . . a . . ."

"Female?" Zane supplied.

"That's right!" Going on her tiptoes, she poked a finger into Thanos's chest and said, "You can take them upstairs. I'm sure the three of you can manage a pot of tea. I'll pick up this mess."

"I can't leave you alone here with the young lothario." Thanos shrugged. "He's looking at you like a hungry man looks at a juicy tart."

"He is?" Tamara turned to Zane and examined his gaze. Now that she was the one feeling rattled, Zane relaxed a little. In fact, he tried for a leer so she wouldn't be disappointed.

Tamara blushed as she turned back to her uncle and pushed on his shoulder. "Yeah, well, I can take care of myself, you know that."

"Right." Thanos, ignoring her meager effort to shove him out of the room, looked over her head at Zane. "Give me your word there won't be any hanky-panky going on down here."

Zane smiled lazily. He and Thanos were off to a fair start. "I never begin things I can't finish properly."

For a moment, Thanos looked outraged, then his frown lifted and he laughed heartily. He thwacked Zane, nearly knocking him off his feet. "A man after my own heart."

Catching Tamara under the chin, Thanos lifted her face and said, "I think he may just do for you, little one." He kissed her forehead. "But you do as I say. Mind your manners, and remember that your aunts and I will be right upstairs."

Zane thought it would be near impossible to forget, considering they butted in more often than not. He imagined if they were anywhere in the vicinity, he wouldn't have guaranteed privacy. Which meant he'd have to wait tonight, no matter how it pained him. When he took Tamara, he wanted the whole night to enjoy himself, to indulge her every need. *Soon*, he promised himself. *Very soon*.

Tamara gazed at him, her eyes burning.

Zane waited until Thanos had escorted both women from the room, then caught Tamara's arm and turned her toward him. "Are you reading my mind?"

She looked startled, laughed a little too exuberantly. "First you accuse me of casting spells, and now I'm a mind reader?"

Put that way, he felt just a little foolish. Until he looked into her eyes.

She had the most incredible green eyes he'd ever seen. They were both sharp with intelligence and soft with innocence. It was a potent combination. Her lashes, a dusky brown, were thick and long, leaving exaggerated shadows over her high cheekbones. Her skin looked and felt incredibly soft, and her mouth . . . Zane groaned softly and bent to kiss her.

She opened her mouth right away, but Zane kept the kiss simple, light. He'd promised Thanos—and besides, he'd meant what he said. There was no point in making this more difficult on either of them.

Against her lips, he said, "Tell me about this imagined intruder."

Her small hands clung to his shoulders. "Not imagined."

He let that pass. "Tell me, Tamara."

She sighed and laid her head on his shoulder. "I can think of a dozen things I'd rather talk about."

"Such as?" Zane coasted a hand up and down her slender back. She was so sweet, so delicate. Her curves were subtle, but *there*, and very enticing.

With his fingers spread, Zane's large hand spanned her back from shoulder blade to shoulder blade. That fact was oddly exciting, exemplifying his harsh maleness to her elegant femininity. He imagined his rough hands on her breasts, her smooth belly, her silky inner thighs.

Damn! Zane stroked her, his fingers barely touching her rounded hip—and he forced himself to stop. He drew a deep breath. "Tell me what you'd rather talk about."

Tamara kissed his collarbone. "I'd like to talk about all the things I want to do to you." Her fingers felt cool on his heated skin, slipping over the nape of his neck, the top of his shoulder. "I've been lying awake at night, thinking about how I'd like to—"

To save himself, Zane pressed a finger to her lips. His forehead touched hers. "Shh. Baby, if you talk like that, I'm not going to be able to keep my promise to Thanos."

Tamara clutched at him, urging him on without even realizing it. "He shouldn't have asked for such a horrible promise."

Zane laughed. "A *horrible* promise, huh?" He stroked her lips, then sighed. "Unfortunately, he's right, and you know it. Your downstairs is no place for an orgy when the upstairs is overloaded with relatives."

A delicate little shudder went through her, and Tamara breathed, "Orgy?"

Zane couldn't resist one more small kiss. He had a feeling he'd be dreaming about kissing her, and more, all night long. "An orgy of pleasure," he explained. "Any thoughts you've got, any sexual curiosities you want to appease, I'm all for it. Remember that."

He deliberately stepped away from her and temptation. "But for now, I'll help you pick up this mess while you tell me why you're so set on believing an intruder is responsible. And don't leave anything out."

FIVE

Zane glanced at Tamara as he began gathering books. Her quick mood swings were almost amusing. Contrary to what he'd told her, he liked her honest reactions far more than the mysterious silence of her Gypsy self.

Right now, she looked disgruntled and rebellious, but he knew in the end he'd win. He always did. His feelings for Tamara were too extreme for him to do less than maintain absolute authority. Considering the nature of their involvement, it'd be best for both of them that way.

He had a stack of books back in the box before Tamara reluctantly began helping. "I don't have any positive proof of an intruder," she admitted, "or else my aunts wouldn't be convinced that it's Uncle Hubert come to haunt us."

"Why would your uncle want to haunt you?" Zane gathered up one old relic that had more torn pages than not. He tried to get them back inside the cover in order, then gave up and just held them in his hand.

"Uncle Hubert strongly believed our family has psychic power." She made a face. "Like the rest of the family, he was really into that sort of thing. We don't, of course, but he thought we did. My aunts are assuming he's haunting us because he thinks we could have predicted his death—so that he could have avoided dying—but we didn't."

Zane sat down and propped his back against the shelf where the box of books had been stacked. The shelf shifted slightly, obviously not sitting level. The old floor had sloped with age, and large cracks ran along the outside wall. "How did he die, if you don't mind me asking?"

Tamara sat, too, crossing her legs tailor-style. "Hubert was a ladies' man, sort of a guru with a following. He got stuck in the sixties and never quite came out."

"Ah. A flower child?"

"Sort of. He was into tie-dye and tattoos and piercings and sex and . . . whatever felt good." She shrugged, but her disapproval was plain on her face. For a Gypsy, she was a prim little thing. "I told him time and again that he'd come to a bad end if he didn't clean up his act. My aunts think I cursed him somehow by saying it."

Zane held himself very still. "But you can't curse anyone?"

"Nope." She held up both hands. "You can stop fretting," she said with a frown. "I already told you, I'm incapable of any real powers."

Looking at her, Zane wasn't at all sure he believed her. Whether she admitted it or not, she'd done something to him. Figuring out what was going to take some time.

Tamara barely managed to control her annoyance. He silently applauded her restraint.

"Still," she said, "they think Hubert believes he was cursed, because he was at a rock concert by his favorite group when a freak storm blew in."

"He died in the storm?"

"Actually, he died in a portable toilet, one of those little plastic houses they use on construction sites. The wind was fierce and knocked it over. He was inside and well . . . when they righted the Porta-Potti the next day, they found Hubert."

Zane tapped the crumbling book on his knee. It wasn't really funny, yet he had the nearly uncontrollable urge to smile. Part of his mood was due to Tamara's expression. She looked so disapproving of her uncle. "Not exactly an auspicious way to go, huh?"

"No." She glanced down at the book literally falling apart in his hands and reached for it. "I guess this one didn't hold up through the fall."

An illustrated page fell out, and she stared. Zane released the smile he'd been holding, and grabbed the page before Tamara could. He lifted it for a closer look. "Ah. Exactly what have you been buying, Miss Tremayne?"

Though her cheeks were bright pink, Zane gave her credit for trying to brazen out the situation. "I buy at estate sales in bulk, so sometimes I get things I hadn't planned on. Obviously what I got this time is erotica, as you can see."

He turned the page, holding it eye level for her, and asked silkily, "Is this something you're interested in trying?"

The illustration was an exaggerated depiction of a man and woman stretched out in the woods atop leaves and flowers, sharing oral pleasure. The ink sketch showed legs and arms in impossible positions, but there was no question about the enjoyment each derived; their eyes, the only facial features visible due to their carnal activity, were glazed with rapture.

Tamara looked like she couldn't breathe, but then her gaze darkened and she peeked up at Zane. Before the words left her mouth, he knew what she would say. And still, hearing her say it, hearing the deepened timbre of her voice, shook him.

"Would you . . . be interested in that?"

Hell, yes, he'd be interested. The thought of tasting Tamara, of her tasting him . . . Thinking it had almost the same effect as doing it. He felt burned.

Zane stuck the picture inside the book and closed it. His heart thumped wildly in his chest, annoying him with the proof of his weakness where she was concerned. She left him breathless with just a few words. What the hell would it be like when he got inside her, when he could feel her squeezing him, hear her moaning, taste her excitement?

"I already told you," he rasped, hoping she wouldn't detect the dark hunger in his tone, "anything you want to do is fine with me."

Her gaze sharpened at his agreement, devouring him, easily sharing with him the images going through her mind.

Her sensual curiosity engulfed him. Everything with Tamara, every word, every conversation, somehow seemed more acute.

She picked up a few more books and packed them away. Idly, as if she wasn't anxious to hear his answer, she asked, "Do you read a lot of erotica?"

He laughed, he couldn't help it. "No. Not since I was a kid and stole Chase's stash to share with Mack." His grin lingered as memories crowded in. He and Mack had spent a week hiding out in the woods behind their home, engrossed in the books—the most reading either of them had ever done—before Cole busted them.

"Chase had some pretty . . . risqué stuff. I remember Mack and I had a hard time not snickering around him after that."

Tamara smiled. "You were young, I gather."

"Old enough to appreciate what I'd found."

"Was Chase mad when he realized you'd gotten into his personal belongings?"

"Mad?" Zane could barely recall ever seeing Chase really angry. He was usually the quietest, but not when it came to Allison. Around his wife, he was an entirely different man. "No, I'd say he was more disgruntled, and determined to make Mack and me understand the differences between fantasies and reality." Before she could ask, he said, "Fantasy is *anything* that gets you hot, no matter how raunchy or ribald it might be. But reality is only what your partner will accept, what will make her happy, too."

Her green eyes glittered at him, filled with questions. "Do you . . . have any fantasies that your partners haven't accepted?"

"A few." Zane shook a finger at her. "And no, I'm not listing them for you."

Tamara bit her lip, then nodded. "Maybe later?"

"Maybe." Damn, but she was killing him in small degrees. A change of topic proved vital. "Chase is pretty laid back most of the time, but Cole, well, he's another matter entirely."

Tamara settled herself comfortably and asked, "What did he do?"

"You have to understand, after our parents died, Cole took over raising us, and he was pretty serious about the whole thing. Whenever he thought we'd gotten into mischief, he lectured. Annoyed the hell out of us, and we'd do our best not to earn a lecture. But God, when Cole got to talking about sex and women, he could go on for hours. And it always came down to the same thing, so most of what he said wasn't even necessary. He could have summed it up in a few sentences, but we always suspected that Cole liked to lecture."

"What did he tell you?"

"Nothing you need to hear."

She straightened. "That's not fair! Why bring it up if you won't tell me?"

Zane leaned forward. "I'll tell if you'll tell."

"You did it on purpose!"

He shrugged. "You answer my questions and I'll answer yours."

Tamara huffed, "Well, since I have a feeling you're going to badger me until I do, sure. Why not?"

"Don't be mad, sweetheart." She ignored him, gathering up more books. Zane didn't like being ignored, not even a little. "Respect women," he said abruptly, determined to regain her attention. "No matter what, no matter where you met her, or what she's done in her past, or who she's been with or why, you give any woman you're with respect."

"That's it?"

"Pretty much. Cole made it clear sex was well and good—"

She smiled.

"—but that sex should be for a reason beyond the physical." Zane laughed, remembering how Cole had always harped on that point. "If you can't at least respect a woman, you have no business being around her. It makes a man look pathetic to go screwing around with a woman he doesn't even like, just to get laid. Cole always said you might as well be paying a prostitute, which definitely smacks of desperation. Since Mack and I never wanted to look desperate, we listened."

"Until now."

"What does that mean?"

"Nothing." Her lashes lowered, hiding her eyes. "I like your brothers."

"Everyone does." She'd said it matter-of-factly, as if she were well acquainted with them, which made Zane frown. "How do you know them?"

"I know *of* them. As I said, I've been to the bar. I've watched them." Her brows lifted. "Your brothers would be pretty darned hard to miss."

"They're all married." His frown became more severe.

"I know. Their wives always look very happy, even when they're arguing with them."

She seemed pleased by that, not at all covetous. Zane nodded. "Yeah, happy about covers it."

"I have another book," Tamara suddenly blurted, "one I took upstairs already."

Zane paused. Her quick switch momentarily threw him. "Erotica?" he asked. He wasn't sure he could handle another conversation on positions. He was already struggling with the last tenuous hold on his discipline.

She glanced at him, then away. "Not exactly."

Aha. The book she'd mentioned earlier. Zane gentled his tone, anxious to hear this tale. "The book that told you to be bold? The one that stated men were slaves to their basic natures, or some such rot?"

"Yes." Tamara picked up the last of the spilled books and shoved them awkwardly into the box. "Only it's not rot. It's a journal of sorts. Written by this amazing woman."

"Anyone I know?"

"Well, I seriously doubt it! She was an elderly woman, and the journal was something she kept hidden from everyone. Not even her family knew about it. She says in the very beginning that what she's writing will be of use to women with aggressive sexualities, women who want to be free, but that not everyone would understand. Certainly not anyone in her peer group. Though her name is nowhere in the book, I gather from what she said that she was from the social elite, and didn't want her affairs to become public knowledge. She explained that her family had already disowned her and that in her social group such things, if they were ever discovered, would be broadcast in the scandal rags."

Zane leaned forward. Much of what she'd just told him was intriguing, but one comment in particular drew his interest. "You fit in the category of 'aggressive sexuality,' do you?"

She floundered. "I . . . well, I don't know."

"You don't know?" What the hell did that mean? Zane wanted to come right out and ask her how many men she'd been with, but at the same time, he wasn't at all sure he wanted to know. He'd always made it a rule not to get overly involved in women's personal lives. Keep it light and friendly—that was his motto.

Her chin lifted. "I feel aggressive about wanting you. And since you were resisting me, I figured I could use some help."

Zane snorted at that, seeing it as a deliberate avoidance of his question. "So you're reading about the private, and evidently racy, sex life of some deceased old lady?"

"It's not like that!" Obviously affronted, Tamara said, "It's sort of a guide, explaining things that she found instrumental in building a wonderful sexual and emotional connection. The journal is divided into sections that detail ways to accomplish different relationships.

"She wanted to share what she'd learned with others, but she didn't dare write a book that would be published, for fear of how society would react." She stood and propped her hands on her slim hips, her expression challenging. "According to this woman, making an emotional connection helps amplify the sexual connection."

"I'll buy that."

"You will?"

"Sure." Zane smiled up at her, and admitted, "I never have sex with strangers. It'd be cold. And I have to at least like a woman to want to be with her, not just find her attractive."

"But . . ." Tamara hesitated, then went on boldly, "You agreed to have sex with me, and you don't like me. And for the most part, I'm still a stranger to you."

Zane considered that for a long moment. "You figure all Cole's preaching went in one of my ears and out the other?"

She shrugged. "At least where I'm concerned."

"Well, you're wrong. I like you just fine." He realized it was true, frowned. "You know, you don't feel like a stranger to me. On some level it seems like I've known you ever since I opened my store. I know we never talked much—"

"You avoided me."

"I didn't exactly avoid you," he said, annoyed at her insistence. Avoidance sounded like the act of a wary man. And he sure as hell wasn't wary of her. He wasn't wary of any woman.

"Yes, you did. Because you didn't like me."

Zane locked his jaw. Through his teeth, he said, "I didn't know you well enough to like or dislike you. It's just that you . . ." *Affected my brain and made me antsy and hot and excited.* "I was just busy getting my business started."

"You found time to date a lot of other women. I saw them with you."

"At the bar?"

"And at your store. You meet a lot of your women there."

His annoyance peaked. "They're not *my women*. We just date. You make it sound like I maintain a harem or something."

She shrugged, unconcerned at insulting his finer sensibilities. "I thought you were proud of your way with women. It's nothing to be ashamed of, you know. I haven't seen any of the women complaining."

Zane pulled himself together once again. It seemed he did that a lot around Tamara. "How'd we get onto my dating habits? We were talking about you and that ridiculous journal."

"It's not ridiculous. In fact, it was the words in the journal that encouraged me to approach you. If I hadn't found that book, we wouldn't be here now."

That was an unbearable thought, and he immediately rejected it. "I'd have approached you."

"Ha!" She tossed her head, flipping her bangs away from her forehead, and glared up at him. "I doubt you'd have even noticed I was leaving until after I was gone—if you noticed even then. I'd have sold my place and moved away and we'd never have shared a kiss, much less anything else."

"You don't know that for sure."

"If it wasn't for that book," she went on, "we'd never have had a chance to enjoy each other. I'd say the book is far from ridiculous. In fact, I'd say we should use it as a guide."

Zane drew back. "A guide? You think I need a goddamn guide to make love to a woman?"

"Don't shout at me. And we're going to have sex, not make love."

Her insistence on that point infuriated him. "I'm not shouting," he shouted.

"You need something," she said, ignoring his temper, "at least where I'm concerned, because it's for certain you hadn't made a move on your own."

Zane growled. Now that he had kissed her and touched her and planned to do so much more, he couldn't believe he'd ever overlooked her. And he damn sure didn't like having her remind him of his oversight.

But he wouldn't admit that to her. He was used to being the one calling the shots. He was used to wielding all the power. But she *had* instigated things, damn it. She'd been quiet and intriguing and she'd lured him in with three little words. *I want you.*

She was far from quiet now. In fact, he'd call her argumentative. Perhaps if he got her back into costume, she'd revert to form and settle back into her mysterious silence. Zane shook his head. He actually liked her much better this way.

In an effort to draw her fire away from him, Zane asked, "Why the hell are you moving, anyway?"

Tamara hesitated, and he said quickly, "Oh, no, you don't. Don't lie to me."

When she looked surprised, he said, "I can see the intent plain in your eyes."

"That's ridiculous."

"Like hell it is." He caught her shoulders and pulled her close. "You don't want to tell me what's going on." He kissed her pursed mouth hard, leaving her bemused, then added, "But I'm afraid I'm going to have to insist."

Tamara pulled away and turned her back on him, her spine rigid, her shoulders stiff. "You can't get around me with sex, Zane."

"Wanna bet?"

She flashed him a glance, then narrowed her eyes. "My problems are my own," she insisted. "I don't want or need to drag you into them."

"You just want me for physical pleasure?" There was a slight acerbity to his tone that he couldn't hide.

"That's right. And I haven't even gotten that yet, so there's nothing more to talk about."

Zane stepped up behind her, close enough that his groin nestled against her soft, rounded bottom. He clasped her shoulders and squeezed gently. "We'll get there soon enough, honey, but not until you tell me what's going on. Fair's fair. We agreed, remember?"

Almost against her will, she leaned into him. "Blackmail? You'll hold out until I 'fess up?"

It was his turn to shrug. "Think of it as concern, not coercion."

"I'm not used to sharing with anyone. I've been the leader of the family for a long time; my aunts and uncle depend on me, not the other way around."

"Your parents died?"

She kept her head down, her face averted. "Yes, like yours, when I was young. Thanos and my aunts took me in."

He noticed that she hadn't claimed they raised her. Because he'd met them, he had to wonder if Tamara hadn't always been the logical, responsible one. "What happened to them?"

Shifting, she finally looked at him. "From what I remember and from what everyone has always told me, they liked to live on the edge. They were daredevils, true Tremaynes, and they got a rush from taking risks and accepting challenges. One night after a celebration, my father raced his car against a friend on a deserted road and . . . Well, it was dark, and rainy. He crashed." She looked wistful, and resigned, as if she still couldn't understand it, but had long ago accepted it. "Thanos is the one who told me."

"Thank God you weren't with them." A sizzle of anger stirred along Zane's nerve endings. How could any parent behave so irresponsibly? He imagined what Tamara must had felt, felt a little of it himself, and it nearly smothered him with compassion.

"Oh, no. They realized when I was very young that I was

different—the white sheep, as you've already heard Thanos call me. They never took me with them when they . . . did dangerous things. Thanos explained that they had wild blood, and that's why they died. He and my aunts were there for me from that moment on."

There was an indefinable sorrow in her eyes as she told that story. The people who should have put her welfare first had instead been out partying and playing with their lives. It sounded to Zane as if they'd totally shirked their duty to her, and in the end, they'd left her alone. He discounted Thanos and the aunts as appropriate supervision. "How old were you?"

"Ten." She shrugged. "But Thanos likes to say I was ten going on twenty-five. He says I no sooner got over my grief than I started organizing everything."

She gave him a small smile. "Try to understand, Zane. I've always been the one in charge, the one who handles problems. It's my way, and Thanos understood that. He helped me to find my place in my new family by letting me take charge. As a child, it made me feel useful, less of a burden. As an adult, it's what I'm used to. My relatives come to me to fix things. All this . . . sharing stuff, your concern, it's not what I was asking for."

"And it's not what you wanted?" He wondered then if she was afraid to share. That possibility struck him deep in his soul.

She looked uncertain. "That's right."

Zane turned her around and looped his arms around her waist. There were some things he intended to be firm on, so she might as well understand that right now. "It's all part and parcel with involvement, sweetheart, at least as far as I'm concerned, so you might as well get used to it. Until you do move, we've got something going on, and I'm not good at standing in the background. Understand?"

She shook her head in exasperation. "You don't have to act like a caveman."

There she went, insulting him again. "Tamara—"

On impulse, she kissed his chin, licked her lips, then kissed his chin again. "Mmmm." Her voice softened, but her meaning didn't. "Spare me the threats, Zane. They won't work."

The spot tingled where her lips had touched, and it was no more than two simple pecks. *On his chin.* "I do not," he stated emphatically, ignoring how intimate those innocent little pecks had felt, "threaten women."

She patted his chest. "Then what would you call it?"

With ruthless determination, Zane reined in his temper and managed to say—with only a partial growl—"You're reneging on a deal. We agreed that if I answered your questions, you'd answer mine."

"I answered your questions on the book."

She was right, damn it. "You're just trying to distract me."

This time her patting was a little harder, tinged with her own temper. She glared up at him. "I can't believe you're being so insistent! It has nothing to do with you."

His control slipped another notch. "As long as we're sleeping together, anything that concerns you, concerns me."

"We're not sleeping together yet."

"Stop stalling and tell me."

"Oh, all right." She wrenched herself out of his hold and paced three steps away.

Zane thought about hauling her back; he *liked* holding her, liked having her snuggled in his arms.

He was just reaching for her when she spoke. And her first words stopped him cold.

S I X

"Someone has been trying to drive us away."

Zane stared at Tamara, not sure he'd heard her correctly.

"I don't know who," she explained hastily, "and I don't know why. But there's been too many small crises for me to write them off as coincidence the way the police have."

"You're not just moving to . . . move?"

"No, why would I? I love it here." A poignant yearning colored her words. "I had a small inheritance from my parents, money they'd earned in the circus and on the road. My uncle put it away for me until

I turned eighteen. As my guardian he could have used the money, and there were plenty of times through the years when we needed it." She smiled at that, as if being broke was part of a series of fond memories.

"I used it to buy their small house. They griped about that, because they'd always considered the money mine and they wanted me to spend it on myself." She glanced at Zane. "They never realized that I wanted to be by myself for a change, so buying the house for them was for me, too."

"How old were you then?"

"Eighteen. Plenty old enough."

Zane shook his head. Hell, at eighteen he'd still been living with Cole, working for him and getting a lot of help as he started college. He couldn't imagine being so completely alone at that age. "How'd you buy this place?"

"I'd saved up money from the jobs we did. I used all my savings for the down payment, and it was just enough."

He imagined she had a very frugal lifestyle, without a lot of room for luxuries or extravagance. Yet, she didn't seem to want for anything—except him. That thought caused a tightness in his chest, and in his groin.

Unaware of his private turmoil, she continued matter-of-factly, "My family is settled and this house is perfect for me. When I was younger and we were on the road so much, I used to dream of a house just like this. I love the wooden floors and the rusty pipes and the high moldings." Sadness invaded her expression before she shook her head, as if bringing herself back to reality.

She clearly thought she had no option except to sell, and just as clearly wasn't going to dwell on what couldn't be. She was too sensible to bemoan things she couldn't change. It was that sensibility, Zane thought, that had enabled her to get a band of loony Gypsies settled in the first place.

"I'm leaving," she told him, "because I don't know what else to do. Everything that happens costs money—money that I can't spare." She shrugged. "So we're . . . moving."

Zane crossed his arms. If there was any way to help her, he damn well would. But first he had to know all the details. "Start with the first crisis."

"A fire."

He cocked a brow and waited.

"That's right. A fire here in my shop. It had been a busy day with people in and out, so I hadn't had a chance to eat all day. When I closed the shop, I went to your bar to get a sandwich and a drink. But you weren't there. I guess you had a date or something, because you weren't at your store, either."

"You were looking for me?"

She shrugged and waved a hand in airy explanation. "I've admired you from afar for some time now. But as I said, you weren't at the bar, so I wrapped up the sandwich, finished my drink, and came home early."

"You've *admired me from afar*?"

"Do you want to hear this story or not?" she demanded.

"Yeah." A feeling of contentment settled over him. "I want to hear the story."

"Then stop interrupting."

Bossy little woman, Zane thought, this time with humor. He realized he was starting to get used to her. And he was liking her more with each minute that passed.

Wondering if she'd be that bossy in bed, he smiled and said, "Yes ma'am."

She eyed him, and must have decided he was sincere, because she continued with her tale. "I always use the outside stairs when I'm going straight home instead of into the shop. But this time I felt that something was wrong."

"You *felt* it? Like a premonition or something?" She kept claiming she didn't have powers, but Zane was sure she did. How else did he explain his obsession?

"I didn't mean it like that! I already told you I'm not psychic." She looked flustered, then went on. "I just used the shop door this time is all. And as soon as I stepped inside, I smelled the smoke. It came from this room, which was a good thing since the door was shut and it kept the damage from reaching most of the rest of the shop."

Zane looked around and only then noticed the blackened corners of the ceiling. The room was small, square, with a shallow closet where Tamara had hung a jacket, and a minuscule bathroom that boasted a plain white toilet and white enamel sink with the pipes exposed. A single bare bulb, hanging in the center of the room, supplied light. It was a storage area in every sense of the word, and at the moment it was packed full of boxes and bags and odds and ends. A fire could have really taken off, with plenty of paper and cardboard to feed on. "Do you know what started it?"

"An old chair that I'd bought at an auction caught fire. The material was threadbare and dry so it went up like kindling. I had planned to reupholster it because I liked the wood trim. It was dark and ornate, and went well with the rest of the decor."

"Eclectic hodgepodge?"

"Exactly."

Zane shook off another smile. He'd have to quit smiling like a fool over every inane thing she said. Otherwise, she'd think he was besotted. And that would never do. "How'd it catch on fire?"

She shrugged. "Supposedly a cigarette. The fire department found a butt down in the seat. Only I don't smoke and no one who works for me does, either. I don't allow it."

"A customer?"

"Not that I know of. I have a prominent NO SMOKING sign. Besides, customers aren't allowed in the back room and they're never left unsupervised, so it's not likely someone could have snuck in there to take a cigarette break."

"Could someone have asked to use the bathroom?"

She shook her head. "I send them to the diner across the street." She began pacing again, her movements punctuated by her explanations. "Luckily I caught the fire early because I can only imagine the amount of damage that might have been done otherwise. As it was, it took me a week to get things cleaned up and the smell out."

She could have been killed, Zane realized. What if she hadn't gone out that night? Or what if she hadn't come home early? If he'd been at the bar when she was there, would she have hung around *admiring him from afar* and then gotten home too late to stop the fire—or perhaps even been caught in it?

A sick feeling stirred in his stomach; it felt remarkably like fear. *For her*.

Damn it, it had to be just a fluke. He couldn't think of a single reason why anyone would want to burn down her small establishment. She wasn't a threat to anyone, didn't offer any great competition to the other businesses in the area. None of it made sense, unless it was all personal. "You're certain your assistant—what's her name?"

"Luna Clark."

Zane did a double take. "Luna?"

Smiling, making her voice deliberately mystical, she said, "Luna, goddess of the moon."

Zane stared. "Uh-huh. Right. So you're certain your assistant goddess doesn't smoke?"

"Just because Luna is a little different doesn't mean she'd lie to me."

"Don't get in a snit. I didn't mean to suggest she would." Then he asked, "Different how? I've never met her."

Tamara grinned. "Except for her coloring, Luna could have been born into my family. She fits right in with them. She believes all the crazy stuff they believe about fortune-telling and fate and ghosts. She's beautiful, naturally flamboyant without a wig or contacts. Half the time I believe she's got mind powers. She usually knows what I'm thinking."

"Does that bother you?" Zane figured one mystical woman was more than enough for him. He'd be happy never to meet Luna face-to-face.

"No. Being around Luna is a riot. The customers love her."

Luna, Zane thought, sounded more than a little flaky. "How long has she worked for you?"

"Around a year. I trust her completely. Besides, she wasn't here that day. She's only part-time."

Zane strode toward her, inexplicably drawn nearer. "Who did work that day?"

"Just me."

"All day?" The sense of fear intensified, only Zane didn't know where it was coming from, or why. He just knew that it was very real, as real as the need to protect Tamara, to claim her. "By yourself?"

"You don't have to say it like that." She rolled her eyes. "My shop is hardly as busy as yours. I can and do work alone quite often. It's no big deal."

A deep breath didn't help. Silently counting to ten didn't help, either. "Are you telling me," Zane asked quietly, "that you *still* work alone? Even though you think someone is out to hurt you?"

She inched back, warily moving away from the bite of his restrained temper. "I never said anyone wanted to hurt *me*. The problems have all been related to the shop somehow. The fire, a dead rat in the toilet that caused all the plumbing to clog up and overflow—"

"Whoa." Zane held up a hand, halting her in midsentence. "A dead rat in the toilet?"

She shifted on her bare feet. "The police said it crawled into the pipes and died somehow, but . . . well, if you'd seen it, you'd know that rat was roadkill. It was disgusting, and I'm convinced it was put there deliberately. Same as the cigarette."

"How?"

"I don't know. That's just it. The window in here is too small for a man to crawl through, and the rest of the place is always locked up."

Zane looked at the window. It was high, narrow. "A kid could probably fit through."

"Maybe. But why would a kid want to?"

He shrugged. Kids did a lot of stupid things, like taking a bet, or agreeing to vandalism for the thrill of it, or for a few bucks. Someone might have hired a kid for the job. It made as much sense as anything else. "Your problems could just be childish pranks."

Tamara bristled. "Childish pranks have ruined my savings account. Repairing the plumbing cost a fortune, not to mention all the cleanup and the fact I had to close for nearly a week. And it wasn't long after the fire had forced me to miss some days, too."

"Do you have a better explanation?"

She sighed in defeat. "I think somehow, someone is getting in without me knowing it. That's why my aunts insist—"

"On Uncle Hubert's ghost." Zane shook his head. "I suppose they choose to believe that because it's less threatening to them than a flesh-and-blood person skulking around, getting in unnoticed."

"I think so." She frowned as she looked up at him, as if she didn't understand him or his level of concern. If it had been up to her, she wouldn't have told him anything—except that she wanted him.

He drew a deep breath. Truth was, Zane didn't understand himself. Never before had he felt so drawn in by a woman's problems. Especially when he'd only kissed her, and most of the time in between those kisses had involved her insulting him. And there was the fact that part of her problems included an eclectic group of relations who had taken turns trying to do him bodily harm.

All in all, Tamara Tremayne shouldn't have been such a temptation. If he had any sense at all, he'd be running in the other direction.

But now he was involved up to his eyebrows. He was worried, damn it, when he didn't like to worry. He felt . . . connected to Tamara and everything that surrounded or touched her, including her problems.

Tamara cleared her throat. "I lost three nice rugs because of the water damage, and several boxes of things that had been on the floor."

"It was the toilet in here?"

"Yes. It's the only one on this floor. There are two bathrooms upstairs, but I only use the one that connects to my bedroom. The other is in the hall in the part of the house that I've shut off."

"You don't use all the rooms upstairs?"

"No. Uncle Thanos and my aunts live in their own home, and I certainly don't need all this space."

He hated to say it, because the idea of an intruder being near Tamara while she slept filled him with rage and helplessness. But the thought wouldn't go away. "Maybe someone got in through that part of the house."

"Upstairs with me?" She looked taken aback by the idea, and damn if Zane didn't feel her anxiety as if it were his own. Then she shook her head, the stubbornness he was beginning to recognize apparent in her expression. "No, the windows are all too high for someone to climb through, and they're locked besides. I even have the hallway door leading to that part of the house locked."

"You put a lock on it?"

"No. It's not uncommon for older houses to have key locks on all the doors."

"A skeleton key?"

"Yes. But the locks are sturdy and I'm a light sleeper. I'd hear if anyone was prowling around."

It was an attempt to convince herself as much as him, and it didn't work. Zane didn't like thinking about her being alone. He wasn't entirely convinced that her prowler was anything more than coincidence and pranks, as the police apparently thought, but just in case, he'd have felt better if she had company.

He'd always written off intuition as coincidence, but now he couldn't rid himself of the feeling that something was very wrong. Tamara wanted him, but he was almost certain that she needed him, too.

It was far too soon for him to propose that he stay over; that would suggest an intimacy that she'd claimed to want no part of. He tried doing the next best thing. "You have a phone by your bed?"

"Yes."

"Call me if anything happens, if you hear anything at night or if you just get nervous."

"Zane . . ."

"Whatever you do, do *not* try to deal with an intruder on your own." He broke out in a sweat as he thought of how she'd tried to race down the steps alone earlier. She hadn't known that only a box of books had fallen; she'd been fully prepared to confront an unknown assailant.

"Zane . . ."

He could tell she was going to refuse. She was an independent woman, doggedly so, and she wouldn't like the suggestion that she might need him. "Promise you'll call me, no matter how silly the reason might seem, or I'm going to suggest to Thanos that he spend the night."

Her eyes flared. "Good God, if you do that, my aunts will want to stay, too!"

He shrugged.

"Do you have any idea how hard I had to fight for my privacy? It wasn't easy getting them settled in their own home!"

He'd want to hear more on that later, he decided. Since he valued his own privacy, and protected it fiercely, he could understand. But this was too important to let go. "Then promise me."

Angry color darkened her cheeks. She didn't like being manipulated any more than he would.

They had more in common than he'd ever suspected.

"Do it for me, Tamara," he insisted. "I know you can take care of yourself, but I'll still worry.

"You're supposed to be a playboy, not a mother hen."

Thoroughly exasperated, Zane asked, "Do you always resort to insults when you don't get your own way?"

Looking contrite, she bit her lip. "There's no reason for you to worry."

"I'm male and you're definitely not. That's all the reason I need."

For several seconds she glared at him. "Oh, all right." After she gave that grudging promise, she actually smiled. "I can tell dealing with you is going to be more difficult than I'd expected."

"You thought things would be simple when you propositioned me?" Zane asked. "No messy involvement or unsolicited caring, just sex? I'd show up when you said, leave when I finished, and not talk to you much in between?"

She looked uncertain, started to say something, then pinched her mouth together and shrugged.

Indignation nearly choked him.

In the past, a no-involvement relationship had always suited him just fine. But at the moment, he wasn't really sure what he wanted. He decided things would last as long as *he* said, and she could just deal with it. Not that he'd tell her so.

Zane turned away from her before she could sidetrack him again.

Hefting the box, he put it back on the shelf. He made sure it was securely stationed this time and wouldn't fall, then took Tamara's hand and started her out of the room. He had more important things to do than moon over his unaccountable feelings for a little Gypsy with too much backbone.

Keeping her safe was first on the list. And to do that, he had to figure out what the hell was going on. He could probably use a little help with that. He'd see his brothers tomorrow, and maybe they could all come up with a logical explanation.

Thinking of the razzing he'd take pissed him off, but he could live with that. He *couldn't* live with leaving Tamara in danger.

"Okay, before I head home," Zane growled, "tell me the rest, and don't leave anything out."

"Zane . . ." She trotted along next to him as he headed upstairs, where her relatives waited. "You're . . . upset?"

She was good at reading him, and he didn't like that much, either. He gave her one sharp nod, unwilling to discuss it. He should have known that wouldn't be enough for Tamara.

She pulled him to a stop in the middle of the stairs. One step above him now, she was on eye level. Her expression turned serious, and curious, and warm. "Why?" she whispered. "Is it because we can't start our new . . . association tonight? Or is it because of that insult business? I didn't mean to make you angry, you know."

It didn't matter this time if she saw his hands shaking. Zane cupped her face and drew her closer until their breaths mingled. "You could have been hurt, Tamara. If you're right, and it is an intruder deliberately preying on you, you could have been killed."

Her eyes widened, in shock both at his vehemence and at the fact that he obviously believed her. Her emotions—relief, confusion, lust—rolled over him in suffocating waves.

"I'm not just upset, honey. I'm goddamn furious." Zane kissed her, to try and block the unwelcome connection, to replace it with pure lust, something he could understand and deal with.

His time as a free man was slipping away, and he knew it.

Cole was at the bar when Zane wandered in much later that night. He hadn't meant to go there. Hell, he'd meant to go home and think about things, maybe get some needed sleep. He'd spent a long while talking to Tamara, hearing about the more recent problems. Before he'd left, they'd made plans to have dinner the following day.

But Zane hadn't gone home afterward, knowing he'd only have stayed awake thinking of Tamara. And so he found himself at the bar. It was a place of comfort, a place to let his brain rest.

Women greeted him as he walked in. They didn't insult him—far from it. They ogled him and smiled suggestively, and his world felt right again.

Dropping onto a bar stool, Zane asked his brother, "Been busy tonight?"

Cole glanced up while filling a mug with beer, then continued to look. With a sudden frown, he demanded, "What'd you do?"

Startled. Zane glanced around, realized Cole was speaking to him, and said, "Nothing. I just got here."

Cole slid the beer to the customer, wiped his hands on a dish towel, and propped his elbows on the bar. He studied Zane suspiciously. "You're up to something."

"I am not!" Zane shifted uncomfortably, laughed a little nervously. There was no way Cole could know what he had planned for Tamara.

"You look just like you used to when you got into trouble."

Zane managed a credible snort. "I never got into that much trouble."

"Ha! I had outraged mothers calling me all the time."

"That's an exaggeration." Zane refused to feel guilty about things he'd done in his teens. More often than not, it had been the females asking him out, anyway.

"You'd stay out too late," Cole continued, on a damn roll for some reason, "go places you shouldn't, like parking, and then break things off as soon as she got serious. . . ."

As if a light went off, Cole straightened. "That's it! You're after a new woman, aren't you?"

"No!" He wasn't after Tamara. Good God, just the opposite. *She* was after *him*. Of course, he was the one who'd been insistent. . . .

"I can see it in your face," Cole said with a nod. "She's got you hooked, doesn't she?"

"*No.*" That was just plain laughable. No way did Tamara have him hooked; he wouldn't let himself be hooked. No woman could affect him to the point that it'd be plain on his face, to the point his brother could take one look at him and—

"If she's a nice woman, Zane, leave her alone."

Leave her alone! Zane couldn't quite hide his irritation. "I know what I'm doing, Cole." At least, he thought he did. But Tamara had a way of keeping him guessing, keeping him on edge.

Affecting him, damn her.

God, maybe he *was* hooked.

"There are plenty of interested females around without seducing one who's hesitant." Cole nodded to the room at large. "Just look around you. Hell, half a dozen are ready and waiting as we speak."

Zane peered over his shoulder and was met with a lot of seductive looks. Beyond feeding his ego, however, they didn't move him one bit. He plain wasn't interested. The only woman he could think of right now was Tamara, and he wanted her bad.

He turned back to Cole and caught his brother's speculative gaze. "Now you can just stop that."

"Stop what?" Cole asked innocently.

"Stop imagining things." Given half a chance, Cole would come up with all kinds of ridiculous notions.

Cole laughed, forced a shrug, and began wiping off the bar. "If you say so."

Gritting his teeth, Zane said, "I am *not* hooked, damn it!"

Several people looked up, making Cole lift his brows and Zane cringe. Zane ran a hand through his hair and then stood. "I'm heading home."

"Don't leave mad," Cole admonished.

"I'm not mad."

This time Cole laughed. "Not hooked, not mad, and not protesting too much, huh?" He hesitated, then said, "Bring her around. I'd like to meet her."

"Not yet." Zane realized what he'd said the second the words left his mouth. He scowled at Cole.

"Well, at least remember what I told you."

"About seducing the unwilling? Ha! I . . . no, forget that." Zane frowned. No way in hell would he explain to his oldest brother that Tamara only wanted him for sex. Not only was it none of his business, it was embarrassing besides.

Cole took pity on him and leaned across the bar to clap him on the shoulder. "You look exhausted. Get on home and get some sleep."

"Yeah, I think I will." If he stayed any longer, he'd be making confessions and telling more than he should. "Give Sophie a hug from me."

Zane made his way out, dodging women and suggestions and invitations. The fresh air felt good, and the thought of his bed sounded great. But Zane knew he wouldn't sleep. He knew he'd think about Tamara, and if by chance he did doze off, he'd dream about her. He had to get a grip.

Tomorrow he'd prove to her that he was still in charge. And before the day was over, they'd both believe it.

S E V E N

They had made plans to get together for a late dinner that night. Because she closed up earlier than Zane, she could take care of a few errands first, shower and change, and replace her garish makeup with something more suitable. She could hardly wait.

Tamara couldn't remember floating through a workday before, but no matter how busy it got, no matter how harried, she felt elated.

Zane had said he wanted to discuss things. She didn't know if he meant her proposition or her problems, but she'd vote for the first. The last thing she wanted was to involve him further in her problems. It was humiliating for one thing; she'd worked long and hard to find a settled life, and she didn't want him to know her financial position was still precarious. A few more setbacks, like the fire and the water damage, could wipe her out completely.

And for another, the book had said to be independent. A man should know you want him before he thinks you need him, otherwise you give him an edge. Tamara thought the book was right, and she intended to keep every edge she could; that was the only way she could deal with Zane Winston and not get her heart permanently squashed.

Luna, who had worked with her that day, eyed her suspiciously. "You've been grinning ever since I arrived."

Tamara tried, and failed, to suppress another smile. "Have I?" She felt like laughing out loud. After all the recent troubles, it was good to be able to concentrate on something else, something positive, especially when that something was tall, dark, and outrageous.

"Uh-huh." Luna looked her over. "Whatever it is, you're glowing—and impatient. You want me to take the money to the bank for you, so you can get freed up a little earlier?"

It wasn't something Luna did often, and Tamara shook her head. "No, that's okay. I can do it. You probably have a date or something tonight, don't you?"

Today Luna had red hair in three stubby braids. The last time she'd worked, her hair had been brown and gelled into a severe bun. Luna changed her appearance from day to day, and the regular customers found her fascinating.

"I have a date," Luna said with a wink, "but waiting is good for him. Keeps him on his toes."

Tamara wished she could be so cavalier. She had no intention of keeping Zane Winston waiting for her. Not only was she far too anxious to stay away from him longer than she actually had to, but she just didn't have the time to waste playing games.

Smiling like a devout sinner, Tamara said, "I have a sort of a date, too."

"What the heck is a sort of a date? You meeting a guy in an alley or something?" As she spoke, Luna went through the routine of snuffing out candles and incense while Tamara took care of the cash register.

After counting out enough money for the next day and locking it away, Tamara stuffed the checks and excess cash into a zippered plastic bag. Luna had already run the credit slips and closed out on them.

Keeping her gaze on the money bag, Tamara admitted, "I'm having dinner with Zane Winston tonight."

Luna halted, then let out a long, low whistle. She propped her hands on her rounded hips and fought with a grin. The grin won. "I'll be damned."

"You know who he is?"

"Honey, there isn't a woman alive in or around Thomasville who doesn't know the Winstons, especially *that* one." She crossed her arms and leaned against the counter. Her black leather pants gleamed in the dimmed light. "It's Zane's antics that have given the Winstons celebrity status."

"Not entirely. Heck, they're all gorgeous, and that's probably reason enough for them to be so popular."

"Maybe," Luna conceded. "But I saw the article the local paper did on him recently. He made the family tavern topless when he stripped off his shirt to serve drinks to a group of women organizing a wedding shower."

"They goaded him into it!"

Luna's eyebrows bobbed theatrically. "The guy's got a stellar chest."

Tamara knew that. She blushed just thinking about how great that chest had felt against her hands and her breasts. "Yeah, he does. His brother assured the reporter that from now on, Zane would be wearing a shirt when he worked there." She couldn't help laughing. "I have the feeling keeping Zane in line is a full-time job for his brothers."

"You know those women asked him to be a stripper at the wedding shower, to surprise the bride."

Tamara had read the whole article—which wasn't the first one on the Winstons. She'd saved them all in an album. "Yep, and Zane refused, saying the bride would never go through with the wedding if she viewed him in the buff."

Both women laughed out loud. Luna pushed away from the counter. "You be careful with him tonight, okay? Guys like that are walking, talking heartbreakers."

"I know what I'm doing."

"Yeah, right." Luna sent her a knowing look. "Honey, *I* know what I'm doing. You're still trying to figure out what it is you want to do."

"I want to do Zane Winston."

Luna did a double take at that bold statement, then chuckled. "I'd wish you luck, but I doubt you'll need any. That one would jump any female who held still long enough."

Tamara didn't bother to explain that at first Zane had unequivocally turned her down. It was too mortifying. She tucked the money bag into the pocket of her long skirt and patted it. "Well, I better get going. I have to get back in time to do a makeover before I go over there."

"He's open late tonight?"

"Nearly every night. He's a workaholic, if you ask me."

"Oh, speaking of work." Luna plucked the appointment book from the counter. "Arkin Devane called and wants to come in again tomorrow. I think the guy is hooked—on you."

Tamara halted on her way to the door. "Me?"

"He insisted on having an hour and a half of your time."

"But . . . that's triple the time I usually spend with a customer."

"According to him, there's a lot he wants to talk about." Luna bobbed her eyebrows suggestively. "And he's willing to pay for it."

"Hmmm."

"Hmmm nothing. Looks like Zane might have some competition."

That comment didn't deserve a response. No one could compete with Zane. Not that Arkin was a bad-looking man, just not in the same league with Zane.

Tamara pictured Arkin: mid-thirties, rangy muscles, light brown hair, and light blue eyes. He was somewhat bookish and overly intense. But she'd liked him on sight and felt a strange affinity with him. He hadn't said as much, but she knew he was in love and was desperately hoping to find a way to win his lady.

She also knew she wasn't that lady.

"I feel a little guilty," Tamara said, "taking money from the sincere ones, you know?"

Luna slipped on her jacket, then gave Tamara a hug. "Deny it all you like, sweetie, but you're a sincere one, too, so I know he's in good hands."

Luna had the annoying habit of seeing through everyone. She insisted endlessly that Tamara had real intuitive abilities. It bugged Tamara that she was partially right, even though she'd never admit it.

Luna grinned her *I know all, I see all* grin, the one the customers ate up. "Don't forget your umbrella. It looks like rain."

Luna went out, leaving Tamara alone with her thoughts. Seconds later, a crack of thunder intruded, proving Luna did at least know her weather. Shaking herself out of her reverie, Tamara slipped on her slicker and grabbed her bright green umbrella. After one last look around the shop, she stepped outside and secured all the locks.

Bloated purple clouds rolled across the sky and the streetlights flickered on. The sharp nip of cold damp air that almost always accompanied a storm made Tamara's slicker insufficient. The first drops of rain began to fall—and Tamara felt an unwelcome gaze watching her. Chills tingled up her arms, her spine.

The bank was only a short walk away, so she never drove there, but today she wished she'd gotten the car from Uncle Thanos.

With the rain coming a little harder now, the sidewalks were slick and all but deserted. Tamara kept a tight grip on the umbrella as wind tried to tear it from her hands. The bottom of her long skirt was quickly soaked, as were her sandals. She cursed the weatherman who had predicted no more than the possibility of a sprinkle.

The bank was in sight when she thought she heard footsteps behind her. Just as when she'd sensed trouble in her shop, an eerie foreboding raced over her nerve endings. She jerked around.

There was no one there, but the feeling didn't abate. Tamara searched the darkened street, trying to see behind parked cars and into the shadows of alleys between tall buildings. Heart racing, lungs compressed with nervousness, she finally turned and jogged the rest of the way to the bank. She was panting by the time she came through the doors.

She did her business quickly, constantly peeking out the wide front window, but she perceived nothing more alarming than hot bright lightning licking across the dark violet sky. Briefly, she considered calling Thanos to come pick her up, but it was almost six and the bank would be closing in just a few minutes. By the time Thanos could arrive, she'd be left standing outside anyway.

Thoughts of Zane whispered through her subconscious, but she shook them off. She would not start imposing on him. He was busy with his own work and he wouldn't close his shop for at least another hour. Somehow she knew he'd come if she called him, but that would seem so cowardly on her part. And she didn't want to start off with Zane seeing her as a coward.

Holding the umbrella steady, she stepped outside. Other than a few people racing to their parked cars, there was no one around. The sidewalk was well lit by streetlamps and security lights at the various businesses; they reflected brightly off the wet pavement and windows. She was not psychic, Tamara insisted to herself, and her premonitions tonight were nothing more than female foolishness. There was no reason to be on edge, to continue standing in the downpour, getting more sodden by the second.

She drew in a deep breath and started off. Despite the assurances she'd just given herself, she couldn't stop her gaze from darting left and right as she walked. Lucky thing, too, because she was only a few yards from her shop door when she saw the man move out of the shadows at the side of the building. He wore a dark ski mask over his face. Despite the gloom of early evening, his eyes shone bright—and he was looking right at her with an arrested expression.

Panic slammed through her.

Tamara didn't think twice; instincts insisted that she run, so she did just that. The opposite side of the street seemed her best bet, so she managed to zigzag across the wet road, then angled back, giving the man in the mask a wide berth. A slick spot on the sidewalk made her stumble, and she dropped the umbrella as she fetched up against a parked van. Pain shot through her upper arm, but it didn't slow her down. She quickly righted herself, darted a look over her shoulder, and took off again. She hadn't seen anyone in that brief glimpse, but the sense of being followed, watched, was still a pounding beat in her heart. Had he followed her? Was he still after her?

She was so anxious, she knew she couldn't begin fumbling with the locked door of her shop; her hands, her entire body, shook uncontrollably. Besides, that would bring her entirely too close to where she'd seen him. She sprinted right past her shop to Zane's. Because of the rain, his door was closed, and she jerked at it, too afraid to look back, for what felt like a lifetime before it opened and she threw herself inside.

Breathing hard, her heart galloping wildly, she collapsed back against the door. Her gaze sought Zane, and then locked on him in stunned disbelief.

He stood by his counter with a beautiful blond woman in his arms. They both stared at Tamara, shock replacing whatever expressions they had worn before her entrance.

The furious drumming of her heartbeat slowed and then almost ceased entirely as she took in the incriminating sight before her.

Zane's hands were on the woman's shoulders, her arms were around his neck, her fingers laced in his dark, silky hair. They stood very close together, upper bodies touching. Intimate. All but embracing.

Shoving hanks of the wet wig out of her face, Tamara searched Zane's eyes. She felt his confusion first, then his annoyance, and finally his unease.

"Tamara . . ." He moved the blonde aside and started forward.

He hadn't been a willing participant in the embrace. Tamara suddenly knew that with a clarity that defied description. Never had an emotion from someone else hit her so strongly. She heaved a relieved sigh, and turned to look out at the darkened parking lot. Rain drubbing against the glass door made visibility difficult. She couldn't see anybody, yet she knew he was still there, knew he was still watching. She felt his panic mixing with her own, confusing her, making her thoughts jumble. Oh, God. What did he want?

"Tamara," Zane said again. He caught her shoulders, trying to turn her. "You're early."

Tamara barely paid him any mind. She scanned the surrounding area—was that a shadow there? No . . . well, maybe.

"It's not the way it looked," Zane insisted, his hands tightening just the tiniest bit, caressing. Warmth radiated from him into her chilled bones. Having him close comforted her, and that was almost as scary as being pursued. She could not begin relying on Zane. He wasn't the reliable sort. Oh, he was a good man, she had no doubts about that. But he wasn't a man who would appreciate having a woman cling to him. She had to remember that.

The blonde cleared her throat—loudly. Zane and Tamara ignored her.

"Tamara, listen to me."

She allowed herself to be bodily shifted away from the door. Her breath was still coming in pants, from both nervousness and exertion.

She could barely get her fractured attention to focus on what Zane said. She stared at him, wishing she knew who had been following her and why.

She shivered.

Zane made a disgusted sound. "Don't look like that, damn it." He lightly shook her. "I was just telling Claire that I was busy tonight. With *you*."

He sounded so . . . concerned. Distracted, Tamara patted his chest while her thoughts spun off in different directions. Would the blasted police believe her this time? There was little enough she could tell them, really. She'd seen a man wearing a ski mask. So what? It was cool tonight, raining, miserable. Lots of people had probably bundled up.

Doubt intruded, edging past her fear. Had he really followed her? Or was he just there, out on errands the same as she was? Tamara couldn't be sure. She thought she'd heard his footsteps behind her, but mostly what had alarmed her was her feeling of being watched, of the man's frustration—and no way would she try to convince the police that she'd been in danger based on a feeling. She could just imagine their reactions to that.

For most of her life, she'd heard the jibes—Gypsies were charlatans, ripping off customers with no more than parlor tricks. And the jibes had been correct.

No, she couldn't tell the police. Something was wrong, she knew that for a fact. But if she went to the police now, they'd write her off as a nut. And then, if she needed their help later, they might think she was just crying wolf. Besides, what could they do now?

Tamara rubbed her forehead, wondering how to proceed.

Zane released her and stepped back. She heard him speaking to the other woman. "You should leave, Claire. Tamara and I have some talking to do." He didn't sound pleased.

Claire said, "You can't be serious. You're turning me down for . . . for this?"

The insult was too blatant for her to miss, even in her distraught state. Eyes narrowed and mean, Tamara focused on the other woman. Oh, her relatives might tease her about being a white sheep, but she knew the power she had when she caught someone in her sights, when she locked her Gypsy eyes on them. The black contacts were great for effect, especially when they accompanied her present dark mood. And no matter what the color of her hair, she was still a Tremayne through and through.

Claire took an alarmed step back.

Though Tamara didn't say a word, the woman quickly donned her raincoat and fled. Tamara briefly wondered if it was safe for Claire to be out there, what with some nefarious type person lurking around in the shadows wearing a ski mask, but the blonde made it safely to her car and drove away. Tamara watched her leave, just to be certain.

Zane made a rough sound behind her. "Terrorizing the locals, Tamara?"

She continued to study the parking lot. There weren't too many places for a grown man to hide. If he was there, she'd have seen him by now. Had she imagined the whole thing? It sickened her to consider that possibility.

"If you think I'm going to apologize, you're sadly mistaken."

Zane's tone drew her away from her concerns. She met his unwavering gaze as her nervousness began receding, replaced by awareness of him. "Okay." Their relationship wasn't the type that required explanations or apologies. She would force herself to remember that, no matter what.

Then she realized that her slicker had blown open when she ran. She was soaked through and through and her makeup was badly botched. No wonder the blonde had been so disbelieving! "I don't suppose you have a towel or anything handy?"

Frowning at her, Zane retrieved a roll of paper towels from behind the counter. "Where the hell is your umbrella?" he asked, as he watched her remove the slicker and drop it by the door.

With the sleeve torn and the lining soaked, it would do nothing to protect her from the weather. She mopped at her dripping face and throat.

"Don't you have enough sense not to run around in the rain?"

She understood him now. He was disgruntled with her and being foul-tempered because of it.

"I dropped my umbrella." Tamara gently wiped away most of the smudged makeup around her eyes and then got a new towel to blot her arms. "It's pouring out there."

"What do you mean you dropped your umbrella?"

Tamara glanced up and then away. Uh-oh. He looked suddenly . . .

angry. And suspiciously alert. The man had too many mood swings for her to keep up with.

When she didn't answer right away, Zane caught her arm and said, "What's going on, Tamara?"

"Going on?"

His jaw tightened. "Don't play games. Something is wrong. I can feel it."

Her brows lifted. Was it possible that he could read her as easily she read him? "No kidding?" It was not a reassuring thought. "Kinda like intuition or something?"

Zane opened his mouth, but nothing came out. His frown turned fierce. "It's clear you're upset about something."

Tamara racked her brain and came up with the obvious reply. "You were here in a heated embrace with another woman. Of course I was upset."

"Bullshit."

Startled, Tamara opened her mouth to reply, but this time it was her turn to play mute.

"Seeing me with Claire didn't bother you a bit." He hesitated as he searched her face, his expression alert. "Did it?"

She didn't understand him at all. His attitude was curious, bordering on hopeful.

"Did you want it to?" Tamara tried to peek over her shoulder again, to look out the door toward the parking lot. It was nearly abandoned. There were no lurking shadows, and even more than that, she had no lingering feelings of danger. Whoever had been there was gone, or at least far enough away that she couldn't sense him anymore.

She couldn't quite muster any relief. In her head she might reason that she'd imagined the danger, but in her heart she knew it existed.

With one finger on her chin, Zane turned her face back to him. "Claire asked me out, I said no because I planned to see you, and she tried to push the issue. That's all there was to it."

Now she felt relief, even though she'd already concluded as much. It was still nice to have him admit it so openly. "Okay."

Exasperation laced his tone. "Just like that?"

Now that the threat was over, Tamara felt safe devoting her full attention to Zane. And it looked like he definitely needed her full attention. He was all but demanding she give it to him.

In a soothing tone, she reassured him. "You said it was nothing and I believe you."

How could she not believe him? She'd felt his sincerity right off. It had been like that from the first. She read Zane more easily than she read others. Throughout her life, there had been people she'd been able to pick up feelings from. She wasn't a mind reader, so she never knew exact thoughts or expectations. But fear, elation, worry—she could sense those emotions in a few people.

When her parents had died, she'd known Uncle Thanos's grief, as well as Olga's and Eva's determination to make her feel welcome as a member of their family. She'd sometimes felt the curiosity of customers, the hopefulness. The scorn.

But it was more than an inkling with Zane. What he felt, she felt as if it were her own. Right now she felt his anticipation, and that brought with it another thought. "Do you plan to see her when you're not seeing me?"

He started to answer and she whirled away, appalled that she'd ask such a thing. "No! Forget I asked that. Really, it's none of my business."

"Tamara—"

"I mean it, Zane. I have no intention of trying to tie you down." The words were hard to get out, but she knew she had to say them. Tamara swallowed hard and added, "If you want to see other women, that's up to you."

Carefully, as if he'd never said such a thing before, Zane muttered, "That's not how it works, Tamara. For as long as we're . . . involved, it'll be exclusive."

Surprised, she stared at him.

He leveled a harsh look on her. "For *both* of us."

Since she had no other prospects, Tamara just shrugged. She certainly had no one else she wanted to see, and she perceived no downside to telling him so. "Fine."

He looked first relieved, then suspicious. "You trust me on this?"

"No, of course not." Zane wasn't a man who could or should be trusted. He was a man to be savored, but only by a woman who kept her wits and didn't expect too much. Like fidelity.

"Damn it, Tamara!" He ran a hand through his hair and glared at her.

"Zane," she said reasonably, "you dance topless on the tables at the bar. You date a different woman every night. You draw customers to your shop with your gorgeous bod alone. Why should you change all that for me?"

His chin jutted forward. After a heavy silence and a look that could scorch, he growled, "Because I said I would and I'm not a liar."

No, he wasn't lying. His earnestness beat at her, wearing her down.

More than anything, Tamara wanted to ask him *why*. Why would he change his habits for her, especially after he'd first turned her down? He'd avoided her, had made his disinterest clear, and now he wanted their agreement to be exclusive?

She wasn't sure the answer would be one she wanted to hear. Slowly, she nodded. "Okay."

"No more doubting?"

"No."

Zane caught her shoulders. "Now that that's out of the way, tell me what spooked you."

Damn, how had he taken her full circle back to the subject she wanted to avoid? "I never said anything spooked me," she hedged.

"You walked in here, soaked to the skin, your blouse all but transparent—"

Gasping, Tamara looked down, but Zane caught her chin and lifted it. Once she met his hot gaze, her blouse was forgotten. "We'll deal with your distracting state of undress in a moment," he murmured. "For now, tell me what happened. And no more lying."

You just had to throw that last in, she thought, scowling at him. He knew she'd lied about not caring if he saw other women. "I thought someone was following me."

Zane stared at her a second more, then cursed as he set her aside. "Why the hell didn't you tell me right away?"

He stalked over to the door, jerked it open, and marched straight into the pounding rain. Tamara ran after him.

"Zane!" The storm had become more violent, rain coming down in a deluge. "Aren't you the one who called me an idiot for running around in the rain? At least I had a good reason!"

He looked between and behind the remaining parked cars in the lot. Finding no one there, he turned and stalked over to the alley between their buildings. Alarmed, Tamara wondered what he intended to do if he found someone.

Lightning pierced the dark sky, briefly lighting the lot. The air sizzled and popped with electricity, while dread churned in her belly. Zane was safe for now, but what if the man had still been hanging around? She would not let Zane be hurt because of her.

Tamara grabbed the back of Zane's shirt. He was soaked through, and now, so was she. "Zane, whoever he was, he's gone."

"You don't know that," he shouted over a loud explosion of thunder that arrived only seconds after the lightning.

"Yes, I do," she yelled back. Zane froze.

Slowly, so slowly it was apparent he had no care of the freezing rain, Zane turned to face her. Water ran in rivulets from his nose to his chin, and dripped off his dark hair, now stuck to his skull. "What do you mean, you know he's gone?"

Tamara twisted her hands together. The rain battered her skin with stinging force. She began shivering. "I just . . . know."

Zane eyed her from top to toes, and his expression hardened. "I'll call the cops." But he didn't move.

"No. It wouldn't do any good." She watched Zane absorb her words, accept them, while her teeth began to chatter. "It's okay now."

Zane looked like a savage, every harshly carved muscle delineated beneath the clinging wet clothes, his dark eyes burning, his jaw tight, his lashes clumped together. Primitive emotions shimmered off him like waves of heat. "That's what I thought," he growled. "Come on."

Despite her assurances and his apparent belief, Zane looked around as he led her into the store, his gaze watchful. This was a side of him she'd never seen, never anticipated, and in a way it was as exciting as it was alarming. He wasn't just a playboy, civilized to the point of urbanity. No, at that moment he was pure, basic male and she couldn't help but respond.

Tamara tried to stop on the welcome mat, thinking to do most of her dripping there, but Zane didn't even slow—and given that he had hold of her arm, she got dragged along with him.

His anger was strong and turbulent, surging against her in forceful ripples. Was it because he realized she was intuitive? Or was it entirely focused on the man who'd followed her? She watched his broad back expand with deep breaths as he led her to a storage room so neatly organized in comparison to her own, it put her to shame.

Tamara was swept along on his emotions, some of them clear, some not so clear. She knew she should be searching her mind for a way to explain the inexplicable, but it was difficult at the moment.

If she told Zane exactly what had happened, would he believe her, or would he accuse her of being a card-carrying swami? His ridicule would he unforgivable. She'd still want him, but she'd never be able to put aside her hurt.

He stopped just over the threshold, shoved the door closed with his foot, and backed Tamara into it. She caught her breath when his hard hips pressed against hers; he was fully aroused, his erection a long, hard ridge between their bodies.

Heat rolled off him, despite the sodden state of their clothes. Tamara followed the progress of a raindrop as it trailed along his firm jaw, down his throat and into the open collar of his shirt. Her belly clenched in sexual awareness—his or hers?

Involuntarily, she licked her lips. Bombarded by sensations, she couldn't quite pinpoint the most prevalent. Desire? Worry? Fear? She tried to draw a deep breath, and drew in the humid smell of Zane's heated body instead. A fine trembling started in her limbs and gained strength the longer she stared at him. "Zane?"

Watching her, holding her gaze captive with his own, he closed his large hand over her breast. His lids dropped to half-mast, his jaw tightened. The feeling was so indescribable, so overwhelming, she tried to flinch away from it. Zane held her secure.

Gently he caressed her, learned her, shaped her in his palm and with his long, hard fingers. When he touched her beaded nipple, his eyes shut briefly. He groaned softly before he opened them again, watching her with a concentration that invaded her soul.

His voice low and rough, he said, "Your blouse and bra are so wet, I can see through them. I can even see your nipples."

Contentment swelled inside her, because he didn't want to question her about the masked man or her intuition. He wanted her, as savagely as she wanted him.

Relieved of that worry, she was better able to focus on what he did to her, to give her full attention to her body. His hand cuddling her breast felt better than she had ever expected. His touch radiated out to make her legs shaky, her fingers tingly. She arched into the steady press of his hips, blindly seeking more. She rubbed her belly against his erection, and moaned at the pleasure of it. With her movements, his breathing came faster, rougher.

Their clothes stuck, cold and uncomfortable, but not a deterrent to the anticipation swelling inside her.

"That's it," Zane crooned with deep satisfaction. He kissed her throat, her shoulder. In contrast to the cold, wet clothes, his mouth was hot, his tongue hotter, leaving behind a burning trail. The clinging material of her blouse bunched in his fist, then rasped across her sensitive breasts as he peeled it away. He kissed her collarbone, lower, dipped his tongue into her cleavage. "I've been thinking about this all day."

Tamara laced both hands into his dripping hair, urging him toward her nipple. The combination of her excitement, the rain, and the cooling temperatures had caused both of her nipples to tighten almost painfully. She needed his mouth on her. "*Zane.*"

"Take it easy." He nuzzled closer while tugging at the blouse and her thin lace bra until he'd bared both breasts completely. She felt physically snared, the material restricting her movements as he pushed it over her shoulders to her upper arms. Her breasts were forced higher by the bunched material and his callused hands.

He continued to kiss her throat, her ear, his mouth open on her as if he couldn't get enough, while his hands caressed and teased. The dual assault was more than she could stand. She made an urgent sound that he responded to by rubbing his thumbs over her nipples and murmuring low, "Damn, you're so soft. I love touching you."

"I can't bear it."

He carefully closed his finger and thumb over one taut nipple and tugged. Her body arched hard as she cried out.

"You like that? You'll like this too." His right arm circled her back and his mouth moved lower. Tamara tilted her head back, breath held in impatience, and still she jumped when his tongue stroked over her throbbing nipple.

She groaned.

"I know." He licked again. "You're very sweet, Tamara."

Even the touch of his breath was a torment. "Zane, please."

His low laugh, gruff with triumph, stroked over her. "Okay, sweetheart." And then he drew her nipple into his mouth with a soft, wet suction that devastated her senses. Her body drew tight, her legs felt liquid.

He sucked, teased. His tongue curled around her, his mouth pulling at her insistently. All she could do was gasp in pleasure and hold on to him.

Zane's arm hooked beneath her bottom and she found herself lifted so that he could reach her more easily. Caught between his solid body and the wall, her stiff, wet clothes tangled around her, she couldn't move. He switched to her other nipple, treating it to the same delicious torment, and just when she didn't think she could bear it a second more, his thick thigh thrust between her legs. With one hand opened wide on her behind, he began moving her against him in a slow hard rhythm that drove her wild. She tried to wiggle away, startled and not just a little alarmed by how quickly she spun out of control. But Zane didn't let her retreat. His dark head stayed bent to her breasts, and his hold on her body was secure, unrelenting, his long fingers pressed deep against her buttocks.

She hadn't been prepared for him, she realized wildly. She had no idea how to react, how to contain herself. Sensations roiled inside her with unstoppable force, and she accepted that she was on the verge of a climax.

The book had said that the first time, a climax was difficult for a woman to achieve. Zane was managing it with distressing ease, and she could do no more than hang on to him.

Then her feet touched the floor again and Zane's mouth was on her own, smothering her cry of disappointment. She'd been so close!

"I know," he muttered gently, again and again. "I know, baby. It's okay."

He fumbled with her wet skirt, shoving it out of the way. She always wore voluminous layered skirts for work, and now she cursed the excess of material as she tried to help bare herself for Zane. She wanted what he wanted, whatever it might be, as long as he didn't let the incredible feelings fade.

When his hand slid over her thighs, her belly, she stilled, frozen with the newness of it, the excitement of it. He wedged his large hand between her thighs, covering her mound in an almost protective way. He didn't move, didn't stroke her. He simply held her that way, the heat of his hard palm both comforting and more tantalizing, and it was so erotic she felt tears sting her eyes.

"I need you now, Tamara," he growled, nipping at her jaw. "Tell me you're ready."

Ready? She'd almost finished without him. If he didn't get on with it, she'd lose her fragile grasp on her emotions and cry with the wonder of it. "Whatever . . ." she started to say, then had to swallow and try again. "Whatever you want, Zane."

She caught his face, kissing his chin, his jaw, biting at his throat. "Just touch me again. *Please*."

"Jesus." He panted as he reached for his belt, jerking at it, frenzied—and someone called his name.

They both froze.

"No," Zane groaned, the word slurred. His face pressed into her neck, his body held rigid as he struggled for control. Their frantic heartbeats mingled, matched. His shoulders looked like sleek steel as he braced himself away from her. "No, goddammit, *no*."

"Zane?" the voice called again. "Where are you?"

"I'll kill him," Zane announced as he pushed himself away from her. Looking at his face, Tamara believed him. His eyes were glittering bright, heavy-lidded, his cheekbones dark with aroused color. His deep chest rose and fell with uneven breaths.

He didn't say a word to Tamara as he turned away.

She watched him jerk the door open and stalk out of the room, menace emanating from every hard inch of his body. She dropped her head back to the wall with a *thunk*, while her heart continued to rap sharply in her chest. Holy moly. *Whew*. She fanned herself, took several deep breaths, but it didn't help. Her body pulsed with unfulfilled need, leaving her shaken and wobbly.

"You better have a damn good reason," Zane all but shouted, "for this impromptu visit."

A different voice, this one amused, said, "What the hell? Did you fall into a puddle, Zane?"

Curiosity was one of her less auspicious character traits. Tamara leaned around the door frame, peeking to see who had come to call. Zane had his back to her, hands on his hips, facing away, but the others weren't—and two male faces locked onto her.

Mack Winston gave a start of surprise, then whistled. "Zane," he asked, "what have you been up to?"

Chase Winston just grinned, a cocky, crooked grin that showed he had accurately guessed the answer to Mack's question. He knew *exactly* what his brother had been doing.

Zane whirled to face her, his scowl dark and deadly, his expression black. She bit her lip.

Busted.

EIGHT

Zane couldn't believe it. He had a boner that would have made Superman proud, and Tamara had gone up like a flame the second he'd touched her. She'd been ready, damn it, *so ready*.

But now he was stuck with his brothers. Oh, he knew good and well they wouldn't just back out politely, regardless of the fact they knew what they'd interrupted. If anything, they'd be more determined to hang around now than ever. Curiosity, and the perverse need to drive him crazy, would guarantee they extended their visit.

He wanted to kick himself. Hard. He'd been caught romping during business hours, his store unattended, his door unlocked. He'd taken total leave of his senses, no doubt about that. His own disbelief was extreme, but he knew his brothers would love ribbing him till doomsday over his lack of discretion. Damn.

Tamara, her face flushed and her lips swollen, stared at the three of them with wide, dark eyes. Zane wanted to erupt in frustration, but he wouldn't give his brothers the satisfaction. With women, he was always controlled. Now would be no different.

He drew a deep breath that didn't do a damn thing to relax him, and said, "Tamara, you might as well come on out."

Looking horrified by that prospect, she ducked back behind the door.

Mack turned to Zane. "You were hiding her?"

"No, of course not."

Unconvinced, Mack said, "She looks like she's hiding."

Zane knew that'd be enough to bring her out. His independent little Gypsy wouldn't want anyone to think her a coward.

Chase crossed his arms over his chest and leaned back against the wall. "Who is she?"

Waving toward the adjacent building, Zane went for the easiest explanation. "She's the Gypsy next door."

Mack, who had seen her several times in the past, whistled again.

"Will you stop that!" Zane no sooner barked at Mack, than he again drew a breath, reaching for that damn elusive control. But it was too late, both Mack and Chase eyed him with satisfied curiosity.

"A Gypsy, huh?"

Chase was having a fine time of it. Zane reigned in his temper with an effort. "Not a real Gypsy, of course. But she looks the part."

At that moment, the jingling of her bell-laden ankle bracelets drew everyone's attention, and Tamara stepped out. All three of them turned toward her. Zane immediately wanted to hide her again.

She was a wreck.

Her wig was sodden, looking blacker than usual, coarser. It hung in crooked clumps, probably because of his hands when he'd been holding her still for his kiss. He could still taste her, how sweet and hot her mouth had been, how stiff her nipple had gotten when he'd drawn on her. His head had nearly erupted with the pleasure of it. He wanted to taste her everywhere—but now he'd have to wait.

Her nose was red, and her makeup was everywhere except where it should have been. Her clothes had been rearranged and overlapped in an awkward way that at least had her decently covered. But it made her look . . . clumpy.

She stood there, narrow shoulders hunched, shivering, the rain dripping off her to form an expanding puddle around her beringed toes.

Looking beyond miserable, she attempted a smile.

Like mute fools, his damn brothers looked at him in disbelief.

Struggling with himself, Zane tried to figure out how to throw his brothers off the scent. At the moment, Tamara looked more like a drowned urchin than a woman who could make a man mad with lust to the point he'd leave his store unattended. They'd never understand why he had lost his head enough to seduce her in his storage room while his business was still open. Hell, he barely understood it.

Then suddenly Tamara's embarrassment hit him. It was such a heavy wave of awareness, pushing at him, smothering him, that he nearly lost his breath. She was mortified, more by his reaction than anything else, and he knew it bone deep.

He looked at her, and saw that she was ready to excuse herself, to claim to be no more than a friend. Her turmoil shamed him, proving his shallowness. He'd dragged her inside, stripped her blouse away from her breasts and touched her and tasted her, and now he was ready to deny it all. He felt like the biggest bastard alive.

Without giving it another thought, he strode forward and threw his arm possessively, protectively, around her shoulders.

She appeared floored that he'd done so, and that gave him a small measure of gratification. It was nice to be able to take her by surprise now and then. It helped to balance the constant state of shock she kept him in.

"Chase, Mack, this is Tamara Tremayne, my neighbor next door." The bold way he edged her into his side proved she was much more than a neighbor; he didn't need to say the words.

Her shivers were so severe, they rattled Zane's ribs where she pressed against him. He needed to get her to her place so she could change. Some hot coffee wouldn't hurt, either. "Tamara, these are my pain-in-the-ass brothers."

Mack and Chase's replies were automatic, without their usual charm. "Hello, there."

"Nice to meet you."

Zane understood; Tamara had that effect on him, too. But it was nothing compared to how she reacted to them.

He'd never seen her tongue-tied before. She'd been deliberately, mysteriously silent plenty of times. But she'd never been speechless. Curving his hand over her shoulder, Zane urged her a step closer and, with a grin, prompted her, "Say 'hi' to my brothers, honey."

"Hi."

Chase recovered first. "I take it you two were caught out in the storm?"

Nodding, Zane said, "Someone was following her—*ooaf*."

Tamara's sharp little elbow surely broke something. Zane glared down at her while he rubbed his midsection, but she just smiled at him.

Then patted him.

Chase and Mack watched with fascination.

"Zane," she said, all sweetness, as if she hadn't just tried to stove in his ribs, "don't bore your brothers with that stuff." Her teeth gleamed briefly in a parody of a smile, and she added, "It doesn't concern them."

Disbelief filled him. "Would you rather they think we were playing in the rain?" She didn't answer, but she looked ready to inflict more harm on his person. Zane narrowed his eyes. He held her elbow this time as a precaution, then said to Chase, "She has this problem with sharing."

"So I see." Amusement flickered across Chase's face.

Mack tugged at his ear. "I have a suggestion. Why don't we take her home and let her change out of those wet clothes before she turns blue? She's shivering so much, her bells are ringing."

Zane looked at her feet and saw Mack was right. Her ankle bracelets quivered, making music even though she tried to hold herself still.

"Her blouse is ripped, too," Chase pointed out.

"What the hell?" How could he have missed that? Zane wondered. Then a thought occurred to him. "Damn, I didn't rip it, did I?"

Slapping her hand over his mouth, her face scalded with color, Tamara said, "It was already ripped."

He circled his fingers around her slender wrist and lowered her hand to her side. He had that awful feeling she was being evasive again. "How?"

Casting a worried look at his brothers' rapt expressions, she lowered her voice. "When I was running, I accidentally ripped it."

"Were you hurt?"

"I'm fine." She stressed that in a way that let him know she wanted him to drop it.

Like hell. "Let me see, honey."

She twisted away from him. "It's not a big deal, Zane."

He didn't believe her, but he knew he'd have a battle on his hands if he tried to force the issue in front of his brothers. Nodding, he said, "All right. Then let's get you home."

Tamara slipped away from Zane before he could stop her. "No, really, that's not necessary."

"Course it is," Chase assured her.

"My apartment is right above my shop. You two came to visit Zane, and I don't want to interrupt. I'll just be on my way—alone, of course, which is how it should be—and you can all have a nice chat." She smiled as if that was that and turned away.

Zane snagged her by the back of the blouse and pulled her up short. "Nice try."

"Zane!" She slapped her hands over her breasts to cover herself as the wet blouse was pulled tight to her front.

He'd forgotten her clothes were transparent. She'd pulled them away from her skin and rearranged herself some before coming out to meet his brothers, but once the blouse touched her skin again, it didn't want to let go. Every fine edge of her lace bra was clearly visible, as well as her puckered nipples beneath.

Mack had his coat off in a flash. "Here you go." He stared at the ceiling as he handed it to her. Chase pretended to be busy examining some new computers on display.

When Tamara didn't take the coat quickly enough, Zane did the gentlemanly thing and stuffed her into it. The sleeves fell almost to her knees. He buttoned the top two buttons, then smiled. Tamara was swallowed up by the dark brown coat, her slim legs barely showing beneath, and the neckline fell almost to her breasts. It was all Zane could do not to laugh, despite her angry expression.

Addressing his brothers, he said, "Come on. We'll walk her over, and we can talk while she changes."

"Zane . . ."

"Quit growling at me, honey. You'll make a bad impression on my brothers."

She glared at him for that comment, and again started to turn away. "Mack."

"Got it." Mack stationed himself in front of the door, barring the way while Zane found his umbrella and Chase opened his own. Tamara looked ready to spit, she was so angry at being thwarted, and Zane decided it was just as well that she get used to it. He assumed he'd be thwarting her a lot, as long as she continued to try to shut him out.

Once through the door, they sandwiched her between them, making certain she didn't get any wetter—though how she could get wetter, he didn't know. She was already drenched. But Zane also wanted her protected just in case the man who'd followed her was still hanging around.

He no longer had any doubts that she was, indeed, in danger. Hell, he'd felt the menace himself, as dumb as that seemed. And now that he knew the menace was real, he'd find a way to protect her—whether she wanted his protection or not.

His heart pounded so hard he felt bruised. He was wet, shivering, his teeth chattering from both cold and nerves. He clamped his jaws together hard, trying to keep from making any noise at all.

One second he'd been alone, well hidden by the shadows and the storm, ready to do what he must, what he had no choice but to do, and then suddenly she was there, that damn bright green umbrella announcing her like a beacon.

He didn't think she saw him today, but he wasn't sure. She'd just . . . taken off so suddenly. Running fast, like her life was in danger. He'd immediately changed his plans, of course, unwilling to take any more risks.

It made him nearly nauseous, each and every time he went in there. He hadn't had a chance to get into her place today; he hadn't had the time before she'd shown up, and he'd been too rattled after to do more than hide.

That was sheer luck on his part, because not long after she'd run into the computer store, a man had stormed outside, looking around. It was a good thing he'd stayed hidden. Even when the rain soaked past his coat and ran in an icy river down his backbone, he hadn't moved from his hidey-hole. He'd stay tucked away until they were all gone, until he knew without a single doubt that it was clear.

But damn, it was hard. He wasn't cut out for this, and he needed to search again—before it was too late.

Zane locked up quickly while his brothers protected her from the storm. Then they dashed across the lot and went, en masse, up the outside metal stairs to her apartment door. Zane and Chase held her elbows. Because Mack had given her his coat, he held the umbrella, making sure they stayed as dry as possible.

The landing was jam-packed with all four of them there, and for a brief moment Zane wondered if it would hold up under their combined weight. He and his brothers each went over two hundred pounds. Add Tamara's one hundred pounds or so to that, and the stairs felt beyond rickety, creaking and groaning with their weight.

"Do you have your key?" Zane asked her.

She tried to dig in her skirt pocket, but the chore proved difficult, given the size of Mack's coat on her and how wet her skirt was. Finally,

Zane reached into her pocket for her. He could feel the sleek firmness of her thigh through the material, and it inflamed him all over again. Damn, but he wanted her, and he wasn't used to holding back, to pulling away after getting so close.

He needed to get her alone, naked. Under him. He wanted to ride her so gently she melted around him, and then not so gently until she screamed out her climax. When he'd cupped her through her panties, he'd felt how soft and warm and wet she was.

He shook, he wanted her so much.

He didn't, however, want to take her against the wall in his storage room. Talk about a lack of finesse. Later, he might even be grateful that his brothers had interrupted. For now, he was still quietly seething, his lust barely banked.

Tamara flipped on the light as soon as they stepped inside. She faced Zane with her hands on her hips. The coat sleeves covered her arms and beyond, so she looked more comical than angry.

He said easily, "Don't start complaining again."

"I'll complain if I want to!"

He unbuttoned the coat, easily dodging her flapping hands, then turned her and wrested the garment off her shoulders.

"Damn it, Zane, if you don't—"

He leaned close to her ear, so close he could brush her lobe with his mouth as he spoke. "You're giving my brothers another peep show, babe."

She whirled, turning her back to them. Over her shoulder, she speared Zane with a smoldering look, and said through gritted teeth, "I'll be right back. Don't you dare say a thing while I'm gone."

Tenderness warmed him. She was so damn cute, so determined to refuse any and all concern. For some reason, she was threatened by the idea that he might actually start to care about her. Zane didn't know why, but he intended to find out.

Her eyes, resembling those of a raccoon with the smudged makeup, narrowed on him, waiting. Zane saluted her. "Yes ma'am."

Her bossy disposition, which had once seemed both annoying and intolerable, now struck him as adorable. She marched away, slim derriere swaying, and Zane stared after her, his mind conjuring wonderful, intimate, carnal images of letting her be bossy in bed—until Chase clapped him on the back.

"You're not being very subtle, Zane."

Mack laughed. "Hell, I'm embarrassed to even witness this. I feel like a voyeur."

"Go to hell, both of you."

His brothers thought that was hysterical. When they finally stopped laughing, Zane told them, "You might as well sit down. I'll fill you in while she showers."

"I thought she told you to be quiet," Chase commented helpfully. He looked around her apartment with interest.

"Yeah," Mack said, piping in, "and you looked like you took her warning to heart."

Oddly enough, their taunting didn't bother him. Tamara was different, and what he felt about her was different. He hadn't quite pinpointed his feelings for her yet—there was curiosity because she *was* different, lust certainly, amusement and concern and protectiveness. What those things all meant collectively, he had no idea. For the moment, he could only make plans to get her alone and in his bed. Or her bed. Or hell, the couch would do. And he wanted to make certain she'd be safe. Once those were both taken care of, maybe he'd be able to stop thinking about her. Maybe.

But he preferred that his brothers not see her as just another woman he wanted to bed. He wanted them to know she was . . . special.

"She'll learn," Zane told them thoughtfully, "that I do things my own way."

"If you say so." Mack sprawled out with a groan on the striped sofa, his arms stretched out along the back, his long legs stuck out in front of him.

Chase walked around looking at the photographs on the walls. Zane hadn't noticed them on his first visit, what with her aunt jumping on his back and her uncle threatening to kill him. Then there had been the ghost who wasn't a ghost at all. . . .

"Are these her parents?" Chase asked.

Zane moved closer to examine the old black-and-white photograph in an antique-looking, ornate oval frame of gold and silver. "I don't know. They died when she was young. She was pretty much raised by two aunts and this enormous uncle who could rival Bigfoot."

"No kidding? Sounds like an interesting family."

"You don't know the half of it." The couple in the photo could have been Tamara's parents. The woman had the same features as Tamara and the aunts: exotically shaped cat eyes, high cheekbones. But the photo was so old, he couldn't tell if she had dark or light hair. The man was big, long hair to his shoulders, mustache, an indulgent smile directed at his wife. It was a nice photo—Zane decided to ask her about it. Later.

Mack clasped his hands behind his head, and his eyes looked drowsy. "She's not your usual type."

The shower started, and Zane moved to the doorway so he could stare down the hall. He pictured Tamara tossing aside the hideous wig, removing her rings one by one, peeling the wet clothes off her body. His heart gave a lurch at the image of her soft skin exposed, those small, plump breasts completely bare. He throbbed.

Shaking his head to clear it, Zane looked at Mack. "What did you say?"

Mack smiled.

"Stop needling him, Mack." Chase sat in the chair facing his youngest brother. "And Zane, stop staring down the hall with such a pathetically lustful expression. Mack's right. It's embarrassing."

Zane sat. There was a lot he needed to discuss with his brothers. And now, while Tamara was busy, seemed like the best possible time. He leaned forward, elbows on his knees, to address his brothers. "I may need your help."

N I N E

"You definitely need help," Mack informed Zane, referring more to his lovelorn expression than to the real issue at hand. "But what can we do?"

Rather than strangle his brother, Zane explained the situation. He told them all about Tamara's troubles, the skeptical police, her nutty family. He skipped the finer details and merely hit the highlights. It was enough. Both Mack and Chase looked incredulous.

Zane heard the shower turn off and the blow-dryer start. He was running out of time. "So what do you think?"

"You're sure she's not just imagining the vandalism?" Chase asked. "I'm not suggesting she'd lie. But the police have a point. Everything that's happened could have been simple pranks or happenstance."

"I had a few lingering doubts myself, until today," Zane admitted. "But when she came through my door—well, I knew then that she was right. Someone was out there. She was really afraid, and from what I've discovered about her so far, she's not exactly a faint heart. She's got a backbone made of iron."

Mack had lost his casual pose and now frowned. "What do her relatives say?"

Zane shook his head. "They think it's a ghost. Their deceased uncle Hubert. Can you believe that crap?"

To his surprise, Chase straightened. "Well now, I wouldn't rule out the possibility."

Both Zane and Mack stared at Chase.

"What?" Chase shifted. "Ghosts exist."

"Whatever you say, Chase." Zane sent a look to Mack which clearly said, *Yeah, right.*

"I'm just saying not to rule it out."

"Trust me, this is a flesh-and-blood person. I'm positive of it." He went on to explain about Hubert and the eccentricities of the relatives, why they might prefer to believe in a ghost than any tangible threat.

"Yeah," Chase said, nodding, "sounds like they fabricated the ghost."

"Don't sound so disappointed, damn it." Sometimes, Zane didn't understand his second oldest brother at all. Chase was the quietest, the most thoughtful—and what ran through his mind was anyone's guess. More often than not, Zane suspected, his thoughts were occupied with his wife, Allison.

"The thing is," Chase explained, "if her relatives really do believe it's a ghost, I wouldn't alienate them with ridicule. Believe me, if you piss off the relatives, you could piss off Tamara, too. They obviously mean a lot to her, given how she's taken care of them."

Zane curled his hands into fists. "How do I help her, damn it, especially when she doesn't want my help?"

They all grew silent, thinking. Finally, Mack leaned forward. He didn't quite look at Zane when he said, "You know who you need to call."

It wasn't a question, but a statement. And Zane did know, damn it. But still he tried to refuse. "No way. I've considered him, but he's usually more trouble than not. And more trouble is something I don't need right now."

"Joe is trained for this sort of thing," Mack argued.

"Joe is trained to seduce women." Their cousin, Joe Winston, was a big, mean son-of-a-bitch. He was between Cole and Chase in age, almost thirty-six now, but age had only made him leaner, harder, stronger. *Nastier*.

He'd given up on law enforcement after a stray bullet had damaged his knee. But even when he'd been on crutches, the women had flocked to him. He had danger written all over him, and for some reason, women seemed to love it.

Joe had played at being a bounty hunter for a few years, a private dick, a bodyguard, and he'd been successful at each job. But he'd been a ladies' man almost from birth.

"He could look out for her," Mack continued, "and she'd never even know he was there."

"Forget it." The thought of his disreputable cousin spying on Tamara, possibly seeing her at vulnerable moments, made him want to howl with possessive fury. Joe would go after her simply because she was different, and because she'd be a challenge.

Chase started laughing and almost couldn't stop. "Oh, this is priceless, Zane. You're worried your little Gypsy will succumb."

Shooting to his feet, Zane barked, "I am not!"

Mack said very softly, "Am too."

Zane squared his shoulders and pointed a finger at Mack. "I'll have you know—"

"What," Tamara said from the doorway, "is all the yelling about?"

Chase and Mack looked up, then their expressions went comically blank, before turning warm and admiring. Zane wanted to groan. He most definitely didn't want to look. But like a magnet, his gaze was drawn to her.

He turned, and there stood Tamara, hair brushed into soft golden curls, exotic green eyes bright. She wore a pair of skinny beige jeans and a long-sleeve, emerald green shirt. A narrow strip of her belly showed between the waistband of the pants and the shirt's hem. Her makeup was gone, her jewelry was gone. He gulped.

Zane was vaguely aware of Mack and Chase slowly coming to their feet. He wanted to knock their heads together. They acted like they'd never seen a woman before. He could almost feel them sorting through their thoughts, trying to decide if the bedraggled, rain-washed Gypsy and the adorable woman before them now could really be one and the same.

It wasn't that she was beautiful, Zane reasoned, attempting to study her dispassionately, from a purely male perspective rather than that of a man already involved.

True, she was cute. Especially now with her expression so disgruntled, her soft mouth set in mulish lines. But her appearance certainly wasn't enough to turn his grown brothers into leering idiots.

Yet there they stood, ogling her.

Zane cleared his throat, but the only one to notice was Tamara.

"Well?" she asked, eyeing him with accusation and suspicion.

Zane shoved Mack in the shoulder, which made him stumble into Chase. Neither of them fell, but it was a close thing.

Returned to his senses, Chase said, "I'm sorry. It's just . . . You look so . . . different."

Mack bobbed his head. "Different."

Tamara scowled at Zane. "You didn't tell them I wear a costume?"

He rolled one shoulder. "Hey, you told me to sit quietly, so I did."

Mack choked over that tale, and while Chase pounded him on the back, Zane moved to stand at Tamara's side.

"Are you okay?"

She bristled, casting conspicuous glances at his brothers. "Of course. Why wouldn't I be?"

Zane wanted to shake her. "You were chased by a guy in a ski mask."

"Zane . . ." She attempted to give him a *shut up* look.

He ignored her. "And drenched to the skin."

"*Zane* . . ."

"And scared half to death—"

"Get out."

"What?" He couldn't believe she'd ordered him out. He was worried. He wanted to hold her and comfort her.

"You heard me." She shoved against him, trying to make him move. He didn't budge, except to blink in disbelief.

He stared down at her, his temper starting to heat. "I'm not going anywhere."

"Oh, yes, you are. I've had it with your bulldozing."

He leaned down to go nose to nose with her. "Hey, *you* came to *me*, remember?"

Her eyes widened, and she looked devastated. *"You told them?"*

Zane drew back, then realized how she'd misunderstood. "Not that, damn it!" He felt the searing intensity of his brothers' interest. The nosy bastards. "I meant today, at the shop. You got scared, so you came to me."

"Oh, that." She shook her head and quit trying to shove him away—probably because she wasn't making any headway. "I didn't think I'd be able to get my door unlocked in time, and I wasn't sure if any of the other stores in the mall were open."

His teeth ground together. "So I was the most convenient?"

"Well, you *are* right next door."

She sounded so logical, his temper ignited. "When I get you alone . . ."

Chase cleared his throat. "Hold that thought, okay?"

Mack made a face. "You're a spoilsport, Chase, you know that? I was all set to hear what grand retribution he had planned."

"You're too young to hear whatever Zane has planned, and you know it."

Zane had all but forgotten his brothers' presence. Tamara could so easily twist him in knots and make him forget himself and his surroundings. He glared at her, letting her know where he placed the blame for his social faux pas.

"We'll discuss this later," he told her, in what he hoped sounded like a calmer, less emotionally charged tone.

Rubbing the back of his neck, Chase said, "Yeah, well, as to that . . . It might need to be much later. That's why we're here. We were hoping you could close up the bar tonight."

Zane's expectations for the immediate future did a nosedive. "Tonight?"

"I wouldn't ask, except there's no one else."

Zane propped his hands on his hips. "Meaning I can't very well refuse?" Man, he hated it when family loyalty forced him to be noble.

Mack tried and failed to control a grin. "Sorry about that. It seems to be the night for kid distractions. Trista is having a sleepover, and I hate to leave Jessica to deal with that on her own."

Tamara politely asked, "Trista?"

"My daughter. She's fourteen, and her birthday is in a few days. She's celebrating with friends tonight—ten of them—and I don't want to miss it."

She blinked at him. "You have a fourteen-year-old daughter?"

Beaming with pride, Mack said, "Yeah. Smartest kid around, and beautiful to boot."

Zane put his arm around Tamara. He was well used to Mack's bloated pride. "Mack would never volunteer the information, since he thinks of Trista as his own, but she came part and parcel with his wife. Jessica had Trista from a previous marriage. I gotta agree with him on the smart and beautiful part, though. And she's so damn mature it's scary."

"Oh."

She still didn't sound like she understood, but Zane figured he could explain that Mack married an older woman later. When Mack wasn't around to object. Zane smiled. He liked Jessica a lot, and she certainly kept his goofy brother on his toes.

"So what are you doing?" Zane asked Chase, still hoping there might be some way out for him.

"Sammy's cutting teeth."

Zane winced in sympathy. "Rough. Did you try giving her something cold to chew on? That worked for me when Nate was doing the same."

"Yeah. It helps, but not for long. Allison hasn't had a quiet minute all week. She's made plans to go out with friends tonight, while I keep the little imp happy—and believe me, closing the bar would be easier than keeping a teething, bossy, female baby in good spirits."

Tamara, looking a little dazed, said, "Sammy?"

"Samantha Jane Winston, five months old and a hellion already." Zane grinned as he said it. He adored his niece, and his nephew. "When she wants to be held, you hold her. When she wants to be fed, it better be right now. She has a yell that could pierce your eardrums."

"Not that anyone lets her yell much," Chase explained. "Especially not Zane. She already knows she has him wrapped around her very tiny finger."

"She likes me the best," Zane confided, earning a scowl from Chase. It annoyed his brother no end that the second Sammy heard

Zane's voice, she started squealing for him. "So let me guess," he said, before Chase could get really put out, "Sophie is going out with Allison, and Cole is watching Nate."

And before Tamara could ask, he told her, "Nate is Cole's little boy, eleven months old now, and not only walking but running—straight into trouble whenever he can accomplish it."

Mack leaned forward in a conspiratorial tone and said to Tamara, "He gets that from his uncle Zane."

Zane reached for Mack, but he ducked away. "Trista and the babies have been to the bar, but usually during the afternoon, which is probably why you haven't seen them. You only go there at night, right?"

Mack and Chase looked at her again, frowning in concentration.

"You've been to the bar?" Chase asked.

"I don't remember seeing you," Mack said.

Tamara muttered, "I try to . . . blend in."

No one knew what she meant by that, but Zane was beginning to understand her. She felt isolated by her family's eccentricities and her occupation. He could only imagine what her life as a child had been like. His arm around her shoulders tightened, and he gave both his brothers a look to let them know to drop it.

Chase was the first to catch on. "Actually," he told Zane, now smiling widely, "Sophie isn't going out with Allison. But we do have some other news for you."

Mack bobbed his head in agreement.

Warily, Zane eyed them both. "What?"

"Sophie is pregnant again."

"What!" A grin caught him by surprise. Another niece or nephew was on the way—it didn't matter to him which. He'd never suspected how incredible babies could be, but he'd found he liked being an uncle. "When's she due?"

"Around October." Chase chuckled. "Cole is a wreck, of course, and so we figured he deserved the night off."

Zane turned to Tamara and lifted her off her feet into a huge bear hug. She clung to his shoulders in startled surprise. "My oldest brother is like a mother hen at times," he told her as he set her back on her feet. The look on her face was priceless.

This time it was his family overwhelming her.

"Especially now that Sophie is expecting again," Mack added. "Her last delivery wasn't exactly easy, and Cole had swore one kid would be it. But Sophie won that argument."

Zane laughed. "Sophie wins all the arguments." He suspected that was because Cole, like the rest of them, hated to disappoint her about anything. "When did she find out?"

"Just this afternoon." Chase chuckled. "She came straight to the bar when Cole was opening up and gave him the news. He's been walking into the walls ever since then."

Glancing at his watch, Zane said, "Damn. I guess I better be heading over that way. I'm surprised he managed to stay there this long. I figured he'd be home, hovering over Sophie, fretting."

"He wanted to follow her out after she told him, but Sophie said she had stuff to do, and made me promise I'd keep him there until eight."

"She's planning a . . ." Mack glanced at Tamara and coughed. "A private celebration, and didn't want Cole home until she was ready."

"Sophie owns a lingerie shop." Zane winked at Tamara. "When she plans a private celebration, no telling what goes on."

Chase added helpfully, "You know, you have about fifteen minutes yet before you'd have to leave, if you want to—"

Zane looked at Tamara, observed her hopeful expression, and shook his head. Without looking away from her, he said, "You two go on. I'll be right behind you."

To Zane's annoyance, Chase walked right up to Tamara and folded her into a big hug. "It was very nice meeting you, Tamara."

Mack kissed her cheek, and even went so far as to bob his eyebrows suggestively. "Very nice."

Flustered, she stammered, "It was nice meeting both of you, too."

It was still raining hard when they opened the door and went out, immediately popping open their umbrellas and pulling up their collars. Cool, damp air blew into the room, and then the door was closed and they were alone again.

Tamara touched his arm, her brows lifted in question. "Fifteen minutes . . . ?"

"Isn't near enough time." Looping his arms around her waist, Zane pulled her into his embrace and kissed her, a kiss of regret, gentle and undemanding. "I'm not a fifteen-minutes kind of guy, honey. When I get you naked, it's going to take me at least twice that long just to get my fill of looking at you."

Her eyes widened. Zane waited for her to blush, for her modesty to kick in. Instead, she blurted, "The book said we should do that."

"Do what?"

She ran her fingers through the hair at his nape. "The journal I told you about? It said new lovers should spend a day just looking at each other, getting used to being naked together."

Zane nearly choked. It made him hot—and more frustrated—just to talk about it. "When you're naked," he informed her, "I can guarantee you I'm going to do more than just look."

Her smiled was pure female mischief. "Like what?"

Eyes gleaming, he whispered, "Like kiss you all over."

"Oh." Her head dropped to his chest and her arms tightened. Zane rubbed her back, wishing that he could stay, and not just to satisfy his lust. He was worried. Despite her show of bravado, he was certain she was a little worried, too. He wanted to hold her, to talk to her. To reassure her.

After a moment, she said, "I like your family a lot."

"They have their moments." *Tonight definitely wasn't one of them.* Knowing he had to go, he reached into his pocket and pulled out an ultrasmall cell phone. He pushed the buttons a few times, setting the phone, did a check, then tried to hand it to her.

She looked at it without taking it. "What is that?"

"Obviously it's a phone." She still didn't reach for it, and he sighed. "I want you to keep it with you." The phone was so slim and small, keeping it next to her person shouldn't be a problem. And that was where he wanted it—on her at all times. "You can push the talk button, and it'll automatically dial me."

Pulling away from the phone as if it might bite her, she asked, "Why?"

He'd expected an argument; everything with Tamara was an argument when she felt he was trying to protect her or help her. He respected her self-reliant nature, especially since he knew it was so important to her. But at the moment, he wished she were just a little less stubborn.

"I don't feel right leaving you after what happened." She shook her head, and he added, "I had planned on spending the night. Tomorrow we could have discussed how to handle this problem."

"*My* problem, not yours."

Zane curled his free hand around her nape and held her still as he bent to kiss her. Her mouth immediately softened and he thrust his tongue inside, tasting her deeply, stealing her breath. Branding her.

When he pulled back, her beautiful green eyes were heavy, and her lips were wet, open. "I'm not taking any chances with you, sweetheart. Now promise me you'll call me if anything happens, or I'll let Cole know I won't be closing the bar after all."

Slowly the fog of desire cleared from her gaze. She heaved a disgruntled sigh, then held out her hand.

Zane placed the phone in her palm and curled her fingers around it, holding her hand in his own. "Keep it with you," he insisted. "In bed, if you go to the bathroom, if you . . ."

"I got it. Keep it with me."

"If you hear anything, anything at all, just push the Talk button."

"You won't be at home."

"I set it to automatically dial another cell phone I have. It's one I normally keep plugged into my car, but I'll carry it with me now."

Tamara nodded, then slipped the tiny phone into her back jeans pocket. "You should go."

"Yeah." He didn't want to leave, damn it.

Staring at her feet, she asked, "What time will the bar close?"

"Tonight? Not until two."

She groaned, then offered suggestively, "I don't open my shop until ten on Saturdays."

Zane almost smiled. "You need to get some sleep. If I come back here, neither one of us will sleep tonight." He again thought of Joe. His cousin would be able to keep her safe when Zane was busy—like tonight. But damn, Joe had always rubbed him the wrong way.

He clasped Tamara's arms just above her elbows and lifted her up, promising himself it would be the very last kiss, and then he'd go.

Though she tried to cover it, he caught her small wince of pain.

He instantly gentled his hold. "What is it?"

She shook her head. "Nothing, I just—"

"I hurt you."

"No, you didn't!" She shifted her shoulder, her expression sulky before she admitted, "I kind of bumped into a van when I was running to your shop."

Going rigid, Zane demanded, "Where are you hurt?"

"It's just a small scratch."

"Where, Tamara?"

"On my arm."

He'd specifically asked her about the rip in her blouse. Why hadn't she told him she was hurt? *Dumb question.* She would consider it none of his business, something to be dealt with on her own.

He stared at her, trying not to let his anger show. "Let me see."

Smug, she told him, "I can't. I'm wearing long sleeves."

No doubt so he wouldn't see her injury. Zane locked his jaw, and solved that problem by catching the hem of her shirt and pulling it up over her head. Tamara tried to stop him with a lot of squawking and complaining and slapping, but she wasn't a match for him. As gently as he could, he relieved her of the shirt and left her standing there in her bra and jeans.

Damn, she was a temptation. Her jeans fit her body perfectly, and her bra, though plain, white cotton, was low-cut and very enticing.

Tamara protested her unveiling, until she realized he was bent on ignoring her luscious little breasts to center his concentration on her injury. Then she became indignant.

Zane took one look at the long red scratch and bruised skin on her upper arm and wanted to bellow. Someone had hurt her, whether deliberately or inadvertently, and there was no way Zane would let it happen again. He made up his mind. He'd call Joe. Tonight.

But he'd also give his disreputable cousin a warning. Tamara was off-limits—and there'd be hell to pay if he forgot that.

T E N

How dare he ignore her when she was half-naked?

Tamara stalked through her quiet house, holding her shirt bunched in her fist as she made certain everything was secured. The latches on the windows were loose and rusted, but thanks to how warped the old windows were, they were tough to open even when they weren't locked. Cold air seeped in around the wooden frames, and made goose bumps rise on her exposed shoulders and midriff as she pulled down every shade.

She barely noticed, she was still so annoyed.

Zane had stripped her shirt off as if she were a child. That had been bad enough, and she fully intended to raise hell with him about it when she saw him again. But worse, he'd ignored her partially exposed body to examine one measly scratch.

Annoyance and stung pride carried her through her house with a stomping gait.

The living room door had a dead bolt, and Zane had listened from the metal landing until he'd heard her click it into place. The door leading to the downstairs, and the door closing off the part of the house she didn't use, both required a skeleton key. She jiggled each of them, making certain they were closed tight.

It had taken her almost five minutes to convince Zane she was fine and she could damn well tend to a scratch without his help. She'd never expected him to be so . . . mollycoddling. Not that she disliked it, because she didn't. And that was part of the problem.

It felt so nice to be tended to, to have someone care.

Zane had surprised her at every turn. She was no longer certain what she'd expected, what she'd hoped for. He seemed so genuine. So concerned and sincere. He wasn't at all like the man she'd read about in the local papers, the outrageous man who bordered on being an exhibitionist, the lady-killer, and the risqué brother. He *was* those things, no way around it. But he was so much more than that.

His happiness over the thought of a new nephew or niece had astounded her. She'd never pictured him with kids, never considered that he might know how to handle himself with children, or be comfortable around them. Yet both his brothers had agreed Zane was a favorite uncle. Sammy squealed at his presence, and Nate emulated him.

Kids were a good judge of character. They knew when someone was innately kind, generous.

Oh damn, she was falling in love with him. She squeezed her eyes shut and tried to deny the truth, but it was impossible. She'd probably been half in love with him even before he'd accepted her proposition. She knew her heart had always thumped erratically whenever she caught sight of him. His laugh had the power to make her stomach flip-flop. And his eyes . . . she often felt like she was melting when she met his eyes.

She'd written all that off as sexual attraction. Every woman who looked at him wanted him, so why should she have been any different, except that he hadn't wanted her in return?

But now she knew it was more. Damn and double damn!

Tamara stopped dead in the hallway and stared blankly at a wall. Love Zane Winston? It was beyond foolish, yet . . . Yet how could she not?

No one had ever tried to take care of her before. She could take care of herself, so it had never been necessary. But it felt nice that he wanted to, that he tried.

Her aunts and uncle had accepted her with open arms, but they were like overgrown children, wallowing in the freedom of their Gypsy spirits, disinclined toward anything that hinted of normalcy, while she'd always craved the mundane. She'd quickly adopted the roll of caretaker, and that setup had suited them all.

But now Zane coddled her, wanting to protect her, worrying about her. He touched her and set her on fire, making her experience things she hadn't even known were possible. He argued with her, but didn't hold a grudge. He put his brothers above his lust, and loved his niece and nephew.

He ignored her body to fret over a scratch.

Oh, he was a very lovable man, and she wasn't immune. Hiding her feelings from him was the key, if she wanted him to stick around. Zane was a bachelor with a capital B. It had taken quite an effort just to get him to agree to have sex with her. If he ever suspected what was in her heart, he'd bolt, she was sure of it.

A clinging woman spouting words of love was guaranteed to drive him away.

Tamara sighed and forced her feet to unglue themselves from the carpet. She couldn't solve any of her dilemmas about Zane tonight, so she might as well quit fretting over them. She had more important things to take care of.

It was still fairly early, but she wouldn't be going back out, so she changed into a sleep shirt and eyed the pile of work on her desk. The sooner she turned in the work, the sooner she'd get paid. It would be a few hours before she could go to bed.

She headed for the kitchen to make a sandwich. On her way past the family room she noticed the blinking light on the answering machine. She pushed the Replay button and listened while she opened the refrigerator.

The voice of her Realtor came on the line. Tamara froze, turning to stare at the machine in horror. There had been an offer on the building. A good one. The Realtor expected her to show up at his office the next day, during her lunch hour, to look it over.

Her hunger gave way to cramps, caused by distress. If the building sold now, she wouldn't have time to spend with Zane. There might not be an opportunity for intimacy.

Could she have gotten so close, only to miss getting to love him?

Zane entered the bar in a rush. He was a few minutes late because he'd had to go home and change. As he darted past the tables to the bar where Cole played bartender, several women whistled to him, a few even reaching out, trying to get hold of him. He was too distracted to pay them much mind, and barely managed a smile.

Cole eyed him as he slipped around the bar. "You just disappointed a lot of ladies."

"What?"

"Your admirers. They're not too pleased to have you breeze by without a notice. First last night, then again today. You ready to tell me what's going on?"

Glancing over his shoulder, Zane eyed the table of sulking women. They waved to him, and this time he winked. When he looked at Cole again, he shook his head. "Sorry, I guess I'm distracted. I've been rushing like hell. I got here as quick as I could."

He hated that he'd kept Cole waiting on such a special night. He knew his brother well, and Cole was likely going nuts wanting to be home with his wife. "Go ahead and take off. I've got it covered."

The place was packed, but that wasn't unusual for a Friday night. They did a hell of a business on the weekends.

Cole finished filling an order, then turned as Zane hung his coat on a hook. Leaning back against the wall and crossing his arms over his chest, Cole said, "Chase and Mack filled me in."

Zane wanted to groan. Instead, he kept his expression carefully impassive. "They told you about Tamara?"

"In great detail." Cole looked Zane over, and smiled. His most out-rageous brother was doing his best to look indifferent. Zane obviously didn't realize it, but that in itself was telling. "They took turns grabbing the phone from each other and shouting into my ear. Around all the laughing, I gathered the Winston curse has taken a nibble out of your stubborn hide."

More like it had bitten off a huge chunk, but Zane wasn't about to admit that. He said noncommittally, "Maybe."

"So that's what had you acting so odd last night."

"I was *not* acting odd." Zane shifted, his tension growing. "I was just . . ."

"I know, distracted."

Chin out, hands fisted, he said, "Yeah," and his stance dared Cole to press him on it.

Far from intimidated, Cole appeared to be barely holding in his laughter. "She sounds . . . unique."

There was just enough inflection in his brother's tone to set Zane's teeth on edge. "You all don't have to keep referring to her as if she's an oddity."

Giving up with a chuckle, Cole held up both hands. "Ho! I didn't mean it that way."

"The hell you didn't. Mack and Chase acted the same." Zane glared at a customer who loudly demanded service, then turned back to Cole. "She *is* different, okay? But in a really nice way."

"That's exactly what Mack and Chase said."

"Bullshit. I bet they told you about the wig, didn't they?"

The customer leaned over the bar. "A wig?"

Zane filled his beer glass and shoved it at him with a glare. "Mind your own damn business."

Still grinning, Cole said, "That's a great way to keep the business healthy, Zane."

Zane was just harassed enough to growl, "Would I be seeing a woman who was odd, damn it?"

"Of course not." Cole's tone was soothing—and filled with barely suppressed humor. "You did say a wig?"

Zane felt his face heat. He hadn't blushed since he'd been a boy. "Sophie's plans for the night are going to be ruined," he growled, "if you don't stop needling me."

In a stage whisper, Zane heard the nosy customer grumbling about women and wigs and curses. Great. Now he had everyone gossiping.

He barely stifled a groan. "Go home, Cole."

"In a minute." Cole refilled two more drinks. He'd hired a couple of new guys, but they hadn't quite gotten a handle on things yet, and were slow to fill orders.

When Cole finished, he reached for his coat. Zane put a hand on his shoulder. "Damn it, I didn't mean to act like a bastard."

"No?" Cole looked amused, not insulted.

"No. I meant to tell you congratulations."

Shaking his head, Cole said, "I swear, Zane, I don't know if I can live through this again."

Zane knew exactly what he was talking about. "You'll be fine. And so will Sophie. She's a trooper."

"Hell, she doesn't even remember how much pain she was in. She talks about the birth like it was a breeze. And I'll be damned if I'm going to remind her otherwise."

Zane felt sympathy for his oldest brother. "You're happy about the baby, aren't you?"

"Hell, yes!" Then he looked around, realized that he'd shouted, and rubbed his hands over his face. "Yes, I'm happy to have another baby, but you can't imagine what it's like to see someone you love hurting that much."

Tamara had only had a scratch, and he'd wanted to beat someone to a pulp. The thought of her going through labor . . . Zane broke out in a sweat and quickly shook off that thought. "Now they know she delivers fast," he assured Cole. "They'll be ready for her."

"They better be, or I'm going to knock some heads together."

Zane patted him on the back, giving in to a reluctant grin. "You know what you need?"

Cole eyed him. "What?"

"To go home and let your wife soothe you."

Smiling, Cole said, "Yeah." Then, "I *am* sorry I interrupted your plans tonight."

Zane was sorry, too. "Are you kidding? I interrupted your plans for most of my life. You were always there for me, so I'm glad to get to pay you back a little now and then."

"Ah, shit." Cole looked away and grumbled, "I just found out I'm going to be a father again, Zane. If you start getting all emotional on me, tonight of all nights, I may have to flatten you just to keep my manly consequence."

Zane laughed. His brother was about the best man he knew. When their parents had died, Cole had taken over without a single complaint. It wasn't until the rest of them were in college that Cole started taking care of his own needs—which included falling in love with Sophie.

Long before he and Sophie had their first child, Cole had learned all the parenting skills he needed by raising his brothers single-handedly.

Zane gave Cole a slight shove. "Get out of here. You're embarrassing me."

Cole turned up his collar. "I'm embarrassing myself." He started to walk away, but paused. "Don't let her get away, Zane."

Zane played stupid by saying, "Who?"

Not in the least fooled, Cole pointed at him. "I didn't raise any dummies. Judging by last night and tonight, you're hooked. Don't do something stupid to blow it." He strode away.

Zane was busy for the next three hours, nonstop. He sometimes missed working at the bar, the activity and loud camaraderie, even though he loved having his computer store. Cole had never expected any of them to stay on at the bar, but he'd made it a very welcome place to be.

The second things slowed down, Zane called Tamara. He didn't think she'd be asleep yet, and he wanted to make certain she was okay. Fretting over a woman was a new experience, and he didn't like it worth a damn.

She answered on the third ring.

She sounded weary, and a bit uncertain. "Zane?"

"What took you so long?" Zane demanded, thinking here he was, worrying like an old woman and she couldn't even be bothered to do as he'd asked.

She yawned into his ear. "Sorry. I was working on some stuff and the phone was buried under papers."

"I thought I told you to keep it on you."

"I can't."

"Why?"

"Because . . ." She sighed in exasperation. "Zane, I'm almost ready for bed."

"So?"

"So I'm . . . not wearing anything with pockets."

Awareness kicked in, and he lowered his voice to ask, "What *are* you wearing?"

Her voice lowered, too. "Just a T-shirt."

His heart punched hard. "Panties?"

"Well, yeah."

His thighs tightened. "What color are they?"

She laughed. "Zane!"

"Tell me. Otherwise I'll go crazy all night wondering."

"They're beige."

"Same color as your skin?"

"Almost."

He groaned, picturing her curled in her bed, the sheet gone, maybe in his T-shirt instead of her own. "Have you been thinking about me?" he whispered.

"You want the truth?" He heard the smile in her voice. "I'm having a hard time doing anything else."

"Good." A slow heat began filling him. "It's crazy here tonight. Cole's hired two new guys, but they're greenhorns and slow as molasses. I've about run my ass off or I'd have called sooner."

"Zane." She said his name in soft rebuke. "I don't need you to call and check up on me."

"But you'll let me do it anyway," he said with insistence.

There was a long hesitation before she answered, resigned. "Yes. I'll let you do it anyway."

"Good girl." Damn, he should be with her. Regardless of what she said, she still had to be a little rattled after what had happened. Zane wished like hell he could get his hands on the man who'd chased her. Every time he thought of her running in a panic—*to him*, despite her protests on that—it made him nuts.

"You know, honey," he said with gentle persistence, "you don't have to be tough with me."

"I'm fine," she said again, and Zane gave up. Sooner or later, he'd get her to let down her guard, to stop shutting him out. He refused to accept any other possibility.

"All right. Go get some sleep."

"Good night, Zane."

"Dream about me." He laughed when she groaned again. She hung up without answering. Zane looked around the bar and decided it was a good time to make another phone call. Things had slowed down a little, the first rush hour over, and he knew if he didn't make this call now, he might not make it at all.

Joe Winston stretched out naked on the top of the quilt and yawned. A cool night breeze whispered through the open window to dry the sweat on his body and lighten the scent of sex. Except for his bum knee, which throbbed like a son-of-a-bitch, he felt good, damn good. About ready to sleep.

The woman next to him immediately rolled into his side. Her hands were graspy, her attitude more so. Belatedly, he realized he never should have slept with her again. Not only had her "harder, harder" demands about taken out his knee, but she was the type to read too much into a second tumble. She'd see it as keen interest rather than the boredom it had been.

Joe held himself still, not about to encourage her.

"I want you to come meet my folks," she whispered significantly, then licked his ear.

Damn, damn, damn. He'd known her only a few weeks, for Christ's sake, slept with her only twice—and this time was an accident, a case of her catching him off guard. But then she was good at that. He'd made it clear he had no intentions of getting serious with anyone, yet she was already making plans for him. Why did women never listen?

Her cool, soft palm moved over his chest, tangling in his body hair and slowly sliding downward. Hell, he'd just finished giving her the ride of her life, and here she was, begging for more!

Her fingers curled around him and she purred triumphantly.

In disbelief, Joe reared up to stare at his cock. He was hard again, damn it, straining against her pale, slender fingers. Unbelievable. He dropped back on the bed with a groan. Done in by his least intelligent body part.

"Joe?" She stroked him with slow, thorough expertise. "Will you come home to meet my family tomorrow? My dad is planning a special dinner for us."

Her dad! Special dinner? He groaned, the sound of mortal man in excruciating pain. It had no effect on her that he could tell.

Someone should have explained the rules of warfare to women. It surely wasn't fair to ask a man such questions while pleasuring him. Everyone knew the male brain couldn't function properly under such provocation.

The ringing of the phone saved him. Joe decided he'd kiss whoever was calling so late. "Hold up, baby," he told her as he coerced his throbbing leg over the side of the bed and his sluggish, aroused body into a semi-sitting position, which forced her to release her death grip on his traitorous member.

She sat up, too, and pressed her lush, naked breasts into his shoulder blades.

"Yeah?" he said into the receiver, trying to ignore the feel of stiffened nipples grazing his heated skin.

"Joe?"

"Right on one."

There was a muttered curse, then, "This is Zane."

"No shit!" He tried to squirrel away from the woman, but she stayed glued to him, disregarding his not-so-subtle hints. "Zane, how ya doing? Everyone okay?"

"The family is fine." A moment of silence, another curse, then grudgingly: "You still up for hire?"

The woman raised herself to her knees, and Joe felt her crisp feminine curls on his spine as she ground herself against him. He squeezed his eyes shut, determined to block her out. "Yeah, yeah. Why?" He laughed. "You got someone you want me to kill?"

"Very funny."

The woman behind him paused. Good. Maybe he could convince her of what Zane had once believed. She started moving again, sinuously rubbing against him, and Joe gave up on that idea.

"You're a real comedian, Joe, you know that?" Zane's tone was so dry, it worked as a distraction for just a minute. His cousin had always been a source of amusement. Joe hadn't forgotten the time Zane had accused him of being no more than a hired killer.

At the time the accusation hadn't been so far-fetched. He'd been in a murderous mood, and if he'd caught the bastard he was after then, instead of over a year later, he might well have beaten him to death with his own hands.

Instead, he'd turned him over to the authorities. Stupid.

"So what's up?" The woman started chewing on his neck while her hands reached around to the front of him. One tapered, painted nail dipped into his navel. Almost desperate, Joe snapped, "Tell me quick, man."

"I need you to keep an eye on someone."

"Family?" he demanded, feeling a surge of rage that anyone would dare to threaten a Winston. Of course, they threatened him all the time. But that was different. He was in the business, and usually the person threatening him had good reason.

"No, a woman."

Joe held the phone away from his ear to stare at it in disbelief. Zane had more damn women than an Arab sheik, but he'd never wanted to protect one of them before. At least, not that Joe had ever heard about.

Putting the phone back to his ear, he remarked, "I'm not a damn baby-sitter."

"Fine," Zane snapped right back, "I'll hire someone else."

"Now wait a minute . . . Damn it!" Joe reached behind himself, caught the woman by the shoulder and moved her to the side. "Will you stop raping me?"

"What the hell does that mean?"

It could have been funny, Joe thought, if he wasn't so tired. "I wasn't talking to you, Zane."

Another silence, then a laugh. "I should have known you wouldn't be sleeping alone."

"I wish."

"Ah ha. Like that, is it?"

"Yeah." Joe didn't go into details, didn't admit he'd been stupid enough—and lonely enough—to let a woman work her wiles on him. That would have ruined Zane's image of him. "So you need me there tomorrow, huh?"

Zane's surprise was obvious. "Well, it doesn't have to be—"

"All right, all right," Joe said, sighing as if he were put out. The woman sprawled on the bed next to him, then stuck her bottom lip out in a rather fetching pout. She was naked and warm and open to him. . . .

His resolve weakened the tiniest bit, but he brought it ruthlessly back under control.

He looked away and held the phone a little tighter. "If it has to be tomorrow, then it has to be tomorrow."

"You're ditching her, I gather?"

"Oh, yeah."

"You're a real bastard sometimes, Joe. You know that?"

He laughed. "I've known it a long, long time." Bastard was one of the least insulting things he'd been called in his lifetime.

"A woman will kill you someday."

"It wouldn't be the worst way to go," Joe said, and then smirked because his companion had just flounced out of the bed. Obviously, if he wouldn't come home with her to perform dutifully for Mommy and Daddy's approval, he wasn't worth screwing. Joe saluted her naked backside as she yanked on her dress, snatched up her shoes, and stormed out of the room.

"What time will you be here?" Zane asked.

The clock on his nightstand told Joe it was creeping toward midnight. He wasn't at all tired now, and though his front door slammed loudly, he didn't trust her not to come back. And he didn't trust himself to refuse her if she did. "I'll get out of here tonight."

Zane laughed. "So she's got you on the run?"

"Avoidance is the better part of valor." Naked, Joe stood and limped to the open window. He was just in time to see the taillights of her car disappear from sight. He scratched his stomach and stretched. "Wanna take me to breakfast in the morning?"

"If you can drag your sorry ass out of bed before noon."

The nightstand drawer held a pen and paper. Joe caught the phone between his shoulder and ear and said, "Give me some details. Who's the woman, where's she live, and what the hell am I watching her for?"

"It's more than just keeping an eye on her, though knowing someone else has her in sight will give me some peace of mind. It seems she's being vandalized regularly, only the cops don't quite buy it."

"Why not?"

Zane sighed. "At best, they're writing it off as coincidence, as unrelated mischief."

"And at worst?"

"They think she's imagining the whole thing." Zane told him about the rat and the fire and even about the toppled box of books, which he had once dismissed. Joe jotted down everything Zane told him, frowning thoughtfully.

"So what do you think?"

Being truthful, Joe said, "I think the lady's got a problem."

"Damn. I was afraid you'd say that."

"Yeah, well, for the record, I don't believe much in coincidence." Once he might have, but he'd learned the hard way that when things seemed off-kilter, they generally were.

"Today," Zane admitted in guttural tones, "someone was hanging outside her shop. In a ski mask. She found the guy when she came back from the bank."

Joe heard his cousin's fury and whistled low. "And that's why you need me to keep an eye on her? Because you can't be with her all the time?"

"That, and I want you to do some snooping. Discreetly. She doesn't know I'm calling you."

"Stubborn?"

"Like a mule. But if you're right, someone is getting into her place. I have no idea how, or why they'd even want to."

Joe felt the tingle of the challenge. It sounded like mixed messages to him. Fires could be deadly, but rearranged boxes of books were the act of a snoop. Rats in the toilet were vandalism, and a man in a mask could be an outright threat. He understood why the cops might be baffled, but then he wasn't a cop. Not anymore. "I'll see what I can find out."

"Great. I appreciate it."

Joe smiled in amusement when Zane added, now with his own dose of menace, "One more thing, Joe. Keep your hands off her, understand?"

Deciding to tweak Zane a bit—just because it was fun—he asked, "A real looker, huh?"

Zane hesitated. "Well . . ."

"She's not?" Joe had to bite his lip to keep from chuckling. "Don't tell me you've fallen for a plain Jane."

"She's not plain!"

"Tall?"

"Not exactly."

"Nice bod?"

"None of your damn business!"

"Let me get this straight now." Joe pretended to be very serious, while his shoulders shook with suppressed laughter. "She's a short, stubborn, not quite plain woman with a body type you don't care to discuss. Hell, Zane, that's a perfect description. I'm sure I'll recognize her right off."

The grinding sound he heard was likely Zane's molars.

"I'm going to kick your ass when you get here."

"I could use the exercise." Then, because he obviously had a real job to do, Joe asked, "Seriously. What's she look like?"

"That depends. And if you laugh, I'm hanging up."

Zane was hedging, and that in itself was unusual. In Joe's experience, a more outspoken, up-front guy didn't exist. Zane was also threatening, but that was nothing new. They'd always gone head to head—which was one reason Joe liked him so much. He could always count on Zane to keep him humble.

"No laughing, Scout's honor."

"You were never a Scout."

Pretending to be wounded, Joe said, "But I wanted to be."

A long groan issued through the phone. "Shut up and listen. Tamara works as a Gypsy."

Another surprise. Joe tried to conjure up an image of what a Gypsy looked like, but the only thing he could think of was the old woman in *The Wolfman*. "You mean like with crystal balls and palm reading and all that crap?"

"Yeah," Zane ground out, "all of that. When she's working, she dresses the part, which includes this long black wig and a good dozen or so rings and dark contacts. Very exotic look."

"Sounds like an interesting woman."

Zane made no response to that, but Joe could practically feel his annoyance. "When she's not working, she's blond, with green eyes. Cute."

"Cute, huh?" For Zane to be so interested, she had to be more than cute. Joe wouldn't be at all surprised to find a model-perfect woman.

"I'm hanging up now."

Joe picked up a balsong knife from the nightstand and sat on the edge of the bed. He flipped it open one-handed, exposing the razor-sharp, lethal blade, then flipped it shut it again, almost in the same motion. "Don't you want to know what I charge?" Open, shut. Open, shut. The knife made a quiet, clinking sound each time he flipped out the blade.

Truth was, he could use a vacation, and this seemed like a perfect time. The woman's trouble sounded like a puzzle, and he was always up to solving a puzzle. Besides, he would enjoy a visit with his cousins, even Zane.

"I don't know. Can I afford you?"

"Helluva time to ask! What were you going to do, wait until I'd finished, then stiff me? Would you have claimed I was too expensive?"

"I have no idea why Chase and Mack thought I should call you."

So it hadn't been Zane's idea to call? Yet, obviously Zane was involved enough that Chase and Mack had thought he could use the help.

Joe opened the knife one last time and examined the edge of the blade. "Cuz they love me, cousin." He chuckled, then said, "Hey, don't sweat it. How about just expenses?"

"I'll pay you the going rate."

He snapped the knife shut and put it back on the nightstand. "No way. You're family. Besides, after hearing about this woman, you couldn't keep me away. The curiosity is killing me."

"*I'll* kill you if—"

"Yeah, yeah, I know. You'll kill me if I touch her, if I sniff her. If I even look at her too hard." He dropped back on the bed with a groan, then stared at the moon shadows on the ceiling. "You know I don't poach, so quit worrying."

It was a novel thing, having Zane jealous over a woman. He'd told the truth when he said his curiosity was stirred. She must be a hell of a babe, regardless of what Zane had said.

A thought occurred to him. "Hey, Zane, you in love with this woman?"

A faint click sounded in his ear, and Joe looked at the receiver, bemused. Zane had hung up on him!

"Well, I'll be damned." He'd been half-kidding, but maybe he'd hit too close to the truth. Maybe Zane had taken the mighty fall, and was still fighting it. The idea was enough to scare any red-blooded bachelor into forgetting his manners, so Joe forgave him for not saying good-bye.

Grinning now, he replaced the phone in the cradle. Rubbing his hand over his bristly jaw, he mentally made a few plans.

Zane in love. Now that was something he definitely wanted to see.

ELEVEN

Tamara heard the shop door chime the next morning. She looked up and saw Zane sauntering in, wearing dark slacks and a gray button-down shirt. He looked tired. She wondered if he'd gotten enough sleep, then immediately berated herself for the concern she felt. She would not start fussing over him. "Good morning."

He kept coming, his long legs carrying him quickly past the reception area to the counter. Flattening both palms on the polished mahogany, he leaned forward and took her mouth in a warm, delicious kiss. Against her lips, he murmured, "Morning."

"Mmmm." Her head swam with the heady taste of him. Lazily lifting her eyelids, she said, "I like greeting the day this way."

"Me, too." Zane straightened, touched her cheek, and smiled. "Do you have the phone on you?"

Shaking her head at his persistence, Tamara patted her pocket. "Right here."

He glanced at her hip, where the phone rested in her deep skirt pocket, and satisfaction mingled with a much warmer emotion. She saw the brief flare of desire in his eyes, before he masked it.

When he looked at her, it was with concern. "How are you feeling today?"

It irritated her that he thought her so weak and insubstantial that a small scratch might cause lingering effects. She pulled up the loose sleeve of her lavender and silver peasant blouse, baring her arm. "It's fine, see? Hardly noticeable anymore."

Zane held her arm, gently stroking with his thumb, then bent to brush it with a kiss. "Looks painful as hell to me, but I'm glad it's not bothering you." He smiled. "I was actually talking about your upset over being chased yesterday."

"Oh." Once it had been over, Tamara wasn't sure what she'd felt. And she was no longer so certain she was chased. Yes, she'd seen a man, but once she'd started running, her fear had obliterated any other sensation. If the man had chased her, she hadn't seen him. It was just as likely he'd run the opposite direction.

Not knowing made her uneasy. She'd thought she was fine. But off and on throughout the night, she'd jerked awake, startled and tense, as if she were being chased again. She felt unsettled, edgy. The whole thing was disconcerting.

Especially since she wasn't positive she had been chased. The man in the ski mask might just have been another poor soul caught in the downpour. He'd looked at her, and there had been something unexpected in his gaze—not really sinister, but threatening in a subtle way.

But had he actually come after her? She couldn't stop thinking about it, running the different scenarios through her mind. She didn't explain any of her worries to Zane because it had *felt* like she'd been chased, and that would be impossible to put into words.

Zane's eyes, dark with concern, met hers. "Did you sleep okay?"

She hadn't—but it wasn't entirely because of the man in the ski mask. It was partly Zane's fault.

She hadn't been able to stop thinking about him and wishing his brothers hadn't interrupted them. Though she had planned to go strictly by the book, upping the odds of her first time with Zane being all she had envisioned, she now thought making love against the wall of his storage room would have been wonderful, too. And that definitely wasn't in the book. She knew. She'd read through it again last night, trying to put herself to sleep after he'd called.

It hadn't worked. She'd lain awake for hours, burning up with the remembrance of his touch.

"Of course," she lied. "I slept just fine."

"You'd have slept better," he promised, "if I could have stayed with you."

Oh, the way he said that. She leaned closer, staring at his mouth. "Yeah?"

"Yeah." His large hand slid around her neck, under the fall of the wig. "I'd have exhausted you."

Tamara almost melted on the spot. She wondered if he intended to exhaust her tonight. It sounded like a fine plan to her.

"I've been thinking," he said, and Tamara hoped the subject of his thoughts was sex. She'd know today if the offer on the building was too good to pass up. If it was, their time together would soon be over. She needed to make every available minute count.

His fingers stroked through the long strands of the wig. "I know your family encourages you to dress this way."

Tamara blinked at the change of subject. Of all the things he could have said, that was the least expected. "Yes, so?"

"I think they're wrong. I've seen you both ways now, and honey, you're fetching no matter what. But without all the props, the real you shines through. I think it'd be great for business if you showed yourself as you really are."

Tamara drew back. "Aunt Olga and Aunt Eva would have a fit."

"So? You're a grown woman and you can do as you please." He brushed her cheek. "Right?"

She wondered if he knew he was issuing a direct challenge. It was probable. Eyes narrowed, she nodded. "True. And it's always pleased me to please them."

Zane tilted up her chin and nibbled on her bottom lip. Her stomach tightened with a sweet ache. "What about pleasing me?"

Her thoughts got muddled whenever he touched her. "Yes."

"Then just give it a try. See what the customers think."

She supposed it couldn't hurt anything. And she did hate the wig. The clothes and the jewelry . . . well, she didn't mind them so much. But the rest of it was uncomfortable and a bother.

Tamara nodded. "I don't have time to change today, but . . . we'll see what happens tomorrow."

Before he grinned at her, she could have sworn she detected a brief flash of relief in his eyes.

"I wonder," he teased, "if your transformation will throw everyone else as hard as it did me."

She remembered his reaction very well, and teased right back. "I doubt anyone else will kiss me over it."

A different voice intruded, sultry and thick. "Oh, I don't know about that."

Zane's head lifted, his expression alert. Tamara watched him as Luna sauntered through the curtain separating the rooms. He was aware of her, but unlike most men, he didn't seem dumbstruck by her appearance—which today was more eye-catching than usual. Her mink brown hair hung straight and sleek from a center part, and her golden brown eyes were highlighted by loads of lush mascara.

Barely contained within a long-sleeve tube dress of pale gold, Luna's very full breasts looked ready to spill free at any moment. Black, high-heeled boots were laced all the way up to her knees, and a chunky black leather belt hung loosely on her rounded hips. She looked chic, sexy, and full-blown, like a movie star pinup.

"Zane, my assistant, Luna Clark. Luna, Zane Winston."

Zane's gaze never wavered from Luna's face; Tamara knew that because she was jealously watching. He nodded. "Luna."

Luna smiled, but didn't come any closer. She fiddled with a thin gold necklace around her throat and said, "If you talk her out of wearing the costume, you might be surprised by the reactions she gets."

Zane's brows lifted. "Meaning?"

"Meaning half the men who come here are already infatuated with her, and it wouldn't take much to make them fall in love."

Zane shifted, turning the slightest bit. He looked to be readying himself for battle, but he gave no verbal reply.

"With the costume," Luna continued, ignoring Tamara's frantic gestures to halt her, "she comes across as part of the props, a little loony, a little whimsical. I bet that's why you overlooked her for so long."

"Who says I overlooked her?"

Luna laughed at that. "This is the first time I've seen you playing kissy-face with her over the counter."

His shoulders tensed. Tamara had no idea what Luna was up to, but she wished she'd knock it off.

"Your point?"

"Most of her innate generosity of spirit is mistaken for part of a con, a way to reel in customers and give them what they're paying for. Without the costume, the whole world will see her for what she really is."

Tamara wanted to slink off in embarrassment. Or else grab some packing tape and use it to seal Luna's mouth.

Quickly, she rounded the counter to stand between Luna and Zane. She tried to laugh, but wasn't pleased with the sickly sound. "Luna is a big kidder."

Proving the point, Luna held her hands together and said in a theatrical voice, "Luna is all-knowing, all-seeing." Then she winked at Zane. "And Luna tells it like it is."

"Luna is becoming a pain in the butt!" Tamara glared at her.

Luna laughed and slipped around the counter to the appointment book. "I wonder, Zane, if you want her to lose the costume because it embarrasses you." Her gaze shifted to Tamara. "Did you happen to meet any of his family lately? Maybe in your Gypsy getup?"

Tamara frowned, but before she could say anything, Zane straightened. His eyes were narrow slits, his dark brows drawn down. "Embarrass me? I don't think so. It was her Gypsy outfit that first drew me in."

Tamara leaped onto that explanation. "True! The first time he came knocking at my door"—she didn't explain that she'd offered herself to him—"he hadn't seen me without the Gypsy costume."

"Is that right? Then I wonder what his motives really are."

Tamara wondered that, too, but she wasn't about to ask Zane now. "Leave it alone, Luna."

Luna grinned. "Don't worry, honey. I won't scare him off. I have the feeling Zane Winston is made of stern stuff. He's not a man to turn tail and run."

Zane, Tamara thought, looked like a man ready to ignite. Tamara took his arm and dragged him out of Luna's hearing. They stopped beside her round table with the hand-crocheted lace tablecloth and the ornamental crystal ball set on a lighted stand. People were often disappointed when they realized she used the crystal ball only for decoration, not to summon spirits.

"She's a little . . . eccentric," Tamara explained.

And though she'd spoken barely above a whisper, Luna said, "That's the pot calling the kettle black, honey."

Tamara growled at her, but Luna didn't look up from where she was checking over names in the appointment book. She did, however, have a small smile on her mouth. Tamara sighed.

"At least you're not working alone today," Zane said, bringing her attention back to him. "I'm glad."

That reminded her of why she'd asked Luna to come in. "I got a call from my Realtor."

As if he, too, realized the ramifications of that, Zane paused. "An offer?"

"Yes."

He surprised her by cursing. "Are you going to accept?"

"I don't know yet. I'm going to his office this afternoon to find out the details. If . . ." She swallowed, hating to say the words. She loved the old building, and she loved the area. She'd so hoped her unsettled days were over. "If it's a good offer, I have to take it."

Zane paced away from her. He walked over to the door and stared out the window. Evidently not caring that Luna was listening, he said, "Will you do me a favor and wait before making any decisions?"

She wanted to say yes. She wanted to wait forever, or not sell at all. But she was a realist. "It won't make any difference. I need to sell."

At this point, Tamara figured it didn't matter if Zane knew everything. She wanted him to understand that she wouldn't leave him without good reason. "Every day my situation gets a little tighter. A good offer right now would be a blessing."

Still without facing her, Zane said, "I could make you a loan."

A heartbeat of silence went by before Tamara caught her breath. She shook her head, incredulous that he'd said such a thing. "No."

"You have options, damn it."

Her temples pounded, her heart ached. "Taking money from you," she said, forcing the words past her tight throat, "isn't one of them."

He put his hands on his hips and dropped his head forward, as if contemplating things. When he looked at her, determination was plain in his eyes. "If the offer is good, it won't go away just because you take a few days to consider it."

"I suppose not."

"Then promise me you'll talk to me before you sign anything."

Luna started laughing, and when they both glared at her, she held out her hands. "Sorry!"

Tamara fretted. She didn't like giving him so much control, because that made him partially responsible. But at the same time, she wanted every second with him that she could get. "I'll tell you what the Realtor has to say."

"You won't agree to anything today?"

"No."

His shoulders relaxed, and he smiled at her. "Tonight, what time will you close?"

With the appointment book open in front of her, Luna said helpfully, "Four o'clock."

"I'll be here at four-fifteen."

Tamara felt breathless again, now for an entirely different reason. "Okay."

Zane walked up to her and kissed her. She was aware of Luna watching, and also aware that Zane didn't care. He touched her chin. "Tonight."

"Yes."

Zane nodded at Luna, who winked, and turned to leave. He'd taken two steps toward the door when it opened and a man stepped inside.

Arkin Devane was early. And even more surprising, another man walked in, right on Arkin's heels.

Zane turned to look at Tamara with lifted brows, curious over this early morning rush.

Arkin smiled his wide, sincere smile and said, "Tamara! I hope you don't mind. I couldn't wait a minute more."

Zane's curiosity turned to a frown. Tamara could feel Luna grinning behind her.

The second man, tall with inky black hair, bulky with muscle, and dressed expensively, looked around the shop with interest. "I gather I'm in the right place."

Arkin moved straight to Tamara and clasped her hands. Tamara struggled not to look at Zane; she didn't want to see his reaction, not when she could already feel the heat of his watchfulness. He was alert, but for what, she didn't know.

"Arkin, you can wait in the first room. I'll be right with you."

Luna, being a proper assistant, stepped forward and introduced herself to the second man. "Did you want an appointment this morning?" she asked him.

The man looked her over, and before Tamara could reach Zane to send him on his way, he said, "Yes, but not with you."

He turned to Tamara. She automatically took a step back, unable to stop herself. The man was just so . . . intense. And the way he looked at her—with barely veiled surprise, now tinged with hunger. Did he have preconceived notions about her, based on her occupation?

She forgot her speculations when he gave a slow, very male smile and said, "I want *you*."

* * *

Zane had never had a sixth sense, except where women were concerned. And then it was razor-sharp. He'd watched Tamara retreat from the man, and everything male inside him went on red-hot alert. He took an aggressive step forward.

Luna touched the man's arm. "I'm sorry, but Ms. Tremayne is booked for the day. You'll need to make an appointment."

Without looking away from Tamara, the man intoned, "I'm Boris Sandor," as if that held some significance.

Tamara glanced at Luna, then at Zane, before turning her attention back to Boris. "It's nice to meet you, Mr. Sandor. My assistant, Luna Clark, can help you set an appointment if you'd like."

He shrugged off Luna's hand. "How much do you charge?"

Annoyed, Luna propped her hands on her hips and lost her ethereal tone. She named a price, which, going by Tamara's expression, was a bit high.

Boris said, "I'll pay twice that."

Arkin stuck his head around the curtain. "Tamara?"

"I'll be right there." She pressed a hand to her forehead. "Look, Mr. Sandor, it doesn't matter what you pay, I'm booked, and I can't leave scheduled clients waiting. If you'd like to see Luna, she's free. Otherwise, you need an appointment like everyone else."

Zane wanted to explode. Damn, it was starting already! He didn't have to see Luna's expression to know she was smirking at his discomfort. He'd had no idea Tamara was so popular, and he sure as hell hadn't envisioned her clientele as male. He'd assumed she dealt mostly with young, fanciful women wanting to know about their boyfriends, or older women hoping to receive a message from a deceased husband or great-great-aunt.

He realized that he really had no idea what Tamara did. She'd told him again and again that she wasn't psychic, though he still had his doubts about that, as well as doubting her ability to cast spells. She'd certainly done *something* to him.

Her front window advertised palm reading, futures told. Run-of-the-mill carnival acts, as far as he knew.

Yet two men, both of them appearing to be reasonable, intelligent sorts, were here first thing in the morning, demanding her attention.

He considered throwing the bulky Sandor out. After all, the man obviously made her uncomfortable with his constant leering, and he was verbally rude to boot. Only the knowledge that she would resent his interference kept him standing there quietly.

When he leaned against the wall beside the door, settling in for the duration of this little confrontation, Tamara sent him an apologetic, dismissive shrug. He ignored it.

He might have enough wit left to let her handle her business herself, but no way in hell was he walking out when he could feel her uneasiness.

She glared at him for not budging, then turned all her annoyance on Sandor. "Luna will give you a card. Feel free to set an appointment for another time."

"Your aunt sent me." He made that announcement as if the queen herself had told him to come calling.

"I'm sure my aunt told you to set an appointment."

"Of course not. She wanted us to get . . . acquainted. As friends, not in a professional manner."

The way he said "professional manner" was very insulting. Zane watched Tamara's mouth thin. "Why?"

"We're from the same homeland."

Zane snorted. "And that would be?"

Sandor turned to him with a show of displeasure. "Excuse me, but the lady and I are having a private conversation."

"In the middle of the shop?" Luna asked, and this time Zane wanted to kiss her for her well-placed zinger. "Besides," she added, waving toward Zane, "he's her man. So of course he's going to listen in."

I'm her man. Zane liked the sound of that, as outdated as it might be.

Boris said, "But your aunt assured me you were unattached!"

"Her aunt was wrong," Zane replied lazily, and he noticed that Tamara wasn't looking at him now, her gaze intently focused on Boris. He didn't like that.

Arkin Devane stuck his head around the curtain again. This time he sounded uncertain when he said, "Tamara?"

Her concentration scattered. "Yes, I'm sorry, Arkin." She started toward the dark curtain. "Excuse me, Mr. Sandor, but as you can see, I'm rather busy. If you'd like to come back another time—"

"Tonight?"

She paused, glanced at Zane, and her face colored. "Ah, no. I already have plans for the evening."

"Then how about lunch?"

Appearing harassed, Tamara said, "I'm sorry, but that won't work either. Luna, will you see if you can fit him in for Monday?"

Zane wanted to laugh at the look on the pompous ass's face. He definitely did not like being dismissed, or put off for so long.

Tamara didn't wait around to see if he accepted or not. She ducked behind the curtain, and Zane heard a door close. At least the fellow she was with now seemed unassuming.

He caught Luna's eye, and she winked at him. "Arkin has an especially long appointment today. Hmmm. Wonder why?"

Her suggestive tone raked along his nerves, and he knew damn good and well she did it on purpose.

"Well, Mr. Sandor? Shall I fit you in on Monday?"

Face red, Boris nodded. "Around noon."

"Sorry." Luna propped both elbows on the counter, leaning forward with the appointment book in front of her. "That's her lunch break." Her breasts fell softly forward, displaying quite a bit of cleavage. Boris gave them an appropriately appreciative look.

Zane struggled with a grin. At first, he hadn't liked Luna much, but now she felt like an ally—when her barbs weren't aimed at him.

"Fine," Boris snapped, recalling himself. "When does she have available?"

"Let's see." Luna took her time looking at the book. Boris took his time ogling Luna's breasts. Pencil in hand, she glanced up finally and asked, "How about two?"

"I'll be here." Without another word, Boris stormed out.

"Oh my, oh my," Luna said. "Someone has a burr under his bottom."

Zane laughed. "You handled him well."

Shrugging, she stuck the pencil behind her ear and grinned. "Part of the job description—handle the crazies."

"Are there many of them?"

"Not usually."

"He said her aunt sent him."

"Her family does that a lot. They're always trying to fix her up." Luna sauntered around from behind the counter. "And just think, thanks to you, the next time Boris sees her, she'll look like herself. Makes you wonder how he'll react to that, huh?"

Zane almost swallowed his tongue. Damn it, she was right! He briefly considered discouraging her from the change, then shook his head. "No," he said aloud. "She's not happy wearing all that camouflage. She only does it because her family makes her feel like she needs it."

Luna's mouth fell open, then she pressed a hand to her heart. "Well, I'll be damned."

"Why?" Zane asked, put out by her exaggerated pose. "What'd you do now?"

"You're authentic, aren't you? You really do have her best interests at heart."

"You believed your own nonsense about her embarrassing me?"

"Yep."

He laughed at her honesty. "For about half a minute, you would have been right. Of course, when my brothers met her, she wasn't just a Gypsy but a soaking wet Gypsy with ruined makeup and a crooked wig."

"And they couldn't understand what the mighty Zane Winston was doing with her?"

Luna was the type of woman you wanted to hug one minute, and turn over your knee the next. With any luck, some guy would do the honors real soon.

"You underestimate my brothers," Zane told her, refusing to react to her sarcasm. "They would never be that rude to a woman, or that crass." And they had known exactly what he was doing, they just hadn't been certain why.

She still looked a little shell-shocked. "You know, Zane Winston, you may be exactly what Tamara needs right now. At least until she sells."

"*If* she sells," Zane insisted, because he was still determined to find a way to fix things for her. And thinking of that, he glanced at his watch and knew Joe would be waiting. "I have to run. Will you be here with her all day?"

"Yes, but Monday she's working alone again, and I have to tell you, you're not the only one worried."

"So we'll both try to keep an eye on her, and in the meantime, I'm working on figuring it out."

"I wish you luck." She sent him a level look and whispered, "As long as you don't hurt her. Because if you hurt her, you'll be the one who ends up sorry."

He realized Luna cared about Tamara, so he didn't take offense at the warning. Instead, he returned Luna's earlier wink and headed for the door. Hurt Tamara? Hell, all he wanted to do was keep her safe.

And make love to her for at least a year.

T W E L V E

Tamara held one of Arkin Devane's slim hands between her own. There were no dimmed lights, no special effects. Music drifted into the room; Luna had turned on the CD player. She assumed Boris Sandor was gone. Which likely meant Zane had left, too, since he'd only been hanging around as a guard dog. She should have been amused by his protectiveness today, but instead, she'd been oddly reassured by it.

She tried to concentrate, to say all the words she knew Arkin expected to hear, but the feeling of unease lingered.

She didn't like Boris Sandor. When he'd looked at her, she felt his concentration like oil, sliding over her skin, clogging her pores. It had filled her with uneasiness. His interest had first been calculated, but had quickly turned red-hot, even intimate. She'd felt his anticipation overtake the dread. Why? What had he been dreading, and why had his emotional state changed? She didn't want to deal with Boris, but he'd said her aunt had sent him.

The level of her awareness had startled her. Zane was the only other man she'd felt like that. Zane was the only man she *wanted* to feel like that.

"Are you all right?"

She met Arkin's concerned gaze and frowned at herself. He paid good money for his time with her, and here she was, daydreaming. "Yes. I'm sorry."

The worry in his pale blue eyes remained. "If it's about me taking up so much of your time . . ."

"No, no, that's fine." She smiled, and squeezed his hand. "I gather we have a lot to talk about."

"But you had to turn that other man away."

Her smile slipped the tiniest bit. "That's okay. I'm sure Luna took care of him. Now, let me see here."

She stared at Arkin's palm, already knowing what she would see, and what he wanted to hear. At the last second though, before she started her discourse on heart lines and hand coloring and finger zones, she looked into his face. It took her only a moment to make up her mind.

Today, Arkin needed the genuine article, and she intended to give it to him.

Tamara squeezed his fingers, then laid his hand aside. "You're obviously in love."

Arkin's eyebrows lifted. He nodded, eager and wary and hopeful. "Very much so."

"The thing is," she told him with a grin, "she's very interested in you, too."

Drawing back, he asked, "How can you know that?"

"To be honest, Arkin, I'm not sure. But I feel it, and," she added gently, "I could feel it only from you." Tamara regarded him. "You realize the truth, you're just too afraid to do anything about it."

Covering his face with his hands, Arkin groaned. "It's true. I'm afraid of messing up, of doing or saying the wrong thing. She's not like me, Tamara. She's. . . ."

Her heart melting for this gentle man, Tamara suggested, "Exuberant? Alive and outgoing and free-spirited."

With a sigh in his voice, he said, "She reminds me of you."

Tamara laughed at that. "You're an attractive man, Arkin. You're kind and responsible."

"And dull as dust."

"That's not true."

"I need help, Tamara." He looked beyond morose. "I always say the wrong thing at the wrong time."

"You've approached her?" She couldn't help being surprised by his initiative. Arkin Devane was not the aggressive sort. More often than not, he entertained himself with books, not women.

"I tried." He winced. "She smiles at me, and I go mute."

Tamara thought of the journal she had upstairs. The first few entries had been on approach, and based on the outcome with Zane, they were quite successful. Again, she took Arkin's hand. "I think I can help you."

His eyes gleamed. "You can?"

"Yes. I found an incredibly interesting journal that's filled with excellent advice. I'll gladly share it with you."

His expression went blank, then hopeful. "A journal?" He half-laughed, somewhat uncertain. "Well, you know how much I enjoy reading."

"Oh, I didn't mean you need to read the whole thing. There's a lot in there that doesn't apply to you, and besides, I'm still reading it myself. But we have plenty of time today, so I'll just go over the pertinent stuff."

Arkin shifted in his seat. "Go over the . . . pertinent stuff?"

Feeling enthusiastic now that she'd made up her mind, Tamara didn't hesitate. "The first thing we need to discuss is what type of woman you're approaching. That's vital to how we handle things."

"Wouldn't it be easier if I read it myself?"

Tamara dismissed his suggestion. "The journal is upstairs. Besides, I can tell you what it said."

Because he was shy, Tamara tried to be as matter-of-fact and blunt as she could, without embarrassing Arkin with unnecessary explicitness. The time flew by, and before she knew it, she needed to leave for her appointment with the Realtor.

Arkin seemed introspective when he finally said goodbye. Considering all the information she'd just shared, he likely had a lot on his mind. She smiled as she watched him leave, hands in his pockets, his head down, deep in thought.

Luna came up behind her. "Tamara, do you know where the astrology charts are?"

"What do you mean?" Distracted, Tamara turned to get her jacket and her purse so she'd make it to the Realtor's on time. "They're right where they always are."

"Nope." Luna followed on her heels. "I had a customer who had questions about her horoscope, but I couldn't find the charts."

Tamara walked to the shelving behind the counter. Running her finger along the numerous books neatly placed there, spines out, she searched for the binder that held the various charts. It wasn't where she'd left it.

Her storage room was disorganized; the rest of her shop was not. Once she sorted through things, she always put them in a specific place so she could grab them in a hurry, if need be.

Propping her hands on her hips, she said, "That's weird. They were here last time I looked."

"When was that?"

"Just a few days ago."

"If you took them out, maybe you accidentally put them away in the wrong spot."

Tamara gave her a look, and Luna said, "I know. Not likely."

Kneeling, Tamara quickly searched through the other books. She didn't have time for this right now. "Well, damn. The address book is in the wrong spot."

Luna knelt, too. "It's even on the wrong shelf." She sounded a little dazed by that discovery. And a little worried.

"Everything is mixed up." Tamara looked at Luna, and saw the same conclusion on her assistant's face. "Someone has been going through our stuff."

Luna plopped down to sit on her bottom. She chewed her lip a moment, then asked, "Do you think one of your aunts was looking for something?"

"They haven't been in since I had the astrology charts out."

Luna's next question surprised Tamara. "Are you going to tell Zane?"

Tamara groaned at the thought. "God, I don't know. I can just imagine his reaction if I do."

"Funny, I was thinking of his reaction if you don't."

Tamara couldn't help smiling. "There is that."

They both stood. Luna dusted off her backside, then brushed Tamara off as well. "For what it's worth, I say tell him."

"I'll think about it. If the offer today is good enough, it may not even matter. None of this will be mine anymore."

"What if all this," Luna asked, indicating the shop, "isn't what they're after? What if someone is after *you*?"

Tamara snatched up the big bag she used as a purse and headed for the door. She didn't even want to consider the possibility, yet Luna's words hung with her, and she felt on edge as she caught the bus that would take her to the Realtor's. But it wasn't just the misplaced items in her shop that had her apprehensive.

Again and again, she felt watchful eyes on her, yet no one on the bus seemed to be paying her any mind. Tamara even looked behind her, and saw no one who should make her feel so suspicious. Her heart tripped with the realization that she was being followed.

Her business with the Realtor didn't take long; the offer was good, but it wasn't quite what she'd hoped to get, what she knew the building was worth because of its location. She breathed a sigh of relief as she wrote out a counteroffer. She'd just gotten a small reprieve. She'd bought herself a few more days with Zane.

The second she stepped outside, she again felt the weight of someone's attention. She didn't detect any real menace, but the intensity of the focus bit into her, making her legs feel like Jell-O.

Trying to hide her nervousness, she made her way to the bus stop. There was a crowd of people there—an elderly couple talking quietly, and holding hands. Several college kids milling around, loaded down with books and using curse words for adjectives, loud enough to make the elderly man scowl at them. There was also a tall, dark man dressed in ragged jeans and a flannel shirt, chatting easily with two buttoned-down businesswomen. The man was big, a muscular, unshaven hulk, disheveled, disreputable, impossible to miss. Tamara shook her head at how the women fawned over him, and how he encouraged them with a sexy smile.

No one seemed aware that they were being watched, but Tamara knew. She still felt it.

During the bus ride, her tension eased. But the second she got off the bus, along with several other people, she sensed the renewed observation. Attempting to be discreet, she studied the people who'd gotten off the bus with her. The group separated, each person going his or her own way and Tamara found herself standing alone. Vulnerable.

Unlike the last time, today the sun was bright and warm, a beautiful spring day. Tamara drew a deep breath to calm herself, and headed down the sidewalk. The lunchtime traffic was heavy, and she was jostled several times. Each touch by a stranger pulled her nerves a little tighter. By the time she turned the corner and could see her shop, she was practically running.

The CLOSED FOR LUNCH sign was in the window. Tamara

quickly extracted her key to unlock the door, then burst inside with unnecessary fanfare. From the other side of the counter, Luna looked up. The New Age music Tamara preferred had been replaced with Tom Petty, and the volume was turned up several notches. Luna had removed her boots as she idly danced. She had a half-eaten sandwich in one hand, a diet Coke in the other.

Tamara locked gazes with her, knowing what she had to do. She sucked in several calming breaths before she finally spoke. "I'll tell Zane tonight."

Luna had stopped dancing the second she spied Tamara's pale face. Now she gulped down the bite in her mouth, choked, and wheezed out, "What made you change your mind?"

"I've been followed again."

It was a few minutes before four o'clock when Zane entered her shop. He didn't see Tamara, but the second the door chimed, she popped up on the other side of the long, polished counter. She still wore her Gypsy costume, but he hadn't expected her to have changed.

Fifteen feet separated the door, where he stood, from the counter, and still he could see the dust on Tamara's nose and the look of alarm in her eyes. When she realized it was him, the wary look was replaced by a tentative smile. "You're early."

"I couldn't keep away." He pushed his hands into his pockets, forcing himself to remain still. Something else had happened, something that had upset her. He was sure of it, just as he was certain she didn't want to tell him about it.

Zane studied her as he considered ways of getting her to open up to him. Her glossy lipstick was gone, leaving her soft mouth naked and twice as appealing. The neckline of her blouse gaped a bit, giving him a peek of cleavage.

When she saw the direction of his gaze, she rearranged herself nervously, watching him the whole time as if she expected him to leap on her. "I've been a little anxious to see you, too."

Zane hid a smile.

She might have instigated their relationship, and she wanted to call the shots, but the last thing she needed was for him to rush her upstairs. He'd have to be patient, even if it killed him. "You're alone now?"

She watched him, wide-eyed and waiting. "Luna left only a few minutes ago."

After locking the door and pulling down the shade, Zane moseyed closer. She had a book in each hand, and a few were sitting on the floor. "What are you up to?"

"Just organizing some things." She hesitated, then said, "Somehow they got out of order."

She bent to push the remaining books into place, and Zane, unable to stop himself, smoothed his hand over her softly rounded ass. She jumped.

As she quickly turned to face him, he cupped his hand around her nape and smiled. She was warm, soft. He couldn't stop touching her. "You have the phone on you?"

"Yes." Exasperated, she frowned at him. "You don't have to keep asking that, you know."

"Just checking." She started to grouse again, and he kissed her. He meant it to be a light, teasing kiss, just enough to still her resistance. But she leaned into him and the kiss lingered.

She tasted so good. He wanted her naked, open, so he could taste her everywhere. His groin throbbed, his testicles pulling tight. He would feast on her, and still it might not be enough.

He closed his eyes for a moment, forcing himself to calm. "Have you had dinner?"

"I'm not hungry."

"That's not what I asked you."

Her hands crept up to his shoulders, then looped behind his neck. "I haven't eaten, but couldn't we eat . . . after?"

His breathing deepened. "If that's what you really want." Damn, how could he be patient if she wouldn't cooperate? More than anything, he wanted this to be good for Tamara, and with the state he was in now, it'd be over before it started.

Her smile was sweet, shy. She left him to wander around the shop, snuffing out incense and pinching out candles. Though she'd watched him lock it, she double-checked to make sure the door was secure.

Her long, wispy skirt flirted around her ankles, and her ankle bracelets rang musically. The late afternoon sunlight coming through the large front window glinted off her jewelry, and left a golden sheen along her skin.

Her movements were graceful and practiced, and Zane accepted that the shop was a part of her, just as his store was a part of him.

He knew how hard he'd worked to make his business a success. How hard had it been for Tamara? She was so young, and where he had his brothers backing him, helping any way they could, she had older relatives for whom she felt responsible. Her burden far exceeded his, emotionally and financially. "How did it go at the Realtor's?"

She turned off the CD player and a heavy silence settled into the shop, mingling with the scented smoke. "The offer wasn't enough. I made a counteroffer."

Some of the tension eased from his shoulders. "This may all work out yet." He made the suggestion uncertainly. He had no real idea of how dire her financial situation might be. She'd said she needed to sell, and knowing Tamara, knowing how headstrong she was, if there'd been another way to cope, she'd have found it already.

"Maybe." It was plain she didn't want to talk about it. She looked at him through her darkened lashes. "Are you ready to go upstairs?"

Inside, Zane smoldered, while outside he maintained an expression of indifference. If Tamara knew how savagely aroused he was, she would probably change her mind and throw him out.

"Yeah, I'm ready." Zane took her hand and allowed her to lead the way up the dim, narrow stairwell.

Tamara closed the door behind him, and turned the key that stayed in the lock. Zane was aware of her in every pore of his body, her nearness, the scent of her, the heat of her skin. Her uncertainty.

She wanted him, but casual sex was unusual for her. That pleased him.

"I need to change out of this stuff," she whispered in a shaky voice, "and shower off my makeup."

Zane fingered the wig. He wanted to feel her own soft curls, not the heavy coarseness of the wig. "I could shower with you."

As she stared up at him, her eyes glittered with sensual awareness. "I've never showered with a man before."

Zane paused. "No?"

"No."

He started to ask her exactly what she *had* done, but he held the words inside. Jealousy was a new emotion for him, and he wasn't ready to broadcast it. "Let's make tonight a first then."

"You don't mind?"

He cuddled her cheek in his palm, enthralled with the velvety, warm texture. He had a feeling she'd be that soft all over, even softer in the places where he badly wanted to touch her, taste her. "Of course not." He liked it that she would experience something new with him. It would forge a special link that she wouldn't be quick to forget.

"I know I gave the impression of having loads of experience. . . ."

"Shh. It doesn't matter." He touched her bottom lip. "By the morning, you'll have all the experience you need."

Her lips parted on an indrawn breath. Because he knew she was nervous and he didn't want her to be, not with him, Zane kissed her. Her lips parted, her tongue accepting his, twining with his. The tempting sweetness of incense clung to her skin, and beneath that, more subtle, was her own unique hot scent. His hands opened wide over her back and drew her into his chest until he could feel her plump breasts cushioned there.

He broke the kiss with some effort, while he still could. They both labored for breath.

In a near daze, Tamara turned and headed for her bedroom. She went straight to the window and opened the blinds, letting in the fading sunlight. It slanted across her desk, just missing the bed. Zane noticed the computer manuals spread out on the desk, but he didn't comment on them. Not right now.

Tamara flipped her head forward, eased the wig off, and ran her fingers through her blond hair, leaving it seductively disheveled. She looked tousled, as if she'd already had sex.

Zane used the wall for support. Watching Tamara transform proved incredibly erotic.

She turned her back to him and removed the contacts. When she faced him again, she stole his breath away. Her hair was in disarray, her eyes now bright green with the kohl liner providing a striking contrast, giving her a more mystical aura than the dark contacts could ever have achieved.

One by one, she pulled off her rings, and it was a type of strip show he would never forget. She worked methodically, slowly. His heart quickened, his cock swelled. Tamara watched him, and as she removed each ring, her eyes grew heavier with arousal.

When her fingers were bare of jewelry, she sat on the edge of the

bed and pulled her skirt up to her knees. As she bent to take off her sandals, Zane forced himself to move.

He went to one knee in front of her. "I'll do it."

The tiny bells on the ankle bracelets chimed as he circled her slim
ankle with his hand. Her skin was warm and silky smooth, and he imagined her feet braced on his shoulders as he drove into her, holding her
hips, refusing to let her retreat from his thrusts.

His hands shook when he lifted her left foot and slipped her sandal
off. Carefully, calmly, he set it on the floor beside the bed. Teasing
himself as much as her, he worked each ring off her small pink toes. He
did the same with her right foot, and when he'd finished, rather than
stand, he parted her legs and moved between them.

Her already raised skirt bunched a little higher, forced up by his
body.

Tamara made a soft sound and stroked her hand through his hair.
"I've wanted you ever since the first time I saw you," she murmured.

Zane laid her back on the bed. Sultry and sweet, she stared up at
him. Her blond curls formed a halo around her head.

He caught her hips and pulled her to the edge of the bed so that the
notch of her thighs cradled him. He could feel the gentle heat of her
mound against his abdomen, even through their clothes. "We're going
to take it slow tonight," he promised.

Lazily, she nodded. He had his hands braced on either side of her
hips, and her left hand circled his right wrist. "We're supposed to look
at each other naked."

Hell yes. "I'll look, all right."

"I mean, according to the book. We're supposed to get used to each
other naked."

Heat curled inside him, threatening his control. He didn't need a
damn book to direct him now. "Just trust me, okay?"

She stared at his mouth. "In this, I do."

That wasn't the answer he would have chosen, but no way would he
argue about it now. Her peasant blouse had a drawstring neckline. He
pulled the neatly tied bow loose, allowing the neckline to expand. The
blouse was tucked into a dark blue skirt of layered gauzy material, and
Zane tugged it free from the waistband.

Without protest, Tamara watched him undressing her. "Are we going to make it to the shower?" she asked breathlessly.

"Yeah." He could barely talk. He was twenty-seven years old, and he couldn't remember ever wanting a woman this much. Her nipples had drawn into tight, small points he could see through her blouse and bra. He couldn't wait a second more and bent to put his mouth over her right breast.

Tamara reacted with a groan, arching her body and clenching her left hand in his hair. "Zane."

He sucked on her, her blouse and bra so thin as to be inconsequential.

"I can't take it," she said in a whimper when he switched to the other nipple. Her hips lifted into his and her legs wrapped around his waist.

Zane slid his hand beneath the small of her back, farther down over her bottom. He lifted her more firmly into him. "You can take this, and a whole lot more."

"No." Her head pressed against the bed, throat exposed, eyes squeezed shut.

"Yeah," He rubbed himself over her. "Let's get to the naked part, okay?"

She froze for a moment before nodding. "Okay."

"I've been thinking all day about getting your panties off you, feeling you wrap your legs around me."

Her lips parted.

"Raise your arms," he instructed in guttural tones. She did, slowly.

Thankful that it was loose-fitting, Zane worked the blouse up, exposing her midriff, her ribs, her lace-covered breasts. She was small and pale and so smooth he couldn't stop stroking her. She lifted herself a little so he could get the top free and toss it aside.

Her puckered nipples showed as dark shadows through the lace of her bra. Zane plumped both breasts together and rubbed her with his thumbs. The hiss of her breath pleased him. The sight of her pleased him.

Getting inside her would please him more, but he was determined to make it last, to devastate her with pleasure.

The bra had a front closure, and he snapped it open with one hand. The material parted, stopping just shy of completely freeing her breasts. Zane bent, nuzzled it away, and found one taut nipple waiting, ready for his mouth. He didn't hesitate. He sucked her deep and then held her close as she lifted into him.

Her fingers in his hair alternately squeezed him closer and struggled to pull him away. She gasped and groaned, telling him one minute that she liked it, and the next that it was too acute, the pleasure too sharp. Relentless, determined, Zane controlled her movements and took his time leisurely tasting her.

A ragged moan escaped her. "Zane, please!"

He sat back to survey her. Her painted eyes were heavy, dilated with need. Her breasts rose and fell with shuddering, uneven breaths, her nipples glistening from his her mouth.

A surge of raw, primitive possessiveness locked his muscles tight. Damn, she was his and he wouldn't let anyone hurt her. He wouldn't let her get away from him either.

Tonight, he'd do whatever was necessary to bind her to him.

It might not be what she expected, but Tamara Tremayne would be satisfied with the results. So satisfied she wouldn't be able to shut him out anymore.

He was counting on it.

T H I R T E E N

Zane fought to subdue the raw emotions and turned Tamara onto her stomach. In the past few days, he'd thought about little else except this moment, having her naked and accepting, ready and anxious for him. Now the time was finally here, and he wouldn't let anything or anyone stop him from taking her.

Startled, Tamara pushed up onto her elbows to stare at him over her shoulder. "Zane, what—"

With one hand at the small of her back, he held her still. The skirt had an elastic waist, without an opening. Zane gave up, too impatient to work it down and off her hips, and instead flipped it up and over her bottom, exposing her.

"Zane!" She attempted to push the skirt down, but got it only as far as the small of her back. Zane bunched it in his fist and moved it completely out of his way.

"Let me look at you," he said in smoky tones, words nearly impossible.

Her panties were stretchy lace, like her bra. He could see the soft globes of her rounded bottom through the material. His lungs compressed, and he rasped, "You have a great ass, Tamara."

Her hands curled into the covers, but she held still.

Zane teased himself, cuddling each cheek in his large hands, squeezing, caressing. She was soft but firm, curvy without being voluptuous. He spread his hands wide, measuring her, letting his thumbs meet at the base of her spine. She wiggled at his touch, prompting him to slowly trace her spine, down, down, over the panties and lower, until he pushed his fingers between her legs and found the damp material there. Satisfaction filled him; she responded so quickly to his touch, even while showing her shyness.

Everything about her fascinated him, inflamed him.

The lace panties were like fancy icing on a delicious cake. But now they were too much distraction. He wanted her naked flesh under his hands, his mouth.

Hooking his fingers in the waistband, Zane stripped them down her thighs to her knees.

With a yelp, Tamara dropped her head forward and hid her face in the bedcovers. He heard her give a soft sigh of embarrassment and soothed her with murmured words, gentle strokes and squeezes.

"Damn." Even with the skirt tucked up around her waist, she was sexy as sin. His erection thrust against his slacks, bringing him to the point of near pain. He couldn't remember ever feeling so taut with need. His skin burned, his muscles ached, his stomach clenched.

Zane sat back on his heels and began unbuttoning his cuffs. "Do you have any idea," he growled, "what I want to do to you?"

She panted, nervous and excited and embarrassed. She didn't speak, but her head moved back and forth on the mattress.

Zane smiled hotly. "Everything. I want to do everything to you." Seeing her stretched out, her white backside his for the taking, was a powerful aphrodisiac. He wanted to slide into her from behind, to feel that soft bottom against his abdomen as he took her. He concentrated hard, knowing what he did and how he did it was important if he wanted her to give over to him completely. And he did.

He wanted Tamara to come to him, to need him for everything, not just sex. In the past, if a woman had asked for more than temporary companionship and mutual physical pleasure, he'd have broken things off to keep from building her expectations, knowing he was a bachelor and damn well intended to stay one.

With Tamara . . . all he knew for certain was that he wanted and needed more. Whether or not it'd last, he had no idea, but for now she was his, and he wanted her to admit it.

"We'll play by your rules, sweetheart, and get used to being naked together first."

That had her peeking, her head swiveling around to watch as he undid the last button on his shirt and shrugged it off his shoulders. He tossed it toward the floor while keeping his gaze glued to her face.

Heat suffused her delicate skin, and she licked her lips. "Go . . . go on," she urged.

Knowing he had her undivided attention, Zane unhooked his belt and slipped it free from the loops. He opened the button at the top of his slacks and carefully eased the zipper down past his throbbing hard-on. And even that touch, with his own hand, was almost too much.

"No," he said abruptly, not about to give up control so soon. "I have to leave my pants on for now, or we're done for."

"But . . ."

"Shh. Trust me, sweetheart. Let me make you feel good."

Her slender, pale shoulders trembled as he touched her, as he dragged his fingers over the inward dip of her waistline, over to her graceful spine, and down to the twin dimples in her bottom. He leaned forward and lightly bit the plumpest curve of her right cheek.

Tamara wiggled and squirmed. Her thighs were clamped tight together.

"Open your legs, sweetheart."

Two heartbeats went by before she slowly edged her thighs just the tiniest bit wider. Again, Zane smiled. She amused him almost as much as she turned him on.

He wedged his fingers between her legs, enthralled with the darkness of his large, rough hand against the paleness of her tender inner thighs. Her body tensed as he moved her legs wide open, letting him see her, every inch of her.

"Beautiful," he murmured, desire twisting his guts and adding to his ache. He sat there like that, holding her steady, open, and looked his fill.

"Zane?"

Her voice was muffled, her face still hidden. Rather than reply, he spread his hands over her upper thighs, parting her more, and touched her glistening pink flesh with his thumbs. Her body shuddered, her legs shifted, and she gave a soft cry.

"So wet for me." He slicked his thumbs back and forth, spreading her moisture, readying her, feeling her.

"Oh God." Her bottom lifted into his hands, begging for more. Her hands tightened in the sheets, her arms tensed with the strain. But he continued, slowly sliding over her lips, opening her, petting her, wanting her as turned on as he'd been ever since her proposition.

And he looked at her, the ultrasoft pink flesh, swelling with excitement. His heartbeat increased with each small gasp she made, until he knew he wouldn't be able to take much more.

"Do you want to come for me, Tamara?"

"I don't know," she whispered brokenly, the words low and rough.

"Well, I do know." Zane stretched out next to her and turned her into his arms. She watched him with dark green, dazed eyes, her mouth open, her nostrils flaring with each deep breath. Fingers damp, he touched her mouth, then licked her.

Tamara moaned and launched herself against him. She was wild, and he loved it, holding her closer as she bit at his mouth, sucked at his tongue.

"Zane, oh God, I didn't expect this."

"I know." Everything with Tamara was harder, hotter, more intense. Hell, he felt ready to come himself, and she hadn't even touched him yet. But touching her was exciting enough to send him over the edge.

He tangled his hand in her hair and tipped her head back, making her back arch so he could reach her breasts. He drew on her nipples, sucking and tonguing and teasing. He pushed her to her back and kissed his way to her soft belly while his fingers combed through her tight damp curls. The hair on her sex was darker than that on her head, a rich, glossy, dark blond.

Again, he parted her, and this time he pushed his finger deep. To his immense surprise, she cried out in mingled excitement and discomfort. Panting, Zane came up over her to stare at her face. He held still while her inner muscles clamped down on his intruding finger.

Her eyes were squeezed shut, her lashes spiked, leaving long shadows on her cheeks.

"Tamara?"

Her hips lifted, adjusted. Her only answer was a shuddering moan. She gripped his wrist with one hand, holding him, while she dug her nails into his shoulder with the other.

Zane could barely breathe. "Another first, baby?"

"Please don't stop."

Slowly, entranced, Zane leaned down and kissed each puckered nipple. He rested his head on her rib cage and inhaled her scent. It took his mind a little time to catch up with his emotions. His pulse rioted and now, above the lust, was a tenderness so deep, so overwhelming he felt on the point of no return.

Very, very carefully, he pulled his finger almost out. Just as carefully, he pushed it into her again, measuring her, testing her readiness. Her nails on his shoulder bit deep, bringing a stinging pain that he relished.

Chiding her, giving his mind time to clear, he said, "You should have told me, sweetheart."

Her hips rose with his next gentle thrust, a rosy blush expanding over her breasts.

"You never wanted me," she gasped, and Zane wondered if she even knew what she was saying. Her eyes were squeezed shut, every inch of her body trembling. He could feel the pulse beat of her heart against his jaw, and around his finger.

Already she was close. Very close.

"I want you more right now than I've ever wanted anything else in my life."

The words hung in the air like a thick storm cloud, and then Tamara sniffed. Big tears seeped from her eyes, ripping out his heart. "You mean that?"

"I mean it."

He kissed her ribs, her cleavage, each breast, and finally her mouth. Smiling down into her beautiful, tear-filled green eyes, he told her, "You are one special lady."

She looked at his mouth. "You know you're killing me?"

His smile nearly became a grin as he maintained the slow, rhythmic in-and-out motion of his finger. "You don't like it?"

"I like it too much." She drew a halting breath, a wave of pleasure nearly taking her, before she continued. "I didn't realize it'd be like this."

He was careful not to touch her clitoris, swollen and taut. "Let's try something else, okay?"

Her answer was a moan of acceptance.

"Easy now." Zane worked another finger inside her. "You are so tight."

She shook her head. "I've never done this."

"I know." He'd thought he understood about her responsibilities, but for a woman as sensual and naturally giving as Tamara to remain a virgin so long, she must have been more restricted than he'd figured.

Another small piece of his heart crumbled, and he decided she was ready now, she had to be ready now. This was something she *would* take from him, and he intended to give it all to her.

"You'll like this," he predicted, and shifting his hand just a little, he found her with his thumb.

Her body stiffened and she turned her face into his shoulder.

"Kiss me, Tamara."

She tried, but she was panting as the pleasure quickly escalated beyond her control.

"Zane!" She reached for him, pulling him to her, kissing his jaw, his neck, biting, squeezing him. Her hands clutched at his back and she moved against him, against his stroking fingers. She cried out, her moans raw and real.

He encouraged her with whispered words and careful touches until finally, all she could do was writhe and gasp.

When her body finally went limp, Zane held her to him, smoothing her soft hair from her face, caressing her bare back, her plump bottom. With her face tucked into his neck, he heard her sniffles. He smiled.

"Hey? You okay?"

She bumped his chin when she bobbed her head.

Feeling emotionally complete, and sexually explosive, Zane managed to say calmly, "You ready for that shower now?"

Again, she merely nodded, but her arms tightened around him.

"Is that a yes or a no, sweetheart?"

It took her a moment, and then she sighed. "Yes, I'm willing, but I don't think I can move."

"Easily remedied." Zane stood, kicked off his shoes, pulled off his socks, and then scooped her into his arms and against his bare chest. The skirt, which had been tangled around her waist, fell into place and something solid bumped his knee.

Tamara, preoccupied with running her hand over his chest, gave an apologetic shrug. "The phone you told me to carry. It's in my pocket."

Her makeup was smudged again, this time by her tears, but it didn't detract from her smoldering sensuality. Her eyes were filled with lazy repletion after her climax, and curiosity at what she knew was yet to come. She was the most endearing, surprising, sensual woman he knew. "I'll take care of it."

Zane carried her into the tiny bathroom and stood her on her feet. He slipped his hand into her hair again, unable to stop touching her. "Towels?"

She looked shy and sweet, standing there on wobbly legs, wearing only a Gypsy skirt and a warm blush. Her breasts were lovely, small but perfectly shaped, her nipples flushed dark. He had no idea how much longer he could last.

She bent and pulled two towels from the cabinet beneath the sink. When she straightened, Zane dropped his slacks and stepped out of them.

The towels fell from her hands. Staring so hard he felt her gaze like a touch, Tamara said, "Oh my."

It hurt to smile. Hell, it hurt to breathe.

It seemed the Winston curse had a stranglehold on him, and he wasn't sure if he should fight it or embrace it. Tamara threatened him in every way he'd sworn a woman never would. Before she'd entered his store and whispered that she wanted him, he'd been doing an admirable job of staying on his given course. Most of his attention had been on growing his computer business. He'd balanced that with his responsibilities to his family. Family, in his book, always came first.

Between his business and his family he'd managed to fit in the occasional woman—like twice weekly—to keep his body sated. He was a very sexual man, and since there had always been willing women, he'd seen no reason to deprive himself.

But now other women didn't interest him at all, and more often than not, Tamara shattered his concentration on business and family. She lurked in his mind, crawled under his skin and into his dreams, and she was easily pushing her way into his heart.

He'd watched his brothers tumble into love, one right after the other. They hadn't fought it, as he'd always intended to. Hell, Cole had sought it out, and Mack had grinned his way to the altar. Even Chase, so quiet and deep, had accepted his fate.

Zane had thought he could keep Tamara in a neatly assigned slot, that he could accept her proposition, get her out of his system, and then get on with his bachelor ways.

It seemed she had the same intent: sexual pleasure, and nothing more. And being the perverse bastard he was, that drove him nuts.

He wouldn't allow it, damn it. Neither the Winston curse, nor any spell his little Gypsy might cast, was going to keep him from doing exactly as he pleased. And at the moment, it would please him to be inside her, to feel her climax while she was under him, moving with him and groaning out his name.

He could see the pulse thrumming in her throat as she stared at his groin. He could have sworn he got harder just from her interested gaze. "Have you come to any conclusions?"

Her focus lifted to his face, but not for long. "Yes."

Zane smiled. "Well, I hope you like what you see, because you're going to be seeing it a lot."

Tamara's heart pounded so hard, she felt faint. Zane was . . . more than she'd expected. She'd known he had a wonderful body; slim jeans and clinging T-shirts had revealed that even before she'd seen him without his shirt.

But now, standing in front of her in the raw, he was the most magnificent thing she'd ever seen. Her legs felt like butter, her skin was hot, her stomach dropped. She couldn't stop staring.

Surely no sane woman would look away from the sight of him. His hips were lean and hard, his legs long and muscled, big feet planted firmly apart, as if prepared for a battle.

She nearly snorted. She had no intention of fighting him. She wanted him, and the pleasure he'd already given her hadn't diminished that desire one whit.

She licked her lips and perceived his slight movement. When she glanced up, his face had gone hard, his eyes dilated. "Can I touch you?"

Her fingertips pulsed with the need to feel him, all of him. His wide shoulders gleamed under the fluorescent light. Nearly hidden beneath dark chest hair, she saw his small brown nipples, and lower down on his abdomen, his navel was circled with the same dark hair. His stomach was flat, ridged with muscles, and she wondered how he stayed in such excellent shape with all the hours he worked. Genes, she decided, thinking of how gorgeous his brothers were, too.

"I want you to touch me," he told her, his voice dark and mesmerizing. One corner of his mouth kicked up. "Hell, I'm counting on it."

Tamara inched closer, but he stopped her, saying, "Let's get you out of that skirt first."

Her mouth went dry. It was silly, considering he'd already looked at her in great detail, but she blushed. "I hadn't pictured it going quite like this."

"Like this how?"

He stared at her breasts, which throbbed, her nipples pulling tight. She waved a hand at the bathroom. "Here, where the light is the brightest."

"I want to see you." His gaze snared and held hers. "And you want to see me, too, remember? Your book said we should get comfortable naked."

He looked plenty comfortable to her. And with good reason. A man couldn't look any better than Zane Winston. "You can be proud of your body."

His gaze heated, moving over her bared upper body. Stepping closer, he caught the waistband of the skirt and worked it over her hips. He brushed it down her thighs, and when he let it go, it dropped to rest around her feet. He stared, swallowed hard as he looked at every naked inch of her.

His voice gentled. "And you think that you can't?"

She wouldn't cower in front of him. "I didn't mean that. But I'm . . . average."

Sliding both hands into her hair, Zane tilted her face up so he could rub his mouth over hers. "No average woman could make me shake with lust, or keep me up at night, or wake me in the early dawn with a wet dream."

She blinked at him. "Wet dream?"

His thumbs brushed the corners of her mouth. He made a low rumbling sound. "Yeah. Not since I was a teen, damn it." His expression was wry, even faintly amused. "But I've been going to sleep wanting you, and I guess that carries over. I walk around with an erection all the damn time lately."

His solid, warm chest beckoned, and she opened her hands on him. "I think about you a lot, too."

He kissed her temple, her jaw, the sensitive skin beneath her ear. "Maybe we've been sharing our dreams. What do you think?"

"Are your dreams about . . . different ways for us to have sex?"

"Yes. And more often than not, they're too damn real for comfort."

She nodded, intrigued by the idea that they might in fact have shared a dream. "I wake up in the middle of the night, hot and tight and achy."

"Do you touch yourself, thinking about me?"

Tamara pressed her face into the curve of his shoulder. She didn't know people talked like this, that such things were discussed. Face burning hot, she admitted, "A little."

A slight shudder ran through him, and his tone was gruff when he asked, "But not to climax?"

Good God, did he need every detail?

"Tamara?" He reached for her breast, his palm rough-textured. His mouth opened on her neck, placing soft wet love bites here and there. Just that easily, he began fanning the fire all over again.

Feeling unsophisticated and clumsy, she whispered, "I don't know how."

Zane froze. The heavy slamming of his heart against her breasts told her how surprised he was. Then he hugged her so tight he lifted her off her feet. "Are you saying," he rumbled against her ear, "the climax I gave you is your first?"

Clinging to him, glad that the way he held her made it impossible for him to see her face, she nodded. "It's . . . it's kind of an elusive thing. At least, it always has been for me. And now, well, it's not at all what I expected."

The words had barely left her mouth and he was there, kissing her voraciously, his tongue in her mouth, his teeth nipping. He was like a wild man turned free. Tamara found herself hefted onto the sink counter, her back against the cold wall while Zane moved her legs apart and continued to kiss her silly.

His hand fondled her breasts, then down between her legs. He cupped her. *"You're mine."*

She tried to rear back, not at all certain what he'd said or how he'd meant it. Surely he hadn't just staked a claim, not when she'd had to fight for his initial agreement, not when he knew she'd be moving away soon. "Zane."

His long fingers probed, stroked, sank deep.

Overwhelmed with the suddenness of his touch, the air left her lungs in a *whoosh*, forcing her to pant. Her body arched, her thighs opened almost of their own volition, and with a groan Zane went to his knees. Through a haze of searing need, Tamara stared, nearly incoherent with shock as he parted her gently and leaned forward. Seeing his dark head between her thighs went beyond anything she'd considered, anything she'd even fantasized.

His tongue touched her. "Zane!"

"Be quiet, sweetheart."

He teased, came closer and closer, and then his mouth opened on her most intimate flesh. Arms rigid, she braced herself with her palms flat on the sink counter so she wouldn't slide onto the floor, a puddle of scandalized excitement.

"Ohmigod." If his fingers had been wonderful, it was nothing compared to his mouth, the wet rasp of his hot tongue.

His face still against her, he said, "I want you to come for me again."

Even his hot moist breath made her shudder. Nowhere in the journal did it say this might happen. At least not this soon. There had been a vague reference in the eighth chapter . . . *ohmigod.*

Her thoughts scattered again when he found that ultra-sensitive spot and suckled. She nearly bucked away from him.

Zane lifted her legs over his shoulders and his strong hands gripped her hips. "Just relax, baby. I've got you," he murmured, and then he was drawing on her again, his tongue flicking, his teeth holding her gently, securely, and she couldn't stop the long, ragged groan of release, hitting her fast this time, like a tidal wave.

The way he pleasured her now was more intense, almost painful as her already ravaged senses exploded again.

"Mmm," he said with so much satisfaction, Tamara almost found the strength to smile. Almost. She felt drained and wrung out and for the first time in ages, totally devoid of tension.

After several lingering tastes, he whispered, "That was nice." Zane kissed her inner thigh, her hipbone, before lifting her legs from his shoulders and allowing them to dangle over the edge of the counter. He stood and touched her chin, his gaze direct. "You're incredible."

Slumped against the wall, more boneless than not, Tamara said, "Ah, it was nothing."

Zane laughed, and in his laugh she heard sexual excitement and male triumph, mirrored by the naked hunger in his eyes. He scooped her up and stepped with her into the shower.

The first blast of icy water revived her before he adjusted the temperature. Watching her, still fully aroused, he soaped his hands while she stood there, concentrating hard on keeping herself upright.

"The book," Tamara interjected, knowing she had to do something, "made it clear that both partners should give. I don't want to be selfish."

A devilish gleam entered his eyes as he worked the soap into a lather. "Believe me, honey, when a woman moans as nicely as you do, she's not selfish."

The water was deflected by his broad back, and only a misty spray reached her. She drew a deep breath and inched closer to him. It wasn't difficult because her tub was short, leaving them little room to maneuver. Tamara touched his shoulder, traced her hand through the water beaded there. "Tell me what to do."

His soapy hands settled on her breasts. "Touch me," he advised. "Any place, any way that you like."

Concentrating, which wasn't easy considering his soap-slippery fingers now rolled her sensitized nipples, she put her hands on his biceps. She loved how hard he was, how his muscles flexed and bunched as he moved.

He wasn't overly hairy, like Uncle Thanos, but a neat diamond of dark hair stretched over his chest, from pec muscle to pec muscle, then made a very distracting trail down his abdomen to his navel, and on again to his groin to frame his large sex.

Tamara chewed her lips, screwed up her courage, and gave in to her curiosity. She reached down and clasped his penis in her fist. He moved to lean against the tile wall. Water sprayed in her face and she wiped it away, intent on examining him. Everything about Zane fascinated her, but his body was of special interest.

She thought he probably had to be larger than average. Surely not all men were that big. She considered asking him, but he'd gone curiously still the second she'd touched him, and now he almost looked in pain. "Am I hurting you?"

"No."

She gentled her hold, stroking him carefully from base to tip, and heard his low curse.

His size intimidated her. Just having his fingers inside her had been vaguely uncomfortable, though pleasure had quickly followed the discomfort.

This though, this was entirely different. He was long and thick, solid, with a velvety soft covering, and her fingers could barely circle him. She squeezed experimentally and watched a drop of fluid appear on the broad head.

Zane's eyes closed as a raw sound of pleasure rumbled from deep inside him. The shower spray pulsated down around him, water streaming over his lean, powerful body. Watching his face, Tamara detected every emotion, every nuance of pleasure that he experienced. And more than that, she absorbed it. Zane was so open to her, sharing each and every sensation, it was almost frightening. He relished her touch, quickly spinning out of control, and she felt it all.

"You like that," she said with awe, amazed at how she affected him.

"Yeah." His voice was hoarse with strain. "I like it. Too damn much." He caught her upper arms and pulled her to his muscular frame. "Kiss me, Tamara."

Still holding him in her hand, she tipped her face up and gave him her mouth. The kiss was lush, slow, consuming. His erection pulsed in a rhythm that matched her racing heartbeat.

"What you did to me?"

"Which part, honey?" He labored for breath, and his legs were locked, braced apart to support them both.

Moving back a little, she brought her other hand up to close around his heavy erection, circling him with both hands now, tracing each vein, cuddling his testicles. She slipped her thumb over the head to test the slippery secretion there.

His expression burning, Zane watched her, so he understood when she said, "You kissed me."

A fine trembling passed through his limbs. "You want me to do it again?"

She looked up, and their gazes locked. "I think I want to do it to you."

"Damn," he groaned, "I can't take it. I've waited too long."

Experiencing her first surge of feminine power, Tamara said, "Yes you can."

Zane laughed and caught her wrists. "No, little Gypsy," he answered emphatically, "I can't."

He easily controlled her as she did her best to convince him. When she realized he intended to get them to the bed first, she quickly washed the makeup from her face and shampooed her hair. Zane scrubbed himself, but not without touching her every so often, slicking a soapy hand over her breasts, trailing his fingers down her spine on the pretense of helping her rinse. He wouldn't let her touch him, catching her hands each time she tried. But that didn't stop him from doing as he pleased to her body, and making her crazy in the process.

When they'd both finished washing, he turned the water off and pushed the shower curtain aside. "I hope you're satisfied that we've met the standards of the book, sweetheart," he said as he reached for the towels, "because I have to get into you. Right now."

The way he spoke so openly about his need for her, and how he wanted to touch her, only added to her growing desire.

In a near daze, Tamara found herself hustled out of the shower, a towel briskly rubbed over her body and her hair, and then Zane picked her up and carried her to her bedroom. He kissed her nose seconds before he tossed her onto the bed.

Tamara only had time to open her arms and Zane was there, moving over her, his mouth covering hers, his damp body sliding against hers.

She still didn't think she'd done her fair share. And she wasn't at all certain he'd fit. But he gave her no more time to worry about it.

FOURTEEN

Zane forced himself to let her go long enough to crawl to the side of the bed and snag his slacks. It wasn't easy, considering what she'd been doing right before he'd ended the shower. Tamara in a curious mood was more exciting than consummation with other women.

He fumbled for his wallet, cursing and sweating, his body in a fever. He was good at donning a condom at the most frantic times; he never took unnecessary chances on parenthood and always wore protection. But now, he felt like an awkward schoolboy and he deeply resented the need to wear a rubber.

It didn't help that Tamara was busy kissing him, trying to pull him back to her. She kept up a rambling monologue that would probably make him laugh after he'd sated himself and could conjure rational thought again.

"You're so big, Zane," she said with breathless wonder, in between hot kisses to his shoulder, his spine. "And so hard."

Her soft hands reached around him, and she attempted to assist him with the condom.

"Baby, wait." Zane knew he was on the verge of exploding. One small touch was all it'd take. He felt her breasts on his back, her pointed nipples rasping him. He felt her breath in his ear, her damp hair tickling his jaw. Damn.

"I know I'm not supposed to like it this first time." She spoke into his ear, breathless and anxious. "I mean, I'm new at this and you're not and you're sort of on the enormous size, so it'll probably—"

In one movement, Zane turned to her, carrying her back down to the mattress and pinning her in place with his body. "It'll be fine, you'll see." The things she said, and how she said them, made him both wild with lust and tenderly amused. "I'm barely bigger than average," he lied. "Trust me."

"I thought"—she gasped as he kneed her legs apart—"I thought men always bragged on their size!"

Zane caught her face. "Shhh. Look at me, Tamara. There's no reason to be nervous. I'm not going to hurt you."

Solemn now, her eyes wary, yet still ablaze with excitement, she nodded. "I know you wouldn't on purpose. You're a very gentle, considerate man. But you're so—oh."

Zane pushed into her, not much, but enough to get her attention. It would be a tight fit, he realized with mind-numbing excitement, and struggled to keep control of himself. Her muscles squeezed at him, contracting at the intrusion. His heart thumped and his pulse surged, urging him on.

"No," he grated through his teeth, fighting the need to drive into her, "don't close your eyes. Look at me."

He wanted every connection to her, mind and body. He wanted her to feel what he felt.

Her hips moved, wiggling in an attempt to accommodate him, and he nearly lost it. The very head of his cock was bathed in her wet heat, her body milking him as small spasms ran through her. It was the most exquisite torture he'd ever endured. She was so tight, so silky and wet.

"Easy," he groaned, as much to himself as to her. "We'll go slow."

Her hands gripped his shoulders. "Will you kiss me again?" she asked shakily.

Zane lowered his head and took her mouth. He meant the kiss to be reassuring, but then Tamara locked her arms around his neck and her legs around his hips and he gave up. With a groan, he pressed forward, slowly sinking into her as her body gradually opened to him. The exquisite friction weakened his resolve.

Tamara didn't retreat, just squeezed him tighter.

He heard her small whimper and lifted his head. "Are you all right?" he asked, destroyed by the idea that he might be hurting her after all.

He did his best to remain motionless, to let her get used to him.

"This . . . this is incredible," she said, and pressed her face into his shoulder. "You're around me and inside me, and the smell of you, the taste of you . . ." She licked his shoulder and groaned. "It's almost too much, but I don't ever want it to stop."

"It won't stop," he promised. "I *can't* stop." Carefully, he flexed his buttocks and went a little deeper, his way eased by how wet she'd gotten, how closely she held him. He withdrew, and pressed forward again. On the third stroke he entered her completely and they both moaned.

Her mouth opened on his chest and she bit him, not a harsh bite, but a hungry one. Her heels dug into the small of his back as she lifted into him, trying to get closer.

He fell into sexual oblivion.

His every thrust heavier than the one before, he pumped into her while a roaring sounded in his ears. His entire body sizzled like a live nerve, every small touch electrifying him, driving him higher until he didn't know if he could survive it, but he knew he couldn't pull back. His hands contracted on her hips, holding her to him.

Vaguely he heard Tamara cry out, but the wave of sensation cresting upward through his body, flooding his mind, obliterated everything else. And then he felt the draining release, the burst of pressure that was both pleasure and pain, and he tensed over her as his body shuddered.

How long he rested on top of her, he wasn't certain. He was horribly afraid he'd fallen asleep, because the sun had set and long shadows crept into the room. The light on her desk glowed, but other than that, the room was dim.

The smell of sex lingered in the air, and the smell of Tamara filled his nostrils as he drew in a deep breath. Their bodies were practically melded together, his head on her breast, her thighs still around him. The steady drumming of her heartbeat sounded in his ear.

He became aware of her right hand on his nape, idly stroking through his hair. Her head was turned, her mouth nibbling on his right hand where it rested beside her on the pillow. Her tongue licked delicately at his salty skin.

"Tamara?" He felt drugged, and struggled to push himself up to his elbows. He was far too heavy to have stayed atop her, yet she hadn't complained, in fact had held him the entire time.

Her eyes were liquid as she looked at him, filled with tears and churning emotion. Her smile quivered over her soft, swollen lips. "You are the most remarkable man," she whispered.

He stroked her hair back from her face, caught a tear that trailed down her cheek. "Sweetheart, why are you crying? Did I hurt you?"

"Oh no." She shook her head, and gave him another beautiful smile. She held his hand to her cheek, rubbing into his palm with sweet contentment. "You have a lover's hand. Did you know that?"

Bending to kiss the corner of her mouth, Zane said, "I'm glad you think so."

She laughed with the delight of a child. "No, I meant that as a palm reader, I can see the defining elements in your hand for a lover. I've been studying it while you dozed."

Damn, so he *had* slept. He was a pig, but God, he felt replete, with both sexual satisfaction and emotional fulfillment. No other experience, no other woman, had prepared him for this. Then he thought about her words.

Her shop window advertised palm reading, and Zane was curious. He smoothly disengaged their bodies, despite her protests. "Don't move. I'll be right back."

But once he stood, he paused to admire her lying there, warm and soft, nestled into the bedding. With a slight blush, she turned on her side, facing him, her soft, slender thighs closing, one arm covering her breasts. A lock of fine, blond hair fell over her eyes and she brushed it away. Her smile was one of sharing, of intimacy.

Zane inhaled deeply. He accepted that he was in deep—and he intended to get a bit deeper.

It took him only a moment to get rid of the condom and splash water on his face. He brought a cool washcloth back with him and sat on the edge of the bed.

"What are you doing?" she asked, eyeing the washcloth with the same fascination she might give to a rattlesnake.

Humor rose in him, sharp and sweet. "Playing the servant."

"No." She started to sit up, and he wrestled her back down. Wrestling with Tamara was more fun than any man deserved. Especially since they were both naked.

When he had her flat on her back again, he said, "This will give me pleasure, Tamara."

Skepticism darkened her vivid green eyes. "You're sure?"

"Positive." She relented, but her shoulders remained stiff, her disposition wary while he bathed her face, her throat, her tender breasts.

A catch in her breath and the sight of her nipples puckering told him she liked the impromptu bath as much as he did.

"I want you to be comfortable." With a gentle, slow touch, he brushed the damp cloth between her legs. Her thick lashes dropped to hide her eyes, and she made a small purr of surprise.

Damn, he loved how quickly she responded to him.

He threw the cloth aside and stretched out next to her, pulling her into his arms. He wanted to hold her all night.

He intended to make love to her again and again before they slept, but she was new to lovemaking and needed time to get used to him. In that, her book was correct.

The hand she'd been kissing was now filled with her breast. "Explain this palm reading business to me," he said as he fondled her. He didn't think he'd ever tire of listening to her, touching her.

Tamara lifted his hand, depriving him of her breast, and kissed the palm. "Here," she said, tracing a thin crease that ran the width of his hand. "This is your heart line. See how long and curvy it is? And it ends between your second and third finger. That means you have a tendency to freely release all emotion and passion that your head would normally block. You have a bigger capacity to experience sensation than many other people."

She twisted to see his face, her smile impish. "It also means you're good at pleasing yourself and your partner."

The twinkle in her eyes charmed him. "And you agree with that assessment?"

"Wholeheartedly." She brought his hand to her mouth again, and this time she bit his baby finger. "See how your little finger is long and straight and sort of leans out to the side? Now that reveals a freethinker, unconcerned with the restrictions of others."

"You're serious?"

"And often accurate."

"Huh. So the services you advertise aren't entirely bogus?"

"Of course not."

She didn't sound hurt by his skepticism, so much as resigned. That bothered him. He didn't want her to accept him as the typical doubting Thomas who didn't understand her. He was more than that, much more.

"I can tell by reading your palm that you're willing to try things."

Trying things held a definite appeal at the moment. Fascinated, Zane studied her breasts, how her nipples were now soft and smooth, her delicate skin a little abraded by his five o'clock shadow. Were her silky thighs scratched too? He cupped his hand protectively over her mound, promising himself he'd shave before pleasuring her that way again.

"What kind of things?" Thoughts of what he intended to do with her and to her made his voice huskier.

Her voice was deeper, too, as she said, "Sexual things."

At least they were on the same track.

"You're not content," she said, "to just make love in the missionary position, on a bed and in the dark."

Zane snorted. "Hell no."

Curiosity brought rosy color to her cheeks. "Where else would you like to make love?" Tamara continued to examine his hand, every so often kissing a fingertip or licking at his flesh.

The "love" word, even in the context of physical love, kicked his heart, making it miss a beat. Infatuation, possessiveness, pounding lust—they were all emotions he could deal with. But love? Jesus, he just didn't know.

As his thoughts progressed, she turned her face against his shoulder, and once again he wondered if she could read his mind. He was the one who'd originally insisted on calling their intimacy "lovemaking." She'd been more than happy to label it mere sex. And here he'd upset her. It seemed that every time he got agitated, *she* was the one to react.

He frowned, reluctant to let anyone into his head. And yet, how could he stop her? Especially when she denied any such thing. It was certainly something for them to discuss, once she stopped being so close-mouthed.

He nuzzled her temple, rubbed his bristly jaw into the soft coolness of her hair. "Before I start sharing fantasies, we need to eat."

He felt her lips form a smile against his skin. "I suppose a man your size gets hungry often?"

"In more ways than one." She lifted her face, staring up at him with invitation. He kissed the end of her nose. "Let's eat, and then," he promised, "we'll trade fantasies."

"The book suggested we should do that. You share a lot of the same philosophies with the woman who wrote it."

Zane stood and pulled her to her feet. After everything they'd already done, she still looked shy, her thighs quickly pressing together, her shoulders hunching as if to hide her breasts.

Patience, he told himself, unwilling to shock her, refusing to let her feel used. But containing his marauding tendencies had never been so difficult. All he had to do was look at her, and his blood raged. Seeing her fresh from his lovemaking had the impact of a wrecking ball on his composure.

Distracting himself, he glanced around the room. "Where is this infamous book?"

Twisting and dipping at the waist, she reached beneath the mattress. Zane clenched his fists to keep his hands off her delightful bottom. It wasn't easy.

She straightened, holding a slim, worn, blue volume with a ribbon poking out from between the faded pages. A marker, he realized, and wondered how far she'd gotten.

Taking it from her, Zane flipped it open. Tamara went on tiptoe to look with him. She pointed. "Right here. Sharing fantasies. It says it's an excellent way to really get to know your lover."

He wasn't sure he'd live through hearing her sexual fantasies, but he was willing to try. "Why don't we check this out while we eat?" He could definitely use some nourishment right now. And filling his mouth with food, while not nearly as satisfying, would keep him from tasting her again.

Tamara held back as he tried to urge her toward the door. "I need to get my robe."

Laughing, Zane pulled the sheet from the bed, tossed it over her shoulders, and lifted her in his arms. "Honey, I like you this way, buck naked. And there's no one in your kitchen to see us, is there?"

"No."

"Then why deprive me of the sight?" Zane strode into the kitchen and plunked her onto the counter next to the refrigerator. He pulled a mock frown when she scrambled to get the sheet around her. "Spoilsport."

He didn't ask permission, just opened the refrigerator and found cheese, mustard, lettuce, milk. "Where's your bread?"

Arms crossed over her breasts to anchor the sheet in place, she nodded toward a pantry. "Over there."

"Stay put." Zane fetched the bread and went about making several sandwiches. "How many can you eat?"

"A half."

He eyed her slim body, practically swallowed by the voluminous sheet, and shrugged. "Okay, but that means we'll have to have dessert, too."

"There's strawberry ice cream in the freezer."

"Perfect." More than perfect, he thought with anticipation.

For the next hour, Zane showed her how to play while giving himself time to recover. He didn't want to admit it to Tamara, but his legs were still rubbery and his pulse still sluggish. She'd zapped him of his strength. He needed all his wits and dexterity to deal with her and the sensual plans he'd made for the night.

The sight of her perched so prettily on the counter did a lot toward helping him reach that goal.

He fed Tamara, occasionally licking one of her fingers, even trailing wet kisses up her wrist to her inner elbow. He found all the places that made her eyes go heavy with desire, and he showed her how and where to kiss him in return.

She enthusiastically complied with all his instructions—even referring back to the book a few times.

"Did you know," she asked, "that women have a biorhythm for when they're most easily excited?"

"Is that from the journal?" He'd read some of the elegant, sloping script, and found it to be amazingly precise and on target.

"Yes." She scooped up the book and thumbed carefully through the fragile pages. "An observant and caring man," she read, "will make note of when his lover is most receptive. A woman can be convinced to do anything if she's approached at the right moment."

"Anything, huh?"

"That's what it says."

"Well now. I think that's terrific information to have. When are you most receptive?"

She lowered her lashes, relaxed enough to flirt, and asked, "What is it you want to do?"

"Everything."

The fluttering of her pulse gave her away. "I . . . I think I'm susceptible to you anytime." She watched him without guile, open and honest.

"I meant it when I said I've wanted you since the first moment I saw you. I think about you most at night, because that's when I'm least busy and I can concentrate more. But you—this—is always in my mind, even while I'm working."

"This?"

"Having you here." Like a lingering touch, her gaze moved over him. "Naked and willing and mine, at least for right now."

His stomach dropped, his chest swelled. "What else do you want? I mean, in life." He was so curious about her, all of her. The more he knew, the better equipped he'd be to deal with the nearly smothering emotions.

She sighed and turned to stare at the floor. "I want to keep my shop. I want whoever is bothering me to leave me alone. And I want to be normal."

Her words hurt him, an actual physical ache that was more powerful than lust could ever be, and more painful than anything he'd ever experienced. "Normal?"

Gesturing, she flapped a hand toward him. "Like you. Like people who go about every day with their regular jobs and their regular lives."

"Not a Gypsy?"

Her lips pressed together. "I'm sorry." When she looked at him, her gaze was clear, all remorse hidden. "I shouldn't be complaining. In so many ways my life has been extraordinary."

"And restrictive."

"Yes. But my aunts and uncle did what they could. And I'm grateful to them. They raised me and loved me, and that's more than a lot of people have."

And it was nothing compared to what he'd been given in his life. He felt spoiled and shallow; he'd pushed through life taking what he wanted, rejecting what he didn't need. He'd had a backup system of love and support and acceptance that he'd often taken for granted.

"I am sorry." Her laugh was self-conscious, frustrated, and it loosened his knees, made his eyes burn and his throat feel tight. "I can't believe I'm yakking on and on like this."

"What?" He bent to look into her face, to see her eyes, her expression. "We can't talk? Can't share?" He kept his tone soft, neutral, carefully hiding the surge of urgency he felt. He wanted, needed, her to tell him more. "Says who?"

Tamara gripped the cloth-covered book tightly. Her hair skimmed her shoulders as she shook her head. "According to the first chapter, I shouldn't be burdening you." She chewed her lip. "It's just that I've never been involved before, so it's hard to remember what I should and shouldn't talk about."

"And here I was thinking that the journal was written by a smart lady." He made a deprecating sound that she immediately reacted to.

"Oh no, we should talk and share. But I don't want you confused over what I want from *you*. Those other things . . . they're not your concern. They're things I'm working out on my own."

How many times, he wondered, had she had to summon up that rigid streak of pride to protect herself, claiming it was what she wanted? How often had independence been her prop for loneliness?

He wouldn't dent her pride for the world, so he let it go. By morning, she'd know in no uncertain terms that she was his in every way, not just within the boundaries she dictated.

She was getting his help whether she wanted it or not, but she didn't need to know that just yet.

For a while they ate and talked about inconsequential things, foods they both liked, movies they had enjoyed. Zane located a few ticklish spots on her—the back of her knees, her hipbones—and he relished her laughter, her small smiles, and her teasing rebukes.

"What else can you do besides read palms?" he asked when they had just about finished all the food. They were both semi-aroused, freely touching and kissing in a lazy, savory way.

Tamara had become unmindful of her nudity. She'd even gone so far as to place the notorious journal aside, and let the sheet drop to her lap, giving him free access to her breasts, letting him do as he pleased. And it pleased him to touch her, kiss her. He couldn't keep from it.

He loved watching her move, the way she gestured with her hands or tilted her head or curled her toes. He'd been with a lot of beautiful women, stacked women, but she had the cutest body he'd ever seen, all soft and pink and petite, with an undeniable feminine strength. He was as enthralled with her as he'd been with his first naked woman. He remembered the fascination then, lying in the sunshine in a field with his junior high school sweetie being very accommodating, giggling as he'd explored with his fingers, moaning when he'd used his tongue to taste her. It had been like having the candy store opened, and everything was free.

He felt that way now, magnified about a thousand times, constantly needing to stroke her or nibble on her in some small way. The ice cream hadn't been dessert enough—he wanted to start at her toes and work his way up.

"I do astrological charts," she said, and even her voice, lyrical and soft, aroused him. "Tarot card readings, and things like that."

She swallowed another bite of strawberry ice cream, then licked her lips. "I do some fortune-telling and predictions of the future, too. Usually that can be based on something the client says." She grinned at him, a wicked, teasing grin. "In other words, a good guess."

"Where'd you learn all that stuff?" Zane finished off his ice cream, and reached past her to put his bowl in the sink. The sheet hung around her waist. He stepped up to her and brought her breasts against his chest. Her accelerated heartbeat kick-started his own. They'd been teasing one another for some time now; he wasn't sure how much longer he could wait.

"I've read books." She slid her hands over his back to his hips, tugging him closer. "I have a whole selection on each topic. When I first came here, I had to fight with the relatives to get rid of the more bogus stuff."

"Like?"

"Using the crystal ball—which is just decoration now. Special light effects, eerie music, incantations, all that. We compromised. I got to apply what I'd actually learned about the craft, and they got me to dress up in my silly costume."

Zane put his hands on her thighs. The thin sheet had absorbed her heat, and with her sitting on the countertop, she was just the right height to kiss. "Your silly costume makes me wild."

She laughed. "It does not."

"It didn't use to," he agreed, "but it does now. I keep thinking about all those rings on your little toes, and all that attitude you have when you're dressed up."

Her lips quivered with a suppressed laugh. "Rings on my toes, huh?"

Trailing a finger over her smooth shoulder, he made his way down the slope of her right breast, stopping just short of her nipple. He watched it pucker, draw tight, just from his teasing. "You're obviously popular with the men, so others must agree with me."

Her breath hitched. "I don't know. I do well enough, I suppose."

Removing all indications of jealousy, Zane tipped up her chin. "You were pretty busy this morning."

She stared at his mouth, and it was easy to know her thoughts now. "Arkin has become a regular only the past few weeks. He's a nice man. I like him."

Logic told him that plenty of women liked nice men. There was no reason for the spike of possessiveness. "And Boris?"

She made a face. "He's a little eerie, isn't he?"

"How so?" True, Zane hadn't liked him, not even a little. And he'd thought him an arrogant jerk, too pushy for his own good. But he hadn't really considered him frightening.

"I don't know. He just made me edgy." She rubbed her arms and looked thoughtful, as if considering her own reaction.

Zane didn't quite understand her uneasiness either. Of course, he wasn't a woman playing at being a Gypsy, determined to stand alone no matter what. Tamara, with her eclectic ways and stubborn disposition, was more vulnerable than most, and from what he could tell, more sensitive than most. If the bastard had frightened her somehow, Zane didn't want him around her again.

With a small sound, Tamara wiggled out of his arms, scooting back on the counter and trying to escape his hold. Zane felt her withdrawal like a punch.

He gripped her arms and lightly shook her. "What is it?"

"Nothing." She pressed away from him.

"Bullshit." He turned her chin toward him. Her green eyes were cloudy with distress. "I can see it on your face, Tamara. Don't shut me out. Tell me what's wrong."

"I don't want you to get mad."

"At you?" She nodded, and Zane automatically pulled her into a hug. She relaxed against him. "Baby, I'm not going to get mad at you. I *want* you to tell me what you're thinking."

A deep breath and several seconds later, she said, "You still think I'm a charlatan."

"What?"

"I understand," she rushed to assure him, ignoring his surprise. "I mean, there's not a whole lot of legitimacy I can lay claim to. But Zane, I truly do want to help people, and a lot of times, I can. Just today, with

Arkin Devane, I was able to tell him things he needed to know, important things."

Mired in confusion, Zane fought to make sense of her words. He didn't doubt her sincerity, and never had. "Honey, what makes you think I'm judging you that way?"

Her teeth sank into her soft bottom lip and her eyes were big, vulnerable. She swallowed. "Because I feel what you feel." Her hand touched his jaw, slid down to the pulse at the base of his throat, her fingertips lightly pressing. "When you're mad or annoyed."

"You feel what I feel?" He didn't mean to sound so incredulous.

"Yes." Hesitation was plain on her face, then she lifted her chin and forged ahead with a near belligerence. "When you're aroused, too. It's . . . a little shocking, how turned on you get."

Her admission should have stunned him, but instead, it made sense. "You're . . . what do they call it? Empathic?"

"To very few people."

Heart racing, Zane asked, "Those people you care about?"

Her gaze never wavered, and she whispered, "Usually."

Cradling her head in his palms, he kissed her eyelids, her nose, her delicious mouth that tasted faintly of strawberries and woman and sexual hunger. "Then know this, little Gypsy. It pisses me off that you won't open yourself to me completely, that you won't trust me to do what I can for you. It makes me madder than hell that anyone would upset you, especially a man. I want you all to myself, and if you left it up to me, Boris Sandor and Arkin Devane and any other man who wants to use your talents would never get within shouting distance of you again."

Tamara blinked at him, her lips slightly parted.

He opened himself to her, sharing as he wanted her to share. "If you know me so well, Tamara, what am I feeling right now?"

Unerringly her hand moved down his side, inward over his hipbones to his groin, and closed hotly around his erection. "Desire. Possessiveness."

His breath hissed at the gentleness of her touch. "I told you before," he said through his teeth, "and I'm telling you again. You're mine. Now more than ever."

He took her mouth, his tongue pushing deep, demanding, and Tamara dropped the sheet to hold him close to her heart.

Zane decided now was a good time to confide a few fantasies to her. His emotions were suddenly so raw, so explosive, it was all he could do to contain them. He had to get inside her, and soon.

He wanted to take her every way known to man. From behind, so he could slip his hands beneath her and stroke her between her thighs, cuddle her breasts. He wanted her over him, so he could watch her pleasure as she came, with free access to her sensitive nipples. He wanted her on her knees in front of him, and he wanted to hear her beg so he'd know he wasn't the only one twisting with need.

He wanted a lot, everything, and he intended to get it.

He lifted Tamara in his arms and carried her into the bedroom. They were both breathing hard, and Tamara frantically touched him everywhere she could reach, her small hands hot and busy, her mouth damp, hungry.

Zane strode to the bed, and just as he laid her on the mattress and stripped away the sheet, the lights went out. He heard Tamara's catch of breath, felt her shock of fear. Then she whispered, "Oh God, he's back."

F I F T E E N

Through the open door, Zane could see how dark the house had gone, not a single light in evidence.

It was silent too, the hum of the refrigerator stopped, no buzz of electricity of any kind. It made his skin prickle and set his senses on alert. "Stay here."

He reached for his slacks and pulled them on, but didn't bother with the zipper or button. Tamara didn't reply, and he knew she was afraid, but he couldn't spare the time to reassure her.

He headed out of the room, enraged that anyone would come into her house when she might have been there alone. And he didn't doubt that someone had. She was empathic—that much he believed with a certainty that touched his soul. She'd know if someone had intruded—and not just any someone, but the same someone. There wasn't a power failure, there wasn't a blown fuse. Someone was in her house.

This was a direct threat to her, and he wouldn't tolerate it. Tamara might not want to admit it, but they'd come to an understanding. She was his to protect, and he'd damn well start tonight.

From his car parked in a vacant lot across the street, Joe saw the house go black in the blink of an eye. He shook his head. Hell, Zane had been at it for hours. His respect for his cousin grew, though after having seen the woman, Joe had to wonder about his choice. She wasn't quite the type he'd always figured Zane would settle on.

Using his finger, Joe stirred the lukewarm coffee in his cup, trying to distribute a packet of sugar. Hell, he was hungry and tired and bored out of his mind. He should just head back to the motel, but some vague intuition nagged at him. That sixth sense had saved his ass more than once, so he wasn't about to start ignoring it now.

The coffee went down in two long gulps. Boredom was a bitch. For a while there he'd entertained himself with thoughts of what Zane might be doing with the black-haired woman who wasn't really black-haired at all but wore a wig. Weird. A little fascinating, but still weird. Zane had never struck him as the type to go after the strange ones.

But even pondering sexual acrobatics had grown old after a few hours. There sure as hell wasn't anything Zane could do that Joe hadn't already done himself. Several times. And likely with more skill.

He smiled. Hell, lately none of it interested him all that much.

Joe studied the building. He looked at the dark upstairs windows where he presumed Zane was going another round. What a stud. Personally, he'd have left the lights on. There wasn't anything prettier than a woman waiting naked for a man.

Unless, of course, they were finally settling down to sleep. It was a little early yet, but hey, sex could be an exhausting business when a man gave it his all.

Joe was smiling at his own sense of humor when it struck him that the faint lights from the downstairs had gone out as well. The entire house was pitch black.

Neat trick, he thought, cursing his slow perception while wondering who had just killed the electricity and why.

The car's interior remained dark and shadowed, the lights disengaged earlier, when he opened the driver's door and slid out. He moved silently, his gun already in his hand, his gaze constantly scanning the area, watching for even the slightest movement. At times like this, he forgot his damn knee and ignored the nagging discomfort. His movements were fluid, as practiced as any human could make them.

The front door of the shop was locked when he reached it, so he slipped around to the side of the building, keeping his back to the brick wall, inching along without so much as disturbing a piece of gravel or stirring up dust. He stuck his head around the corner, trying to locate the back door.

There wasn't one.

A faint scraping sound reached his ears, coming from the other side of the house. Joe moved, running flat-out and circling around the back. The security lights from Zane's computer business were bright enough to carry across the alley, but faded as they reached the metal stairs leading to the upper story of the building. Joe had great night vision, or he'd never have seen that the door at the top of the stairs was ajar.

"*Fuck.*" Nothing made Joe madder than realizing he'd made a mistake. Here he'd been watching the front of the house—hell, Zane was upstairs for Christ's sake!—and someone had slipped up the side stairs.

He'd taken two somewhat hobbling, pain-filled steps toward the stairs when he heard the *whoosh* of movement behind him. Joe turned, his eyes zeroing in on a moving shadow. Too far away to chase and catch, a body dashed into the darkness. There was little for Joe to commit to memory. The person had dressed all in black, and even the face was covered.

Joe looked back at the upstairs door. More cautiously now, in case the runner hadn't worked alone, he climbed the stairs. They were rickety, and some noise was unavoidable. He flattened himself against the outside wall, peeked inside and detected nothing but darkness. He slid his bad leg in, felt the way was clear, and ducked his body inside.

With the help of the moonlight, his eyes were quickly adjusting. He could make out a couch, a table. To his right, an interior door stood open, probably the door that led to her downstairs shop. He glanced at it, but kept his eyes moving, searching, unwilling to let anything else get past him. He'd learned through experience that staring too hard, especially in the dark, shattered your awareness. A little focus was good, too much could be deadly.

Through the open door he heard a noise, that of shuffling feet, and a muffled curse.

Zane.

Joe took a hasty step in that direction, then ducked as his instincts screamed a warning. A whistling filled his ears and something *whooshed* past his head, coming far too close for comfort. Another swing, but the aim was off and the object—something flat and hard—smashed into his shoulder.

Without so much as a grunt of pain, Joe turned for a tackle, his gun held tight. He collided with a small, slim body and they went down in a clatter of disrupted furniture and knocked-over knickknacks. His hands encountered bare skin—silky bare skin—but before he could get a good grip, something toppled onto his head with a resounding *thunk*. Stunned, he slackened his hold, and the body slithered away and up.

"Tamara!"

Zane's roar would have scared a dead man out of his grave, if the thunderous footsteps racing up the stairs hadn't already accomplished just that.

Joe reached out and caught a piece of material as it drifted over his arm. It snagged in his fist, then went loose and empty.

"Goddammit." He struggled to his feet, his eyes searching—and a flashlight came on.

Joe found himself staring at a woman.

Small, blond, wide-eyed, and sweet.

Buck naked.

Well hell, talk about shattering a man's focus.

He couldn't hear over his madly drumming heartbeat. Was someone following, hands reaching out, ready to catch him even now, despite his rapid flight? Fear, disgust, was a bitter taste in his mouth, making his stomach churn. Puking was a very real possibility.

When he could run no more, his lungs burning, his heart straining, he slowed, labored for breath as his ears continued ringing. He ducked behind an old abandoned truck parked in an alley and waited. Silence. Nothing but dead silence, thank God. He shook all over.

She was supposed to be out! He'd heard her say so with his own two ears, so what was she doing at home?

It was a long minute before he accepted that he was truly safe yet again. His heart gradually slowed, but his thoughts churned. Holding his side, cramping, feeling the sweat on his face and back, he came out of his hiding place and began hobbling home, defeated, frustrated.

He was wrong, so wrong to do this to her. He knew it, accepted his guilt. But then, when in love, the heart and mind knew no conscience.

He would do what he had to do.

Tamara's teeth chattered, she was so afraid.

The flashlight's beam bounced wildly around the room when Zane shoved the tall, intimidating man staring at her. The man stumbled and went down on one knee, wincing in pain, but he still stared. Hard. Unrelenting. Of course she recognized him.

She didn't know what to do, how to help Zane. She clutched the journal, ready and more than willing to use it against the man's head if necessary. But then Zane stepped in front of her. She was in the shadows again.

"He's the man from the bus stop," she told Zane urgently, her breath catching in small gasps. She struggled to peek over his shoulder, to keep the man in her sights while Zane struggled to get the sheet around her and still hold the flashlight in one hand. She didn't want Zane to turn his back on the big bruiser. He was quiet now, but he had a gun, which he clutched in a large fist hanging loosely at his side. He looked more than capable of murder or any other number of misdeeds.

"Hold still, damn it."

Confusion closed in on her. Zane didn't act the least worried about the man—all his concentration was on covering her. Who cared if she was naked, if the man planned to shoot them anyway? And why did he just stand there, watching as Zane covered her?

When Zane was satisfied that she was decent, he turned and shone the light directly in the man's face.

He flinched away. "Hey, damn it, knock it off!"

At his gravelly tone, Tamara stepped forward to swing the book again, and to her surprise, though he was blinded by the light, the man caught the book in midair, wrapping the long fingers of his left hand around it and wrenching it away from her. She heard the aged fabric cover rip, saw a section of pages drop out.

She hastily backed up again, and scowled. "You're ruining my journal!"

"Lady, you're the one trying to bludgeon me with it!"

Zane smirked. "I see your reflexes are still good."

"Lucky for me, or she'd have knocked my damn brains out."

"Quit cursing." Zane now sounded more amused than annoyed.

"Go to hell. But first, tell me what's going on." His gaze, when it landed on Tamara, was flinty—but quickly softened. Speculation flared in his eyes, then interest. She squirmed.

Zane puffed up in renewed outrage. It was rather amazing to see, even in her state of confusion. "I swear to God, Joe, if you don't stop leering—"

The man shook his head. Tamara got a glimpse of a small gold hoop in his ear and longish, silky, blue-black hair that matched the beard shadow on his lean jaw.

"She was naked, Zane," he said in a dry voice. "Sorta took me by surprise, ya know?"

Zane took a threatening step forward, his arms rigid at his sides, and once again the flashlight beam scattered around the room.

Tamara jumped between the two men and jerked the light away from Zane. She wanted to know what was going on, not watch a display of testosterone one-upmanship. "I take it you know each other?"

Zane gestured vaguely. "He's my cousin, Joe Winston."

Suspicion rose in her, ugly and raw and mean. "Your cousin?"

Zane scowled. "Yeah."

"He followed me today," she informed him. "On the bus, when I went to the Realtor's."

A little surprised, Zane cocked a brow at Joe.

Joe shrugged. "She's good. I have no idea how she spotted me."

Every volatile emotion she'd just experienced—fear, panic, anger—coalesced into a fiery rage. She readied herself to blast Zane, to maybe get the journal back and use it on his head this time, when he whipped around to face her and growled, "Why didn't you tell me someone followed you?"

Indignation cut through her. She sputtered several seconds before spitting out, "Why didn't *you* tell *me*!"

He leaned into her fury, giving back his own. "I was trying to protect you! If you wouldn't keep shutting me out, maybe it wouldn't be necessary!"

She sputtered again. "I didn't ask you for protection!"

"I know. You won't ask me for anything except—"

Her hand slapped over his mouth. "Don't—you—dare."

Joe laughed as Zane caught her wrist and carried her hand to her side.

"You may not want my protection, but I'm giving it anyway. And God knows you need it." Using his hold on her wrist, he tugged her closer. "And didn't I tell you to stay in the bedroom?"

"Zane!" Did he have to outright announce their relationship that way?

Joe made a *tsk*ing sound. "Now, children . . ."

Tamara reached for the battered journal, wanting to smack him a good one for scaring her so badly, and finding his unwanted audience a good enough reason.

Since Joe was so tall, about an inch above Zane, it was easy for him to hold it out of her reach. "Easy, love. Before you start trying to scatter my brains again, do you think we could find some lights?"

Relenting went against the grain, but she saw no option. "I have candles."

"I don't think that's necessary." Zane flipped the flashlight around the room. "The downstairs is still locked."

"I know." Joe, too, looked around. "The fuse box?"

"That's what I assume. How else could he have gotten the whole house to go dark at one time?"

They both looked at Tamara, brows raised, expressions identical though their features were polar opposites.

She almost laughed. Zane stood there, tall, lean, beautifully masculine, a man who oozed charm and sex appeal through every pore, every breath. A man who made her want him just by being.

And next to him, Joe, who looked darker, meaner. She doubted his cousin even knew how to spell charm, much less employ it. He didn't ooze sex appeal—he shouted it. It fell off him in chunks.

"You two are pretty intimidating, you know that?" Then she poked Joe in the chest. "Only I don't intimidate that easily."

Zane slung an arm around her shoulder and hauled her close. "Now Tamara, don't abuse my cousin. As annoying as he is, he's trying to help."

"*Trying* to help?" Joe asked with mock offense. "I got here in time to scare off your intruder. I'd say that's a little more than trying, considering you don't look like either of you were prepared to do battle."

Zane, hair rumpled and eyes heavy, had on unbuttoned and unzipped slacks, riding low on his muscular hips. He was barefoot, barechested . . . her heart punched into her ribs. He looked *so* good. She squirmed beneath the sheet as her heart turned over and her toes curled.

Zane's muscled arm around her shoulders went taut. "You saw someone?"

"Ran off past your store, down the street. I could have given chase, but I didn't know if you'd need me in here."

"Damn, I understand and I appreciate the concern, but I wish you'd run the bastard to the ground."

"I'll get him next time."

Tamara slipped away from Zane—and was promptly hauled back. She nearly lost her sheet, which got Joe's attention and had Zane snarling again.

"Where's the damn fuse box?" he demanded.

"That's where I was going," she informed him with just as much heat, and again tried to move away.

"You'll go with me. We can't be sure that whoever did this is entirely gone."

"Your cousin said he saw him run away."

Joe cleared his throat. "Yeah, well, that doesn't mean there was only one guy."

Tamara felt no sense of intrusion, no sense of threat. Whoever had been there had left. But she merely shrugged. If it'd make Zane feel better to keep her close, she had no quarrel with that.

Using the flashlight and trailing her sheet, she led the way to the metal stairs. On the outside wall, to the left of the entry door, the fuse box stood open. The main breaker had been flipped.

Tamara clicked it over and the house buzzed to life. A glow poured from her bedroom window, adding shadows that hadn't been there before.

Joe and Zane stared at her, Joe in open-mouthed wonder, Zane in vexation. They presented a united front—against her.

Clutching the sheet a little more closely, she squared off with them. "What?"

"That's a damn stupid place for your fuse box."

Joe grinned. "I'd have put it more delicately than that, but he's right. At the very least, you should have a lock on it. Hell, anyone could come in here and—*omph*!"

Tamara didn't hang around to see if the big buffoon liked getting hit with the flashlight more than the journal. She doubted she'd hurt him, though. His abdomen was as hard as Zane's.

Marching in the door, she briefly considered slamming it behind her, and contented herself with stomping to her bedroom instead. "Insufferable, insulting . . ."

Zane said into her ear, "Do you have to entertain every damn male relative I have?"

She yelped. She hadn't known he was following on her heels. Rounding on him, she thumped his bare chest with a fist. "Damn it, don't sneak up on me!"

"Quit stalking off, and I won't have to."

Tamara stopped at the bedroom door, gestured for him to precede her, then went in and slammed the door. She couldn't remember ever slamming a door before, but then, she'd never dealt with a hardheaded, autocratic male before either.

Jumping right into her grievances, she said, "I don't appreciate having a watchdog that I know nothing about. And I most definitely don't want you poking fun at me or insulting me in front of other people. And while we're on it, don't you ever run off in a dangerous situation and expect me to just cower behind."

Zane pulled her to her tiptoes and kissed her hard. "Joe stays until we figure out what's going on. If you don't like it, tough. I refuse to apologize for worrying about you." He kissed her again, this time sliding his tongue deep until she softened in his hold. He said against her lips, "I didn't mean to insult you, and for that I apologize. But if we're ever in another dangerous situation, you can damn well believe I'll tie your sweet little ass to the bed if that's what it takes to keep you safe."

His words were so low and seductive and filled with tenderness, it took Tamara a moment to absorb their meaning. When she did, she jerked away. She started to let loose on him—but the look on his face did her in. Damn, he looked so . . . affectionate. Perhaps people in a relationship always carried on that way. She just didn't know.

She swallowed hard, suddenly overcome by all that had happened. Her stomach pulled into a knot. "Someone," she whispered, "was trying to get in my house."

He nodded slowly. "With you home." His big hands smoothed up and down her back, comforting, protecting.

"I don't know what to do."

"Pack. You'll stay with me until we figure out what the hell is going on. With Joe on the case, it shouldn't be long. He's good at this kind of crap."

"I can't." Tamara knew what Zane's expression would be without looking at him. She stepped over to her dresser, dropped the sheet and found a pair of jeans. Forgoing underwear, she stepped into the soft denim and zipped up. A T-shirt was next, followed by a red pullover. She had no idea what she'd done with her shoes, but from beneath her bed, her slippers peeked out. She went to her knees to retrieve them.

When she straightened, her feet now resembling white bunnies, Zane crowded against her.

"You're coming home with me, Tamara."

Hoping to placate him, she put one hand on his naked chest. Warmth and security rose from his hard flesh—it'd be so easy to give in to him, to let him take care of her problems. But there were some facts she couldn't overlook. "Everything I own is here, Zane. Everything. I'm not leaving it. What if he comes back?"

"Exactly."

"No." She shook her head, not quite meeting his eyes. He wouldn't understand; his life was full in so many ways. Compared to him, her most valued possessions were few. "This is my life. I can't just abandon it to be ransacked."

His brows pinched together, warning of a full-blown rage. Tamara hugged herself to him.

"I've had a fire, Zane, a flood, snoops. Today, I realized someone had been going through my shelves. I have no idea why, what he was looking for, but a lot of things had been displaced. Someone got in here and rifled through my things." She shuddered. Saying it out loud made it somehow worse, more real. "I don't like this, Zane."

He hesitated, his body thrumming with near violence that she knew wasn't directed at her. "Why the hell didn't you tell me?"

"I was going to, but you distracted me with sex."

Something dangerous flashed in his eyes—possession, protectiveness—then his strong arms came around her and held her tight. "All right. If you won't come home with me, I'll stay here with you."

"You don't have to do that."

"I'm staying."

Iron laced his words, and she swallowed her sigh of relief. "Thank you."

Zane tipped up her chin. "Honey, no matter what your journal says, there's nothing wrong with leaning on me a little."

She worried her bottom lip between her teeth. "There's . . . there's a chapter on intimacy leading to more. I didn't want to do that. I didn't want to start something that you don't want to finish, and I *can't* finish."

"And why can't you?" He smoothed her hair, brushed her temple with his thumb, snugged her hips up to his, and wrapped her in his heat and scent and comfort.

She felt like a limp noodle, weak in body and mind. "I'm selling, remember?"

"And where will you go?"

A question she couldn't answer. God, would this night never end? "I don't know. We've worked the circus before, small fairs, places like that."

"The circus?"

He sounded appalled, forcing her to dredge up a smile of reassurance. "Every kid's dream, right?"

"Was it? Don't lie to me, sweetheart. Tell me the truth."

"The truth, huh?" The truth, in her opinion, was ugly. It wasn't something to be hashed over, but she could pick and choose her words. She shrugged, willing to share a little of the past life she'd never been suited to. "I hated constantly changing friends, forever attempting to build new relationships."

"So finally, you just gave up?"

"My aunts and uncle became my friends."

"It's not the same as kids around your own age."

"No. But you know what bothered me even more? In the circus, it's never quiet, and you're never alone, where you can just think. My parents loved that chaos, the continual excitement, and so did my aunts and uncle. But I used to dream of just being all alone, maybe sitting in a rowboat in the middle of a lake, or out in a field with only the bees buzzing."

He caressed her, his rough palms moving up and down her back. "Which is why you like living alone now?"

"Yes." Zane looked far too grim to suit her, and she attempted to lighten the mood. "Maybe I'll just relocate, start a smaller shop somewhere else."

His dark eyes were so intent, so probing, she felt more naked than she had before getting dressed. He touched her face, his fingertips gliding over her chin, her nose, smoothing out her puckered brow.

"If Joe finds out who's doing this, you wouldn't have to sell, would you?"

Confiding in anyone, leaning on anyone, was as uncomfortable as a toothache. Because of the way she'd grown up, she'd never done it, didn't know how, and could already tell she wasn't going to like it. But Zane was a mix of tumultuous emotions, cresting against her reserve like a continual wave, wearing her down, smoothing away her worries. He was aroused—but he was always aroused whenever they were alone together. She was getting used to that—or, rather, accepting it. He was also tenderly concerned, openly caring. He wanted her, not just for sex, she realized, but for more.

She shook her head, unwilling to start an internal debate on that subject. What he wanted, how much he wanted, would remain a mystery until he told her outright. It was too important for her to play guessing games. She could sense his feelings, but she wasn't a mind reader who could dissect his every thought with accuracy.

"I lost a lot of money," she said wearily. "The shop does fine, but not when there are a lot of unexpected expenses. It . . . put me behind. Recovering enough financially to stay here would be difficult."

"Do you have some upkeep for your relatives?"

"Not a whole lot." She felt protective of them. They never asked for much, and after all they'd given her, she didn't mind helping them now that they were older. "Because their house is already paid for, their expenses are minimal."

Turning away, Zane picked up one of the software manuals on her desk. He flipped through a stack of notes there, picked up and examined a disk. "And what is all this?"

She flushed. What she did outside of being a Gypsy was just so . . . personal. Stiffening her spine, ready to accept any jokes he might feel compelled to make, she said. "Strange as it may seem, I'm a technical writer."

He glanced at her over his shoulder, his gaze full of censure. "Not strange, honey, so don't put words in my mouth." Laying the manual aside, he crossed his arms and rested against the edge of the desk. "I just want to know more about you, about your situation."

"You don't think it's funny, the contrast in the two professions?"

"You're a jumble of contrasts, so it makes sense that you'd seek other outlets." His voice gentled. "You're a complex woman, Tamara Tremayne, and I find I like discovering all the different angles."

She sucked in some necessary oxygen for her laboring lungs and deprived brain. The emotions he felt now were layered and varied and too entwined for her to even begin to sort them out. They mixed with her own emotions, until she felt light-headed.

"Is it hard work?"

Her heart raced at the sincerity of his question. She loved her computer work, but it wasn't something she'd ever been able to share with anyone.

A burst of light, like a ray of sunshine, cut through everything else, warming her, filling her up. She smiled, this time a natural smile. "It seems I have a knack for making the complicated sound simple." It was a boastful statement, but with Zane, she felt free to lose her modesty. She knew he wouldn't mind and that, in fact, he'd expect no less.

"I work with a software company on getting instructions down in a user-friendly way. Our work mode varies, but generally I sit with the programmer and get trained how to use the software. I document the smallest details, then organize everything and write a manual on how to use it."

"This is added income?"

"Yes." She could tell he'd misread the particulars, and her smile widened. "I'm not working in the coal mines, Zane."

"No, but I've seen your light on late into the night, and now I know why. The job you have is already full-time. You haven't left yourself much time for you."

The irony of his statement amused her. "Gee, how is it you've seen my light on, unless you were just leaving your job, too?"

"One job, Tamara. Not two."

"The technical writing is something I enjoy." How to explain it, she wondered. And how much should she explain? "It's . . . serendipitous."

His gaze softened, his shoulders softened. A small, understanding smile turned up the corners of his sensuous mouth. "Part of that 'normal lifestyle' you were talking about earlier?"

"Yes."

Zane watched her a moment more, then started to close his slacks. "We've got a lot to discuss. And if I know Joe, he's probably out there snooping around right now."

Startled, Tamara's brows shot up. "Snooping? In my house?"

"Yeah." Zane shrugged. "It's sort of what he does now."

She barely heard him, having already turned away. Long, anxious strides carried her out the bedroom door and down the hallway. But Joe Winston wasn't snooping. Nope. His big body was lounged out on her sofa, long legs in disreputable tattered jeans stretched out in front of him. He was engrossed in the journal.

A pair of black-framed reading glasses perched on the end of his slightly crooked nose, looking horribly out of place against his rugged and whiskery face. His golden earring glinted under the soft light of the end table lamp. His chiseled mouth was pursed in contemplation.

On the seat next to him, the pages that had gotten torn from the book when she'd hit him with it had been smoothed out flat.

Without looking up to acknowledge her presence, he muttered, "I never figured Zane for the type to need instructions," then he turned another page.

Heat rushed into her cheeks. Behind her, Zane threatened Joe in the most lurid way imaginable.

Joe glanced up, unconcerned with Zane's ire. "A lot of it is hogwash, but you know, some of it is right on target."

Zane took two long steps forward and snatched the book from his cousin's hand. "I sure as hell don't need you to clarify for me."

"Well, not after reading that book, anyway." Joe calmly folded his glasses and slipped them into his jacket pocket.

Tamara hid a smile. Zane's cousin epitomized outrageousness, possibly even more so than Zane. No woman could take him seriously.

"We weren't using the book as a guide," she said.

"No?" Joe stood, his gaze piercing Tamara, holding her to the spot. "Well, if it's just an experiment, count me in, love."

Zane grabbed him by the front of his shirt and twisted. "I'll count you out if you don't leave her the hell alone."

"Zane!" Alarmed, Tamara stepped between them. "What's the matter with you?"

With a shove, Zane released Joe. "He's coming on to you, right in front of me."

Even during Zane's attack, Joe hadn't looked away from Tamara, and now humor lit his dark blue, heavily fringed eyes. "He's jealous, sweetheart, anyone can see that. Seems Zane has a possessive streak, at least where you're concerned. I don't remember him getting his shorts in a bunch over any other woman."

Heart racing, Tamara dared a quick look at Zane. She expected immediate denials, a resurgence of his anger, something volatile.

He surprised her. No longer rigid, a mocking cynicism lit his eyes and a smirk made his sexy mouth go crooked. "Let me guess. This your way of helping out, Joe?"

Joe shrugged. "Just call me your guardian angel. Left to your own devices, I was afraid she'd throw your sorry ass out."

"He's staying here tonight," Tamara announced. She was uncertain what the two of them were prattling on about, but she felt it necessary to defend Zane just the same.

"Not smart," Joe said immediately.

"She refuses to come home with me." Zane caught her hand and pulled her to his side. "She doesn't want to leave the house unprotected. I can understand that."

"Ah." Joe tipped his head at Tamara and said with a shrug of acceptance, "Then I suppose it makes sense after all. Zane definitely shouldn't leave you here alone. But," he added, "we'll have to set up a few safeguards first."

"Tonight, and more tomorrow."

"That's what I was thinking."

Tamara leveled a look on both men. "You're thinking without my input, and I won't have it."

Joe laughed, and she had the suspicion it was at her expense. "I should get out of here and let you both get to sleep." His gaze warmed. "You have to be exhausted."

"Joe . . ."

"I gather there's no point calling the police."

Zane again looked ready to brawl, but he subsided. "I'm calling them. I just don't think they'll do anything."

"Any idea who might be behind this?"

"An idea, yeah. It'd have to be someone with access to a key, someone with a motive."

"Someone you already don't like?"

"That's right. But my not liking him is incidental to the facts."

Joe pondered the possibility. "The bad guys don't always look bad or act bad, you know. Don't get it set in your head or you're liable to miss other more likely possibilities."

Zane nodded. Standing beside him, Tamara bristled. "You have about two seconds, Zane Winston, to tell me who you think tried to break in here."

His grin wasn't at all nice this time. It was predatory. "He wanted to see you, and you turned him down. He knows your relatives—"

Tamara picked up on his train of thought. "And my family has keys for emergency use. He could have gotten one from them without them knowing."

Their gazes locked, and they said together, "Boris Sandor."

SIXTEEN

Zane held the tattered journal against his bent knee. Next to him, Tamara stirred just a little. He soothed her with a hand on her hip, stroking slow and easy. He loved the feel of her, both under his hand and beside him in bed. Warm and sleep-heavy, she sighed.

The chapters on sexual satisfaction had been incredible. They'd gone through most of them last night when Zane realized Tamara was too upset to sleep. Joe had promised to hang around outside until sunup, even though they were both relatively certain their visitor wouldn't be back that night. Tamara had seemed stunned by such an offer, but Joe assured her that surveillance was nothing new to him.

The police, as Zane had suspected, could do no more than make out a report and promise to drive by occasionally. Since Joe was already there, the offer was unnecessary.

Zane smiled now, reluctantly admitting to himself that Joe had been the hero of the night. If it hadn't been for him, the intruder might have been the one to stumble onto Tamara naked. The thought made Zane shudder. Deep down, he trusted Joe implicitly, or he'd never have asked him for help. If it had been a stranger ogling her, he'd have been tempted to kill the man.

He supposed he'd have to thank his cousin. Zane grinned as he imagined Joe's reaction to sincere gratitude. Coming from Zane, it was liable to give Joe a heart attack.

Zane chuckled softly, looking over at Tamara's tousled hair and slightly parted lips. In a very short time, she'd become so special to him, so precious.

As per the damn book's instruction, she would accept sexual satisfaction from him. Accept, demand, revel in. In all his mature years, he'd never met a woman who more equally balanced his sexual drive, taking and giving. During the night, he'd suggested things in a heated whisper, and she'd accepted openly, hungrily, drowning in anything and everything he wanted to do.

His body reacted now to the memory, and that was nothing short of a miracle. He'd let her drift off to sleep only a few hours ago. He should have been dead to the world, carnal activity beyond him, for at least a day. Possibly two. But just feeling the heat of her next to him, hearing her soft breathing, made his sex stir in anticipation.

He wanted her again.

He wanted her always.

Zane turned another page and skimmed the text. This was the part of the book Tamara hadn't bothered to share with him. It detailed ways to make your lover fall in love. But she didn't want love from him.

She'd asked him for sex, and like the most noble of negotiators, she refused to try to take more.

Tough.

Zane had never needed much sleep, usually five hours tops, but now he was nearing exhaustion. Still, he didn't want to sleep, didn't want to waste a single second of this opportunity. Getting Tamara to lean on him, to trust him and accept him in every way, wasn't going to be easy. Because, he realized, she didn't know how.

She knew how to stand on her own, how to take care of others and get through life any way she could, but she didn't know how to ask for help, or how to accept it, because she'd never been given the opportunity to learn.

He discounted what her relatives had done for her as a child. Of course they'd taken her in; she was family and that's what family did. He'd bend over backward and walk on his hands for his brothers if that's what they needed from him. And now, by association, his brother's wives and children had the same loyalty. *That* was life, that was the course you took when you had family. There wasn't a single doubt in his mind that any of his brothers would do the same for him.

Which reminded him. Joe now had an inkling of what Tamara meant to him, but he should clear it up with Cole, Chase, and Mack, too. Just on the off chance something happened to him, he wanted her taken care of. He didn't want her to have to sell and start over. He didn't want her to be on her own, ever again.

Share your fears, your dreams, your hopes for the future.

The journal held a lot of insight, not only on sexual satisfaction, but also on falling in love. After reading it, Zane felt he knew the woman who'd written it. Her loneliness and her determination were there on the page, seeping through the words, sharing personal things if only someone cared to see them. Things Tamara could relate to because she was alone and lonely as well.

His heart ached.

He'd never said those three incredible little words that could change a man's life. Now they burned in his throat, wanting out. But Tamara wasn't ready for that. He needed to woo her, he decided with a smile. He needed to follow the instructions of the manual and share his heart bit by bit, before making it an offering.

All his ruminations had brought his mind and body into agreement. He did indeed need Tamara again. Was she sore? She sure as hell hadn't complained last night, and he knew she could use the sleep now. But the combination of love burning behind his eyes and in his heart, joined with the slower, hotter pulse of desire, had his hands shaking.

He'd never been in love and he wanted, needed, some form of confirmation from her, even if only physical.

With infinite care, he eased the sheet off her body.

Being accommodating, she turned to her back, put one arm over her head, and snuggled her sweet bottom into the mattress. Looking at her brought all the swirling emotions and sensations together into a razor-sharp point.

His hand on her pale, slender thigh, urging her legs wide, looked dark and rough. The contrast maddened him, made it hard to breathe.

Her scent clung to the sheets, to him, to the cool morning air around them. Drifting his long fingers through her crisp pubic curls, he watched her body shift, awaken. Her belly sucked in a little, and he had to kiss her there, had to dip his tongue into her cute little navel.

Her hand settled in his hair, and in a sleep-foggy voice she said, "Zane."

There was satisfaction in her tone and he chose to think affection as well.

"I missed you," he whispered, kissing his way up her torso, nibbling on her hips, each rib, until she squirmed and he could hear the growing excitement in her sigh.

She twisted to see the bedside clock. "It's been only a few hours since you . . ."

Her voice trailed off, delighting him with her continued reserve when she opened her body so completely to him. "Since I loved you silly?" he asked, and kissed the small vertical worry lines between her slim brows. "I love loving you."

Her frown deepened. Zane hid his grin, knowing he'd confused her, that she was unsure how to take him or the words he'd slipped in. *Sate yourself*, the journal said, *on the pleasure you give your lover*. Wise words from an obviously wise, caring woman. He intended to follow the instructions to the letter, and all the while he'd talk to her, tell her things that she'd be unable to respond to.

Light as a breeze, his fingers continued to tease over her, dipping every so often through her curls to touch warm, moist flesh. Teasing. Tempting her into that whirlwind of carnality.

"You are so soft."

"You're not," she said, and reached down to circle her hand around his throbbing cock where it pressed into her thigh.

Zane let her hold him, squeeze him; God, he loved her touch. He loved her frowns and her independence and her vulnerability. He loved everything about her.

Her breath caught, then her gaze skittered to the journal, open on the bedside table. "You've been . . . reading?"

Uncertainty warred with her growing pleasure. He could see it in her beautiful green eyes. "You read it," he explained, "and I wanted to know what you'd found there."

Balanced on his side, he put his right leg over hers and pinned her down, keeping her legs open. She was wet now, her tender vulva swelling, readying for him. Slowly, with infinite care because he knew he'd been excessive through the night, he pushed his middle finger into her.

Her back arched and a small catch in her breath thrilled him. "Does that feel good, sweetheart?"

"Yes."

"You're not too raw?" He worked his finger in and out, pressing deep so that his knuckles rubbed against her distended clitoris, then withdrawing to tease the soft swollen lips, before pressing in again.

She tangled her fingers in his hair. "Kiss me."

He withdrew again, readjusted his hand, and caught her small clitoris with his fingertips. He tugged very lightly. "Here?"

"Zane!" Her thighs opened more, struggled against the restraint of his.

"Or here?" He leaned down and licked one begging nipple. His tongue swirled around and around until he heard her long, broken moan. "Like this?" He sucked her deep.

Her body twisted, writhed against the sheets. The pleasure would be sharp, he knew, after all the loving they'd done. She was ultrasensitive, and her body quaked, trembled. "I can't," she cried, pressing her hips into the mattress, trying to pull away.

"Shhh," he said against her breast. "My tongue is softer. It'll be easier for you."

"*No . . .*"

He wasn't sure what she protested, the pleasure he'd give her, the use of his mouth, or her own wavering uncertainty.

Zane sat up and threw the sheets completely from the bed. Tamara's body, flushed and taut, stretched out like a sacrifice before him. He wanted to devour her until she screamed his name and said those three words he felt bound to hold inside.

Kneeling between her thighs, he caught her breasts in his hands and roughly caressed them. "You have the most delectable body I've ever seen, Tamara."

Neck arched, eyes closed, she whispered, "Yes."

She wasn't even aware of what she said, he realized, pleased with the results he'd gained. He thumbed her nipples and watched her strain for more. Her breasts flushed, swelled in his hands.

"So sweet," he whispered, and bent to take her into his mouth again. She lifted, the open juncture of her thighs pressing into his abdomen, warm, silky wet, making him insane. He drew on her nipple while he caught her thighs and held them. It would be so easy to slide into her now. It wouldn't take more than six hard, fast pumps to put him into nirvana.

He wanted more.

Blindly groping across the head of the bed, Zane found his pillow and snagged it with a fist. He lifted away from her delicious breasts, leaving her nipples darkened, glistening wet. He caught her slim hips and lifted, pressing the pillow beneath her, making an offering of her lush heated sex. Moisture gathered in his mouth as he looked at her, hungry for the taste of her, for her pleasure.

He traced the delicate pink flesh with one fingertip, his chest working like a bellows, never able to get enough air. "Open your legs wider for me, sweetheart."

She moaned softly, squirmed, fisted her hands in the sheet next to her hips.

"Do it, Tamara."

"It's too much."

"And not enough. I know. Do it."

Tentatively, in small degrees, her legs spread open. Zane stared at her lovely face, eyes squeezed shut, teeth sunk into her bottom lip. The hair at her temples was damp with sweat.

God, he loved waking her like this.

"Wider," he ordered and saw her mouth open on a groan. Her thighs quivered, stretched wide.

"Yes." He lowered his head and took one long, leisurely lick, swirling around her clitoris so that her hips left the cushioning pillow and she cried out.

He did it again, and again, teasing her, giving her just a little, but not enough. Anchoring her in place, he kept her legs spread with his hands tight on her upper thighs. On the sixth lick he lingered, suckled, and she screamed out her climax, making him shudder with the pleasure of it.

She felt boneless, her limbs limp, her body dewy. He rested his head on her thigh and continued to toy with her—light, gentle touches that kept her aroused but didn't cause discomfort to her sensitized nerve endings.

After a while her long, deep breaths began to quicken once more. Satisfied, Zane turned his head, seeking her again with his mouth. This time he was gentler, slower, nuzzling into her, nibbling, until her long ragged groan, hoarse with nearly painful pleasure, split the quiet morning.

He blew on her, cooling her, teasing again. Moving up her body, he kissed her lax mouth, smiling against her lips. "You're incredible."

No response. But that didn't bother him. He rolled to his back and pulled her atop him, letting her body drape over his chest and hips like a blanket. He spread her thighs in one smooth movement and pushed his erection into her wet heat. She was so wet, she accepted him easily, and he was content to simply hold her like that for a time, connected physically in all ways.

The journal had emphasized the importance of holding. He'd never had a predilection for difficult women, but he wanted this difficult woman to love him. He wanted her to feel everything he felt, and hoped she understood it when she did.

Sexual tension vibrated in his every pore, but a lot of the urgency he'd felt earlier, prompted by a need to claim her, had diminished. She was his; he'd made up his mind and now he just wanted to enjoy her in every way he could think of.

She mumbled into his chest, her heated breath a taunt on his skin, "You're not wearing a condom."

Zane kissed the top of her head. Because he loved her, he wanted to give her choices. Now wasn't really fair because she was literally spent, limp as a drugged fish, but fairness seldom came into play when you were in love. His reasoning sounded weak even to his own mind, but he didn't give a damn.

"I want to feel you, and just you," he explained. Still, he asked, "Do you care?"

She hesitated, and he held his breath. Her soft hair tickled his chin, her heartbeat thumped in time to his own. Her body welcomed him, holding him snug in slippery wetness and sizzling heat.

"No."

That one simple word broke his control. It said and meant so much, more than he'd dared to hope for so soon. He cupped her bottom, held her steady while he began to thrust.

Tamara struggled to sit up, inadvertently deepening his penetration. They both groaned. He felt her womb, felt all of her. She braced her small hands on his chest and like a siren, whispered, "Let me."

Keeping still was about the hardest thing he'd ever done. Her every movement enflamed him, the way she shook her fair hair over her shoulders, arched her neck, pushed her breasts forward.

With concentrated deliberation, Zane forced his fingers to unclench on her hips and raised them to her breasts. He cuddled them, stroked her nipples as she lifted, fell, lifted, fell. Her movements were unpracticed, but enthusiastic.

"Roll your hips," he told her in a rasp, knowing it would increase her pleasure.

"Like this?"

It was his turn to arch, and they both moaned at how deeply he entered her.

Her thighs strained, the sleek muscles pulled taut. She clasped him, her sex pulling at him like a voracious mouth. He fought hard not to come yet, to hold off until she'd taken her own orgasm one more time.

"I don't believe this," she whispered a few minutes later when he felt her tightening around him, milking him.

He clenched his teeth to keep words of love unsaid. Watching her, seeing her beautiful face twisted and real with the savage pleasure of their lovemaking, was a gift he'd never forget.

She cried when the last spasms had left her, and Zane turned her beneath him, licking at her tears and driving into her hard and deep and rough, once, twice . . . He threw his head back and shouted as he came.

Tamara managed to get one arm around him when he fell heavily atop her. They were both sweaty, heat pouring off their bodies, adhering them together. She made a sound, like wonder or disbelief or . . . *love.*

God, let it be the start of love.

Puckering required more dexterity than he could summon, but he moved his lips against her neck, the only reply he could muster.

He was just thinking life couldn't get any better when a fist rattled the bedroom door and Thanos's voice rang out, imperative and angry.

"Tamara! Are you all right? Answer me, damn it."

"No," Zane mumbled, unable to reconcile his sluggish brain and depleted body to the fact of intrusive relatives right now, at this precise moment. Relatives he hadn't heard enter the house. Relatives who were loony, and apparently angry to boot. "No, no."

The small, warm body cushioning his stiffened alarmingly.

"They not only have a key," Zane managed to mumble, "but they use it?"

Taking him and his debilitated body by surprise, Tamara became a small whirlwind and threw him off. He almost slid over the side of the wrecked mattress to the floor. He was just stabilizing himself when a naked thigh came over his head and Tamara scrambled to her feet.

"Just a minute, Uncle!"

Zane reached for her wrist and missed. Seconds later his slacks hit him in the face. "Get dressed," she hissed, then scurried around the room grabbing for clothes. Her movements were awkward and jerky, but then, she'd just come several times. He was shaky, and he hadn't lost his senses nearly as often as she had.

Feeling very put upon, Zane dragged himself to a sitting position on the side of the bed. His knees were rickety, damn it. "What are they doing here?"

Tamara's face was pale, her eyes filled with mortification. "They come every Sunday."

"And you forgot to tell me this?"

She fried him with an evil glare. "You distracted me."

From the other side of the door. Thanos said, "I can hear every word."

"Go away!" Tamara wailed, her face bright red.

Incredulous, Zane stood, waited to see if he'd fall flat on his face, and when his legs didn't give out, he pulled on his slacks.

Thanos's booming laugh reached them. "I'll be in the kitchen with the others. I gather you could use some coffee. Don't dally or I'll be back."

Yanking a shirt over her head, Tamara ordered, "Hurry. Finish dressing."

"Tamara." Zane caught her and held her still when she struggled. "Honey, I know this is a little embarrassing—"

"Ha!"

"—but you're a grown woman and this is your house. You don't have to explain anything to anyone."

A look of absolute incredulity crossed her face. "Explain? I think they understand already!" She paused, looked at his chest, and touched a small bite mark over his pectoral muscle. She remarked in distressed tones, "A shirt. You definitely have to put on your shirt. And shoes, too. I don't want my aunts eyeing your naked feet."

"Who gives a damn about my naked feet?"

"I do!" She tugged on the same jeans she'd worn the night before, glanced in the mirror, and hastily fingercombed her hair. "This is just awful."

"Well." Zane sat on the edge of the mattress to don socks and shoes. God forbid he should flaunt his damn feet. "That's a great way to lacerate a guy's ego."

She looked harassed. "I don't mean *you*. I mean *this*—getting caught, facing nosy relatives." She paused to say with heartfelt sincerity, "You were . . . indescribable."

Still without his shirt, Zane stood and folded her close. "Shh. They'll hear you." But he was grinning and couldn't seem to stop.

She covered her face and dropped into his embrace. "I can't believe I forgot about them. I can't believe we didn't *hear* them. They always knock first. Who knows what they thought when I didn't answer."

"We know what they're thinking now, that's for sure." He slid his hand beneath her tangled hair and clasped her nape. "But don't worry about it. We have plenty to distract them with this morning."

She groaned as a new reality intruded. "Last night is almost a blur. Do you realize whoever broke in could have come back today and we wouldn't have noticed?"

"Which is why," Zane told her, seeing the perfect opening, "you're not going to argue with me when I have an alarm system installed to cover the doors and windows."

"No, I don't—"

"I know. You don't need or want my help." He pressed his thumb over her lips, and when that didn't appease him, he replaced his thumb with his mouth. This kiss was filled with the love he not only accepted, but relished.

She inspected his face, and Zane wondered how much of what he felt was apparent to her. How much of it could she perceive? When her gaze softened, he assumed she was aware of at least some of the emotional depth she'd taken him to.

"You make me feel like a high schooler on prom night, Tamara, waiting to see if I'll be asked to dance. I don't like it."

"Oh Zane." Her tone was apologetic, concerned, as it always was when she feared she might have hurt him somehow. "I don't want to make you feel bad."

"That's a start, sweetheart." He kissed her again and then set her away from him. "I want you protected, so I'm taking care of an alarm. It doesn't ingratiate you to me in any way. It doesn't tax me financially and you don't owe me anything in return."

"Zane . . ."

"And it means nothing more than that I care. Because you sense my emotions, you surely already know that, right?"

It was an admission, plain and simple, but not one that would threaten her independent nature.

Green eyes dark and intense, she nodded slowly.

Relief flooded through him in near painful pleasure.

"Excellent." He touched her cheek. "I want to do what I can to see that you're safe when I'm not with you. Okay?"

Every line of her petite body bespoke exasperation and uncertainty. "How am I supposed to respond to that?"

Zane caught her face in his hands and said with as much seriousness as he could muster when his body was so sated and his heart so full, "I know you don't have much practice at this, but you could just say 'thank you.'"

She worried her bottom lip between her teeth. "But . . ."

"No buts, sweetheart. No doubts. You either trust me or you don't." He added, unable to stop himself, "Trust me, Tamara."

She sighed. "You keep saying that, though what it has to do with trust, I don't know."

"It has everything to do with trust."

As if pondering world peace, she considered what he said. Zane thought she took far more time than the situation, or the proposition, warranted. It was her uncle bellowing down the hallway that the coffee was ready that helped her make up her mind.

In a rush, she said, "Okay," and almost as an afterthought, "Thank you."

She started out of the bedroom in a rush. Zane caught her, pulled her back, and stuck the cell phone in her pocket. "You're to carry it on you at all times, remember?"

Tamara rolled her eyes and took off again—the phone with her.

Loving an independent, headstrong Gypsy with meddlesome, wacky relatives wasn't going to be easy.

But not loving her was the impossible alternative, so like each of his brothers before him, Zane smiled as he accepted his fate.

The Winston curse had struck again.

S E V E N T E E N

Tamara prepared herself as best she could to face her aunts and uncle. It wasn't easy, being so distracted. Zane cared. Not just about the wonderful physical relationship they'd started, but about her, as a person. His affection washed over her like a soothing hand, giving immeasurable comfort, unqualified support. She'd never experienced anything like it before.

It was both pleasurable and frightening.

She hated being vulnerable, like a small child once more, unsure where she would go or what she would do after her parents' death. The thought of moving again was bad enough, but at least that was her decision, a way of maintaining financial security rather than sitting around and waiting to lose her shop.

Above all, she needed to be in charge, even in failure.

Zane's attention kept her utterly out of control, with her mind, her body, her emotions.

Her heart.

She knew how to handle most situations—by pushing forward with sheer strength of will and stubborn determination. She'd learned to do that as a means of survival, even before her parents had passed away. Her relatives were on the money when they called her a white sheep. Compared to them, she was so sedate, she bordered on dull. To them, she *was* dull.

What they found exciting and carefree, she found intimidating and unstable. She wasn't meant to be a Gypsy, at least not the mobile kind. She wanted to keep her stationary life. She wanted to keep her shop.

She wanted to keep Zane. *Damn.*

Ignoring the aching in her heart, she plastered a serene smile on her face and stiffened her backbone, primed to face her aunts and uncle and all their speculation.

No way was she prepared for the guest they'd brought along.

She stopped dead in her tracks when she saw the man sitting at her small kitchen table, sipping coffee with elegant grace.

Zane, following close on her heels, ran into her. He grabbed her shoulders to steady them both. Tamara accepted his heat, his strength at her back.

They were both frozen for a mere heartbeat before her temper detonated and she lurched forward.

"You!" Ready to commit murder, to gain retribution for the night's fright and the other deeds that had cost her so much, Tamara reached for Boris. Her fingers caught air and she drew up short when Zane snagged the back of her jeans.

Sublime confusion on his aristocratic face, Boris Sandor observed her with one raised, sardonic brow. "Excuse me?"

"What the hell are you doing in my house?" she roared. Her vibrating anger was slightly diffused by the fact Zane had her up on her tiptoes, his hold on her waistband unrelenting.

"Calm down, Tamara," he told her in a nearly bored voice that only she realized was laced with real menace. Oh, he was furious all right, but he was also more collected. That only annoyed her further.

"Let me go," she said to him.

"Will you control your volatile tendencies?"

It was there in his voice; he wouldn't let her go unless she could restrain herself. Though she knew he was right, it galled her. "For now."

He acknowledged her concession with a smile. "Just keep in mind, sweetheart, that I'd hate to have to kill him with your relatives looking on."

The relatives gaped at each other in fascinated awe. She was used to Zane now, but they certainly weren't.

He continued, saying, "Better not to provoke him until we've had a chance to talk."

That made sense, damn him. They did need to understand the motives behind the break-ins. And she didn't want Zane killing anyone, especially not for her.

Her aunts kept giving her horrified looks, and her uncle had risen from the table, alerted by her fury.

Thanos's bushy beard quivered as he demanded, "What is it, little one?"

Glaring at the intruder, Tamara asked, "Why is he here?"

Boris Sandor slowly came to his feet. He was immaculately dressed in gray trousers, a dark blue sweater over a silk shirt, and polished shoes.

The contrast to the rest of them was striking. Her aunts wore loose, colorful dresses layered by either a shawl or a home-knit sweater, and Thanos was in brown jeans and a flannel with rainbow striped suspenders. Behind her, Zane's hastily buttoned shirt hung loose from his waistband and had wrinkles from a night on the floor. Her own clothes were rumpled and slightly askew.

Boris Sandor's annoyance slapped against her. Once again, she was surprised by the depth to which she experienced him. It made her feel queasy.

"Ms. Tremayne?" Vague distaste threaded through his icy politeness. His gaze encompassed her from ears to toes and back again. "My God, is that truly you?"

Both her aunts jumped in to explain, anxious for a new tack to take, other than her embarrassing outrage.

"She's forgotten her wig."

"She seldom looks so . . . rumpled."

"Apparently we've interrupted"—Olga shrugged helplessly—"something."

The scattered statements ended with more wide-eyed conjecture. Their confusion was apparent, as was their curiosity.

The emotions in the room were high; Boris's ugly contemplation, her aunts' and uncle's confusion, speculation. And Zane's barely leashed anger. Her head throbbed. She wasn't used to feeling so many people at one time. She felt overloaded, weighed down.

The only way she could think to get through this was to take charge.

She cleared her throat, thrust up her chin, and avoided her aunts' gazes by staring at Boris. "Yes, you've interrupted. But that doesn't tell me why the hell you're here."

"Tamara," her uncle growled. "I'd like you to explain your behavior."

She felt heat flare in her cheeks, and the touch of Zane's body on her back. Her chin went up another inch. "You knew I wanted him."

Mouths dropped open, eyes widened. Boris made a sound of derision.

On a choked laugh, Zane said, "I think he means your temper, sweetheart, and your reaction to your . . . guest."

Embarrassment was lost beneath invective. Oh, she could tell them why she objected to Boris!

Aunt Olga beat her to the punch.

"My word," she exclaimed, "she's been debauched."

Eva clasped her hands to her generous bosom. Even with the start of cataracts, her black eyes were piercing and bright. "You think?" Then to Olga, "She's showing signs of the Tremayne passion."

Olga, who also looked dumbstruck, yet thrilled, cried, "But it's for the wrong man! It was supposed to be Boris."

"*What?*" Tamara couldn't quite believe her aunts' audacity. It was obvious to one and all what they had blundered into that morning, and they persisted in the delusion she might be interested in Boris? Forget that they didn't know he was a criminal of the meanest sort, ruining her business for heaven only knew what reason. Forget that she barely knew the man.

Zane, tall and proud and gorgeous beyond compare, stood directly behind her. His large hands were on her shoulders in a proprietary display, a display she in no way objected to. She leaned into him.

They could *see* him.

Surely they didn't for a single moment think she'd trade down for Boris? The mere thought had her curling her lip.

Boris cleared his throat. "Perhaps this isn't the most auspicious time for me to call."

Zane's fingers tightened. "For what you have in mind, Sandor, there won't be a better time."

Olga stepped forward. "Don't be so hasty, young man. It's good for a woman to have suitors scrap over her. And Boris is better suited for what we have in mind."

Tamara gasped. "For what *you* have in mind?"

Thanos tugged at his ear. "He's wealthy, little one, and influential. There's a lot he could do to help us, and he understands our people."

"I'm from the homeland," Boris reminded them.

Tamara felt the throbbing waves of Zane's anger, but could think of no way to reassure him. She said with dripping disdain, "Since when do we need anyone's help or influence? I can handle my problems on my own."

Zane's hands moved from her shoulders to lightly encircle her throat, as a gentle reminder that *he* would help.

She absently patted his hand to let him know she accepted him, then continued. "And you say he understands our people? Then he's one up on me, because I sure as hell don't."

Horrified, Olga turned to Boris and patted his shoulder. "She's a white sheep, never quite getting into the swing of things, if you know what I mean."

Eva added, as if it were a sin, "She's . . . steadfast."

With courtly condescension, Boris murmured, "I do understand." His gaze was hungry as he scrutinized Tamara.

Tamara wanted to distance herself from the physical interest she sensed in Boris, which conflicted with his emotional disdain. He didn't like her, but he wanted her.

She stepped back, and found herself encompassed by Zane. There was no reason for her to cower, no reason for her to let Boris frighten her. She was here, as Zane had said, in her own home. She wouldn't tolerate Boris's haughty imposition.

"I was born and raised in America," she said. "Only my most distant relatives were foreigners. Your claims don't mean a thing to me, Boris."

Dismay had her aunts fretting and Thanos shaking his head. Tamara decided to get it all on the table. "Besides," she sneered, "I don't associate with disreputable scoundrels."

A collective gasp stirred the air.

Zane's gaze first met with Tamara's, then swept the room to include each of her relatives in his disclosure. "He's the one who's been harassing Tamara, breaking into her shop, setting fires and causing the plumbing to flood. He's the one forcing you all to move."

Boris slammed both hands down on her table. His face turned a mottled red and his eyes bulged. "How dare you! I've done no such thing and I refuse to stand here and be besmirched by the likes of you."

Zane merely grinned at Boris's contempt. "Can you prove it wasn't you?"

Thanos crossed his massive arms over his chest. "I can see you care for her, Zane, but wild accusations won't win her over."

"This isn't a contest, damn it, and she isn't a prize."

Tamara's nerve endings tingled with Zane's outpouring of annoyance. *On her behalf*. She had to think of a way to defuse the situation. It would break her heart if her beloved uncle and Zane got into a fight.

Thanos said, "No? Then what is this all about?"

"He wouldn't understand," Boris sneered. "Loyalty to family is obviously beyond him."

Tamara sucked in a startled breath. Oh no. She knew, even if Boris didn't, that he'd just crossed the line.

With eerie calm, Zane set Tamara to the side of him and took two measured steps toward Boris. "I don't know what you're up to, but you can forget it right now. She's not alone anymore."

Olga took exception to that. "She's never been alone. She's been with us."

Anger swirled around Zane as he turned to her aunt. He was polite, even gentle when he spoke, but Tamara knew the turmoil he contained.

"No? What has she gotten from you? Complete acceptance for the woman she is? Or a lot of pressure to be what she isn't?"

Olga and Eva glanced warily at one another.

"Have you given her unwavering support?" Zane demanded.

"Have you tried to understand her and her needs? Or have you forced her into a mold that best served you?"

"Zane," Tamara whispered uncertainly.

"She's a Tremayne." Eva made that statement as if it explained everything.

"She's a woman first." Zane didn't back down.

"That's enough," Thanos remarked quietly, moving to stand beside the two older women.

"Damn right it is. Enough of costumes and veiled insults—"

"Zane, they've never meant to insult me."

"Yet they do," he answered, looking at each of them in turn, "every time they suggest that you don't measure up."

Olga looked aghast, her wrinkled face going pale. "Dear God, we love her."

"Then let her be her own woman."

Tamara shook off her shock. Never in her life had she stood idly by while her relatives were badgered, not by spectators, not by law officials. She wouldn't stand by now, not even for Zane.

His defense galled her, even as his understanding melted her heart.

"I can deal with my relatives on my own, Zane Winston."

He turned, not the least put off by her imperious tone, her bristling attitude. His smile was intimate, private, and he said, "But you no longer have to."

He meant it. His earnestness was a live thing, drumming in time to her heart. But he didn't understand her aunts and uncle, didn't know how difficult it had been for them to take on a little girl.

She cleared her throat. "Maybe . . . maybe you should go."

"Me?" Incredulous, he pointed at Boris. "What about him?"

"I can deal with him."

"Like hell." Zane crossed his arms much in the same fashion as Thanos. Standing near one another, they looked like mismatched bookends. "I'm not taking one step out of here, babe, so forget it."

Boris pushed himself past the table to face off with Zane. He was nearly as tall, older by a decade, heavily muscled. Yet, there was no comparison. Zane was competent and strong and self-assured, while Boris appeared bloated with bluster.

"How dare you speak to her with such a lack of respect!"

Zane looked down his nose at the older man. Ignoring the question, he took a step forward and forced Boris to retreat. "You tried to break in here last night, didn't you?"

"No!"

"You're trying to run her off, and I'm curious why."

"That's absurd!" Boris was quickly wheeling backward now, and he bumped into Thanos.

"You get your jollies by terrorizing women alone, is that it? Only she wasn't alone last night, was she?" Zane caught him by his shirt collar. "She won't be alone ever again."

Tamara went light-headed at his words. *Ever again.* Her heart thundered, her stomach dipped. What was he saying? Surely not what she . . . no, that was ridiculous. Numb in the brain, she muttered, "I was not terrorized, Zane."

Boris pushed his hand away. "And I did not attempt to come into her home uninvited."

"I don't believe you."

Thanos asked, "I think you need to back off, Zane."

Blank disbelief filled Zane. "You still champion him? After what I've just told you?"

Thanos shrugged. "I don't know about that. I need to give this all some thought. But Boris wasn't here last night, that I do know."

Tamara moved to Zane's side, giving him her silent, unquestioning support. He accepted it by taking her hand. "How?"

With another shrug, this one of apology, Thanos admitted, "Because he was with me till very late."

"With you?" Then with more suspicion, "Doing what?"

"Having drinks, sharing conversation." Glancing at the aunts, back at Tamara, Thanos winced. "Planning your future."

A red haze clouded his vision. Through set teeth, Zane growled very softly, "*Planning her future?*"

With his own show of bluster, Thanos said, "It's an uncle's duty to see that—"

Zane interrupted him. "Did I plan into this future?"

Thanos cut a quick look at Boris, and that more than answered his question. "I don't fucking believe this."

"Zane!"

The two aunts looked ready to swoon. Thanos scowled darkly. "You'll watch your mouth, young man."

"Yeah, right. I'll watch my mouth while you try to push her off to this joker?"

Boris sputtered. "I've had just about enough of you. I agree with Ms. Tremayne. You should go."

Zane's eyes glittered. "Why don't you put me out?" His hands curled into fists, the need for physical violence boiling up inside him.

Boris, looking uncertain, turned to Thanos.

And then Tamara was there, standing in front of him, a small smile on her beautiful face. She touched his chest, his face.

"Zane, I really would like it if you'd calm down."

His jaw felt too tight to speak. Through set teeth, he repeated, "I'm not leaving here."

"Of course you're not."

Boris cleared his throat. "I thought perhaps we could spend the day together, Ms. Tremayne. Your uncle tells me your Sundays are free."

Her gaze still locked on Zane's, she said, "My uncle is wrong. My Sunday is very taken."

"Well," Eva mused briskly as she patted her streaked black and gray hair back into a tidy bun. "It's apparent she's made up her mind."

"But she works so hard."

Zane drew a calming breath and turned to Olga. "What did you say?"

"She works so hard to make ends meet. And Boris is rich, so . . ."

Zane shook his head. "You're worried about her?"

"Yes, of course."

Eva nodded in agreement, and Thanos looked grim.

"You're all so concerned, yet you'd leave her alone with him?" He nodded toward Boris with the same regard he'd give a worm.

"This is outrageous." Looking to Thanos to back him up, Boris said, "He's spewing outright slander. You know I didn't come here last night."

Every muscle on Zane's body bunched. He wanted, quite simply, to drag Boris outside and beat the hell of him. Not just because he'd been troubling Tamara, but because her family had chosen him.

Too bad.

Thoughtful, Thanos scratched his beard. "But someone apparently was here."

Tamara patted Zane's chest and turned, then she leaned into him until her bottom was snuggled up against his groin. Damn. Zane knew she only wanted to offer support, to share some of her own calm, but if she kept that up, he'd be embarrassing them both.

She said to Thanos, "Someone shut off my electric and tried to waltz right in." Here she glared at Boris. "He had a key."

Olga and Eva looked at each other, then at Thanos. Thanos said, "We didn't give him a key."

"Of course you didn't," Boris agreed. "Why, Ms. Tremayne and I haven't even gotten properly acquainted." He unwisely added, "Yet."

Surging with intense fury—partially based on jealousy and possessiveness—Zane reached past Tamara and caught Boris by this shirtfront. He rattled him like a paper bag. *"You're not getting anywhere near her."*

"Zane!"

He was damn sick and tired of her remonstrating with him. With Boris gasping for air at the end of his arm, Zane said, *"What?"*

"You told me to control my volatile tendencies."

"Yeah. So?" Boris made a strangling sound and Zane shook him again. Olga and Eva watched, like captivated viewers of a train wreck, while Thanos appeared pensive over the whole thing, unmoved by Boris's reddening complexion.

"So," Tamara said in exasperation, "you have to get a grip. This isn't going to solve anything."

"It'll make me feel a helluva lot better."

She actually laughed. In the middle of everything happening, with her family trying to hoist her off on a criminal and the criminal leering at her with lascivious intent, she managed to laugh. Damn, she was something else.

And she was his.

Zane let Boris drop, gagging and gasping and cursing, back to his feet. "All right," he said, addressing Thanos, "if it wasn't Boris who broke in here last night, then who the hell do you think it was?"

"All I know for certain is that he didn't get the key from me." Apparently affronted by the very idea, Thanos added, "I would never be so careless with my niece."

They all ignored Boris as they considered the possibilities. As Joe had said, it wasn't always as obvious as it seemed, though no way was Zane ruling out Boris as a probable.

Olga clutched at her throat and Eva pressed her hands together. Almost in unison, they cried, "Uncle Hubert!"

Boris, having regained a modicum of his aplomb, rasped, "Who the hell is Uncle Hubert?"

Zane smirked at him. "The family apparition, of course."

Boris cast on him a look of scorn. "Hogwash."

Just that easily, he alienated Eva and Olga.

Zane, seeing his opportunity, turned to the quailing women. He slipped his arm around Olga's frail shoulders and patted Eva's delicately veined hands. "Not a ghost this time, ladies. We saw him running off. He's flesh and blood." Zane deliberately didn't mention Joe; the fewer people who knew about him, the more effective he could be.

"Someone really did force his way in here?" In a quick turnaround, Eva and Olga rushed to Tamara. "Our poor baby! Are you okay?"

While the women were occupied smothering Tamara with concern, Zane narrowed his eyes on Boris. "Get lost."

"I'm ready to leave," he announced in cultured tones. "But I'll be back."

Zane opened his mouth, and before his rejoinder could reach any ears, Tamara said, "Not without an appointment."

And Boris agreed, "Whatever it takes."

E I G H T E E N

Luckily for Zane, the customer's conversation was sufficiently mundane that he didn't need to pay close attention. Truth was, he could barely think at all and the condition got worse every day.

For two weeks now, Tamara's business had been booming. Not only was Boris the bore still hanging around, doggedly it seemed, but Arkin Devane showed up more often than ever, as did a dozen other men. Though a scattering of women also called, her clientele consisted largely of the male persuasion. It made him nuts.

Tamara had done no more than present her own naturally sensual, seductive self to the world, and the male populace had fallen to its knees.

As the customer's monologue drew to a close, Zane handed him a receipt, bade him farewell, and went to peer out the window. Two women and a man loitered on the walk in front of the old house.

The upside to all the attention Tamara had garnered was that her financial situation was more stable than ever. She might even recover her losses. The Realtor had presented her with another offer for the house, but it still wasn't quite as much as she had countered. Because of all her good fortune of late, she'd been comfortable in negotiating for a higher price. Zane didn't even want to consider the day when the offer might be good enough. There was no way he was letting her go, even if he had to take out a loan and buy her damn building himself.

But he wasn't stupid, so he hadn't told her that.

The downside to all her added business was that she worked more hours. Which meant she had less time to spend with him. He'd actually cut back on his hours, not that it had done him much good. Her days were busy.

But her nights . . . well, her nights belonged to him.

Smiling, Zane pictured her in his mind as she'd looked that morning, with her green eyes bright, only lightly made up, her blond hair bouncing with natural curl, and her boundless energy.

God, he loved her energy. The way she made love with him each evening, and most mornings, boggled his mind. Other than his one overly emotional slipup, he'd used protection every time. Because he cared so much about her, he forced himself into fair play.

Tamara had made even that especially tantalizing, by learning how to put the condom on him—slowly. So slowly that he wondered if he was a little masochistic for enjoying the torture.

She was creative and, in the tradition of her heritage, free-spirited. They'd made a rather sexy game of the journal, trying everything the author suggested, and embellishing on a few.

More and more Zane wondered about the woman who'd patiently organized so many erotic details—if she'd died happy, if her life had been all it could be. Did she write out of a need to share her happiness, or to try to help others find what she couldn't?

One night, after he'd loved Tamara into near exhaustion, she'd voiced the same concerns. Though they'd never met the woman, her journal had given them great insight into her personality. Her caring and loving nature had come through on paper, and had endeared her to them. Whoever she might have been, Zane felt sure she'd been a very special woman with a very large heart and a zest for life and love.

Now that he held Tamara every night, he couldn't imagine sleeping without her. He hadn't mentioned leaving her home, and neither had she. He'd simply picked up more items from his place as he needed them, and now all his shower and shaving supplies were in Tamara's bathroom, and her closet held a good portion of his clothes.

Sometimes, in the early evening, he'd sit in bed, pretending to read, and watch her work on the computer. She was intense then, her slim brows narrowed in thought and her face, in the blue light of the computer, endearingly studious. When she'd finally shut off the computer, he'd put aside his book and open his arms.

A new alarm system had been installed, and a floodlight mounted on the side of his building was aimed at her lot. There had been no more run-ins with masked men in the middle of night, no more dead rats or small fires. Zane had no reason to remain with her except that he needed her; he hoped she understood that.

It still enraged him that Boris had an alibi. It didn't matter in the long run, because Zane wasn't convinced that Boris was innocent. Perhaps he hadn't been there that particular night, but it was possible, even likely, that he'd paid someone to do his dirty work. Until Joe actually caught someone, Zane wouldn't be able to let down his guard.

"Brooding again, I see."

Zane wanted to groan. He'd "hired" Joe as an assistant to give him a reason to be close to Tamara, to snoop around and check into things. But having him in the store all the time was trying. The women who usually flirted with Zane now divided their time with Joe. Zane didn't mind on a personal level because Tamara was the only woman who interested him. It just nettled that Joe might think he was stealing the women's attention.

"I see you forgot your name badge again."

Joe grinned, unrepentant, then rubbed at the left side of his chest.

"Hell, I nearly pierced my nipple with the damn thing. Get a stick-on name tag and I'll wear it, but no more pins, thank you. Besides, I don't need it. Everyone knows me already."

True enough. The women whispered his name in hushed excitement and the men grumbled about Joe's policy of "ladies first." It didn't matter how long a male customer had been waiting, if a woman walked in, Joe moved to assist her. He was the worst sort of employee, but Zane wasn't about to fire him.

"So what has you mooning this time?" Joe asked.

Zane moved away from him. "Just anticipating closing time." Which was still several hours away, damn it.

Seeing through Zane's lie, Joe said, "She's a sweetie, I'll give you that. It'd be hard not to think about her."

Zane wondered if Joe had his own mind-reading abilities. "I can do without your experienced opinion on the matter."

Joe laughed. "You wanna hear what I've found out about your buddy Boris, while the crowd is gone?"

Zane jerked around to face Joe. "You've found out something?"

"Of course. What, you thought I was a totally ineffectual snoop?" He snorted. "That doesn't say much for you, since you hired me."

"You've been here all morning and it's damn near lunchtime now! Why the hell didn't you say something sooner?"

Joe shrugged. Along with not wearing a name tag, he refused to dress up for his bogus job, preferring to stick with jeans and T-shirts and boots so scuffed they had to be ten years old. His hair was too long, his earring too damn noticeable, more often than not he forgot or refused to shave—and the female customers adored him. It was a good thing Joe didn't know anything about computers, or he'd likely have accepted some of the inquiries on home service.

"Your place is busier than I expected." He clapped Zane on the shoulder. "You run a helluva business, cousin. I'm impressed."

Zane sliced his hand through the air, dismissing the compliment in favor of hearing more important news. "What did you find out?"

Propping his hip on the counter next to the cash register, Joe retrieved a knife from his pocket. He flicked it open, then closed—an annoying habit he had. "Boris is married."

Of all the things Zane had expected, that wasn't anywhere on the list. "No shit? The bastard has a wife?"

"A wealthy wife. Not that Boris comes from a poor background. His family was well-to-do, but lost a lot in the last ten years or so. I gather he married as a way to restore the family financial standing."

Pacing, Zane muttered, "This is incredible."

"And he's not from Romania, as he supposedly told Tamara's uncle, but his wife is. Very Old World. Her family dates back to some impressive and influential names."

I'll kill him, was Zane's immediate thought. But first he had to find out what Boris wanted with Tamara. Then he could work him over. He flexed his hands, imagining them around Boris's thick neck. "What do you think he's up to?"

"Can't tell you that, but I can tell you that his wife's family is not the type who'd take kindly to news of his activities." Joe flipped the knife open again, polished the blade along the denim on his left thigh, and held it up to the fluorescent lights to admire the shine. "If they knew he'd been sniffing after another woman, the proverbial crapola would hit the fan."

"You're sure he and his wife aren't separated?"

"Nope. I could find no mention of it, and this isn't the type of family who puts up with separation." He closed the knife and slid it back into his pocket. Hopping off the counter, he crossed his arms and said, "You marry, you stay married. Finito."

"I've got a really bad feeling about this."

"Rightfully so. It proves without a doubt that you're dead-on, that Boris is unprincipled to say the least, and up to something sinister at the most."

"He's going to be seeing her again today." And Zane intended to be there. Damn, at least now he had something solid to use against Boris. Surely this would make her relatives detest him as much as Zane did.

"Yeah, well, I'd put an end to that real quick."

Zane flashed Joe an irritated glance. "I tried reasoning with her. She's convinced that as long as Boris is minding his manners and paying for her time, she should indulge her relatives by pretending to give him an opportunity to woo her."

Joe shook his head in a pitying way.

Because his attitude mirrored Zane's own, there wasn't much he could say.

Of course, that didn't stop Joe. "You should know better than to attempt to reason with the female brain, Zane. Take the guy aside, break his nose, make him understand that he's to get lost and stay lost." Joe cracked his knuckles. "And if you're not up to it, I'm game."

It was no less than what Zane wanted to do, but he found himself laughing. "You've become a bloodthirsty cynic, you know that? Besides, this isn't the Stone Age. Women are allowed their own thoughts and choices."

"More's the pity." Joe shook his head. "If I was ever gullible enough to fall in love—which is doubtful—it'd damn sure be with a woman who knew how to listen."

Before Zane could react to that by knocking Joe on his ass, a laugh sounded behind them. They both turned, and found Cole and Chase standing there. Chase pointed at Joe. "You're going to eat those words one day."

Cole nodded. "I just hope I'm around to see it."

"Not me." Zane hefted a box of keyboards and carried it to an empty shelf. "I don't want to be anywhere around. It's a bitch to get blood out of clothes, and it's for certain, the woman in question would flay him alive."

Totally unconcerned, Joe laughed. "What are you two rogues doing wandering loose today? Where are your little ladies?"

Zane knew Joe had spent quite a bit of time visiting with Cole and Chase at the bar. Mack and Jessica had gone there several nights to join in. They all got along well, and Mack had laughed, explaining how the women at the bar had doted on Joe. Zane didn't care how many women chased him, as long as he didn't go after Tamara.

"Actually," Cole said—and Zane felt his brother's gaze boring into him—"our wives are visiting Tamara, along with Mack."

Zane dropped the box as he spun around. "What?"

"Yep. Sophie was pretty annoyed that you hadn't brought her around to meet the family yet, and she got Jessica and Allison all riled, and like a female militant group, they headed off. We decided to follow along just for the hell of it."

Zane marched to the window and looked out. It was quiet in front of the Gypsy shop now, no more customers standing around. Were they all inside already? What would his darling sisters-in-law say about him?

Since marrying into the family, they'd taunted him endlessly for his bachelor ways, his overindulgence in female attention. And Zane had encouraged them by being more outrageous than ever. He enjoyed his sisters-in-law and loved bantering with them.

Would they blather on to Tamara about his disreputable ways?

Damn, he didn't want the fragile bond he'd forged with Tamara disrupted. She'd forgiven him for his outburst with her relatives, especially considering they'd paid heed to him and had quit pressuring her about the damn wig and dark contacts. If anything, they were doubly pleased that she could attract so much attention without artificial devices.

She'd also quit pushing him away at every turn. He wouldn't go so far as to say she'd accepted his help graciously. But she'd only frowned a little when he installed the spotlight and aimed it her way. She'd complained that it'd shine in her bedroom window at night.

Zane remembered her slow smile when he'd told her that he liked being able to see her clearly when they were in bed together. She trusted him with her body; she was beginning to trust him with her pride. Soon, she'd trust him with her heart.

He said abruptly, uncaring who paid heed, "Watch the place for me," and headed for the door. He had to get over there to make certain no one got her thinking too hard on his less sterling qualities.

Cole laughed and met him at the door. "Not me! If you're running over there, so am I."

"Why?"

"To watch, of course."

"Me too," Chase added, hot on their heels.

Zane stopped, frustrated, wondering what his customers would think if he simply locked his door for a few hours.

Leaning against a wall, Joe stretched and put his arms behind his head. "Go on, Zane. You can leave everything to me."

Appalled by the idea, Zane said, "You've got to be kidding."

Cole and Chase caught his arms and started out, dragging Zane backward. "Joe will do fine."

"Ha!"

"Do you want to visit Tamara or not?"

Joe stood there, utterly confident as usual. He even went so far as to grin. "No need to thank me, Zane. You know I'm always glad to help out. But send over some lunch, will ya? I'm starved."

"We'll see to it," Cole assured him. "It's the least Zane can do."

Zane considered knocking his brothers' heads together, but then he thought of Tamara getting her ears filled, and he relented. "At least let me walk in under my own steam."

They released him, but not without a few more good-natured jibes. Considering how he'd riled them when they were falling in love, Zane figured he had it coming.

They marched next door, and Cole's long stride suited Zane's impatience just fine.

In an offhanded voice, Chase asked, "Ready to give in to the Winston curse yet?"

Zane reached Tamara's door with the gaudy painted sign and flashing light. He turned the knob. "I gave in two weeks ago, if you want the gory details. Now I just need her to succumb." He walked into the foyer with the sound of Chase's and Cole's boisterous laughter behind him. Damn fools. Didn't they understand that this was serious stuff?

His female relatives were clustered around the counter when he entered. Mack stood close by, holding his wife in front of him, and they had Tamara encircled. The music from the CD player had been turned low to allow for easy conversation.

Smiling, flushed with pleasure and unrestrained laughter, Tamara was a sight to steal his breath. Today she had her hair pulled back on one side with an enamel comb. Dangling earrings brushed her shoulders. She still wore the enticing, flirty jewelry and sexy, flowing skirts. But her makeup was different, subtle, her lips a glossy peach instead of bright red, her long lashes dusty brown rather than inky black.

He liked seeing her like this, a part of his family, a part of his life.

Chase and Cole shoved past him, nearly knocking him over.

Jessica noticed them first, and she turned her big chocolate brown eyes on Zane.

Oh hell, he thought, and braced himself for a raucous joke of some kind that would undermine all the progress he'd made with Tamara. Instead, Jessica winked, then looked over her shoulder at Mack. His doting brother kissed her temple.

Allison, still laughing, turned and held out a hand to Chase. He went to her without missing a step. Those two, it often seemed, spoke on some private plane that no one else could hear. Zane had always thought it a little strange, but now he envied them their rapport.

Cole didn't wait for an invite. He strode forward and looped his arms around Sophie's waist, settling his big hands on her still-flat belly with paternal affection. Sophie positively glowed.

Zane swallowed a lump. Damn, he wanted what they all had. He hadn't at first, only because he hadn't fully understood the completeness of it, the depth of emotion. He knew they were happy, knew marriage suited them, but he'd thought himself different, thought he needed more time to enjoy life and his freedom. He was a real dumbass on occasion.

Tamara looked up and her beautiful green eyes lit at the sight of him. "Zane! I thought you were working."

She separated herself from the group and came to him. Her smile was warm, and the bells on her ankles tinkled. She made his heart race, his pulse quicken. Aware of their amused audience, Zane restrained himself and indulged only in a light kiss.

Tamara stared up at him. "What's wrong?" she asked in a soft whisper. "You're fretting or something."

Her ability to understand him no longer seemed threatening. In fact, he counted on it, so she'd know he was sincere in his declarations—when he got around to declaring himself.

"I missed you," he murmured.

He heard Chase snort. "More like he felt compelled to come here and defend his honor."

Bemused, Tamara asked, "Defend your honor from what?"

"Not what," Cole said, ignoring his wife's attempts to hush him, "but who. Our wives do like to give him a hard time."

Sophie elbowed Cole hard enough to make him grunt. "That's not true! We *adore* Zane."

Mack, ignoring his sister-in-law, added, "Blissfully content married women refuse to believe that any man can be happy without a wife to keep him that way."

Looking like an imp, Jessica said, "But Zane's so sexy and sweet. He can't help but attract scores of women." Mack promptly growled, attacking her neck in a tender assault that had her laughing. She amended her statement. "But not as sexy as Mack! No way!"

Allison peered over the top of her glasses and addressed the assembled group. "Chase is by far the sexiest, but that's beside the point. We all adore Zane and want nothing more than to see him . . . happy."

Wondering if he should strangle the lot of them, Zane snarled,

"Then you should be deliriously satisfied, because I *am* happy." At least he would be if they didn't scare her off.

To his surprise, Tamara sighed. "It must be wonderful to have such a large family."

Damn, there she went again, ripping his guts out.

Cole asked, "Was it lonely growing up alone?"

Just then a door opened and the black curtain moved. Luna and Aunt Olga stepped out, two clients behind them.

Tamara smiled at her aunt. "I had my aunts and uncle to keep me company."

Olga grinned at her, then sent an "I-told-you-we-loved-her" look toward Zane.

He ground his teeth together, but no one noticed with the buzz of the two clients setting future appointments and saying their good-byes.

Zane had a few moments to consider Olga's continued aloofness toward him. She was still a little ticked, but she had obviously listened. All three of Tamara's relatives now appeared to support her more, encouraging her in her uniqueness. They even claimed to like Zane well enough, yet they forever sang their litany of praises for Boris.

He forced himself to smile at Olga now. "It's nice to see you again, Olga."

"I'm working today," she informed him loftily. "We decided Tamara needed more help, especially with all the added business." Her pointy chin went into the air, her black eyes challenging. "And I wanted to give her some time off. She deserves it."

Zane looked down at Tamara in time to see her grin. "It's true," she said. "They've been wonderful."

Luna, looking as outrageously delicious as ever with her golden brown eyes alight and her mink-colored hair loose, said, "She even has time for lunch." Then she winked. "Of course, your relatives have already claimed her, and invited the others to join them."

Zane was curious as to what others, when the door chimed and Thanos and Eva walked in. He'd wanted a few minutes alone with Tamara to talk to her about Boris. Once she knew the scoundrel was married, she'd surely tell her relatives and they'd quickly toss him off the prospective beau list. But now it looked as though he wouldn't have a chance, not with his brothers and sisters-in-law organizing a damn tea party.

Introductions were made. Olga and Luna volunteered to stay behind and watch the shop in case anyone dropped in, and the rest prepared to go up to Tamara's home to dine. Zane remembered Joe and his request for food. He whispered to Tamara that he had to feed him, and Luna overheard.

Zane wondered if Luna had super powers, because it seemed the softer he spoke, the more clearly she understood him.

"A new assistant, Zane?" she asked.

Though he'd told Tamara to keep Joe's identity secret, he had half-expected her to confide in Luna anyway. He was pleased that she hadn't. "Yes, just hired in the last few weeks."

Luna's lips curled with feminine curiosity. "I'm going to run out to the deli. Want me to stop over there and see what he wants?"

Zane already knew what Joe would want from Luna, but if ever there was a woman who could hold her own, it was Luna Clark. He smiled, very pleased at the prospect, and said, "That'd be great. Thanks."

She gave him a suspicious look, but smiled. "No problem."

Zane expected to order pizza for their lunch, but he wasn't overly surprised to see his sisters-in-law had taken care of it. The feast they supplied was more like dinner than lunch, with carry-out fried chicken, potato salad, biscuits and honey, and a chocolate cake for dessert. They refused to let Tamara do a thing—other than her job. They wanted to know their horoscopes, have their palms read, and Sophie even asked if Tamara could tell her the sex of her baby.

Sitting close beside Zane, Tamara laughed. "I can't predict the future. All I can tell you is that you don't really care if it's a boy or a girl, you just want a healthy baby."

Astonished, Sophie stared at Tamara and said with awe, "How did you know?"

"You're the type of woman who loves with all her heart. That doesn't leave room for conditions. Besides, you now have a son, and Allison has a daughter, and you're content with that mix."

There were murmured agreements among Zane's relatives as to Tamara's accuracy, and prideful boasts by Tamara's relatives for the same reason.

Excited, Sophie stuck out her hand. "And my palm? What does that tell you?"

Tamara studied her hand. She glanced at Zane, then around the room, before tilting her head at Sophie again. "This won't embarrass you?"

Nonplussed by the question, Sophie drew back. "Am I going to be found lacking?"

"Of course not." Tamara inhaled, then lightly traced a fingertip over the very base of each of Sophie's fingers, where they met with her palm. "This is the E zone. You see how this area is plumper and softer than the other areas of your fingers? Well, that means you're a person who loves to touch, and especially loves the pleasures of the body."

Cole choked on his raspberry tea. Sophie gave a twittering, pleased, but self-conscious laugh.

In typical brotherly fashion, Mack and Chase saluted Cole.

"You work in a boutique, right?"

Sophie nodded, wide-eyed.

"That's a little unusual. Generally speaking, a woman with hands like yours would be more likely to be a massage therapist or have some other type of physical contact work."

Cole said, "Well, she does like to—*omphf*."

Sophie glared at him, and in a stage whisper said, "That is *private*, Cole Winston."

He laughed, set down his glass, and scooped her into his lap. "All right, sweetheart."

Since they were all used to Cole cuddling Sophie, most especially when she was pregnant, the brothers and their wives ignored them. Thanos and Eva, however, along with Tamara, couldn't help but smile at their affectionate display.

Jessica stuck her hand out. "I'm next."

And so it went, each of them taking turns having Tamara read their palms. Thanos and Eva added their own colorful and mystic predictions to Tamara's study-based readings, and they all acted like old friends.

Zane took pleasure in watching Tamara charm his family. It put him that much closer to winning her over.

He supposed he owed his sisters-in-law gratitude rather than suspicion for their impromptu visit. When Allison gave him an inconspicuous thumbs-up, he knew he was right. Damn, he was a lucky cuss to have such a wonderful family.

Soon, they'd be Tamara's family, too.

NINETEEN

Tamara breathed a sigh of relief after everyone had gone. As enjoyable as it had been, she was impatient to spend some time alone with Zane. She'd made a decision that she hoped to discuss with him.

They walked Zane's relatives back downstairs to the door. Luna had returned, but her lunch was left uneaten on the counter while she fumed, pacing around the shop. Tamara and Zane shared a look of concern.

"What's the matter?" Tamara asked, never having seen her assistant in such a state.

Luna's smile was gloating, wicked. "Nothing. *Now*."

Zane winced. "Uh-oh. Does this little upset of yours have anything to do with Joe?"

She snorted loudly. "I wouldn't allow that moron to upset me." Then she stormed into the backroom and slammed the door. Hard.

Tamara cleared her throat. *Oh dear*. She certainly hoped Joe had survived whatever had passed between them.

Cole put his arm around Sophie and broke the uncomfortable silence. "We need to get going. I have some new guys working for me, but they haven't entirely got the hang of it yet. Leaving them alone at lunchtime was iffy."

Mack grinned. "We had a teacher's in-service day, so I was able to go out for lunch. But I have conferences starting soon, so I have to go, too."

"And I have a woman showing up in half an hour for her portrait." Jessica embraced Tamara and whispered in her ear, "He comes from good stock. Hang on to him."

Not knowing what to say to that, Tamara laughed. But Jessica's hug galvanized the others and she got passed around from person to person as they explained the jobs and people they needed to get back to. Being a businesswoman herself, she understood. It was apparent they'd taken time from their busy lives to meet her.

Did that mean anything? A glance at Zane, who wore a vacuous smile, didn't tell her a thing.

Luna returned to the counter. She went about business as usual, but she still looked a little rattled when Arkin Devane came in a few minutes early. Tamara promised him she'd be right there, and because he was a regular and knew the routine, she sent him ahead to the room to wait for her.

"Will you be okay out here?" she asked Luna. "Or would you rather I have Aunt Olga take over?"

Olga, who was busy dusting all the knickknacks scattered about, looked hopeful.

Luna scoffed at the concern. "I'm perfectly fine. Perfectly. Fine." She added, miffed, "I don't know why you'd think I'm not."

"Well," Tamara admitted with some humor, "you have little bits of what looks like egg salad in your hair, and you keep cursing under your breath."

Luna snatched a hand through her hair. "Well damn! I thought it all went on him." She looked at her fingers, now holding bits of boiled egg, and made a sound of disgust. "Must have splattered on me, too."

"Him?" Zane asked, full of interest.

"Your new hire." She made a face, and her eyes flashed. "I threw his sandwich at him, but only because he deserved it."

Grinning, Zane said, "I'm sure he did."

Tamara had the suspicion that Zane was thoroughly enjoying the mental picture of Luna attacking Joe. She bit back a laugh.

Luna sent Zane her haughtiest look. "If he's worth whatever you're paying him, he's cleaning the floor right now." So saying, Luna again stalked off to the tiny bathroom in the backroom.

"Good heavens," Tamara muttered, but she could barely hear herself above Zane's laughter. "What in the world do you think happened?"

Still chuckling, Zane wiped his eyes. "Joe happened, and God, I'd give a hundred bucks to have been there."

"Zane Winston, you're terrible. He's your cousin."

"And he's entirely too cocksure of himself where women are concerned. You know, if I had to venture a guess, I'd say Joe likely acted like himself and Luna rightfully took exception."

"He can't be that bad."

Zane hugged her. "Sweetheart, I swear, he's a good deal worse."

The door chimed again, and this time Tamara groaned. "Darn it, why is everyone coming early? I wanted a chance to talk to you."

Zane smiled down at her. Those warm, intimate feelings of his drifted over her with the coziness of a posh blanket.

"They're early," he whispered, "because, like me, they're eager to see you."

"Oh Zane." Words of affection, of . . . *love*, were just about to escape her when another, colder voice broke in.

"I see I'm interrupting yet again."

Teeth bared in a parody of a smile, Zane turned. "Boris."

Boris looked past Zane to Tamara. With his normal pompous disregard for propriety, he said, "I trust you're ready for me?"

Tamara's smile wasn't much better than Zane's. "You're early, so you'll have to wait for a bit."

That brought him down a peg. He scowled in disbelief and disappointment. "But I had hoped . . ."

Zane rumbled with anger. "Why don't you just leave, if you don't have time to wait till your damn appointment?"

Tamara wished he *would* leave. She needed to talk to Zane, and with Boris's entrance, the need became nearly desperate. She wasn't sure what was wrong, or what Boris wanted, but she thought talking to Zane about it might help clear things up.

She trusted him, she realized with some consternation. In the past, she never would have entrusted someone else, relied on someone else to help her understand a situation and deal with it. But Zane had worked his way into her life, into her confidence.

Into her heart.

Now, she couldn't imagine not sharing with him. The sudden insight was both disturbing and oddly liberating.

She was anxious to share her new insights with Zane, to tell him her astounding revelations, but of course Boris didn't go away. Beyond her own emotional upheaval, she picked up on Boris's determination, his hard insistence, the darkness of his thoughts that seeped into her mind like thunderclouds.

He pretended an indifference she knew to be the direct opposite of what he really felt. His smile was a barely veiled sneer. "I'll wait, of course."

A wave of sickness made her suck in her breath.

Zane quickly put his arm around her. "Are you okay?"

"Yes. I . . . I'm fine." She fashioned a smile, as much to reassure Zane as to fool Boris. She didn't want him to know what she felt. God, she'd figured a few things out only that morning, and now Boris was back and everything was coming to a head. She had to talk to Zane.

Bringing her attention back to him, Zane asked, "Do you need to sit down?"

"No." She couldn't take the chance of alerting Boris by acting like a fainting dolt now, so she searched her brain for some innocuous bit of conversation, something everyday and mundane. She came upon the perfect tidbit. "I wanted to talk to you about the journal."

The reflection of sensual, satisfying memories plain in his dark eyes, Zane murmured, "Is that so? One of my favorite topics." His smile gentle, he added, "Planning something new? What page are you up to?"

A wave of heat flooded her cheeks. Boris had taken a seat on the sofa in the foyer, but he made no pretense of ignoring them. His attention was openly, fixedly, set on their conversation.

That was fine. At least he wouldn't suspect anything when she led Zane upstairs.

Tamara cleared her throat. "Actually, I was thinking of giving the book away."

She'd shocked him. Zane frowned as he said, "Give it away? Why?"

Since Boris knew nothing of the book or what it contained, she felt safe saying, "To another client. I've been sharing parts of the book with him, and I think that may be the main reason he's coming around so much. If I give him the book . . ."

Zane caught on. He took her arm and steered her out of hearing distance of Boris. He moved her over by the stairs that led to her rooms. "Arkin Devane?"

"Yes." With complete honesty, she admitted, "I feel horrible taking his money and his time when all I do is relay parts of the journal to him. It's not fair to charge him for that, because it's not my advice or insight, it's straight from someone else."

"He gets the information from you, though."

"Yes. But . . ." Tamara hesitated. Zane gave her so much, it was time she became more honest with him. He deserved at least that much. It took a fortifying breath for her to be able to say, "He's in love."

"With you?"

She laughed at his bristling annoyance. "No, not with me. With someone else." She put her hand on his neck and smiled up at him. "Now that I'm so . . . happy, I want everyone else to be that happy, too."

A heartbeat passed while Zane searched her face, then he gathered her close. "So you're happy, huh?"

"Remarkably so."

She felt his smile against her temple. "With me?"

Leaning back to see his face, she nodded. "I didn't know it was possible to be this happy."

His expression softened, grew intent. "Damn, I wish I was alone with you right now."

"Me, too." Impishly, she reminded him, "There's tonight, of course."

He became arrested, then groaned. "Don't."

"Don't what?"

Laughing under his breath, he said, "Don't look at me like that, don't talk like that. God, you'll make it impossible for me to walk."

Delighted with his open response to her, she said, "You affect me the same way."

"Damn it." He closed his eyes and said, "That's it. One more word and you'll miss the next three appointments."

Tamara laughed. "You're so easy." Then, to get them back on subject, she pointed out, "You see? We don't need the journal anymore. Don't you think we should share it? That the author would have wanted us to share it?"

"Maybe. But I've grown partial to it, you know. I feel . . . protective. I don't want to give it to just anyone."

She smiled at this further proof of how sensitive Zane could be. "Yes, I know. But it'll be in good hands. Arkin's a wonderful man, and I'm sure he'll feel the same as we do."

Zane looked at her mouth. "You're sure it's some other woman he's fixated on?"

"Yes. I keep telling you and Luna that he's not really here for me.

It's because I understand him and his shyness and I have the book to help him."

"Well, God knows I'm all for weeding out your gentlemen callers."

Tamara couldn't help but laugh again. She found it hysterically funny whenever Zane pretended to be jealous.

Her laugh died in midbreath. "Oh no."

"What is it?" Zane caught her arms. Alarm darkened his eyes. "Tamara?"

"You don't sense it?"

"Sense what, damn it?"

Urgently, feeling like a fool for not realizing the truth sooner, she said, "We need to go upstairs for a minute."

Zane's bafflement was plain, but he didn't argue with her. He turned to Luna. "We'll be right back. Can you hold down the fort?"

After one long, searching glance at Tamara's face, she gave Zane a salute. "Not a problem."

They were barely up the stairs and through the door before Tamara said, "Boris is the one."

"What one? The guy who's been trying to ruin you?"

"Yes."

Grabbing her shoulders, Zane barked. "Did he say something to you? Did he touch you?"

"Shh. Calm down, Zane." Tamara bit her lip in slight uncertainty, but then she shook her head. This was Zane. She trusted him, and he'd never laughed at her. Not once. "He hasn't done or said anything. I just . . . I *feel* it."

Zane didn't allow himself to relax. Tension vibrated off Tamara, as did her hesitancy. But she'd trusted him, confided in him. "How long have you known?"

"Almost from the beginning. I couldn't be certain, but I knew something about him didn't seem right. Whenever he was around, I felt his . . . evil. He was so easy to read—"

A new anger washed through him, one constructed of jealousy. "I thought other than family, I was the only man you could read." He'd assumed, based on what Tamara had told him, that she cared about him whether she admitted it or not, and that was what facilitated her ability to know his feelings. "I know damn good and well you don't care about Sandor."

"Of course not. He makes me nauseous, the emotions in him are so black and ugly and thick. But that's precisely why I can read him. Strong emotions, of any kind, are sometimes apparent to me. It's just that most people don't feel that strongly."

"You're losing me, Tamara."

She rubbed her forehead as she considered how best to explain. "It's like with your relatives. Sophie is easy to know because her feelings for Cole are so powerful. And the same is true of Cole. Love sort of pours off him when he looks at his wife, when he looks at you or your brothers."

"That's how you knew Sophie didn't have a preference for the baby?"

"Yes. And it's how I know Arkin Devane is in love, and how I know your cousin Joe is basically a very good, honorable man, and how I know . . ." she drew a steadying breath ". . . that Boris is a very bad man."

Zane propped his hands on his hips and dropped his head forward to think. "If you knew this, if you could feel what kind of man he was, why the hell did you let him hang around?"

"I wasn't certain if he was the one who'd done all those things to my shop. Sometimes I felt him, but sometimes, like the night of the break-in, and the night I was followed, it was different somehow. Fractured. Not as strong or as negative." She shook her head. "Not Boris."

"Maybe he hired someone to do those things for him, but it still doesn't explain why the hell you didn't say something to me sooner."

"I knew if I did, you'd get all macho and protective and you'd try to put a stop to his visits. Then I'd never be able to find out what he was after."

Zane fought the urge to shake her. "You still don't know, do you?"

Tamara was shaking her head when a voice from behind her said calmly, "Perhaps I'll enlighten you."

In one swift movement, Zane had Tamara at his back. And then he saw the gun, a polished thirty-eight, in Boris's meaty hand. Fear tightened his throat. If Tamara got hurt . . . He felt her pressed against him, felt her quickened breath on his shoulder.

She wouldn't be hurt. No matter what, he'd make sure of that.

Boris must have come up the outside stairs, Zane realized. It was the only other entrance. But the alarm should have gone off. . . .

Tamara went on tiptoe to whisper in his ear, "I didn't set the alarm.

We were here, and there were visitors, and I, well, I only use it at night or when I'm away."

Zane wanted to groan. Instead he asked. "What the hell do you want, Sandor?"

"Why, to set the record straight, of course." Waving the gun, he motioned them away from the stairway leading to the shop and quietly stepped past them to close the door. Zane's heartbeat stuttered and nearly died each and every time the barrel pointed at Tamara. He would not let this maniac hurt her.

She said, her voice laced with nervousness as she peered around him, "Don't you dare be a hero, Zane Winston." Her hands knotted in the back of his shirt and she shook him. "I mean it."

Boris laughed. "A hero? My dear, he can hardly do battle with a bullet."

"I asked you what you wanted." Zane spoke in order to keep Boris's attention away from Tamara.

"Well, first, I wasn't the one who broke into your home. And no, Mr. Sherlock, I didn't hire anyone to break in, either. That would have been too risky."

Zane could barely move with Tamara clinging to him like a vine, but that didn't stop his mind from churning. Boris was older, heavier. Zane was quick, his reactions razor-sharp. Adrenaline pumped through him. He could take Boris. He might get a bullet in the bargain, but that was a chance he was willing to take. "You think I'm going to believe you?" he asked, buying himself more time.

"Why would I lie?" Boris acted almost cavalier about the situation. "You see, I did start the fire and cause the flood. It was easy enough to pay a disreputable sort of fellow to pry open the old storeroom window and toss in a burning cigarette butt." His expression hardened. "Unfortunately, she came home too soon, and the fire was extinguished before it could do the job."

"What job is that?"

Boris ignored him. "And the rat in the toilet was a brainstorm. A slightly more difficult feat, requiring a child who could fit through the window, but luckily, I'd hired a family man. He had a son who was just the right size."

"You used a child?" Tamara demanded, not bothering to hide her loathing.

Boris shrugged. "The boy thought it was a lark. I believe he enjoyed himself. And it stood to reason that if the place flooded, everything on the floor would be destroyed. Again, misfortune smiled on me." He glowered at Tamara, his jaw tightening, his lip curled. "She'd already removed it from the boxes in the storeroom. I know because I paid good money for a man to go through her garbage."

Tamara went on tiptoe to see over Zane's shoulder. "I'd already moved what? What are you talking about?"

Just that easily, Boris's composure slipped. *"That goddamned journal!"*

Both Tamara and Zane froze. Zane backed up a tiny step, crowding into Tamara, forcing her to back up, too. The farther from Boris she got, the easier it'd be for her to escape while he distracted Boris with an attack.

"Hold still! Neither one of you is going anywhere."

"What do you want with the journal?" Tamara asked, edging out from behind Zane, thwarting his efforts. He tried to stop her, but she moved too quickly for him.

Boris shrugged, collecting himself as if he hadn't just shouted, as if he didn't have a gun pointed at them. "It's rightfully mine." He grinned, an evil baring of teeth. "My aunt Felicia wrote it."

Zane casually strolled across the room until he was once again standing in front of Tamara. "I don't buy it."

He appeared taken aback at Zane's doubt. "It's true."

"The woman who wrote that journal was generous, open, and warm." Zane shook his head. "A coldhearted bastard like you couldn't possibly have the same blood."

Boris snarled. "She was a whore, fucking anything that got close enough and then having the audacity to actually write about it."

"That's not true!" Tamara again left the dubious safety of Zane's back. "She wasn't detailing conquests! She wanted to share emotional connections and physical pleasure. She was a sensual woman who enjoyed male companionship. That's only natural."

"She was a vulgar bitch behaving below her station. What she did was plebeian, and if society found out, they'd crucify not only her, but every man she named as well."

"Which would cause some mighty repercussions, wouldn't it? I have the feeling some of her partners were influential men, men who wouldn't take kindly to being named. Why didn't you recover the journal sooner?" Zane asked.

Boris shook his head. "When the bitch died, I was glad to be rid of her, and I had all her belongings sold. But I didn't know about the ridiculous journal until I cleaned out her safety-deposit box and found a letter about it. She actually wanted me to give it to a friend of hers. Can you imagine?" He shuddered. "Luckily the company who handled the estate sale kept a record of transactions. It was easy enough to track it here, but more difficult to recover it. Now, though, I'll finally be able to destroy the goddamn thing."

Tamara was nearly beside herself. "But *why*?"

Again moving to block Tamara from Boris, Zane whispered, "Because his wife's family is traditional in the extreme, and they move with the upper crust. If they found out about the journal and knew it had the ability to damage their reputations, they wouldn't be content with just destroying it. They'd want any and all links to it gone."

Boris, looking surprised by Zane's information, didn't argue the point. "They'd disown me, damn them and their insistence on supercilious deportment."

"You said that with a straight face, Boris," Zane taunted, "but you know better. From what I understand, they abhor scandals and leave nothing to chance, especially if it concerns their good name and their standing in the community." He looked Boris in the eyes and said, "They wouldn't risk letting you walk free with all that information in your head. They'd get rid of you, permanently, and you know it."

Boris trembled with rage. Zane wanted him to tremble, he wanted him to quake with fury. The more out of control the man got, the more mistakes he might make.

"Once the two of you are dead and the journal is destroyed," Boris spat, "they'll never know, will they?"

Zane snorted. "If you shoot that gun, everyone will hear. The downstairs is crowded with customers and relatives and employees. The police will be here and you'll be taken away. But then, prison might be better than what your wife's family will have planned."

Very slowly, Boris raised his gun hand and aimed at Zane. Madness gleamed in his dark eyes. "Maybe I won't shoot you, then. I'd planned to burn the journal. Hell, I'll just burn the whole shop. It's a blight on an otherwise modern area anyway. The police will assume the fire was caused by whoever broke in here. God knows, Ms. Tremayne, you've lodged enough complaints lately."

"Thanks to you."

"I'm sorry, but I can't take all the credit. It seems you're racking up enemies left and right."

Why would he still lie? A sickening suspicion curled in Zane's gut, making him cramp. "She saw you outside her building one night, Sandor, wearing a ski mask."

"No."

"Then it was someone you hired."

"Not I."

"Damn you, you shut off the electric and tried to break in."

He shook his head with mock regret. "As I said, I can't take credit for that."

Tamara literally heaved with anger. "You went through my belongings, rearranged my books."

He sniffed. "I haven't been in your shop except for the appointments, and the one time Thanos brought me over. Ah, he had such grand hopes of us getting together, you know." He slid his lecherous gaze over Tamara, lingering on her breasts, her hips. "I must admit, the thought of taking you wasn't completely displeasing. You've a certain . . . raw appeal with your vampish clothes and rough manners. Quite took me by surprise."

It was all Zane could do to keep from lunging at him. He wanted to tear Boris apart for leering at her that way, but he had to ensure that Tamara wouldn't be hurt by his actions.

Then Boris shook his head. "I had hoped to get close enough to you to simply steal the book. Otherwise, I assure you, I'd have no use for a Gypsy fraud with cheap tricks." He sighed with regret. "Now I'm afraid this little conversation is over. Both of you, into the bedroom. It'll be a fitting place for you to die."

Zane planted his feet apart, let his arms hang loosely at his sides. "I don't think so, Sandor."

"You refuse to cooperate?"

Zane shrugged. "Why should I make it easy on you?" Damn it, he needed more time to think.

The gun aimed past him. "Fine." Boris grinned again. "I'll shoot her first, and then you. Everyone will think it a murder/suicide, that you acted out of jealousy, perhaps even jealousy of me. Her relatives are in my favor, so that would seem logical to them."

"Luna will know you came up here."

Zane was proud of how brave Tamara sounded. He could hear the quivering in her voice, but she wasn't going hysterical on him.

"Your fine assistant, my dear, bid me adieu and watched me leave in a fit of annoyance over your delay. She thinks I'm at home by now, brooding over being scorned."

Zane's last hope vanished. There was nothing left for him to do but take Boris by surprise—and hope for the best.

T W E N T Y

Bare-chested and short on temper, Joe sat stewing behind the register. Two female customers, the only ones in the store, continually favored him with funny looks—admiring looks—but it did nothing to lighten his mood. He still couldn't believe what had happened. What he'd allowed her to do. Why, if he ever got within three feet of her again, he'd . . .

"Joe!"

He looked up when the same crazy broad came barreling in. He quickly stood, a demonic grin spreading over his face as he prepared for battle.

"Back so soon?" he drawled, gaining the attention of the other two women who watched in frozen fascination. "You should know I let you get away with flinging food at me once, but I'll turn you over my knee if you try anything like that again. Don't think I won't."

She kept coming, moving at a fast clip. There was a harried, nearly panicked look in her big golden brown eyes that took him by surprise.

Joe backed up. Not sure what the hell to make of her, he muttered, "That was one of my favorite shirts, you know."

Luna grabbed him by the chest hair, and he howled. Using her secure hold, she brought his face down to hers over the counter and hissed, "I don't know what the hell is going on, but Boris Sandor just snuck up the outside stairs to Tamara's, and she and Zane are both up there."

"Ah, shit." Joe leaped over the counter in one smooth move. Thank God Luna let go of his chest hair when he did, otherwise his chest would have sported an impressive bald spot. He didn't have his gun on him, but before he even realized it, his knife was in his hand and open, the razor-sharp blade gleaming under the fluorescent lights. "Go call the police."

"Already done. They're on their way, but I was afraid to wait."

"Good girl." He was aware of her clipping along behind him, out the door and across the lot.

"Tamara and Zane went upstairs," she whispered, very close on his heels. "When they didn't come back down, Boris said he'd reschedule his appointment. He'd never done that before, so I peeked out the window when he left and I saw him go around the side of the building. I got there just in time to see him pry the door open and waltz in."

"The alarm didn't go off?"

"She only sets it at night."

"Shit." Joe stopped to push her flat into the brick facing of Tamara's building. "Stay back."

"No."

A string of near-silent curses tripped off his tongue. "Damn it, woman, do as I say."

"Go," she urged him, and gave him a shove to get him moving again.

Not seeing any hope for it, Joe muttered, "You make one single sound and so help me God, I'll throttle you."

He didn't wait to see if she heeded his warning. On light feet, ignoring the stiffness of his busted knee, he dashed up the metal stairs. The door there was closed, but not locked. It let out a tiny squeak when he opened it. Luna was so silent, if it hadn't been for her breath on the back of his right ear, he wouldn't have known she was still there.

Voices carried to him, and he crept forward, his knife at the ready. He peeked around the kitchen door to the hallway, and he saw Boris standing there with a gun. A simple thirty-eight, but hell, they were deadly if you had a decent aim. And at that close range, how could he possibly miss?

Fingers spread, Joe reached behind him and flattened his free hand on Luna. As attentive to the current situation as a man could be, he still realized that his hand was on her belly, and that she felt very nice. *Damned irritant.*

Luna immediately stilled, not out of intimidation, he was certain, because a herd of wild buffalo wouldn't intimidate that one, but out of common sense. She knew he was about to act, and didn't want to get in his way. Joe gave her points for intelligence, if not for discretion or moderation.

"Once I have the journal," Boris said, disgustingly smug, "my aunt Felicia's disgrace will be forever dead, buried with her where it belongs."

Joe drew back, his body perfectly balanced. A balsong knife wasn't really meant for throwing, but the distance was short and he was good, very good. He'd locked the knife open and had not a single doubt that'd he hit the mark.

In that final moment before the blade would have sliced through the air, another voice intruded, screaming, "Bastard!"

Joe paused, senses heightened, and stared, incredulous, as a slim man threw himself at Boris. Both bodies tumbled. The next few seconds were chaos.

Boris cursed, Zane yelled, and the gun went off with a deafening roar.

"*Stay here.*" Joe pushed Luna back just to make sure she knew he meant business, and a second later he entered the fray. If he hadn't been so worried for Zane and Tamara, for innocent bystanders, *for Luna*, he'd have actually been having fun.

Zane couldn't credit his eyes when Arkin Devane opened the stairwell door and crept forward. *Jesus*, he thought, *were they working together?*

Then Boris made his threat, and the meek and mild Arkin went into a red-hot frenzy. His screech of fury nearly drowned out the blast of the gunshot. Zane bore Tamara down to the carpet and covered her with his body, his arms over her head, protecting her as best he could.

She made a muffled sound that might have been a protest. Zane tightened his hold while Arkin and Boris wrestled for control of the gun, but since Boris was insane and much heavier than Arkin, Zane knew where he'd put his money.

"Stay down," he instructed Tamara, and started to rise so he could ensure Arkin's success.

Tamara rolled to her back and clutched at him, her voice desperate and high. "Zane, no!"

"Shh. It's all right, baby." He pried her fingers loose and bounded to his feet. To his right, he saw Joe lunge forward. The gun went off again, and Zane caught his breath. Arkin slumped back with a painful groan.

Boris lumbered to his feet. "Miserable little . . ." He aimed at Arkin, who writhed on the floor while a sluggish flow of blood pulsed from the top of his right arm.

Grinning evilly, Joe kicked out and the gun went flying. Zane grabbed Boris by the shoulder, flung him around, and did what he'd wanted to do since he'd first met the man. He drove his fist into his face.

Cartilage gave way with a satisfying crunch.

Boris yowled, grabbing at his nose and staggering drunkenly under the impact of the blow. Tamara, disregarding orders as usual, scurried on her knees to the gun and picked it up. She aimed it at Boris.

"You broke his nose," Joe remarked to Zane in a barely winded voice. He sounded impressed.

Ignoring his cousin, Zane motioned to Boris. "C'mon, Sandor. I'm not done."

Boris shook his head. "No, no." Blood poured from between his fingers, made his words choked and garbled, and already his eyes were turning black.

Flabbergasted, Joe said, "You're quitting because of a bloody nose?" Then with utter disdain, "You big baby, that's pathetic."

Slowly, Zane shook his head. "Oh, no, he's not quitting." He grabbed Boris, hauled him forward. "You held a gun on her," he said, and punctuated his words with a hard punch to Boris's midsection. Boris doubled over, spewing more blood.

"*Eeuw.*" Luna made a face as she sauntered into the room. "That's disgusting. What a mess."

Joe, after giving Luna a sidelong glance, laughed and bent down to Arkin. "You okay, buddy?"

"I'm shot!" Arkin clutched at his upper arm and rolled back and forth, his knees pulled up in the fetal position.

"Yeah, well, I can see that." Joe held him still with one hand, and lifted away the bloody edge of his sweater to peer at the wound. "Doesn't look too bad to me. Luckily he hit your arm and not your chest."

"*Luckily?*" Arkin quit wailing long enough to fry Joe with a look. "It hurts like hell!"

Unconcerned, Joe shrugged. "Gunshot wounds are a bitch."

Luna edged closer, looking over Joe's naked shoulder at the fallen man. "You've been shot before?"

Joe glared at her. "None of your damn business."

She lightly touched a mark on his shoulder. "Here?"

Shuddering, Joe rasped, "Yeah," and then he shook his head, cursed, and scooted out of her reach.

Zane wrapped a fist in the front of Boris's shirt and hauled him close yet again. His anger was a live thing, needing release. He'd get that release with Boris.

But, proving what a coward he was, Boris held both hands up to cover his face and began pleading. He wasn't much sport, Zane thought in disgust, and flung him away. Boris dropped to his knees, moaning.

"Zane?" Tamara trembled, causing the bells on her ankles to chime musically, and the gun in her hand to jerk. But she managed to keep it pointed at Boris.

Gently, Zane covered her hand with his own. "Let me have the gun, honey."

"Oh no." She shook her head hard, making her blond hair fly. "You're going to shoot him."

Joe cocked a brow at that, interest lighting his eyes. He looked almost . . . hopeful.

"No, I'm not." Zane kept his tone as even and calm as possible, especially since he knew Tamara was likely experiencing her own feelings, and his as well. It was a lot for one small woman to deal with.

She turned to look him straight in the eye. "Yes, you are. You can't lie to me."

Zane smiled. "I'd like to," he specified. "But that's not the same as I would." And he added, "You can trust me, honey."

Her big green eyes stared up at him, and she blinked. "Oh, Zane. I know that." The gun went limp in her hand, and Zane took it. He held Tamara close with one arm and handed the gun to Joe. "Here, you can shoot him."

Tamara stiffened, but Joe only laughed. "Very funny." He palmed the gun and squatted down by Boris. "You hear that, old man? I get to shoot you."

"*No!*"

Tamara curled into Zane. "He won't really . . . ?"

"Nah." But Zane added as an afterthought, "At least, I don't think he will."

Joe agreed. "I won't. Shooting him would only add more mess to Tamara's place, and he's caused her enough trouble."

Tamara relaxed, leaning into Zane and turning her face to his shoulder.

"That is," Joe went on, "I won't shoot him as long as he just lies there and stays quiet. Give me a reason, any reason, and I'd be glad to give him a little taste of what he gave your buddy there."

"Arkin Devane is not my buddy." Zane reached for Luna, dragged her next to Tamara, and told them both, "It's okay now. I can hear the sirens. The cops will be here in just a few minutes."

Luna patted Tamara. "Being females, and thus weak, we're supposed to comfort each other, right?" She smiled. "Well, don't worry. We're fine."

"Tamara?" Zane wanted to hear her speak to him before he put even three inches between them.

"Yes." She smiled. "I'm okay. Just a little . . . shook-up."

"Adrenaline," Joe remarked. "Comes in real handy when you need it, but it's tough to shake off afterward."

Zane squatted down next to Arkin. "What the hell are you doing here, Arkin?"

Arkin moaned, putting his head back and letting it loll on the carpet. "Tamara didn't show up, so I came to see why. I saw Luna follow Boris, and I followed her." He swallowed hard. "I figured something was up when she ran up the stairs with that other fellow, and he had a knife."

"How are you involved in this, Arkin?"

He moaned again. "Please."

"Jesus," Joe said with loathing. "They don't make 'em very tough in

Thomasville, do they? All this pleading and whining is about to make me puke."

"He saved us," Tamara protested, ready to defend her number-one client.

"No." Zane narrowed his eyes. "I have the feeling Arkin was saving the journal."

"It's true." Arkin opened his eyes long enough to look at Tamara. "I'm so sorry. So very, very sorry."

Pulling away from Luna, Tamara went to him. She knelt down next to Zane and slipped her hand in his. He clasped her fingers warmly.

"Sorry for what, exactly?" she asked.

"I . . ." He choked, swallowed hard, then continued. "I'm the one you saw that night in the ski mask." In a rush, he added, "I wasn't chasing you, I swear. I was just looking for the journal. But then you came back early and . . ." He managed a shrug and a self-conscious smile. "We both had quite a shock."

"And the other night?" Zane asked. "You're the one who cut the electricity?"

"Yes." He turned his head away, hiding his shame and shutting out Zane's contempt. "I heard her tell Boris she was going out. I didn't think anyone would be at home. I'd already checked everywhere downstairs and couldn't find the journal."

"So," Tamara said, "you realized I'd taken it upstairs and you were going to steal it from me?"

"Yes. You told me you had it upstairs, when we talked about . . ."

"The lady you're in love with," Tamara said as the truth dawned.

"How the hell did you get in?" Zane wasn't over the edge enough to batter a man already shot, a man with tears in his eyes, a man curled up like a damn baby. But—he wanted to.

"The Realtor selling her place. I stole the key from him, had a copy made, and then returned it."

"You wanna tell me how you managed that?" Zane tried to keep his tone even for Tamara's sake. She looked more shocked than ever.

"I know him. The Realtor, I mean. We went to college together."

Somewhere behind Zane, Joe laughed. "Tidy."

"Do you mind?" Zane wondered how the hell Joe could be enjoying himself now, but it was plain to see he was having a ball. He always had been a man who thrived on trouble.

"My rearranged books." Tamara whispered the words more as a statement than a question.

"That was me." Arkin added in a heartfelt rush, "The journal should have been *mine*. Felicia was such a dear friend, such a lovely woman. I taught her piano, you know."

Zane and Joe shared a look, but Tamara had all her attention on Arkin. "You were friends?"

"Yes. She told me about her journal, and promised to share it with me. Like you, she understood me."

Zane turned. "You said there was a note in her safety-deposit box, Sandor. Is that who she left it to? Arkin Devane?"

"I don't remember, damn it."

Joe said, "My trigger finger is twitching. Look at that! Damn, I can barely keep from—"

Discolored eyes opening wide, Boris said, "Yes! Yes, it was Arkin Devane."

Arkin's pain-filled expression softened, his body relaxing for the first time since he'd been shot. "She knew I was falling in love," he whispered to no one in particular, "but that I needed some . . . help. She promised to give me the journal. Then she died and Boris"—Arkin managed to raise his head enough to glare at the other man—"had all her things sold, everything, even her most prized possessions. Suddenly everything she valued had been handed off to strangers."

"The estate sale," Tamara said.

"Yes. I tried to buy the journal, but it had been packed away with the rest of her library, and you bought it all."

"Like Sandor, you got that information from the estate sale company?"

"Yes."

"And that's why you sought me out, why you started coming to me."

He nodded, looking more miserable by the second.

"Why didn't you just ask me for it outright, Arkin?" And then, with some hurt, "I thought we had become friends."

"We *are* friends!" He gulped, and more tears gathered in his eyes. "You're one of the kindest women I know. But Felicia had kept the book private. If I started asking about it, if I mentioned it to *anyone*, others might have discovered it. The scandal she'd so hoped to avoid might still have come about. She didn't deserve that. She'd already been so badly mistreated by her family."

"Boris and his relatives?" Zane asked.

"Yes. They never understood her. She'd shamed them merely by being her own woman, and they'd disowned her. I almost had a heart attack when you had that flood"—Boris got another glare, this one even darker—"and you threw away all those boxes of things. I was so afraid it was gone forever, and then you mentioned it to me and you were sharing it with me. I knew it was upstairs, and I tried one last time to get it. But then we talked more, and I . . . well, I realized that I didn't need to steal it, not from you. I didn't use the key again after that."

He squeezed his eyes shut. "You understood. You read Felicia's journal with the same emotion and acceptance as I'd have given it."

Zane dropped back on his behind with a curse. "I don't believe it. All this over a journal."

Boris groaned. "She was a blight on the family. I had to recover and destroy that damn book before my in-laws found out, before good men got ruined, before—"

Joe nudged him with the toe of his boot. "I hear the police coming up the stairs. Looks like you won't have to worry about any of that after all."

But it wasn't the police who came barreling through the door. Cole and Mack stumbled into the room, their gazes searching, frantic. When they spotted Zane, Tamara at his side, both of them healthy and whole, they slumped against each other, wheezing and gasping for air.

Zane caught Tamara's arm and helped her to stand. "What are you two doing here?"

Cole, his hands on his knees while he bent forward, trying to catch his breath, nodded toward Luna. "She called us. She saw Boris sneaking in and told us she had a bad feeling."

Mack did his own huffing and gulping, and now flopped limply against the wall. "Her bad feeling gave *me* a bad feeling," he said, "and we got here as fast as we could. Of course, we ran into the damn police, sirens blaring, on the way."

"Which only worried us more."

Smiling, Tamara went to each brother and hugged him. "Thank you."

"Chase came, too," Cole told them, finally able to straighten on his shaky legs enough to put his arm around Tamara. Mack crowded in on her other side. "But there was a group of customers milling around your parking lot looking confused, so he went to check things out there."

"Oh hell." Joe jerked upright. "I left your place empty when Luna told me what was going on."

Zane hesitated only a moment, and then he reached for Joe. Taking him completely by surprise, he pulled his cousin into a tight bear hug. "I'm glad you did, Joe. Thanks."

At that moment the police charged into the room, weapons at the ready. Joe turned to them and said, "Here, you better take this gun." He grinned stupidly, wavered, then clutched his bare chest. "I think I'm going to have a heart attack."

The bar was crowded when Tamara wended her way through the door. She heard a laugh and lifted her head, seeing Zane on a bar stool, sipping from a steaming mug. Cole, holding his baby niece, Sammy, against his shoulder, chatted with Zane while Chase alternately served drinks to the customers and joined in. It took her only a moment to locate Mack, situated at a nearby table with Trista, his teenage daughter. Joe was seated there, too, cuddling baby Nate, with the wives positioned around him. Her heart gave a funny little catch at seeing them all together.

Poignant regret. Pain, smothering and stark. And a silly flare of hope.

She stopped, attempting to gather her thoughts, to shore up her weak female emotions so she wouldn't embarrass herself. In that instant, Zane looked up and his smile lit up the room.

He smiled at something Cole said and started her way. Tamara watched the women watching him. Two called out to him, making him pause. Another grabbed his arm; he leaned down to listen, then laughed.

Within thirty seconds, he stood before her. His welcome, his warmth and his scent wrapped around her in comforting familiarity.

It had been two weeks since the awful debacle at her home. In that time the bloodstained carpet in the living room had been replaced, the bullet hole in the ceiling from the first gunshot had been repaired. And Zane had all but moved in with her.

Just that morning he'd sat on the edge of the tub and watched her put on her makeup. He'd made them coffee and she'd fixed toast. He'd kissed her good-bye at her front door, then sauntered across the lot to his store. It had all seemed so domestic, so . . . lasting.

Tamara reached up and touched his face. "Hi."

He tilted his head. "You're a little late," he said softly. "My brothers have been razzing me about getting stood up."

Tamara dropped her gaze to his throat. "No woman in her right mind would ever stand you up, and you know it."

With one finger beneath her chin, he lifted her face again. "What's wrong, sweetheart?"

She drew a deep breath, prepared to tell him. And suddenly Joe was there, hooking an arm through hers and dragging her to the bar where the others waited. He balanced year-old Nate in his other arm. The baby had dark hair, vivid blue eyes, and looked like he could have been Joe's son instead of Cole's. Nate chuckled happily as Joe made him bounce.

Trista, Mack's daughter, leaned into his side while Chase refilled all their mugs of hot chocolate. The women had left the table and were now in various positions with their husbands. Zane trailed indulgently behind her as Joe stole her away.

Pretending to be gallant, Joe brushed away imaginary dust on a stool right in the middle of the family clan, then, despite Nate's sturdy little body, he bowed. "Take a seat."

Zane slid into place beside her, not saying a word but giving Joe a look that plainly told him to seat himself elsewhere.

Joe just grinned. "Pretend all you want, Zane. But I'm on to you now. You're crazy nuts about me. Hell, I may even be your favorite cousin."

Zane rolled his eyes. It amused Tamara how Joe now needled him endlessly, ever since that ill-advised hug, and Zane complained every single time.

"I'm sorry I'm late," Tamara told them all, still a little bemused by the attention they bestowed on her.

Sophie crowded closer. "So what did you decide to do with the journal? Zane said you'd made a decision, but wouldn't even give us a clue."

Tamara glanced at him behind her, then cleared her throat. "That's probably because he disagrees with me. But I gave it to Arkin. It was rightfully his all along, and he never did any damage to my place."

Zane, clearly disgusted by her choice, said, "She even forgives him. Can you believe that? It was bad enough that she didn't want to press charges, but—"

"He did save your asses," Mack pointed out.

Jessica objected. "I think Joe had as much to do with that as Arkin."

"Yeah," Cole said, "all Arkin did was get shot."

"And that saved Zane from getting shot," Tamara pointed out, "because he was just about ready to jump Boris himself." Tamara nodded when they all stared at her. "It's true."

Joe shifted the baby against his chest. His dark blue eyes warmed on her face. "How do you know what Zane was going to do?"

She faltered. No way would she tell them she was empathic. She merely shook her head.

Allison sniffed. "Everyone knows a woman in love is attuned to her man."

Chase reached over the bar and stroked her cheek with one finger. "And husbands are attuned to their wives, too."

Allison grinned shamelessly while Mack and Cole said, "Hear, hear."

Joe shook his head. "Any man worth his salt knows what a woman wants and how she thinks. Especially at select times—like in bed."

Zane groaned. "For a man bent on staying a bachelor, you sure seem to enjoy holding the babies."

"*Other* people's babies," Joe said, putting emphasis on the first word. "They're great to hold and cuddle—and then hand back to their papas." To demonstrate, he started to hand Nate over to Cole. But Nate had other ideas, and knotted his chubby fists in Joe's hair, just over his temples. Joe yelped, then gave up with a laugh.

"You should get a haircut," Zane suggested, but Joe pretended not to hear him while he went about growling into Nate's neck.

Propping his arms on the bar, Chase brought the conversation back around. "Olga and Eva are pretty downcast that it was Boris, not a ghost."

A genuine smile found its way past Tamara's sadness. "I know. Aunt Olga feels guilty that she blamed poor Uncle Hubert for Boris's misdeeds. Now she's certain he'll come haunt her for discrediting him."

They all laughed, but Chase said, "Hmm. I wonder."

Zane bent to her ear. "So where were you? I was starting to get worried."

Knowing she couldn't put it off any longer, Tamara turned to face Zane. It was cowardly of her, but she preferred to share her news right here, among his family, where she knew she couldn't break down and cry and embarrass them both.

Forcing a smile that hurt, she said, "My Realtor called."

Zane hesitated in the act of picking up his hot chocolate. After just a second, he took a healthy swallow and set the mug back down. "Is that right? What did he have to say?"

Hoping she looked happy rather than despondent, Tamara said, "I was offered my full asking price."

Though noise continued in the bar, everyone around Tamara had gone silent. The brothers exchanged worried glances and Joe ducked his head, whistling low. The wives were all staring at Zane, waiting to see what he'd do.

He narrowed his eyes on Tamara. "I assume you turned it down."

"I . . . no." Holding a smile was nearly impossible. Her eyes burned. "I told him I'd have to get back to him."

"There's no reason for you to sell, you know."

Nervously pushing her hair behind her ears, she stammered, "My finances are . . ."

Zane cupped her cheek and repeated, "There's no reason for you to sell. Not now."

His meaning dawned on her. "We've been over that, Zane. I won't take a loan from you."

"You won't have to. Now that I've moved in, I can pay my share. That'll cut your expenses in half, right?"

Tamara glanced around her. Not a single one of his family made any pretense about listening in. They were engrossed.

Her throat felt tight, and she cleared it. "You intend to . . . keep living with me?"

"Damn right."

"But . . ." She wasn't sure what to say. Everything was up in the air, nothing was settled.

"You could be pregnant."

His statement caused a stir of whispers and inhalations among his family. Tamara scowled at him. "I'm not."

Zane shifted. He looked down at the floor, at the ceiling. He propped his hands on his hips and made a sound of disgust.

Joe bit back a laugh, which seemed to galvanize Zane. He pierced Tamara with a look and said, "You *could* love me."

She caught her breath. It hit her—everything he was feeling, everything he thought, the depth of his emotion. She couldn't seem to drag in enough air for her starved lungs. Tears stung her eyes, overflowed, and she smiled. "I do."

This time Joe went ahead and laughed, a big whooping laugh. Chase snatched Nate out of his arms and Mack shoved him right off his bar stool.

Zane never even bothered to glance his way. "I love you, too," he said to Tamara.

And she whispered back, "I know. Now."

As Zane pulled Tamara close for a heated kiss, Mack looked on and rubbed his hands. "Well, then, there you go. It's all settled."

E P I L O G U E

"She's beautiful."

"Yes. She'd have looked even prettier if she'd worn the red dress."

"Perhaps. And a tad more makeup."

Thanos hushed Olga and Eva. "She couldn't wear red to a wedding, even if it was the dress you both wore."

"Antique lace and hand stitching. It'd have to be taken in some for her."

"Especially in the bust," Olga agreed, "because we are more endowed than our little Gypsy, but still—"

"But it wouldn't have been appropriate," Thanos insisted, "not for Tamara."

Eva sniffed. "A Tremayne can do as she pleases."

He agreed, and said with a grin, "She did that."

Tamara heard her relatives whispering, but she didn't mind. They'd taken her marriage to Zane rather well. According to Eva, Zane was just outrageous enough to please their free spirits.

Thanos had given her away, looking extremely dapper in his tux, his beard trimmed and his smile bright and proud. The aunts stood together as mothers of the bride, alternately crying and whispering since the music started.

Tamara felt wrapped in a cocoon of love, the emotions emanating from her relatives, her soon-to-be in-laws, and the incredibly handsome groom.

To her side, Luna stood as maid of honor, with Sophie, Allison, and Jessica lined up as bridesmaids. Next to Zane, Cole was best man, with Mack and Chase and Joe in line behind him. The minister kept things blessedly short, which was good since her heart was so full, she had a hard time concentrating.

Zane touched her chin. "I do."

She stared at him, sighed, and said, "I know you do."

Cole choked, which prompted a round of masculine coughs. Tamara's aunts twittered in delight, and Thanos let out a booming chuckle.

Zane grinned at her. "Almost your turn, sweetheart."

"Oh!" She knew her face was red, but fortunately the veil hid it.

When asked if she took Zane as her husband, she managed to say quite properly, "I do."

Stifling his own smile, the minister said, "I now pronounce you man and wife. Zane, you may kiss your lovely bride."

Zane carefully lifted her veil.

Tamara looked at him, at his beautiful smile and the naked love in his eyes. She trembled, shook, struggled for breath, and in the next instant she hurled herself into his arms. "I love you so much!"

Laughing, Zane caught her to him and twirled her around.

Olga whispered loudly, "Oh, that girl does me proud," and Eva agreed.

Being a good friend as well as an assistant, Luna cheered, and everyone else followed suit.

An hour later, they were cutting the cake when suddenly the lights went out. Tamara froze, Zane cursed. A low rumble of confusion drifted through their guests. Then Aunt Eva wailed, "It's Uncle Hubert!"

The lights came back on as quickly as they'd gone out. "Sorry," came a low masculine voice from the other side of the room, "I, ah, leaned on the main switch." Joe, a look of apology on his face, stood next to Luna, her hair disheveled, the bodice of her gown askew. They were in front of a narrow corridor, and they both looked guilty.

Chase rubbed his hands together. "And the curse continues," he said with relish. All the Winstons—all but Joe—gave a mighty cheer.

Tamara laughed. And to think she'd wanted a *normal* life. How silly.

Lori Foster is a *USA Today* bestselling author who has written many romances. Visit her website at www.lorifoster.com.